NATURE'S REWARD

They moved silently about their morning routine, drinking coffee, and eating breakfast, but the looks that passed between them said far more than words could ever tell.

Faith watched Jonas chop down a tree. He looked comfortable in the task, even happy.

"You do belong here, Jonas," she said. "You are beginning to love this land nearly as much as I do, aren't you?"

"That land and you," he answered and pulled her to him. He kissed her mouth with all the hunger he had suppressed for so long.

Faith sought the passion of his embrace and gave herself up to the fierce sweetness. The world seemed to be only the touch of his lips, the haven of his arms . . .

Taylor—made Romance From Zebra Books

WHISPERED KISSES   (3830, $4.99/$5.99)

Beautiful Texas heiress Laura Leigh Webster never imagined that her biggest worry on her African safari would be
the handsome Jace Elliot, her tour guide. Laura's guard-
ian, Lord Chadwick Hamilton, warns her of Jace's dangerous past; she simply cannot resist the lure of his strong
arms and the passion of his *Whispered Kisses*.

KISS OF THE NIGHT WIND   (3831, $4.99/$5.99)

Carrie Sue Strover thought she was leaving trouble behind
her when she deserted her brother's outlaw gang to live her
life as schoolmarm Carolyn Starns. On her journey, her
stagecoach was attacked and she was rescued by handsome
T.J. Rogue. T.J. plots to have Carrie lead him to her brother's cohorts who murdered his family. T.J., however, soon
succumbs to the beautiful runaway's charms and loving caresses.

FORTUNE'S FLAMES   (3825, $4.99/$5.99)

Impatient to begin her journey back home to New Orleans,
beautiful Maren James was furious when Captain Hawk
delayed the voyage by searching for stowaways. Impatience
gave way to uncontrollable desire once the handsome captain searched *her* cabin. He was looking for illegal passengers; what he found was wild passion with a woman he
knew was unlike all those he had known before!

PASSIONS WILD AND FREE   (3828, $4.99/$5.99)

After seeing her family and home destroyed by the cruel
and hateful Epson gang, Randee Hollis swore revenge. She
knew she found the perfect man to help her—gunslinger
Marsh Logan. Not only strong and brave, Marsh had the
ebony hair and light blue eyes to make Randee forget her
hate and seek the love and passion that only he could give
her.

KATHRYN HOCKETT

WILD WESTERN FIRE

ZEBRA BOOKS
KENSINGTON PUBLISHING CORP.

ZEBRA BOOKS are published by

Kensington Publishing Corp.
475 Park Avenue South
New York, NY 10016

First printing: February 1994

Printed in the United States of America

Author's Note

When the gates of the West were opened to settlement, new modes of travel were needed. For generations, a few brave souls had traveled west of the Mississippi River along well-worn wagon trails and old Indian trails. The Santa Fe Trail and old California Trail had been established during the California Gold Rush days of 1849. It was along the old California Trail that the first transcontinental railroad was completed in May of 1869, with the new rails running from Omaha to San Francisco.

The clouds of gray smoke that billowed skyward from locomotives crossing the vast, open plains west of the Mississippi to Santa Fe or San Francisco were not an uncommon sight. People were becoming used to the sound of the train whistles and whirling wheels over the tracks. Nevertheless, most of the nation was still amazed that a great part of the American continent could be crossed by rail in a week's time as opposed to the several months it took to travel by any other means.

In the late 1860's and early part of the 1870's Oregon was not as thickly populated as some of the southwestern states, for the Northern Pacific Railroad was still only a dream father north and would not become a reality until 1880. In the meantime, travelers to the Northwestern Pacific States—Oregon and Washington—had to be content with less modern forms of travel.

It was not unusual in the last years of the 1860's and early ones of the 1870's to see caravans of prairie schooners, horses and wagons with a cow tied on behind, traveling the same roads as the stagecoaches. Not everyone could afford to travel by stagecoach. Many immigrants and people of moderate circumstances made do with whatever means they could muster, which was in contrast to the mode of transportation being used to the south.

The Donation Land Act in Oregon in 1865 opened the way for settlement in a vast virgin territory—one hundred and sixty acres of the most fertile soil in the Willamette Valley abundant in water and timber. There was rich black farm soil waiting to nurture many forms of farm produce. The weather was comparatively mild near the seacoast, the rainfall plentiful. The Columbia River gave excellent opportunity for shipping.

With the exception of Portland and Seattle, the vast country of Oregon and Washington was still a wilderness compared to the southern states such as Texas and California. The fur trappers and Missourians had long before carved out small clusters of buildings that had developed into townships, many of which were crisscrossed by water. The Willamette Valley was known for its orchards, flowers, nuts and wheat crops.

In that vast new territory, our story takes place. A young woman comes west to homestead and learns to deal with the elements and her solitude. When a daring young man, on the run because he has been framed for a crime he didn't commit, seeks her land as his haven of safety, they are both thrown into an adventure and romance neither of them had counted on.

Part One:
Where the Heart Is
1869

"No truer word save God's was ever spoken,
Than that the largest heart is soonest broken."
—Landor, *Epigrams*

One

The train station was crowded with people, all carrying boxes and bags of various shapes and sizes. Pushing through the throng, suitcase in one hand, satchel in the other, her purse dangling precariously from her shoulder, Faith Tomkins moved toward the platform as fast as she could. But it was no easy task to maneuver through the often immovable throng.

"Excuse me!"

From St. Paul, Faith had traveled by steamship to St. Louis. From St. Louis she had taken a train to Omaha. Now she was hurrying to catch another train from Omaha to a place called South Pass in Utah. Then she would take a stagecoach to her final destination—Portland, Oregon. A lot of traveling for someone who had never before left her hometown of St. Paul!

"I beg your pardon."

The mixture of people waiting to board the train was a curious one. There were a few women and children but mostly the crowd was made up of men. And a seemingly rowdy lot. Though it was usually Faith's way to be friendly, she remembered her mother's warning about strangers and kept her gaze focused straight ahead. She felt isolated. Lonely. More than a little ill at ease as she juggled her belongings.

"Please let me through!" It was exasperating to her that she couldn't see over the hat tops. Her view was completely blocked by those people who were much taller than she. All Faith could see was the dark-gray smoke that belched from the incoming train's engine.

A whistle screamed and she heard the brakes screech as the train pulled into Omaha. Her heart lurched as she realized that it must be the very train she was waiting to board.

"Oh, please," she murmured in distress. "I don't want to miss it." *And be stranded here in an unfamiliar place.* The thought was unsettling and caused Faith to be more persistent in her quest to push herself through the human forest. Her assertiveness paid off when she was at last afforded sight of the long black train as it came to a full stop.

Faith watched as a throng of passengers alighted from the flat-roofed cars that resembled boxes on wheels to be hugged and squeezed as they threw themselves into the arms of those waiting for them on the platform. For just a moment she was reminded of the family she had said goodbye to in St. Paul and fought against a mist of tears. She had left her mother, father, and five sisters to travel west and couldn't help but feel a twinge of homesickness, an emotion she tried to push aside. Starting a new life with her fiancé, Henry would be well worth the sacrifice.

"Henry!" Just speaking his name aloud conjured up so many pleasant memories that any apprehension she might have had was quickly laid aside. Henry was the kind of man any young woman dreamed about. She had made the right choice! She just knew she had.

It took a long time to empty the train, a tranquil respite from the pushing and shoving, but as soon as the passengers had disembarked, the crowd began its impatient stampede again. The piercing whoosh of the steam engines blasted from full-bellied boilers continuing to send thick black smoke into sky. The brakeman raised and lowered his kerosene lantern. The train was getting ready to begin its journey, to chug and puff down the maze of tracks that reminded Faith of a Chinese puzzle.

Faith heard the conductor call "All

aboard!" as she waded through the stampede of people who at least were headed in the same direction now.

"Ouch!" she cried out as a misdirected elbow caught her in the ribs. The culprit didn't even say he was sorry. Certainly he was no gentleman, she thought with an indignant sniff. Nor was that her only "wound." She was pinched and prodded, and her toes were stepped on several times along the way. It seemed to be every "man" for himself and Faith was certain that before this was over she would be covered with bruises. And all the while her two pieces of luggage seemed to get heavier and heavier.

Oh how she missed Henry's strong arms, she thought, succumbing to her disappointment that he would not be traveling to Portland with her. Originally she was to have met her fiancé here and then journeyed with him to their new homestead. When she had arrived, however, Henry was not there to meet her. He had left a letter instructing her to take the deed he had given her as a wedding present and go on to Oregon on her own. He would meet her in Portland in two weeks, just in time for their wedding, he had said. It seemed the railroad had one last surveying job for him before they let him go.

"Ah, well, we'll have the rest of our lives to be together," she sighed, remembering the fervor with which Henry Wingham had

14

courted her. There had been many moonlit nights, walks in the garden, quiet candlelight dinners, evenings at theater, gifts of candy and flowers. Henry was handsome, dashing, and charming—how could she help but love him?

One night he had surprised her with a velvet case that had revealed a splendid diamond ring. Was it any wonder she had said yes to his proposal?

"Tickets. Tickets. . . ."

For just a moment she panicked, fearing she had lost hers, but a search of her reticule revealed it to be safely tucked at the bottom. Faith set the large suitcase down just long enough to enable her to retrieve the ticket from her purse. How glad she was going to be when all this traveling was over and she could settle down . . .

"No!" With a gasp she saw that a tall dark-haired man had plucked up her suitcase. She was just about to admonish him as a thief when he flashed her a wide, friendly grin.

"Looks like you could use a little help, miss." He tipped his wide-brimmed Stetson. "Allow me."

For just a moment she was going to tell him that she could manage very well on her own, but something about his hazel eyes melted her icy reserve. His were kind eyes. And that suitcase was so very heavy. "Thank you," she said instead.

"My name's Winslow. Jonas Winslow." He raised his eyebrows in expectation. "Mrs. . . . ?"

Did she dare tell him her name? For just a moment she was unsure. A woman traveling alone had to be careful. But dear God, some of those other men were ogling her so openly that it made her flesh crawl. This Winslow man at least seemed to be a gentleman.

"Tomkins."

"Mrs. Tomkins."

The truth slipped out before she realized it. "It's *Miss. Miss* Tomkins."

"How do you do, *Miss* Tomkins. . . ." Once again he smiled, revealing deep dimples in his cheeks. He was a decidedly handsome man, something Faith tired not to notice.

"I'm soon to be a missus," she quickly amended, just so he would know not to trifle with her. "My fiancé is a surveyor with the railroad."

"I see." Jonas Winslow cautiously scanned the waiting passengers. "And is he in the crowd somewhere?"

"No . . . no . . ." There was no use in lying. "We . . . we were supposed to travel on to Portland together but . . . he's been delayed. He's going to *meet me* there, however," she emphasized, handing her ticket to the conductor who had by now grown more than a little impatient.

"Well then, I guess it's up to me to look out after you in the meantime," he boldly whispered in her ear as he likewise held forth his ticket. "At least for a while. You see, I'm going to be on the very same train." Jonas was pleased at the thought of having this pretty blue-eyed, auburn-haired woman as his traveling companion. It would make a tedious journey more interesting.

"Look after me?" Faith was hesitant. For all his congeniality he was after all a stranger. "I wouldn't want to be a bother."

His hazel eyes twinkled at her. "Believe me, it will be no bother." When she still didn't capitulate, he added, "Really."

"Well . . ." She was weakening. As she looked at the other men boarding she decided that maybe it wasn't really such a bad idea. Being a woman alone made one so very vulnerable. "All right."

"Come on then, Miss Tomkins. I'll be your protector, at least until we reach the end of the line." The hand he laid on her shoulder as he guided her up the train's two steps was gentle.

"It's Faith. My name is Faith," she revealed. Certainly if they were going to be journeying together she could forego formalities.

"Faith."

Most of the wooden benches aboard were filling up rapidly but Faith's self-appointed traveling companion spotted two vacant seats at the farthest end of the passenger car. He offered Faith the window seat, then secured his suitcase and both of hers underneath the bench just as the final whistle sounded. He took his place beside her just as the train pulled away from the platform.

Faith thought how the traveling cars reminded her of boxes on wheels. Certainly they were just about as uncomfortable. And crowded. Being cooped up with so many other people made it so hot. Worse yet, it was up to the passengers to take care of their own needs.

It was noisy inside the train as bags clunked together and people chattered. Faith made use of the confusion to steal a long look at this Jonas Winslow. He was dressed in a dark-gray suit with matching double-breasted vest, a white shirt, red tie, and black leather boots. The only thing that separated him from an easterner was his wide-brimmed black Stetson and the angle at which he wore it—a jaunty angle that made him look more cowboy than dude. He was obviously a strong man, broad of shoulder, narrow in the hips, and long of leg.

"So, you're going all the way to Oregon, huh, little lady?" As he suddenly focused his

18

eyes on her, Faith blushed at having been caught staring.

"To take advantage of the Donation Land Act, yes," she said quickly. "My fiancé and I are going to homestead near Portland. In . . . in Milwaukie." She remembered the name of the town by association. There was a Milwaukee, Wisconsin, in the state that bordered hers.

"Milwaukee? I've been to a Milwaukee, but not one in Oregon." He shook his head. "No, never heard of it."

She felt the strange need to defend her soon-to-be new home. "It's in the Willamette Valley and is a paradise, or so I've been told." She mimicked Henry's words. "Rich black farmland, rivers, orchards, flowers. A perfect climate. The ocean . . ."

"Does sound like a veritable heaven, but homesteading there will mean hard work." Dubiously Jonas eyed the petite woman who was dressed so properly in a full-skirted dark-blue traveling suit and matching bonnet. She seemed too fragile for heavy toil, more the type for velvets and laces.

Faith laughed softly. "I'm used to working hard. My father owns a flour mill and my mother runs the boardinghouse where many of my father's workers stay. There was always something for my five sisters and me to do."

"Five sisters?" He wondered if they were all as attractive as this young woman.

For just a moment Faith could see their faces as they had tearfully said goodbye. She reached for her own handkerchief. "Hope, Charity, Patience, Prudence . . ." She blushed faintly as she said the last name. "And Chastity."

Jonas repeated the names, amused. "Faith, Hope, and Charity. Patience, Prudence, and Chastity. It sounds as if you come from Bible-reading folks."

"Mama was. Papa never looked at it. Mama was the one who named us." She sighed, remembering how her father had insisted that he would name the boys when they came along. Though he had said he wasn't disappointed not to have any sons, Faith suspected he had lied. "And now I'm leaving them all behind." She dabbed at her eyes with the corner of her handkerchief, quickly recovering her composure. "How about you? Do you come from a big family?"

"Nope. Just me. I'm an only child, you see . . ." Jonas tried to keep the bitterness out of his voice. He was an only child all right. Left abandoned at an orphanage. Even now he couldn't even think about his early years without anger. But he'd survived by his wits and with his smile. Ever since then he'd been a loner, never really relying on anyone but himself when he got into trouble.

"Oh . . ." The way he had answered her seemed to indicate to Faith that he didn't really want to talk about his family. She quickly changed the subject. "Just where are you headed?"

"Well, one might say, little lady, that I'm disillusioned with city life. Too many people. Too much hustle and bustle." Jonas pushed his hat farther forward as he leaned his head back against the bench and crossed his legs. "I thought maybe Omaha would be different, but it was just more of the same, although a little more rustic." And dangerous, too, with all the hard-headed ranchers and farmers roaming about who didn't cotton much to his gambling ways. "Thought I might see what San Francisco is like, seeing as how it's at the end of the line. I've heard it's a land of opportunity." He didn't want to tell her that he was a gambler, figuring that somehow he'd earn her disapproval so he said, "You might say that I'm . . . I'm an 'entrepreneur.'"

"Oh." Faith didn't know exactly what that was, but it sounded impressive. "And . . . and I'm sure that you're a good one."

He grinned. "I try to be, little lady. I try to be." Indeed, he was skilled at his true profession. *Too* skilled, the last group of ranchers had said when they threatened to send him out of town on a rail. Jonas was not just a card player, he was a professional who had made his way in life by playing cards since the age of thirteen. A gambler in the true

21

sense of the word, he came out the winner an ungodly percentage of the time and knew exactly what hand of cards his opponents were holding. A bizarre skill perhaps, but one that had enabled him to live a life of ease.

"And so you're going to San Francisco." Faith wasn't at all certain that Mister Winslow had made a good choice. From what she had heard of that city, it was filled with vice, but she wished him well nonetheless.

"Yep!" Jonas settled back in his seat. It was going to be a long journey, but it sure would be more pleasant with feminine company. Too bad the young woman was engaged, for she really was quite comely. Had circumstances been different they might have had a bit of fun aboard the train. As it was, he'd have to remember himself. He had enough problems without a jealous fiancé chasing after him for an indiscretion. That had happened to him more than once. This time he'd be sure to act the perfect gentleman.

The steady, pulsating rhythm of the train wheels was mesmerizing, and for a long time Faith occupied herself by listening to the clatter, immersed in her own thoughts and memories. Was this all a dream? Would she wake up and find herself back in her bedroom at home? No, this journey was real. Henry was real. And so was the promise of a happy life, a new beginning. She was getting married, and there was only one thing marring the perfection of it all: her father's deep disapproval of the man she had chosen.

"He's a bit too bossy for my liking, missy. Why can't he just stay here in St. Paul and not go traipsing around to some godforsaken part of the continent, eh?" Her father had paused in his paperwork to look up at her sternly over the rim of his spectacles, and though she had tried to reason with him, he had stuck to his opinion. Faith would regret her decision, he had said over and over. She was determined to prove him wrong. The marriage would succeed. After all, hadn't nearly every female in St. Paul set her cap for Henry? Even her mother, who usually espoused the opinion that no man was good enough for her daughter, had given her approval to Henry Wingham. And every one of her five sisters had given him the eye. Faith had felt very proud the day she told them all about the upcoming wedding.

"Humph! If he were any kind of a man he'd have the wedding ceremony in a civilized part of the country where you could have your family attending," Andrew Tomkins had grumbled. "Instead, he insists on your tying the knot miles and miles away. Strange! Irritating."

Faith had tried to explain that Henry had wanted to have their wedding be symbolic of a new beginning and a new life by marrying in their new home territory, but though she'd tried to make her father understand, it had only caused Andrew Tomkins to resent Henry all the more. So much so that he had been the only family member who had not come to tell her goodbye. That still hurt Faith deeply.

"Oh, Papa!"

"What did you say?" Jonas Winslow's voice cut through the fog of Faith's thoughts, wresting her back to the present.

Faith hadn't realized she had spoken aloud. "The . . . the seat. It's getting just a bit uncomfortable," she said, not wanting to confide her troubles to this stranger. She shifted nervously in an effort to ease her numb backside.

Without a second thought to wrinkling his fine frock coat, he took it off and folded it, fashioning a cushion for her. "I've traveled enough to know that passengers have to bring their own blankets and pillows if they want a soft ride. Here . . . perhaps this will help." He handed her the coat.

"Oh, no. I just couldn't . . ." But Jonas Winslow wouldn't take no for an answer. Faith was thankful to have met such a gentleman. "Then thank you again." Although she didn't know anything about Jonas Winslow, his nearness made her feel safe and content.

"There, you see," Jonas said softly. "Isn't that better?"

"Oh, yes." She settled herself down to comfort. Looking out the window, Faith watched as the landscape of Omaha sped by, the city soon giving way to the checkerboard of farmland.

"The railroads have turned the empty West into a cornucopia, a land of plenty from what once was barren wasteland." Ah, yes he thought. There was money to be made because of this little invention. "Lumbermen send logs by rail. The fruits and harvests of California are transported to markets in many different places of the country." And of course there was another boon the railroads had brought as well, Jonas thought. Suckers. The kind of men who were perfect to be plucked. Men who couldn't say no to a game of cards.

They had traveled for a long time, so long that Faith's stomach rumbled in hunger. On the way to Omaha the conductor had stopped the train briefly so that the passengers could get sandwiches and coffee from a small depot lunchroom on the train platform. But it didn't appear that such a stop was going to be made this time. Again, however, Jonas Winslow saved the day.

"I don't suppose you packed a lunch?"

Faith shook her head. "No. I . . . didn't have time."

"Then by all means . . ." Reaching under the bench, he brought forth a small canvas bag. Inside were several beef sandwiches, two apples, and a piece of pie which was wrapped in a sheet of newspaper. Faith took one of the sandwiches and a bright red apple.

"Thank you. You are very generous." The food was a godsend and soon perked up her spirits.

"I've been on trains that traveled west before and I knew they wouldn't have depot eateries along the way. 'Be prepared' is always my motto."

He seemed so at ease, so knowledgeable. "You must have traveled by train several times before."

"Hundreds!" Jonas shot back. He doubted that there were very many miles of track that he hadn't crossed at least once in his travels.

"Oh, my!" For just a moment she envied him.

"I'm part Gypsy, I guess," she heard him say.

"It would seem so." Again she concentrated on the scenery, feeling excitement at the thought of the new life that awaited her. Listening to the clatter of the train wheels, she could almost imagine them saying, "Henry. Henry. Henry."

"So, you're on your way to Portland," she heard Jonas Winslow murmur, more to himself than to her.

"Milwaukie, actually," she corrected. "Unfortunately I'm going to have to take the stage since the railroad hasn't laid tracks there. At least not yet." Henry told her it was just a matter of time until the whole continent was zigzagged by the railroad.

"The stage, huh." Again she noted his gentle touch as he laid his hand on her arm. "Well, you be careful, you hear." His tone of voice told her he really meant it.

"I will be." Suddenly she wanted to express her gratitude to him for being so kind to her. Opening her eyes wide, she offered a sincere invitation. "If . . . if you are ever up Oregon way, please stop by and look in on Henry and me." Fearing she might have been a bit impetuous, she added, "I know Henry would like you." *She* certainly did.

"Yeah, sure." Jonas was a ladies' man who usually rankled men. He wasn't at all sure this new husband of hers would really welcome him if he accepted such an invitation.

"I mean it. Henry would like you and you would like him." She spoke sincerely from the bottom of her heart. "Think of the offer as being from one friend to another."

Friend? Jonas had never really had one, hadn't really trusted anyone long enough for that kind of relationship. Though Jonas acted as if he might accept Faith's offer, he doubted her ever would. What the hell would a man in his profession ever do in such a remote area of the country? Oregon. Ha! Not his kind of place, he thought. No, Oregon was the last territory he ever intended to visit.

Two

The pulsating clomp of horses' hooves was unnerving as, several hours later, the stagecoach bounced and lurched over the rutted road. Faith tried to brace herself to avoid the jolts, but she was less than successful. Now and again the coach would hit a big bump and in turn her head hit the hard wooden roof of the coach. This ride aboard the California State Company's stage was *not* pleasurable.

She certainly hoped she would reach her destination all in one piece, Faith thought as she muffled a cry of pain. She felt queasy from the motion. She longed for the comfort of the train. Even if the benches were hard and the tracks not completely smooth, at least the ride had been tranquil compared to this. Though the wood-burning, potbellied stoves inside each car had made the interior smoky at times as well as warm, that was far better than this choking dust from the road that teared her eyes, made her choke, burned her throat, and covered her hair and clothing with grime. As Faith suffered another jolt, she decided that stagecoaches most definitely weren't the place for proper ladies.

Even so, she knew that it could have been much worse. Upon boarding the stage, she had been told by the driver the rules of travel. When a wheel sank in sand or mud, everyone was expected to walk for miles beside the coach to ease the weight, he had said. They would leave their luggage and water buckets inside. Everything else had to be carried. Men should be prepared to push the coach from hip-deep mud if the necessity arose. When an accident occurred, all passengers had to be ready to give the driver a hand. Thankfully there had been none. At least not yet.

I wish I could have continued on the train, she thought. Unfortunately the railroad didn't reach as far as Oregon and she had no choice but to make do with this bone-jiggling mode of transportation. But yes, it could have been worse. Usually they tried to pack as many passengers in as possible, giving each passenger an area that was only about fifteen inches square. At least she had room to stretch her legs.

"You look frightened, sweet thing."

Only one other passenger was on the stage

right now, a black-haired, mustached man with mischief in his eyes who seemed to undress her every time he looked in her direction. He made her extremely uneasy.

"Want to come over next to me? I can put my arm around you for protection." Even the man's low baritone voice gave her the jitters. Faith missed Jonas Winslow, her former traveling companion.

"No. No, thank you. I'm fine." She tried to hide her nervousness beneath a facade of calm, wishing all the while it was Jonas sitting near her. Jonas had been completely charming. His easygoing manner and interesting conversation had put her at ease, turning what might have been a long, tedious journey into a seemingly short jaunt that had ended much too soon. When the Union Pacific had at last stopped at the station in Promontory Point and they had told each other goodbye, she to go by stagecoach and he to take the Central Pacific on in to San Francisco, she hated to see him leave. It was unusual for Faith to be so terribly forward, but she had actually thrown her arms around his neck and hugged him.

"Take care of yourself, Jonas," she had whispered. "And thank you for being so . . . so . . . *nice*. I'll never forget you."

He had seemed almost embarrassed by her gratitude. "Thank you for making my trip so pleasurable." He had winked. "If you weren't about to become a married lady, I just might have tried to convince you to run off to San Francisco with me."

"And I just might have gone if it wasn't for Henry," she had teased. And in truth, if it hadn't been for Henry she just *might* have.

"You know, I really envy him," he had said softly, the sincerity in his voice evident. "He's one lucky man!"

For just a brief moment their eyes had met and held in a look so potent that Faith shivered. Remembering propriety, she had forced herself to look away.

"Goodbye."

"Goodbye and good luck, Jonas . . ."

She wondered now how things were going for him. Undoubtedly he'd have reached San Francisco by now, while she was still bouncing along on her way. He'd seemed so happy about his trip. He had made no secret of the fact that he was anxious to leave Omaha. He had said that he had lived there long enough not to want to make it his permanent home, though from the looks of him he might have made a good wrangler. Certainly he was muscular enough.

Now, what was it he had told her he did? Ah, yes. He was an "entrepreneur." She'd have to remember to ask Henry exactly what that was. A businessman of sorts, she supposed. She had wondered at the pearl-handled revolver she had glimpsed protruding from his vest when he had removed his coat. But then, a man had to protect himself on the road, didn't he?

"Godspeed, Jonas."

Faith's own journey had been long and exhausting. From the moment she had reached Promontory Point and boarded this stagecoach, she had sensed that she was in for quite a time. The driver seemed to be in a terrible hurry, as if his very life depended on traveling as rapidly as possible. With orders that all passengers were only to sleep a few hours at the rest stops and should be up before the crack of dawn, the surly little man had set the coach's six black horses into a lively gallop, stirring up a goodly amount of dust. Choking grit drifted through the open window like a thick, dark cloud. Despite fits of coughing, however, Faith had to admit that even this annoyance was bearable when she thought of the happiness that waited her once the journey was over.

"Mrs. Henry Wingham. Faith Wingham. Mrs. Faith Anne Wingham." Feeling light-hearted, she said her new name over and over again to herself. Oh, it seemed too good to be true. She was excited about her new life in Oregon. How wonderful it would be to be married to Henry, she thought as the stagecoach bounced along the steep road.

From time to time she looked out the window at the huge rocks, flowing creeks, and tall trees. It certainly was a rugged terrain, wasn't it? A far cry from the flat lands the train had chugged through. Perhaps much too rugged, she suddenly thought in alarm as the stagecoach weaved up a mountain road. Then there was the terrifying descent. Hairpin curves. Sometimes she couldn't even see the lead horses when they disappeared around the bend. The brakes smoked and the coach rattled. Faith took a deep gasp of air as the wheels of the stagecoach loomed too close to the edge. The embankment only reminded her how far she would fall if there was an accident.

"Sorry you came out here, sweet thing?"

The dark-haired man's voice startled her, reinforcing her dislike of him. For one moment she had been able to forget his presence. "I just wish the stagecoach wasn't going so fast, that's all."

Her heart was beating so loud that she was certain he could hear. Perhaps if she clutched the satchel in which she was carrying her wedding gown, held it close to her heart, she could slow its hammering.

"Has to, if it's going to keep to schedule." The man looked at his watch. "Don't the vehicles travel this fast where you come from? Wherever that is."

"Minnesota."

"Minnesota, huh?" He shrugged. "I've never been there. Must be a nice place, though, if it turns out women as pretty as you. Peaches-and-cream complexion, auburn hair, big blue eyes. Just to my liking." As he spoke, he reached out to caress a stray curl that had slipped from beneath her bonnet.

"I beg your pardon, sir!" She voiced her outrage as she backed away quickly. "I'm certain my future husband would take great exception to your familiarity with me."

"Just trying to be friendly, sweet thing. Just trying to be friendly." Taking out a cigar, the man struck a match on the sole of his boot and lit it, then made great show of savoring each puff. The smoke made Faith sneeze, but the activity did, however, at least stop his advances for a while.

Faith wished that the two women who had been traveling with them earlier hadn't gotten off at the last stop—a small place called Eugene, which seemed to be a collection of tiny houses clustered together. She longed for their company now and didn't like being alone with this overbold weasel.

"Abigail Scott and Cloe Gordeon," she said to herself, remembering them. Abigail was an opinionated, parasol-wielding matron who would have soon put him in his place. Mrs. Scott looked as if she could take good care of herself and anyone else near by.

Faith remembered listening as Mrs. Scott had talked on and on about her personal business in Eugene. She had been proud that she was a new landowner and had revealed that women owned fifteen percent of the land there and were gaining more rights all the time. Her friend, Cloe Gordeon, seemed a bit less forward than Abigail, a rather frail, demure young woman as a matter of fact. She, too, however, had proudly boasted of the land she and her husband had come to claim.

Suddenly the coach hit a bump in the road, jarring both passengers. It was all Faith could do to keep from hurling right onto the lap of the offensive man. With a frantic gasp, she shoved her hat back off her forehead and pushed the feather out of her eyes.

"What in heaven's name . . . ?"

Leaning out the window, the dark-haired man was shouting obscenities at the driver. "Damn it all to hell, you old son-of-a-bitch! Watch where the hell you're going!"

Faith was quick to come to the driver's defense. "It might not have been his fault."

"Yeah, and then again it just might have been." It took several minutes for the man to cool his temper. He sat back in his seat, but seemed very preoccupied with looking out the window. Every once in a while he would glance at his watch and Faith could only suppose he feared he was going to be late for some appointment.

Well, at least whatever the problem, it has

taken his mind off me, Faith thought, but her relief came much too soon.

"Now, as to you, sweet thing . . ." Boldly he reached out and touched Faith's knee as if to prove to her just how little he feared her husband-to-be. "It might just be a heap better for you if you were a bit more friendly." Whereas Jonas Winslow's smile had warmed her, this stranger's grin left her shivering. He seemed by every word and deed to be a thoroughly unscrupulous cad.

"I'm being just exactly as friendly as I feel I should be," Faith retorted hotly, for a moment wishing she had Jonas's revolver in her possession. "And if you ever dare touch—"

She might have said more, but just then, too men with flour sacks over their heads that showed only their eyes rode alongside the coach. If there had been a cloud of dust before, now it was a virtual dust storm. The sound of horses' hooves was deafening.

"My God!" Faith had heard of stagecoach holdups, but even in her wildest imaginings, she had never dreamed it would happen while she was a passenger. "Those men!" Frantically, she pointed out the window.

"Well, well, well . . ." With no great show of alarm, the dark-haired man beside her merely puffed on his cigar.

"We're going to be robbed!" Despite her loathing for her fellow passenger, Faith

37

turned to him for help. "What are we going to do?"

"The driver will try to outdistance them," he answered very calmly.

"Outdistance?" Poking her head out the window, Faith frantically urged the stagecoach driver on. "Dear God! Hurry! Hurry." As if she were holding the imaginary reins, she clenched her fists. "Come on! Come on!"

With a snap of the whip and a stream of curse words, the driver kept the horses traveling the winding road at an astonishing speed, but with the bulk of the coach to drag them down, the horses weren't any match for their pursuers. Much to Faith's dismay the gunmen finally brought the stagecoach to a complete halt at the top of the hill.

"Thought you'd never make it, Clancy!" the passenger inside called out to one of the men as he opened the door.

"Clancy?" He knew the robbers! "Why, you're one of them," Faith blurted out, hardly realizing the words had escaped. Quickly, she covered her mouth with her hand lest she say more.

"Sure enough, lady!" Without a twinge of remorse, the man got out to join his partners in crime. He motioned to Faith to join him. "Now be a good little girl and join the driver over there at the edge of the road. Keep your hands on top of your head like he's doing," he said, pointing in the driver's direction.

Though Faith's knees were quaking, she managed to comply. Desperately, she looked around her for a way of escape but decided that such a show of bravery would be foolish. She couldn't run fast enough to escape a bullet.

"And hand over your jewelry."

Faith was too stunned to do as she was ordered. How could this be happening to her? Certainly it wouldn't be happening if she was still in St. Paul!

"I said, your jewelry!" Yanking at her hand, the man who had traveled so deceptively beside her pressed his fingers against her ring. "Now."

Slowly Faith pulled the diamond engagement ring off her finger, remembering how light of heart she had felt when Henry had slipped it on her finger. Controlling the urge to hurl it in the stage robber's face, she demurely handed it over. She'd get it back. She had to believe that.

The men were thorough and unrelenting in their quest for valuables. Though the real reason for their attack was a wooden box filled with gold, they also tore her large suitcase apart. Dresses were scattered about everywhere, as well as all her unmentionables.

"Oh la la. Look at them corsets and petticoats." One of the masked bandits made sport of modeling one or two pieces of the undergarments, much to Faith's mortification.

"And just like a woman, she's hidden her money pouch among all the lace." Triumphantly the second robber held up the leather item.

"Noooooo!" Every penny Faith had in the world was in there, except for the emergency money she had hidden in her bodice. But she didn't expect any plea for clemency would do any good.

"Hand over that other suitcase you're carrying."

Faith was devastated. She couldn't give up the satchel! Inside were pictures of her family and the white satin-and-lace gown her mother had made for her. "Please don't take this one," she pleaded, her eyes filling with tears. "My—my wedding dress is inside."

"Oh, boo hoo." One of the hooded men circled around her and tugged at the small suitcase, but Faith held tight.

"Please . . ." Her eyes sought out the man who had ridden in the stagecoach with her, though why she expected any help from him she didn't know.

"Am I supposed to be sympathetic?" He scowled angrily at her but pushed his companion's hand away when he would have yanked the small suitcase from her hands. "Your wedding dress, huh? A wedding dress might bring a good price. If the lace is good."

Faith wasn't too proud to beg. "Let me keep this at least . . ."

He seemed ready to give in to her plea, but his cohort in crime interceded. "You said we intended to keep everything, including that old coot's rifle." The hooded man was obviously peevish.

"Yeah. I suppose I did." His voice was curt, but much to Faith's relief he let her keep the smaller suitcase. "Throw all that baggage and those mail sacks down here, Joe. Clancy and I will catch it and fasten it on to the horses." For a moment he turned his back on Faith. "Good old Clancy. You did bring a horse for me and a packhorse as well." He grinned. "Always knew you were my man and that I could trust you."

Lurching forward, one of the hooded men grabbed once again at Faith's small suitcase, but she clutched it desperately. This was even more necessary to her than the money. She just couldn't let anyone take it! "No!"

"Listen, lady . . ." The man's demeanor was threatening.

Faith again turned to her former traveling companion for help. "At least let me keep the pictures of my family and my fiancé. And . . . and my wedding dress. My mother made it for me." Her eyes flashed defiance. "I won't let you take everything!"

The dark-haired man pushed his wide-brimmed brown hat back on his head and looked her over while he nibbled on the edge of a matchstick. For some reason he seemed to decide to let her keep the small suitcase. "Well, I suppose we can let you keep those few items. Don't want you to think I'm a complete villain." He eyes her with a measure of respect. "Guess I always did have a special fondness for spunky women."

"Thank you!" For just a fleeting moment she nearly liked him. "And in return I'll forget I ever saw you." Strange, she thought, that while the others were masked, this man showed his face.

"If you know what's good for you, you will do just that." Walking over to her, he cupped her chin in his hand and looked deep into her eyes. "And who can say. Maybe we'll meet up again some time and can continue where we left off when my friends appeared." With a deep, throaty laugh he let her go and turned away.

"Goodness gracious, I certainly hope not," Faith mumbled beneath her breath. She was so glad to be retaining her most precious items that she just nodded and gave him a crooked, reluctant smile when he turned around. Little did he know that the deed to her new property had been sewn into the hem of her wedding dress. Harry had insisted that she take this wedding present with her until he could join her, but it had been *her* idea to conceal it in such a manner. All of a sudden she felt very clever. She wasn't as naive as she might have appeared.

A thunder of hoofbeats announced the bandits' departure. Bending down, Faith picked up the scattered contents of her suitcase, stuffing the underwear and dresses inside and closing the lid. Since the clasp was broken, she had to tie it all together with a length of rope the stagecoach driver gave her.

"Damn vultures!" With a grunt, the driver dusted himself off. "I'm going to be shanghied when I get to Portland without that gold." Putting his hand on her arm, he helped Faith back to the coach.

"My money is gone. My ring!" she mumbled. But at least she hadn't lost everything. She could make do until Henry arrived, if she was frugal. With a sigh, she settled back in her seat as the stagecoach started up again. What a story she would have to tell her fiancé! Closing her eyes, she thought for a moment about Jonas Winslow. What was he doing at this moment? Probably settling himself in at some fancy hotel in San Francisco, she thought. In that moment she envied him.

Three

Jonas took a puff on his expensive cigar and grinned as he looked around at his elegant surroundings. Now this was what he deserved—a hotel with crystal chandeliers, ornate mirrors, red velvet chairs, marble floors, Turkish carpets, and mahogany paneling from wall to wall! A man could quickly get used to this kind of luxury. He certainly had in just the two hours since he'd arrived.

"Yes, sir, San Francisco is exactly what I thought it would be," he affirmed aloud. And more. It was a city thick with those who had made their fortunes in the shipping industry, in gold mines, and the railroads. They were sheep just waiting to be fleeced and, best of all, from what he'd seen, they all enjoyed gaming and betting. Men here seemed driven to placing bets—on turtle races, jumping frogs, cockfights, bare-knuckled boxing matches which lasted until one of the fighters was knocked unconscious, or games of chance such as keno, roulette, klondike fare, blackjack, and poker. The card games were more up Jonas's alley.

"Hello, stranger!"

As Jonas looked up to see the willowy redhead in her black satin dress who had perched herself so sensuously by his elbow, he added beautiful women to the list of San Francisco's delights. "Hello yourself."

"May I sit down?" Before Jonas could answer, she moved with all the grace of a sleek cat, slithering into the empty chair beside him.

"Be my guest." He'd be a fool to turn down such promising company. "May I offer you a drink?" She nodded, and Jonas picked up his decanter of brandy and poured a glass for her and one for himself.

"My name's Red," she said, leaning over so that her breath tickled his ear.

"Red, huh." Her name was so obvious that he couldn't help but grin. That thick shining hair of hers was certainly red all right. "Mine is Jonas."

"Jonas." The way she said it, so low and husky, was seductive.

Jonas took a long, slow slip of his liquor, envisioning the start of a very pleasant friendship. Looking at the cleavage she so provocatively displayed, he decided that this was a woman he would really like to know better.

"Where are you from?"

That wasn't a question Jonas could easily deal with. "Here, there, and everywhere," he answered evasively. "How about you?"

"Chicago." Taking his arm, she leaned against him. "I came to further my fame on the Barbary Coast. And I have," she said proudly. As if to make certain that he would know just who she was, she pointed to a large poster on the wall. It displayed her painted likeness, a dimpled smiling image dressed in an emerald-green low-cut gown with "Red Danberry, San Francisco's Nightingale" emblazoned in gold letters.

"You." Jonas looked from Red to the portrait, deciding it really didn't do her justice. "Well, if your singing matches your beauty, then I can look forward to a rare and special treat."

She didn't reply to his compliment, but the look in her eyes told Jonas that he had made a hit. After a while she asked, "Tell me, Jonas, is your skill at cards as great as your charm?"

Not wanting it known that he was a professional gambler, Jonas just shrugged. "Like most, sometimes I'm lucky and then again sometimes I'm not." It was perfect that she was the one who mentioned cards first. Jonas suspected that she might be a lookout who not only kept an eye out for cheaters, making certain the house profits were high, but also the bait to lead men into a game or two. Well, that was really what he wanted. Still, he played it very cautiously waiting for her to cajole him into joining a table of gaming-room patrons. It wasn't long before she did just that. Jonas affected a jaunty air as he walked to the table. He had the feeling that this was going to be his lucky night.

Taking a seat beside him, Red Danberry introduced him to his fellow card players. Slowly Jonas's eyes swept over the other men at the table. The man to his right was tall and wore spectacles, the man to his left was mustached and balding, and the one across from him had a large nose and eyebrows that were thick and grew together. They were ordinary-looking men in their thirties and forties but paunchy from lives that excluded any real work. Men to whom the good life had come relatively easy, he thought. The type that made it easy on his conscience.

"Are you going to deal, Red?" one of the men asked, eyeing her up and down with a gaze that could have started a blaze.

"Sure, why not!"

Jonas watched as she shuffled the deck with a skill that proved she was anything but a novice. He had the feeling she would bring him luck, an intuition that was quickly soured when he looked at his cards. The hand he had been dealt was a poor one, but he didn't even flinch. A big part of being a successful gambler was keeping a "poker face," hiding one's real emotions. Despite only having a pair of fours, he leaned back in his chair and hid his disappointment, even betting a dollar. He'd bluff the others. Wasn't that his forte after all?

"Draw?" Red's voice was soothing.

"Yeah." Discarding two cards, Jonas optimistically drew two more. They didn't do him any good. He'd hoped to at least get two pair, but he had drawn two losers. Still, he kept his composure, grinning all the while, wider when Red boldly fondled his knee beneath the table.

"Your turn Danner," the man sitting to Jonas's right said to the man on his left. It was obvious by his smile that he thought he had the winning hand.

"I fold." With a disgruntled snort, Danner threw in his hand.

The man across the table took his turn to draw. After taking a quick peek at the cards, he threw out two dollars in change. "I'll see you two and raise you." His cheek twitched in agitation, a movement Jonas sensed was a dangerous sign. He didn't like the man with the thick brows. Didn't like him at all. A warning of some kind pricked at him. Well, maybe he'd get out of this game after the current hand was played.

The man on the right added his stake to the pile of money in the middle of the table. Tension tingled in the air.

"I call." The man with the thick brows announced his two pair, then reached for the pile of money. Before he could take it, the man to Jonas's right reached out and put a stranglehold on his wrist.

"Not so fast." His hand consisted of three aces and two jacks.

"That's impossible!" came a shout from the man to the left. He threw down his two aces. "There aren't five aces in any deck of cards. You are a cheating bastard."

All eyes turned toward the self-proclaimed winner, Randolph Vanduvall, as the man across from Jonas reached for his gun. He was not quite fast enough. Pulling his own revolver, the man to the right pointed it straight at his accuser.

"Now, wait a minute . . ." Without even thinking, Jonas drew his pearl-handled gun just as a shot rang out. The eyes of the man across from him showed a flicker of astonishment, then he fell forward. "I'll be damned."

From out of nowhere a crowd of men suddenly appeared, a plump, gray-haired man at their head. Taking Red's arm with familiarity, looking daggers at Jonas all the while, he erringly proclaimed the culprit of the deed.

"That man. He's the culprit." Pointing his finger right at Jonas, his voice held a tone of certainty. "He killed Randolph Vanduvall."

Four

Faith was relieved when, cracking the whip, the driver started the horses back on their journey. With a groan, the stagecoach rolled down the rutted dirt road that led to Portland. Needless to say, it was an exhilarating ride. Bracing herself against the side of the coach, she held her breath, hoping against hope that there wouldn't be any more outlaws lurking behind the bushes to take them unawares.

"One robbery is enough to last me for a lifetime," she mumbled indignantly, patting that place in her bodice where her emergency funds were hidden. Well, at least not all was lost. Thanks to the small stash of money and the deed she would be able to survive for a time. But oh how glad she would be to see Henry!

All along the way Faith let her imagination wander. What would Henry have done if they had been together when the bandits robbed the stage? Would he have stood up to them? Fought those rogues for her honor? Kept them from stealing nearly everything she had? She tried to place Henry in the position of hero, but somehow, although Henry was kind and generous, he was rather more bookish and businesslike than most western men. Henry probably would have been very diplomatic and would never have done anything to upset those bandit rogues. He would have tried to reason them out of the robbery. And as glib of tongue as he was, he might very well have succeeded.

Dear, sweet Henry. In Minnesota he had worked with his father's law firm of Wingham and Carney and had been blessed with the "gift of gab" all men of his profession seemed to have. Among the "eligibles" he had been considered an excellent catch, coming as he did from an aristocratic family. That he also had good looks, an education, and charm had made him doubly sought after. With all the women in Minnesota giving him the eye, however, he had wanted *her* and had made no secret of that fact.

Clutching the hem of her wedding dress, where the deed was hidden, Faith reflected on the past. Henry Wingham had made Faith feel special. Wanted. As if she were the most important woman in the world. How then could she have helped falling in love with him. And soon they would start a new life together in that place her father had called "that uncivilized wilderness on the other side of the world."

Faith couldn't help but smile at her father's perception of the beautiful, forested place in which she would make her new home. Why, it had been a state now for almost ten years. Hardly uncivilized. Henry said it was the perfect place for a landowner to become prosperous.

"A perfect place . . ." She sighed, anxious to get to her destination. She had done about all the traveling she wanted for a while. It would be good to stay in one place. To take a bath, sleep on a feather bed again. With Henry.

Faith felt a surge of emotion. Looking around her at the empty confines of the stagecoach, she realized she had never felt so alone in all her life. Not that she wasn't relieved to have parted company with that lecherous man, that villain who had robbed them. No, it was just that she suddenly wished she had someone to talk to. Someone like that Abigail Scott. Or Jonas Winslow. Someone who might at least have some idea where they were.

"Driver!" Poking her head out the window, she tired to get his attention. "How much farther?" She was becoming very impatient.

But it was like trying to talk to the wind.

Whether he just didn't hear her or didn't want to respond, the stagecoach driver didn't even turn his head. Faith looked around her, but she couldn't tell whether or not they were coming to a town. She *could* tell, however, that they were in for a storm. The sky had totally changed since the last time she had looked. It was cloudy. Gray. There was a dampness in the air.

"Just what we need. A rainstorm." What would it do to her hairdo? To her clothes? To the roads? Henry had warned about the rain, telling her that it was what would make their homestead green. Optimistically, Faith also thought of how good the moisture would be for her complexion. Wasn't that what Henry liked about her. He had said she always saw a rainbow behind every cloud.

Faith remembered how everyone in St. Paul had been amazed when Henry had decided to leave his father's firm and go to work as a surveyor for the railroad. Everyone except Faith herself. She understood that a job with the railroad would better prepare him for his new life in the West. A life she was soon to be a part of.

Once again Faith's thoughts turned to those first days with Henry. He had courted her for six months before making his decision to go to Omaha, Nebraska. A few weeks before leaving, he had asked her father's permission to marry her. It had been granted grudgingly. After all, Faith was the eldest at twenty-four. It was about time one of the girls planned to marry, he had said. He couldn't imagine why she had decided to remain single for so long. Faith suspected that despite his anger at her traveling so far away and his objections to Henry, her father had said yes to the marriage because he wanted grandsons.

"He's the perfect husband for you," Faith's mother had said. As always, she had thought about Faith's happiness.

Faith had tried to hide her independent nature, but her mother and sister Hope, the two family members who were closest to her, knew she was tired of city life and longed for adventure in the West. Though her father had been as grumbly as a bear, Henry had been enthusiastically approved by the female members. All five of Faith's sisters had admitted to being a wee bit jealous of her approaching marriage and had told her that Henry had given her one of the prettiest engagement rings they had ever seen. And now it was gone! Stolen by those . . . those awful men.

Faith touched her finger, missing the sparkle. For just a moment she felt a bit sorry for herself. Her eyes misted with tears but she hastily blinked them away and scolded herself. It could have been much worse. She could have lost her life. As it was, she still had some money and the deed, the precious deed. And quite a story to tell Henry when he arrived in two weeks.

A growl of thunder caused Faith to look out the window, there to gaze at a vast forest. Beautiful green trees as far as the eye could see. What magnificent country. How could it not help to lift her spirits. No wonder Henry had loved it so. It was like a continuous garden, wildflowers interspersed with the other foliage. She wondered if Portland would be just as green and hoped that it would.

Henry had purposely chosen a place near Portland, named Milwaukie. As she had told Jonas Winslow, it had the same name as a town in Wisconsin that was close to neighboring Minnesota, their home state. There were no towns in Oregon named St. Paul, the place where they were both from. But it was close enough. He said it would bring them luck. She smiled as she thought of Henry's thoughtfulness in choosing Milwaukie and admired him for selecting an area where he felt she would be more at home.

But would she ever get there? For just a moment the journey seemed unending. How tired she was of being alone on this road. The sound of a human voice would certainly warm her spirits. As it was, all she could hear now was the roar of thunder, the thumping sound of rain as it began to fall on the top of the coach, and the unrelenting sound of horses' hooves.

It was late in the afternoon before the stage finally came to an end at the mouth of the gulch along which they had been traveling. The approach to Portland from the east was a very narrow, very winding road that was scary for travelers and a holy terror for the stagecoach drivers. But it was beautiful. Spongy woods and lushly ferned hills that shaded the roads sometimes let in little sunshine, Henry had told her. That was hardly the problem today with the rain tumbling from the skies. But sun or not, a kaleidoscope of distant images and colors caused Faith to gasp in wonder as she came closer and closer to her final stage of the journey.

The Columbia River gorge was up ahead. The view was enough to make her head swim. The cascades rolled eastward in a series of uneven greenery, the three great peaks of the Oregon Cascades in the distance: Mount Hood, Mount Jefferson, and the Three Sisters. There were several waterfalls and odd rock formations, some of the falls tumbling from overhanging cliffs.

The city of Portland itself seemed not much different from any other she had seen along the way. As the stagecoach groaned through the mud traveling down the main street, Faith was afforded a full view of the sprawling metropolis that shone through a curtain of raindrops.

Faith could hardly wait to meet Henry and get to Milwaukie, but for tonight and several nights to come she would have to stay here.

Ignoring the rain, the driver jumped down from his seat, opened the stage door, and assisted Faith down to ground level. She held her suitcase and walked, ankle deep in the mud. The only refuge from the storm seemed to be the depot tearoom, and she hurriedly darted in to it. Wet, her hair stringing, looking like a waif, she wondered if Jonas Winslow would have been so gentlemanly if she had looked then like she looked now.

Five

Jonas shivered as he fought down a surge of panic. Flattening himself against the cold wood of a saloon alcove, he waited as a police wagon rumbled by. He had to find a place to hide. But where? The whole damned city was looking for him.

I have to get away from here! he thought, feeling a surging tide of desperation. San Francisco would be his doom if he didn't get free of it as soon as he could.

Pushing past signs that lured the unwary to saloons and brothels, he fled into the night, shivering as the sound of gunfire shattered the stillness. He'd been spotted. Damn it all! If only for just a fleeting moment he could make himself invisible.

"It's him all right, Sergeant!" a patrolman declared.

"Are you sure?"

"As sure as I am that I'm Irish!" The

sound of tramping feet announced that they were following Jonas.

Never in his life had he run so fast! Up streets and down. Through alleys. Leaping over boxes and barrels. Ducking beneath wagons. Dodging carriage wheels. How he covered so much territory in so little time Jonas would never know. Certainly he'd never exhibited any athletic prowess before this, but suddenly he found himself at the edge of the city. Pausing for just a moment, he took a long, deep breath, drawing the wet scent of San Francisco Bay into his lungs. He was trapped! Fool that he was, he had cornered himself.

"And so, Winslow, it comes to this," he muttered. The water looked cold, but not nearly as icy as he would be if a bullet took his life. He had to jump! There was no other choice. Or was there?

An earthen checkerboard was a welcome sight. God bless farmers! Jonas let a long sigh of relief tear from his lips as he spotted a cornfield far to his left. The tall stalks offered a hope. Better than taking a chance on drowning. It was a long shot, but he knew he had to try. With strong determination to survive, he set his feet to flying.

Three shots rang out, barely missing Jonas's tall, muscular frame as he darted in and out amidst the high-waving cornstalks.

Only his dark head bobbed up from time to time.

"Damn fool policeman," Jonas muttered. He'd shot Jonas's expensive Stetson right off his head, but Jonas couldn't put himself in more danger by going back to fetch it now. He'd just have to buy a new one at the first opportunity.

"I don't suppose it matters that I am innocent!" he called out. Gunfire was his answer.

My God! he thought to himself, his hazel eyes blazing anger, directed mostly at himself. Why had he not just left well enough alone? When he had drawn his pistol to stop that argument he hadn't even really known those men. It hadn't been his concern that they were fighting over a damned poker game. He should have minded his own business.

As it was, a man was shot, stone-cold dead. Another man, apparently the assassin's friend, had accused Jonas of committing the murder. To cover his own guilt, of course. Such details hadn't mattered, however, considering that Jonas was standing there with a revolver in his hand when the policemen had walked in.

Jonas relived the incident in his mind as he paused in his flight. He wondered how a perfectly enjoyable evening could have suddenly gone so wrong. He had instantly fallen in love with the architecture and the atmosphere of San Francisco. The women were beautiful, the hotels luxurious, and money seemed to flow as easily as water from a fountain. It had seemed as if he had finally found a permanent home. How could he have ever known that an innocent game of cards would be his undoing? Or that a man's jealousy would nearly mean the end of his freedom forever?

Jonas darted from shadow to shadow, trying desperately to lose his pursuers. Scrambling up the hill, he shivered as the sound of gunfire again shattered the stillness.

Cards and women! When was he ever going to learn? That red-haired nightingale hadn't even been worth the price he'd have to pay if he was caught. Why hadn't he noticed that that man from Nob Hill was upset over the attention she had been paying Jonas earlier in the evening!

Hell, I can't help it if I'm irresistible to women, he thought. Besides, how was he to know she was the paramour of that short, paunchy, balding man. She should have told him. Now that loud-mouthed lout of hers would have the last laugh when he saw Jonas put behind bars for the rest of his life because of his lousy testimony. Damn it! But they would have to catch him first.

Jonas ran for his life, not even daring a glance over his shoulder. He'd just arrived in San Francisco. Didn't have a friend anywhere nearby who could vouch for him. Even so, any damn fool with half a thimbleful of sense would know he hadn't fired that shot. The barrel of his Colt had been as cold as ice when he had been apprehended and dragged off to that miserable jail cell. But then, such a detail really wouldn't matter if someone of influence wanted to see him caged.

Every once in a while Jonas stopped to catch his breath and to see if he was still being followed. From the appearance of things it was evident that he had evaded his pursuers at least for the time being. He was nevertheless aware of the fact he was now wanted for the murder of a complete stranger.

It was a puzzle, he thought. Though there were several pieces, they just didn't all fit together. Right now he didn't have time to figure it out nor to learn how or why he'd been framed, or by whom. He would let that mystery go unsolved. He had to get far away. Someday he would return to San Francisco and do some investigating, but right now the most important thing was to get across the border into another state. But not on foot. He needed a horse and some food.

A horse and food. It sounded so simple, but at that moment he might as well have been wishing for the world. Still, he was determined.

It was dark. That much at least was in his favor. With the sun down, it would be difficult for anyone to follow him. If he could somehow get to that farmhouse up ahead and "borrow" a horse, along with whatever other supplies he could find, he might get out of this fix. *Might.*

If he rode all night long he could be out of the state by daylight, he realized. *If.* A lot rested on that little word. And yet the very hope that escape was entirely possible made him feel a whole lot better. He could get away if he kept calm.

Sitting very still, Jonas contemplated his next move, then crept quietly toward a large wood barn up ahead. Once inside he found out that it was warm and cozy. So much so that he was nearly tempted into staying put and relaxing—until he remembered his predicament!

Climbing into the hayloft, Jonas peered down at two dapple gray horses eating from their trough of oats. He was in luck. Though this farm certainly wasn't the home of monied people, he figured these two horses would be just what he was looking for.

He warned himself that he was stealing. The thought troubled him. Gambling and taking from the rich was one thing, but stealing from common folk was another. But he had no other choice. He was a desperate man. His very life was at stake if he stayed anywhere around here. He didn't know if these horses could even travel very fast. But what the hell! What else could he do?

Before he started out again, he had to map out in his mind the direction he wanted to take. Over toward Nevada? No, there were too many tinhorn gamblers there. Undoubtedly, it would be one of the first places his pursuers would look. There would be handbills and pamphlets galore offering a reward.

Oregon popped into his head then. Yes, that was it. Oregon. The image of wide, long-lashed blue eyes came immediately to mind. Now, what was the name of that little lady he'd met on the train? Tom . . . Tom . . . *Tomkins.* That was it. But what was her first name? He remembered her telling him that she came from a family of six daughters.

"Faith." Yes, that was it. Three of the girls had been named Faith, Hope, and Charity. He couldn't remember the names of the others, but that didn't matter. All he wanted to remember was the eldest of the girls—Faith Tomkins, soon to become a married woman.

Jonas always had an excellent memory. Now he forced himself to remember the details. She had been on her way to marry a man by the name of Henry. Wing-and-a-ham. Henry Wingham, a surveyor for the railroad. She was going to their homestead in Oregon where her soon-to-be husband would meet her. By now they were probably married and in possession of a nice piece of farmland.

A hiding place and much more. A good opportunity. If he could get there, he might be able to land a job at their place, at least until the heat died down. And who could tell but that the little lady and her husband could mean a whole new chance for him, Jonas thought. "Faith," he whispered again. Fate had certainly dealt him a good hand when he'd come across that little lady.

Jonas tried to remember more details. They'd parted company at Promontory Point and she had taken the Overland Stage. As she left she had told him to look them up if he ever came up Portland way. Milwaukie was the name of the town. Probably some godforsaken place where hardly anyone ever came. A place where people were gullible. Perfect.

"Faith Tomkins."

What a stroke of luck! Perhaps being kind to a woman traveling alone would pay off. When he'd helped her with her luggage and she had insisted that he come visit her in Oregon, it had been a turning point in his life, though he hadn't know it then.

"Ah yes, Faith, my dear." The more he contemplated the idea, the more he realized it was the only way. "It appears that we are going to meet again, Faith Tomkins, and much sooner than either of us realized."

Six

Looking out the small window of the stage stop tearoom, Faith couldn't help thinking of the rhyme she and her sisters had repeated when they were children. *Rain, rain go away.* Was it ever going to stop? There were so many things to be done and here she was trapped by this torrent.

"Rain, rain go away. Come again some other day," she mouthed between sips from her teacup.

Foremost on her mind was whether she would be able to find a place to stay the night. The storm was making her arrival in Portland difficult. She had hoped to find a hotel or boardinghouse, but the muddy streets, the rain, and the approaching darkness would handicap such an effort.

A helpless, sinking feeling swept over her as she realized the seriousness of her predicament. She was alone in a new place with very little money. Friendless, with nowhere to go. It was raining buckets and from the looks of things the tearoom would soon be closing. A sign on the wall said that it was open from sunup to sundown. Well, what sun there was would soon be setting.

Faith was tired. It had been a long and grueling day. Giving in to her sagging spirits and exhaustion, she put down her teacup and used her folded arms as a pillow and laid her head on the table. Closing her eyes, she tried to calm her muddled thoughts and think of what she should do, where she should go.

She suddenly felt a light tap on her shoulder. Looking up, Faith saw a tall woman with kind gray eyes and an abundance of salt-and-pepper hair pulled severely back from her face and held in a chignon by a multitude of hairpins. A kindly, motherly face.

"Is there something wrong, lassie?" The woman's voice, like her expression, mirrored her concern.

Wrong? So many things had gone wrong today that Faith wouldn't have known where to begin. Wordlessly, she just sat there as a mist of tears stung her eyes. She still had high hopes for her future, but she was most assuredly getting off to a very bad start. At the moment she was just tired and discouraged.

"There, there, now don't you cry." Pulling

a handkerchief out of her reticule, the woman promptly handed it to Faith.

"I—I won't." But she did. The tears she had suppressed after the stage coach robbery now fell as fiercely as the raindrops. Having at last found someone who would listen, Faith let her story out, punctuating it with sniffles and sobs. She babbled about Henry, about their dreams of a life together, and about her train journey from St. Paul. She grimaced as she spoke about the bumpy ride aboard the stage. Lastly she related the awful moment when she had faced those gun-toting ruffians who had stolen everything she owned.

"They didn't!"

"They did." Faith blew her nose. "Or nearly did, that is." She touched the small suitcase leaning against the leg of her chair. "Everything but this and the clothes on my back."

Pulling out a chair, the woman sat down beside her, clucking her tongue in sympathy. "You poor, poor dearie." She reached out and patted Faith's hand. "Ah, but it sounds to me as if you were very brave. As for myself, I might have fainted dead away."

"I couldn't! I had to keep my wits about me. I had to think of Henry and what he would have wanted me to do." Cautiously, she failed to mention anything pertaining to the deed or the money tucked away in her bodice.

"Henry?"

"My fiancé. He's going to meet me here in two weeks. We're going to get married then." It was so good to finally have someone to talk to. "In the meantime I have no place to stay." Faith was just about to ask her to recommend a good hotel, but before she had the chance, the woman spoke up.

"Would you like to come home with me?" When Faith hesitated, the woman added, "I have a husband, two sons, and two daughters. The elder girl is just about your age."

It was tempting, but Faith had always been taught never to impose. Besides, as nice as she was, this woman was after all a stranger. "Oh—oh, I couldn't."

"It would be no trouble." The woman added emphatically, "Really."

Faith looked out the window. It was still pouring. "That horrid rain." Reaching up, she touched her hair, brushing at her rain-dampened curls. "I must look a mess."

"You look a wee bit like a drowned mousie." There was gentle laughter in the voice.

Faith couldn't help but smile. "And I feel like one, too."

"Then why not come home with me, lass. You can dry your hair before our hearth, have some warm broth, and slip into one of my daughter's nightgowns."

A fire! What Faith would give for such

warmth. Still, she shook her head. Somehow she'd make do, she thought, looking around her. The tearoom was a small area built right off the room where passengers waited to board the stagecoach. The wallpaper was tan and brown and had an allover pattern that looked like huge "S's." There were four round tables for two. Cups hung from pegs on the wall and two kerosene lamps hung from the ceiling. A potbellied stove in the far corner was used to heat the water to make tea, but it didn't throw off much warmth. The hard wooden floor didn't even have one small rug. There was nothing at all of any softness that could serve as a bed. Even so, Faith's pride prompted her to refuse.

Just as she was mouthing her thanks to the woman, the proprietor of the tearoom walked to the door and changed the sign from Open to Closed. The other three patrons, all men, hastily made their exit.

"Ladies . . ." The proprietor spoke in a tone that clearly said he expected them to leave.

Getting up from her chair, Faith's would-be benefactress moved toward the door. "I repeat, you are welcome to come home with me for the night, dearie."

This time Faith accepted. It appeared she had a choice of walking the muddy streets all alone or going home with this woman.

"All right I will, but I didn't mean to be a bother."

Faith's savior gave her a warm hug. "You're not a bother at all. Besides, I'd want someone to do the same thing for my Mary if she were in a similar situation."

Faith felt as if the weight of the world had suddenly been lifted off her shoulders. "Thank you. Thank you from the bottom of my heart . . ."

"Margaret." She stuck out her hand, taking Faith's in a firm grip. "My name is Margaret MacQuarrie."

"I am Faith. Faith Tomkins, soon to be Faith Wingham," she said, thinking of Henry. This act of kindness was just one more thing she had to tell him when he arrived. Perhaps their stay together in Oregon would be just as promising as she had first supposed. Surely this woman's kindness had wiped away Faith's misgivings. Even braving the rain didn't bother her as much, now knowing that she had somewhere to go.

"My buggy is down the street at the livery stable. Even though I've lived here for quite a while I was caught without an umbrella, so I'm afraid we will get a wee bit wet. It can't be helped."

"That's all right." Faith's shoes were already ruined, her dress wet. The feather on her hat was drooping, and her hair was a sopping mass. Even so, there was a bounce to her walk now as she stepped over the puddles and fought the deluge of raindrops. Side by side with Margaret MacQuarrie she trudged through the muck and mire. At the end of the street was the buggy, just as the woman had promised. A buggy with a black canvas top. Picking up her sodden skirt, Faith pulled herself up and settled herself on the leather-upholstered seat.

Faith had thought that the stagecoach driver had been daring, but it turned out he had been tame compared to the manner in which Margaret MacQuarrie guided her buggy down the quagmire of rain-soaked streets. Despite the canvas top, raindrops catapulted down Faith's face. And yet in a strange way, despite the discomfort she felt a strange sense of exhilaration. Meeting Margaret MacQuarrie seemed to be a favorable sign that all would go well in this new state that she and Henry had chosen.

Jonas Winslow rode the dapple gray at a furious pace up and down the hills outside of San Francisco only to find this was a city surrounded by water. There was the Pacific Ocean to the west, San Francisco Bay to the east, and San Pablo Bay to the north. He had thought to ride horseback into Oregon but clearly his knowledge of the Pacific coast left much to be desired. Nor could he even think of going south. Undoubtedly every law-man in the city was looking for him. The vigilantes would all be out combing the streets. Clearly he would have to reassess the situation.

Sitting astride his stolen horse, Jonas looked back for just a moment at the city of San Francisco. It had shown promise of being an exhilarating place. Exciting. Now he was being forced to leave because of something he hadn't even had a hand in. Gritting his teeth, he drew in a deep breath and pushed forward. He couldn't look back again. He had to push on. He was now a man on the run. A man with his back against the wall. He was trapped by the water unless . . .

A boat! That was what he needed. He could sail across the bay, go out to the ocean and right up the coast. Of course. It was per-fect. Better by sea than by land. "On to Port-land," he almost shouted in relief.

Jonas was even more determined than ever to reach the city Faith Tomkins had men-tioned. He had been thinking about it as he rode up and down the hillside trying to find an escape. Portland was just the place. It would be somewhere to hide out for a while and at the same time win back his money. No doubt Portland was bursting at the seams with men of means—landowners, lumber-jacks, miners. From what Faith Tomkins had said, it would be a great city for a gambler to stalk. Best of all he doubted that in Milwaukie he'd have much competition, unlike the San Francisco area where gamblers were as plentiful as a dog's fleas.

Jonas looked around him. Fog was rising over the hills of San Francisco, a perfect cloak for his getaway. So much the better. And even more helpful, there wasn't a ripple or a wave upon the blue expanse of the bay. He hoped the ocean would have as smooth sailing. If he could find something on which to sail, he thought of guiding the dapple gray in the direction where several boats, ships, and barges bobbed about.

Square-rigged grain ships, whalers, clipper ships, purse seiners, and one-sailed fishing boats dotted the waterfront. Swarthy sailors meandered around in boisterous fashion, singing boatsongs or ditties of a more vulgar nature. Determined to be inconspicuous, Jonas hurried to dismount and, slapping the gray on the rump, sent it along on its way.

It was unthinkable to try to book passage on a ship or a California clipper just recently unloaded of its valuable goods. There would be a chance of recognition, too many questions asked, and the possibility he would be apprehended. A fishing boat, however, was a different matter entirely. They could come and go as they pleased unlike the larger ships, which were burdened with inspections and regulations.

"A fishing boat!" There was one manned by a Genoese crew and another by a group of smiling Sicilians. Giving in to his gambler's nature, Jonas tossed a coin. The Sicilians won. Now the only thing left to do was to convince them to take him along.

Seven

Sitting on the calico-cushioned, high-backed rocking chair in the bedroom, Faith watched as raindrops gently spattered the window. She had thought she would only spend one night with Margaret MacQuarrie and her family, but because the rain had lasted for several days, she had stayed longer. She had enjoyed her visit, and had been taken into the hearts of the whole MacQuarrie family.

Smiling, Faith remembered the frantic drive through the rain to the large two-story frame house on Front Street, not too far from the sawmill that Margaret's husband, Ian, owned. After helping unhitch the horse and securing it in the barn, Faith had followed the Scottish woman down the path that led from the carriage house to the kitchen entrance. Stepping inside, dripping wet, she had been enveloped by the warmth radiating from the black cast-iron cooking stove. Two pretty dark-haired girls were standing near that stove, busily cutting vegetables and stirring a big pot of stew.

"Faith, my dear, these are my two daughters Mary and Caitlin. Mary and Cate, this is Faith Tomkins. She is going to share your room tonight," Margaret had said.

Like their mother, the two dark-haired girls sported wide, cordial smiles. They had welcomed Faith into the household, helping her to dry off. Since brown-eyed, eighteen-year-old Mary was just an inch shorter than Faith and likewise slim, her blue wool dress fit Faith perfectly. Although Mary's shoes were a tight fit, she did not complain.

Margaret's two sandy-haired sons, Lachlan and Cameron, were likewise amiable. Ian, her husband, seemed a bit gruff at first. A slightly balding man, rugged in build, he seemed a perfect match for Margaret. Studying Faith suspiciously over his spectacles, he had plied her with a dozen questions as they all sat around the dinner table. After hearing of Faith's trials and tribulations, his attitude softened and he, too, seemed to accept her. It was his suggestion that she stay on until the weather cleared. After dinner he had even serenaded their guest by playing his bag pipes to the tune of "The Flowers of Edinburgh" and "The Reel of Tulloch."

"Now, off to bed with ye, lassies. Candles

and the oil for the lamps are expensive," he had cautioned at the end of his recital.

Faith had followed Mary and Caitlin to their bedroom upstairs. After changing into one of Mary's flannel nightgowns and warming her cold bare feet on a large soapstone which had been heated in the fireplace and wrapped in a towel, she had gotten into bed. Made of maple with rope springs, a thick pad of straw and feather mattress on top, it had been brought all the way from Scotland, or so Mary said. Though it was uncomfortable sleeping three on a mattress, she had quickly fallen asleep snuggled between the sheets and under several of Margaret's handmade quilts.

Faith couldn't help thinking now how lucky she had been that Margaret had come into the tearoom. What might have been a catastrophe had instead turned out to be a time of making new friends.

She was content here. Indeed, the MacQuarrie family house was perfect. There was a pond in the front yard upon which ducks and geese swam about, an old mill building complete with a water wheel, a pump house, barn, and carriage house. Apple and cherry trees abounded near the mill. Terraced land flanked the pond and fed it with water from a gently moving stream, a stream which had nearly swollen to a creek because of the rain.

The rain, after days of fog and muddy

streets, was slowly coming to an end now, however. Like a bold warrior the sun was valiantly trying to push aside the clouds. When Faith realized that with the sun would come her departure, a prick of remorse flashed through her, but she knew she couldn't stay here forever, no matter how cozy and safe a haven it was.

"What, up already, Faith?"

Recognizing Mary's voice, she turned around. "I couldn't sleep."

"My, what a wee earlie birdie you be." Sitting up and stretching her arms over her head, Mary MacQuarrie yawned, then nudged at her gently snoring sister. "Up, up, sleepyhead, we've a hundred chores to do."

Succumbing to her sister's prods, Caitlin, the younger of the two by four years, bolted out of bed, immediately grumbling that she was always given the hardest work. "Why am I always the one to have to churn the butter, sweep the floors, and do the scrubbing? My hands will look like an old woman's before I'm seventeen. I'll end up an old maid."

"Not here you won't," Mary guffawed, tugging on her sister's long hair. "Men are always in need of a pretty little worker like you. Besides, they outnumber us at least ten to one."

Faith had learned the men in the area were mainly government agents, lumberjacks, miners, trade post operators, hunters, trappers, fishermen, and foreigners from overseas and across the Canadian border.

Likewise, Margaret and Ian had come to Prineville from Canada twenty years ago. Ian had come to work in the mines, but seeing the vast, lush green forests, he had gotten a better idea. He had wisely realized that lumber would be worth just as much as gold. He had foreseen that there would be a great deal of building in the future and had moved his new Scottish bride and newborn daughter to Portland where he had started a lumber mill on the bank of the Willamette River. It had proven to be a booming business that had kept growing. Now he supplied lumber not only to Oregon but to mine owners, railroad workers, to the ship yard and all those building settlements and towns in California, Montana, and Idaho.

"Ten men to one." Caitlin made a face. "And most of them dirty, loudmouthed, and disrespectful." Walking to the small dressing table, she poured water from a china pitcher into the wash basin. "I want to marry a gentleman. Like Faith's Henry."

Henry. The reminder of her fiancé made Faith's heart quicken. She had been eagerly counting off the days until they were together. There were nine days left until their appointed meeting at the land office. Nine days. To her it might as well have been a hundred. Ah, well, she thought, joining the other two young women in going about their early-morning dressing and grooming. Once she and Henry were together, all this waiting would prove well worthwhile.

Margaret MacQuarrie was already working in the kitchen by the time her daughters and Faith arrived. A pot of porridge bubbled on the stove, and the enticing aroma of bread baking in the oven made Faith realize just how hungry she was. Forcing herself to ignore her gently growling stomach, however, she joined Margaret in peeling the potatoes to be fried for the morning meal.

"The rain is lifting. I—I'll be leaving soon." She couldn't take advantage of the MacQuarries' hospitality any longer.

"Oh." Margaret raised her graying brows. "To go where?"

"A hotel or boardinghouse—"

Before she could even finish her sentence, the Scottish woman was shaking her head. "Of a surety you will not! You're a woman alone without a husband or family to care for you. I won't hear of it!" Despite Faith's insistence, Margaret was determined that she would stay put until her future husband arrived. "As a matter of fact, now that the rain is lifting, Ian has come up with a splendid idea. A barn raising!"

"A barn raising?"

Mary, just back from gathering eggs from the chickens who cakewalked around the loft in the barn, was quick to explain. "A wonderful reason for a fun social gathering. Good food, good music, and men!"

Margaret clucked her tongue. "Mary Brie! Hold your tongue, lass." She turned to Faith. "A barn raising is surely much more than that. It is a community gathering meant to help newcomers get a start. Ian is going to supply the lumber so that some of the young men can build you a barn and a place to stay on that new land of yours." The whole family participated in the lumber mill business. Ian was the foreman, both sons cut and sawed logs beside the other hired men, Margaret kept the books, and the girls provided what general help they could. As if reading Faith's mind she added, "You and Henry can pay him back a little at a time once you get on your feet."

Despite her pride, Faith had to admit it was a wonderful idea. How surprised Henry would be. "I don't know what to say but thank you." Putting down her half-peeled potato, she grabbed Margaret's hand and gave it a grateful squeeze. "I'll never be able to repay you for all you've done for me. You've a heart of gold, Maggie."

"Oh, go on with you now." Margaret Mac-Quarrie brushed off the compliment, but her smile showed she was pleased. "That's the way not only of the Scots but of we Oregonians as well. When you're way out here, far away from the rest of the country, people soon learn to help each other. Besides, it's the godly way."

"And you're an angel!" She was anxious to detail the goodness of Margaret MacQuarrie in a letter to her mother and five sisters . . . And about Jonas Winslow, too.

Looking out toward the changing colors of the morning sky that lit up the rocky shoreline, Jonas knew himself to be one hell of a lucky man as well as a damned good card player. Having been met with a firm "no" when he had approached the curly-haired Sicilian fishing boat captain, Jonas had tried nearly everything to get him to change his mind. He had even offered Antonio Giaconi money, the one thing Jonas was always loath to part with. Still the answer had been no. Then Jonas had been inspired. Knowing that all men were gamblers at heart, he had conned the captain into playing just one hand of cards. Poker. His gold pocket watch against the chance to travel with Giaconi and his crew up to coast to Astoria in Clatsop County.

Jonas chuckled as he thought of his marked deck of cards. Antonio Giaconi hadn't had a chance. Now he was on board this skiff, skimming through the waters of the Pacific. If he smelled more than a little like

83

the fish that shared the boat, that was the price he had to pay, at least until he reached the town and had a chance to bathe.

The turbulent water whipped and churned around the boat. Grabbing tightly to the side, Jonas cursed softly. He was lucky, yes, but that was not to say that this had been a smooth ride. Not by a long shot. At least, however, the turmoil in his stomach had finally subsided. Jonas added the duty of sailor to his imaginary list of jobs. Jobs of which he had an extreme dislike. Never would he sail in a boat again.

"You are sorry you came, eh?" Antonio Giaconi asked the question in a deep-throated rumble.

"Sorry?" Jonas shook his head. "Not sorry at all!"

In truth he had had little choice, seeing as how his life depended on it. He had not revealed that fact to the captain, though. Instead, thinking about Faith Tomkins, he had conjured up the story of hurrying up to Portland to stop a wedding. Knowing how romantic and lusty the Sicilians were, he had told Antonio that he and the woman he loved had argued foolishly, that she had left him and gone to Oregon. Having received her letter informing him that she was marrying a logger, he was risking his life to put an end to the marriage once and for all. He intended to sweep her off her feet, carry her away, and marry her himself as she had wanted in the first place.

Antonio laughed. "Ah, true love. I think perhaps at heart you must be Sicilian. No?"

Running his fingers through his wind-tousled black hair Jonas grinned. "Perhaps." In the meantime as the waves got fiercer he could only hope that he would arrive all in one piece. He wondered what the odds were of this fishing boat capsizing, but tried to push that thought out of his head. The boat would make it. Giaconi and the others looked to be able seamen. He hoped.

Eight

After all the days of rain and bone-chilling dampness, the sun was a welcome sight as it hung over Portland's horizon. Although there were still puddles here and there, the streets had dried sufficiently to allow buggies, wagons, carts, and horses to once again pass over them with ease. Among those vehicles were the buggies, two-wheeled logging carts, and lumber wagons belong to the MacQuarries.

The small parade careened down Grand Street, headed out of town in the direction of Milwaukie. Following behind on horseback were Margaret MacQuarrie's sons, Lachlan and Cameron, as well as several mill workers and family friends. Young, strong men all who were well prepared to put forth the muscle and energy needed to build Faith a new barn.

Heading the procession was the buggy driven by Margaret with Faith, Caitlin, and

Mary crammed tightly inside. This was no easy task considering that they were wearing petticoats and crinolines beneath their Sunday best—cotton and calico checks and prints sent up by clipper ship from San Francisco. Margaret's dress was a royal blue with bell sleeves, Caitlin's was dark pink decorated with ribbons and bows, and Mary wore a brown-and-gold check. Faith herself was fashionably clothed in a new dress of forest green edged in black piping, an extravagance, true, but one she felt would be compensated for once Henry arrived.

Faith had likewise used her "emergency" money to pay for the food that would be served at the get-together after the barn raising. One of the wagons carried boxes and baskets loaded with homemade pies, fried chicken, biscuits, cold baked potatoes, apples, pears, and cherries. Ian had donated a large wooden barrel of beer and a small keg of apple cider for the ladies.

Looking behind her, she counted at least fifteen men, all of whom would undoubtedly have hearty appetites. Ian had promised that with so many men helping out, the raising of Faith's barn would be accomplished in a single day. Whereas a house went up slowly, barns were usually laid out on the ground and raised immediately, with the roof put on later.

"Papa sketched a drawing from an old

standard barn design," Mary informed Faith as they rode along.

Ian MacQuarrie had gone out to the site of Faith's property the day before. Seeing that it needed clearing, he had taken the matter in hand, removing rocks and cutting down some of the trees near the site where the barn was to be erected. Loading the chopped logs, he had brought them back to town to replace some of the seasoned and dried lumber he would be using today. A barter of wood for wood. That way Faith's debt would be lessened.

Faith calculated how much money she owed Ian MacQuarrie thus far, minus the chopped trees from her land. Quite a sum. And yet what he and his family had given her was beyond any monetary measure. Somehow she and Henry would find a way to show their gratitude, she thought.

As Faith looked out toward the road, her face suddenly turned pale and her breath caught in her throat. Putting her hand to her mouth, she gasped. A knot of indignation and anger coiled in her stomach. Passing the buggy on horseback from the opposite direction was a man she recognized all too well. The man who had been her fellow passenger on the stage. The accomplice to the stage robbery. The very villain who had nearly ruined her life.

"Faith, what's wrong?" Mary laid a hand on Faith's shoulder.

She wanted to answer, but it was as if her vocal cords had become paralyzed. All she could do was to point toward the man and gasp again. Somehow she managed to choke out, "It's him!"

"Him?" Caitlin cocked her head. "Henry?"

"No!" Faith shook her head so violently that her bonnet tumbled to the floorboards of the buggy. "The man. The man who robbed the stagecoach!"

Mary and Caitlin snapped around to see, but he had vanished over the rim of a hill.

"Margaret! We must turn around." Faith was intent on pursuing the cause of her distress, but with all the vehicles on the road it was impossible. It galled her that the culprit would go unapprehended. Still, she now knew that he was in the vicinity. If it was the last thing she did, she would track him down and make him pay for his evil deed.

It was a short, pleasant ride south to Milwaukie, yet the beauty of the scenery was marred to Faith's eyes. All she could think about was the humiliation of that moment when she had been so callously terrorized. "Faith, are you all right? You've been so silent all along the way." Caitlin was concerned.

"I'm fine," Faith answered, but she was far from that. She could hear the men's laughter, could visualize those white masks and the slits that had revealed cold, cruel eyes. But most of all she could remember that sneering face, could feel the touch of his hand on her chin as the leader of those wolves had told her they might well meet again. Oh, yes, they would. She would see to that.

"Portland folk pride ourselves on how law-abiding we are, but I must admit, lass, that the city does have its criminal element." Margaret MacQuarrie flicked at the reins in irritation. "Mainly in the north end, where that one must have been headed."

"Loggers and sailors out to celebrate after months in the wilderness or at sea go there," Caitlin added.

"It's there that the—the women of ill repute are called 'the daughters of Aphrodite,'" Mary whispered behind her hand, evoking a stern reproach from her mother.

"Respectable citizens try to pretend the district does not exist. And you would do well to do that, too," Margaret cautioned, as if somehow reading Faith's thoughts. "What is done is done and you will only put yourself at risk if you go poking your nose in dangerous places."

It was good advice, but even so, Faith was determined to make that awful man pay for his actions. When at last they arrived in Milwaukie, however, she was able to put her vengeful feelings aside. She savored the sights, sounds, and fragrances of the area that belonged to her. The scenery was graceful and peaceful. A veritable Garden of Eden, or so Margaret said, with its abundance of trees and wildflowers. A small stream across the far end of her property looked muddy right now, but what a boon it would be. If she and Henry worked very hard, they had the chance to become prosperous here. She was sure of it.

Margaret walked along by Faith's side as she leisurely explored. "Well, how do you like it?"

For just a moment Faith had shivers up and down her spine from the beauty of it all and the knowledge that it belonged to *her*. The feeling she had at that moment equaled how she felt when Henry kissed her.

"I have to pinch myself to realize I'm not dreaming." Oh, if only Henry were here to share this moment with her. She thought about their upcoming wedding, visualizing how it would be. They'd be married outside, of course. They'd say their vows under the big apple tree, its branches spread out like a canopy.

The sound of pounding disturbed Faith's reverie. Ian and his workers had cut all the wood the day before, taking great care that all the pieces would fit. Now they were putting the pieces together. Their tools were few—a square, a compass, a straight edge, hammers—but their logic was abundant.

"Weather has a great deal to do with the planning of a barn. I hope you don't mind that Ian took it upon himself to pick the spot," Margaret said, shielding her eyes from the sun with her hand.

"Oh, no. To the contrary. I'm grateful." Ian had told Faith that long before the axe fell, a barn builder had to plot out the routes of sunshine and wind, the slopes of drainage, and determine how the seasons might affect the barn site. Living so close to nature made people "weather wise." Faith had heard the men speak of the barn being placed "well into the weather."

"He knows how to plan for the health and comfort of the animals and for the protection of barn timbers and stored grain."

In silent fascination Faith watched as the men worked. First they set the foundation timbers in place with a heavy hammer called a commander. Then they assembled the pieces out on the ground. Because it rained frequently in the area they used wooden nails, knowing that metal ones would rust. Wood against wood also made for a strong structure. Using ropes and pulleys, the men hoisted the barn walls and hammered them into place. Large wooden shingles completed the sides.

The roof likewise was assembled on the

ground. The front and back rafter sections looked like a large triangle with a kingpost up the middle. It, too, was lifted up by way of ropes and pulleys until it rested atop the walls. The result was a simple, beautiful structure without embellishment. After chiseling the date into a section, the barn was erected and a branch was put atop it to bring good luck. Margaret had said the barn-raising ceremony went all the way back to the Druids.

Faith stepped back to look, pleased with the sight of the big barn with its loft and double doors.

As the men worked, the women set out the meal, placing it on a large, planked table the men had erected. It seemed that a handsome red-haired fellow named Noah Brickerage had taken a shine to Mary's biscuits as well as to Mary herself. At first merely admiring her from afar, he later used his hunger as an excuse to hang around the table. Taking off his shirt, he preened like a rooster, showing off his firm muscles.

"Careful, sister," Caitlin hissed. "That one looks like trouble to me."

"Pooh. I'm not afraid." Mary coquettishly batted her eyelashes at the young man. A few minutes of flirting soon led to a walk down by the stream—but in full view of her mother's watchful eye.

Handing Faith a cup of cider, Margaret

sighed. "Ah, but I worry. Having such a bonny daughter is what has put gray hairs on my poor head. Woe is me to have two."

For just a moment Faith was terribly homesick. "My mother always said the same thing. She had six."

"Six!" Margaret's eyes were wide. "Poor woman. And was she gray?"

Faith smiled. "Completely."

The celebration after the barn raising was a success. There was hardly a crumb of food left, and the barrel and keg were drained dry. The sound of chatter and laughter blended with the crickets' serenade. Later there was music provided by Ian on his bagpipes, Lachlan on his fiddle, and Cameron on his guitar. Ian even did a Scottish jig. Soon everyone was dancing and kicking up their heels until they were exhausted. Then, sooner than Faith would have liked, it was time to go home. Everyone headed toward their buggies, wagons, and horses. Everyone, that is, except Faith.

"Faith? Lassie." Margaret took her by the arm to lead her toward her buggy. "What's wrong?"

A melancholy mood had overtaken Faith, a deep desire to at last have her own home. The barn was just a beginning, yet somehow it signified a change in her life. "I wish I could stay here tonight," she confided to Margaret. But that was unthinkable. It would be chilly, damp and maybe even dangerous. Still, Faith took one long, last look at the structure.

Nine

A cold spray of ocean mist splashed Jonas in the face. *A rude awakening to be sure,* he thought, opening his eyes wide. "What in hell?"

For a moment he was confused as to his whereabouts, but then the sight of the big basket of fish beside him and its offending smell reminded him all too well. The fishing boat. He let his eyes roam over the familiar wooden confines of the single-sailed, round-sterned, broad-beamed and flat-bottomed rig that was Antonio's pride.

The small fishing boat had been in constant struggle with nature and the sea. Fortunately it was sturdier than it looked, though last night he had been certain he would be swept overboard by the waves or that the small five-crewed boat would be thrown against the rocks on shore. But somehow the *Al Di La* had survived, and all aboard as well.

"Ah, you are awake, *mio amico!*" Already moving about with fishing nets and poles in hand though dawn was just streaking the sky, Antonio came to Jonas's side. Since he was the only one aboard who spoke English, he was the only one Jonas could converse with.

"Yes, I am awake." Jonas sat up, feeling as if he had aged a hundred years. Sleeping on the hard wooden deck, on top of the damp and cold, made his bones creak. He was sore in every joint.

"I promised we would not capsize," Antonio said cheerily.

"I really didn't think that we would." Jonas lied between his teeth, trying not to reveal his pain as he moved about. Last night he would have laid ten to one odds on the *Al Di La's* sinking. "When are we going to reach shore?"

"Soon. Astoria is right up ahead." He pointed northward, then handed Jonas a corner of a fishing net, setting him to work with the other four men.

Wishing he had never set foot on this boat and vowing never to set foot on another, Jonas set about his appointed task, securing the net to the side of the boat by two ropes, colliding with two of the fishermen as he did so.

He wondered if he would ever be able to

eat salmon again. "And just what is this Astoria like?"

"It is the roughest town in Oregon. A fishing village at the mouth of the Columbia River." Astoria had been the Pacific Fur Company's base of operations many years ago but unregulated trade had caused many evils and rivalries to spring forth. Antonio had informed him the rival traders would offer security and assistance to their own countrymen.

"Saloons?" Jonas's interest was suddenly piqued.

"Many. And gambling dens and bawdy houses, too. You must stay clear of them, my friend."

"Stay clear of them!" After the miserable time he'd had aboard the boat, they sounded like a great deal of fun. And there was money to be made.

"*Sì*, stay away. Many a man has either lost his life in a dark alley there or ended up on a boat headed for China."

It was a warning Jonas remembered only until the *Al Di La* pulled ashore. Land! What a welcome sight! Jonas wasn't really sorry to leave Antonio and his other traveling companions. It had been rough sailing over hundreds of miles of treacherous waters. Still, Antonio had been friendly and he would miss him a little. On the journey inland the Sicilian had shared many fascinating seafaring stories with him. The ones about men being "shanghaied" into involuntary labor aboard ships made his flesh crawl. He would have to be careful, he cautioned himself as they tied up at Astoria. The waves, the surface swirls and rippling dark water lapped at the side of the boat.

Jonas squinted as he took in the view. All along the shoreline were log warehouses, piles of timber, barrels. Crates were being loaded and unloaded. Here and there a ship was having its hull or sails repaired, or some other repair. Soon his companions would be on their way again after taking on a few needed supplies, but he intended to stay a while. Walking backward, Jonas wished Antonio a safe trip and waved to him until he was out of sight.

Jonas pushed his way through the throng of male bodies on the dock, then along the planked sidewalk searching for a gambling hall that appealed to him. Although there were some small shops, hotels, and private homes farther inland, a good part of Astoria was taken up by saloons and brothels. He needed money if he was going to stay the night in a hotel. But where would he get it?

A steady stream of men were making their way in and out of the seedy saloons and gaming halls on both sides of the street. As the doors opened he could hear swearing and other violent noises. They all looked to be refuges or criminals of every description. He carefully avoided those places.

He finally came to a fairly decent-looking place called the White Whale and entered. He made his way to the bar along the far side. All in all, it didn't seem very different from the lower-class liquor and gaming halls of San Francisco.

"A whiskey. From an unopened bottle if you please." Jonas watched as the bartender tore off the seal and uncorked the bottle.

As the liquid fire warmed him, Jonas looked around, assessing the place. The patrons seemed to be largely made up of loud-mouthed, swarthy sailors, staggering and pushing each other around. The barroom seemed to be the loafing place for many of the strange-looking characters he had seen along the streets. This was obviously a violent, crime-laden area, for from across the room he could see one man with a missing ear, another with a hook for a hand. Many here seemed to be living in squalor and destitution. Certainly there was no evidence of the gold watches and diamond stickpins he had seen in San Francisco.

He asked himself if he should stay, or go. Would he get in trouble here? Trouble? Not anything he couldn't handle. He was well able to defend himself in any fair fight. Still, he had to admit that he would have left this place immediately had his money not dwindled away too close to nothing. He had to replenish it before he could afford a place to sleep tonight. Like it or not, he would have to try his hand at a card game or two.

He soon spotted a small group of gambling men collected at the far end of the hall, away from the noisy bar, where they could concentrate on the cards. That was where he wanted to be. Gambling seemed to take place, he supposed, on every waterfront along the Pacific. Looking around the room, he had kept his eye on the several tables of gamblers he had seen earlier, over near the wall. Several men were beginning to gather near a table, where a game was just breaking up and another about to start. Walking over, he asked if he could join them.

He regretted his request as soon as his eyes swept over them. The men looked to be of a less than amiable disposition, Jonas thought as he viewed the knives, brass knuckles, and other weapons freely displayed. Should he turn around, hightail it out of this place quickly? he wondered. No. He would play the game good-humoredly and use his cool cunning to the best of his ability. And even if he should hold a losing hand, his fingers would not tremble, his expression would not change. Nor would he be so foolish as to win too much money. Just enough.

"Deal me in, gentlemen."

The game was well under way when a

short, dirty, evil-looking man approached Jonas, offering him a drink and a voyage to the South Seas. There was a ship at the dock looking for sailors, the man said.

"I'm not a sailor," Jonas quickly answered, hoping he didn't smell too much like fish. He pointed out that he would be little help as a crewman and then declined the man's generosity in offering a bottle. Jonas certainly did not intend to become stupefied by drink. He had gotten himself in enough trouble in San Francisco because of liquor and women. He had to watch himself among this rowdy crowd.

Jonas watched as the sleazy man moved away, seeming to prefer bonafide sailors. Let someone else end up with a knot on his head. Jonas did not believe his story. Thanks to Antonio he knew all about "Spanish fly," which was often put into drinks to knock a man senseless. He had no intention of being shanghaied, but he knew he would have to keep his eye on that grimy little fellow and his drinks.

"Who was that?" he asked the man next to him, trying not to sound overly interested.

He was told that the man was named Doyle Cox. He was a friend of the owner of the White Whale, a man by name of Mike Pitts, said to be a well-known stagecoach bandit. Pitts owned many establishments in other parts of the country, from Denver to Astoria.

No one dared to cross him or reveal his true identity. He paid his employees well and they in return were loyal to him. His yearly income from robberies netted him a goodly sum of money and his power and influence was enormous. The sleazy little man was in Mike Pitts's employ.

"Mike Pitts," he mumbled. It was a name Jonas had to remember, at least while he was in this dangerous town. Hopefully that wouldn't be for long—just long enough to put a little bit of money in his pocket.

"You." The man next to Jonas reminded him that there was a game in progress. "You stayin' in or foldin'?"

Jonas held three jacks and two queens, but until he had fully assessed the men he was playing with, he decided to be cautious and just watch. He didn't want to win too soon. "I fold," he said, throwing his cards facedown on the table. What a shame. It had been a great hand. With a shrug, he watched as the stakes were raked in by one of the other men.

It was a long night. A dismal night. After that first good hand, Luck didn't smile on Jonas for a long time. Then, just when he was going to pull out so as not to come away from the table penniless, his luck began to change. A full house gave him his first win of the evening.

"About time," he said with a grin.

Jonas's supreme command of the intricacies of the card game made him win again—and then again. He remained unruffled by any distractions. Finally, after winning a respectable though small amount of money, he collected his bounty and left the gaming hall. Since it was too late to travel any farther, he decided to stay in Astoria, but just for the night. He'd find a hotel, have a bath, a bite to eat, then get some sleep. He'd be on his way to Portland first thing in the morning.

Jonas whistled a tune as he walked along the boardwalk. Deciding to look Faith Tomkins up was one of his better decisions. At least it would be if he played his cards right. From the looks of her, she was rather well-to-do. A real lady. What had she said her fiancé did? Ah, yes. He worked for the railroad. Just the right kind of profession. He would know men with influence and could introduce Jonas to an opportunity or two. And now the Winghams held title to several hundred acres of land. It was perfect.

Jonas paused for just a moment. Damn if he didn't have the uneasy feeling that he was being watched. Turning his head, he looked behind him. No one there.

He walked on, quickening his steps, turning around from time to time. He was anxious now to get inside somewhere. Anywhere. Roaming these streets was clearly dangerous. He spotted a hotel that looked to be fairly decent just up ahead. Not exactly the luxury he hoped for, but it would have to do, he thought as he headed there. But he didn't reach the hotel in time.

Suddenly, as if from out of nowhere, two men appeared. Jonas recognized one as the sleazy little man from the gaming hall. Each was holding the end of a fishing net as they came at him. Jonas walked headlong into it. He was defenseless. Trapped like some fool fish. He felt the cords of the net press into his flesh as the men pulled the net tightly around him. Still he struggled.

"He's a strong one. Better subdue him," he heard one of the men say. Then he felt something hard strike his head. Jonas struggled against the terrible darkness that pressed down on him.

Ten

A stillness hung over the land—a peaceful quiet that was broken only by the sound of birds and the gurgling of the stream that flowed down the hill. Sitting all alone on the seat of the MacQuarries' wagon, Faith let the calm solitude soothe and enfold her as she looked at the symbol of her newfound happiness. The barn. Proof that when people worked together in friendship a miracle could happen. Just as a miracle had happened when she had met Henry and his love had touched her heart.

"And soon we'll be together," she murmured under her breath.

Faith had nearly died of impatience counting the days until their meeting. Taking Margaret's advice, however, she had forced herself to keep busy so that the time would pass more quickly. Driving back and forth from Portland to her Milwaukie homestead, she had kept occupied with the very pleasant task of getting things ready for Henry—things like fixing up the barn with homey touches.

Faith had decided that while their house was being built she and her new husband would live in the barn, so she had brought out a mattress, bedding, water pitcher and basin, candles, a small cookstove and a few meager supplies there. She had made the loft into a bedroom, complete with curtains at the tiny window. Built with a trapdoor that could be pulled up and latched at night to keep out wild animals, the loft could be a cozy place, especially for a newly married couple, she thought with nary a sign of a blush.

"Home." The word had a tuneful ring to it. As soon as Henry picked the spot where he wanted the house, they would have that to look forward to. It was like a picture out of a storybook, the land was so beautiful. And practical as well. There was timber for buildings, a source of water, and a magnificent view of trees and grass that went on for miles.

Faith thought about the wonder of it all. How at first it had just been a dream. Hers and Henry's. Now that dream had come true and was unfolding right before her eyes, just like the sunset that was spreading out on the horizon, touching the land. If the roads left a great deal to be desired, they would just have to do their best to overcome it.

Flicking the reins, sending the horses down one of those bumpy pathways, Faith headed back to Portland. Though she didn't travel the same bone-jiggling speed as Margaret, she still rolled along at quite a pace. She didn't want to be on the road after dark. Margaret had warned against a woman being alone and the stagecoach robbery was still fresh in her mind. Besides, Ian might have need of the wagon, she thought, hurrying along. As if giving credence to that thought, Ian MacQuarrie was waiting for her by the barn as she rambled up.

"Faith." The look on his face was indescribable. Not his usual stern look. Not a smile. Not even anger. Just a look that told her that something was very wrong.

"What is it?"

Usually so fastidiously involved in his care of the horses, Ian now seemed far more concerned with her. Without even unhitching the animals, he helped her down and immediately led her toward the house.

"Margaret!" That something had happened to the woman filled Faith with sudden fear.

"She's fine."

"Then?"

Opening the front door, Ian gently pushed her inside. "You have a visitor."

"A visitor!" How could she not think of

Henry? "Where?" Her tone gave proof of her elation.

"In the par—"

Without even letting Ian finish, Faith burst into that room, her emotions soaring. Henry was here! He'd come a day early and had found out she was staying with the MacQuarries.

But it wasn't Henry waiting to see her. It was a tall, thin man dressed in black whose frown spoke of some kind of trouble. He tipped his head and watched her as she swept through the door. "Miss Tomkins, I presume."

"You presume correctly." Why she took such an instant dislike to him she could not say, but she did.

He pointed toward the green velvet settee. "I think you should sit down."

"Sit down?" She preferred to remain standing. A person was only told that when something bad had happened. "My mother? My father? My sisters?" A chill tickled her spine. "Henry."

Without any hesitation he told her. "I'm afraid something terrible has happened."

An accident. That thought consumed Faith's mind. Clutching at the man's sleeve, she pleaded, "Take me to him."

He cleared his throat and carefully removed her hand as if it was offending him. "I'm afraid that is impossible."

"Impossible?" The expression on his face terrified her. "Impossible why?"

He blurted it out. "I'm afraid he's been killed, Miss Tomkins."

"Killed?" Her voice was a mournful cry. At the same time she refused to listen to the voice reverberating in her ears. The truth was far too painful.

Now that he had broken the news, the man droned on, telling her how her fiancé had been killed only hours before he was going to retire from his surveying job to head for Portland, Oregon. "Whiskey peddlers and gamblers. A violent, drunken bunch." He related how they had followed the supply trains with the intent to steal. Running wild and shooting blindly, they had sent a bullet flying directly into Henry Wingham's head. There had been no doctor to attend to his wound, just a roaming minister to say a prayer for his soul. He had died instantly.

"No. It is a mistake." A dreadful mistake.

"I wish it was, but I'm afraid it is not!" As if to give further proof, he handed her the death certificate. "We didn't have time to locate you so—so we went ahead with the funeral."

Funeral. She had not even been allowed to see him one last time.

"There was a small gathering of his fellow workers."

Tears stung Faith's eyes as she looked at

110

Henry's name on that loathsome piece of paper. Her knees felt weak, her head spun, and for a moment she was afraid she might faint. Sinking down on the chair, she closed her eyes, pressing her fingers to her throbbing temples. She wanted to hold him just one more time, to see his eyes brim with delight and love. But she couldn't. He was gone.

"Oh, dear God!" Putting her hands to her face, Faith gave vent to an uncontrollable flood of tears. Henry was gone. She would never see him again. He was gone. The pain of grief and loss wrenched through her like a knife, so piercing she was certain she could not bear it. Sobbing, she gave vent to the full fury of her anguish. He was gone and the desolation was shattering. It wasn't fair. It just wasn't fair. She felt a vast emptiness where her heart was supposed to be.

"I'm sorry." The messenger of the grim news tipped his hat again and quickly left.

Margaret MacQuarrie was quick to try to bring comfort. "Faith. I'm so sorry."

Somehow Faith choked out his name. "Henry . . ." The aching sense of being all alone overwhelmed her, but she fought to gain control of her emotions. Tears wouldn't solve anything. Certainly they couldn't bring Henry back. Angrily, she wiped her eyes with the back of her hand. She had to be brave. Henry would want her to be. But what was she going to do? The little money she had left would not allow her to survive much longer. The thought that they would never meet again brought forth a fresh storm of weeping.

Eleven

Pain throbbed violently through Jonas's head, tormenting him back into consciousness. As he opened his eyes he painfully tried to remember what had happened. He'd been caught in a net, just like the fish Antonio had ambushed in the ocean. Those two men had thrown a net over him and then thumped him on the head. That accounted for the lump and the soreness.

A stab of pain shot through his head and he tried to move his hands with the intent of massaging his temples. He gave an outraged shout when he realized he couldn't move them. A tall support beam ran from ceiling to floor and it was to this that he was securely connected. Those evil men had tied his hands behind him.

"I've been shanghaied!" he uttered in dismay. There could be no other word for it. Undoubtedly he'd been robbed as well.

The revelation was galling. He had traveled all over the place, gotten himself in and out of every kind of predicament, including escaping from the men pursuing him for a murder he had not committed. Yet here he was tied up and left to languish God knew where.

He lay perfectly still, listening, trying to adjust his eyes to the dim light. His thoughts were a jumble and he tried to sort them out. Just where was he? Where had they taken him and why?

Antonio's warning about the place he had called Swilltown came quickly to mind. The fisherman had told Jonas about the men who set upon poor unwary strangers with the purpose of taking them on board some vessel that was headed out to sea. Fit subjects for scurvy, he had called the victims. Men who hadn't even a Chinaman's chance of regaining their liberty. He'd cautioned Jonas about dark alleys and drugged whiskey. A man all too often traded a week's wages for a night of entertainment only to lose his life in a dark alley, he had said. Jonas had taken care not to drink anything that might be spiked and he'd stayed away from alleyways. The Sicilian hadn't warned him about fish nets, though!

His pulse quickened at the thought and, stiffening his muscles, Jonas turned his head and looked around. One old cracked oil lamp cast just enough of a glow to reflect on the walls of the windowless dwelling. A storehouse of some kind, he thought hazily. He realized he wasn't alone. Several men had likewise been taken captive by that sleazy little bastard who had been at the White Whale. Jonas counted fifteen of them. Luckless seamen all, who like himself, would find themselves aboard a ship unless something was done and fast.

Being aboard the *Al Di La* had been enough for him. Jonas was determined not to fall victim to such a fate. Though Antonio had told him that shanghaied men never got out of their bonds, he would pay no attention to those words. He would escape. Somehow. Being a sailor just wasn't in his plans.

Jonas thought carefully. First, above all, he had to get free of the ropes that held him. He could fight with the best of them, but he had to be able to wield his fists. Fighting against dizziness, he slowly rose to his feet, balancing against the pillar. Purposefully, he moved the ropes around his wrists back and forth, up and down, to weaken them. If only there was a piece of metal around, a nail perhaps. But to his annoyance, there wasn't.

"Hey, mister." Realizing he couldn't do it all alone, Jonas nudged the man lying beside him with his foot. "You wouldn't happen to have anything sharp, would you?"

Opening his eyes, the man looked up at

Jonas with glazed eyes. He was under the influence of something. Opium or laudanum probably, put in a glass of wine or some other liquor.

"You won't get any help from him," a deep voice rasped in the darkness. "He drank enough drugged whiskey to subdue a whale. But I'll help you, if you promise to help me in return."

"Help you? Of course." His answer was a logical one.

"And the others, too. No man should be forced to go to his death at sea. And that's just what this will turn out to be. Have no doubts about it."

Jonas was in a bargaining mood. Besides, it only made sense. "We'll get them all out if possible." It would be a small army. Surely then they could go up against any of the thugs that might set upon them.

"All of them. That would do my heart good after what has happened." Slowly crawling on his side toward Jonas, the burly, red-haired man soon positioned himself by the support beam. Raising himself up on his knees, his bound wrists touched Jonas's. "There's nothing sharp in here. They took everything. We'll have to try and untie each other's ropes without cutting them. We'll do it somehow."

It would have been a difficult task under any circumstances. The ropes were tied tightly, there was little light, and worst of all, it was difficult to maneuver the knots with his hands behind his back. Still, Jonas the other man knew they had to try.

"The name's Peter. Peter Seton."

Jonas thought a moment before introducing himself. He couldn't take a chance on anyone knowing his real name, at least until he had cleared it, so he said, "My name's J. W." It wasn't a lie.

"Glad to meet you, J. W." Breathing hard as he tugged at Jonas's ropes, Peter asked, "How did they get you?"

Jonas hated to reveal the humiliating moment, but after taking a deep breath, he blurted, "I got caught in a net, then hit on the head. You?"

Peter Seton explained that he and five of the others had been set upon while being entertained in one of Astoria's many brothels. "A pretty young woman caught my eye. She had peaches-and-cream skin and curves in all the right places. Unfortunately she was a decoy to catch fools like me."

He told a story that was much worse than Jonas's own. In the brothel he had gone to for entertainment, he had soon found himself in dire trouble. He had been held by two thugs while another searched him. All his valuables had been stolen, his clothing stripped off to be replaced by shoddy cast-offs, and he had been forced to sign a document that assigned him as a sailor aboard a ship heading out to sea. His companions had it worse when they refused. They had been bludgeoned until they had given in.

"Those bastards!" Jonas swore beneath his breath. "Why? What do they get from it?"

"One hundred dollars for each man they bring in as a sailor."

"One hundred dollars!" The idea of someone making that kind of bounty from his suffering enraged Jonas. He picked and pulled at Peter's ropes with a frenzy that made him ignore his bleeding fingers.

"Depending on the need of sailors, sometimes it's even more."

"Blood money!" He'd get free if it was the last thing he did. But it was so hard. Whoever had tied the ropes had done so with the intention of making certain that they *stayed* tied.

"Hurry. Before they all come back." Peter explained that at dawn they would all be loaded into boats and rowed out to the ships that were to be their doom. The chance of escape would be impossible then.

"They'll be back. And when they are, we'll be ready for them." Jonas gritted his teeth, murderously angry. That spurt of fury somehow gave him the strength and agility of fingers to at last free his companion. In turn he himself was released. "Now the others."

One by one the other prisoners were untied. Those who were drugged were helped to stand upon their feet. Jonas, Peter, and two other men banged down the door, but before they could push through it, four large armed men entered, brutes all of them.

"Get back! Get back before you get shot full of holes." A likely threat, seeing as they were all brandishing pistols. Still, Jonas couldn't abide the thought of turning coward now. As he looked at Peter he could almost see the same thought turning over in his mind. It was either now or never.

"Now!"

At the signal, Jonas, Peter, and the others threw themselves forward. Shots were fired, guns were grappled for, two sailors fell, but in the ensuing scuffle, the mutineers were victorious. Courage, and the fact that they outnumbered their captors, gave them the advantage. Now it was the captors who faced the barrels of their own guns.

"Tie the bastards up. Let them see how it feels." Being the winner in this battle gave Jonas a feeling akin to having a winning hand of cards. Taking charge, he only relaxed after the four men were secure in their bonds. "We'd better get the hell out of here before someone else comes." Reaching down, Jonas was elated to see that one of the men was carrying his very own pearl-handled revolver that had been taken from his person when he was apprehended. Quickly he reclaimed it.

"Where are you headed now, J. W.?" Peter Seton's voice cut through the noise of the rescued men's jabbering voices.

It took Jonas a minute to realize he was talking to him. "Portland. Then on to Milwaukie. There's a pretty young woman I aim to see there."

Peter Seton patted him on the back. "It's a small world. I'm headed to Portland myself. I live near there. I'm a logger. I brought a wagonload of timber to Astoria to be used for ship building. Now I'll be heading back."

Jonas grinned as he realized that fortune was smiling on him once again. Peter Seton had a wagon. "Mind if I ride along?" He ran his hands up and down over his pockets. "It seems that I've been robbed. I don't have any money."

"Don't worry." Peter was instantly agreeable. "I'd enjoy the company. Besides, I might well owe my life to you." Dusting himself off, he headed for the door, giving Jonas a push in the same direction.

If the lumber wagon that Peter Seton headed for looked anything but comfortable, Jonas didn't care. He pulled himself up and took a seat beside the red-haired man. After what he had experienced he wanted to get as far from Astoria as he could. Besides, what more could he ask for than a free ride out of town?

It turned out to be an interesting ride. Peter was anything but dull. As the lumber wagon rolled along, he told Jonas about himself and how he had fought in the Civil War on the side of the Confederacy.

"Hope you weren't a damned Yankee!" he jested to Jonas.

Jonas shrugged. During the war he hadn't taken sides. It seemed safer that way. Not wanting to be a soldier any more than he had wanted to be a sailor, he had stayed far away from anything to do with the war, going west instead. "Nope. I played it safe and minded my own business."

"Sometimes I wish *I* had." Peter Seton had an exciting tale to tell about his own experiences. When the retreating Union Army had left the steam frigate *Merrimack* behind, he had been among those Rebels who had recovered it and transformed it into the first "wonder weapon" of the Civil War. The ship had been cut down to the waterline, sheathed in armor, and armed with a powerful broadside that spelled death to any fleet of transports the North dared send within her reach. Renamed the *Virginia,* it had been a thorn in the Union Navy's side.

"So, you were a sailor. No wonder they wanted to shanghai you." Jonas grinned. "They were probably Yankees."

"Undoubtedly." Peter Seton laughed. "But it doesn't matter now. What does matter, though, is that you had the fortitude to stand up against them. Few men have had that."

"I get seasick, that's all." Jonas hurried to change the subject. "So, you're from Portland. Don't suppose you know a pretty young woman who just arrived there. Her name is Faith, as in faith, hope, and charity."

Peter nodded. "As a matter of fact, I do remember her. Auburn hair. Blue eyes. Staying with the MacQuarrie family until she gets settled. I helped build her barn several days back."

"You don't say." It seemed to be another good omen. The world was getting smaller all the time. "Well, it just so happens that I've come a long way just to see her." And see her he would. Soon now. Very soon.

Twelve

Faith stared up at the blackness of the ceiling. The shock of Henry's death had worn away to some extent but not the pain. Even an ocean of tears could not wash away that heartache. Henry was gone. She would never see his face again, never hear his voice, join in his laughter, feel the touch of his lips and hands.

Henry was dead. Though she didn't want to come to terms with such a sad reality, it was true. She had planned to love him and live with him *always*—but it turned out there was no such word. Like a candle in the wind, life could be snuffed out just as his has been. Thoughtlessly. Violently.

Murdered! That was what the man bringing the message had said. Henry had been shot by whiskey peddlers and gamblers. A tragic, senseless death.

At first Faith had been filled with anger,

with a thirst for vengeance. She had sworn and she had raged. The obsession to find and punish Henry's killers had nearly overcome her. Then there had been only the sorrow. Henry was dead and with him had gone all her dreams.

Suddenly she was afraid. All her life there had been someone to look after her. Her father, her mother, her sisters, and then Henry. Now she was far away from St. Paul and there was no one. No one but the MacQuarries, bless their souls. Kind people and friends, it was true, but not her permanent guardians. She couldn't stay here forever and take advantage of their kindness. Where then?

Go back home, a voice seemed to say. *Go back to your family, to the security, to the warmth that shielded you.* "Yes, go back," she murmured. Under the circumstances, it seemed so tempting to return to the safety of the family hearth.

Back to the boredom.

"No!" Go back and give up all her dreams? "No!" Despite what had happened, Faith realized that she wanted to stay.

Strange, but even though she knew she wouldn't be sharing a life here with Henry, she just couldn't imagine returning to St. Paul. She was an adventuresome girl. She longed for freedom. For a new life. For opportunity. There were more dangers than assurances facing her, she knew that. And yet there was a feeling of hope illuminating through her sorrow. Somehow she would make it on her own.

A name and a face came immediately to mind. Abigail Scott, the woman she had met briefly on the stagecoach. *She* had made a new life for herself after the death of her husband, had taken on the responsibility of her own land. Why then, couldn't she do the same?

Faith would not admit defeat. The land she owned was in the Willamette Valley—the most fertile spot in all of Oregon. How could she give it up? There was water, soil, game for food, wood for fuel, and an ideal climate for growing things. It was as Henry had promised—a veritable Eden. If it now meant that Eve would be without her Adam, perhaps that was God's will.

God's will. Another flood of tears welled up behind her eyes, but she refused to let them fall. She had to regain control if she was going to make it on her own. No more tears. Not now. Not ever, if she could help it. She had to be strong. Living here would demand that.

"I can do it. I *will* do it!" She knew that meant watching her every penny, working hard, and making tough decisions. But she would do it! Somehow. Some way. Her resolution gave her a strange sense of peace. Closing her eyes, she immediately fell asleep.

When the first glow of the sun peered over the horizon, she awakened, anxious to get started. There was so much to be done. So much to be learned. She had only begun. There was land to be cleared, trees to be felled, rocks to be moved, plowing to attend to, seeds to be planted.

Faith hurried to dress in a faded dress of blue calico that Mary had discarded. All the while, her fingers trembled as she mentally made her plans. She would proceed as if Henry were beside her. Live in the loft and oversee her acres. Work would make her new land prosperous, and, better yet, it would keep her mind off Henry and his tragic death. But she would need at least one man to help her. Someone she could trust. Someone who would either do the work for a small piece of her land or would work on credit until her efforts turned profitable.

Hurrying to the kitchen to talk to Maggie, she was disappointed that instead of encouraging her plans, the Scottish woman tried to dissuade her. "Doing such a thing when you have a husband to protect you is one thing, living there alone is another, lass."

"But, Maggie!" Picking up an egg, Faith

cracked the shell and let the contents slide into the bowl she held in her hand.

"I would never, never let Mary or Caitlin even *think* of such a thing." Margaret Mac-Quarrie attacked the potatoes, mashing them in bold, quick strokes that emphasized her opinion, then forming them into patties to be fried. "The men you'll find here, except for my Ian, Lachlan, and Cameron, are rough. They drink to excess, quarrel and womanize all the time. They'll take advantage of a woman alone."

"And just what else can I do, might I ask?" Disappointment made Faith's tone sharp as she asked the question. She had been so certain that Maggie would applaud her decision.

Margaret MacQuarrie paused to push back a stray lock of her hair and looked at Faith determinedly. "You should go home. Back to the parents who love you."

"No!" It was out of the question. Faith had made up her mind and there was no changing her decision.

"Because you quarreled with your father over Henry." Maggie clucked her tongue. "It will all be forgotten. He'll be only too happy to have you back."

"No. Not because we quarreled. Because when I really think about it, I wasn't happy there." Faith spoke the words without even thinking, suddenly realizing that what she said was the truth. She *hadn't* been happy. Not really. "That's why I so freely agreed to go away with Henry. There I was just one of six daughters. Here I'm *me*. Faith Tomkins."

Margaret put the potato patties on the grill and stoked the iron stove's fire with wood from the woodpile. "Then stay right here with Ian and me. We think of you as part of our family, and all the children love you."

The invitation was issued with such warmth that Faith had to smile. "I know, and I am so grateful. No one could have been better friends to me." Faith broke another egg into the bowl. "But I need to make my own way. Staying with you was never meant to be anything other than temporary. I don't want to be a burden."

"A burden?" Maggie gasped her outrage at such foolishness. "I say again that you are welcome to stay here." In an effort to convince her, she recited a long list of advantages to such an arrangement, including a nearby dressmaker who got all the latest fashions from New York by way of fashion plates.

"And work as a schoolmarm, I suppose."

Maggie smiled. "Sure and it is a wonderful suggestion."

Faith shook her head. "No, Maggie. I should have done that in St. Paul. I came here so that I could own my own land."

Maggie was full of ideas. "Then if the land is so important to you, lease it out. Have

128

someone else work it and give you rent. It's a thing that is done all the time."

Faith sighed in frustration at Margaret's attitude. "It wouldn't be the same." Gently, she touched the older woman's hand. "I want to do this, I must. Even if I try and fail, at least I will have tried. Please understand."

There was a silence before Margaret spoke. "I suppose that I do." She wiggled her index finger under Faith's nose. "But I don't think that means I'll just let you go traipsing off without checking up on you. I will and Ian will and Lachlan will and Cameron will. No woman should be living off alone, toiling morning to night without having someone to answer to. Why—why, anything could happen."

The conversation was interrupted as the rest of the MacQuarrie family trailed into the kitchen to see what was being prepared for breakfast. Breakfast was a solemn time for Faith as she showed respect for Henry's passing. Having little appetite, she ate only an apple and bit into a fried potato cake, listening as Ian MacQuarrie did the talking.

"Peter Seton is back. Got a good price for the lumber I sent all the way to Astoria with him," he informed his wife. "Only to have the money stolen, or so he said."

Margaret's tone was scolding. "Sending him to that Sodom and Gomorrah. Shame, shame on you, husband." Seeing his stunned expression, she said, "Oh, don't be surprised that I have heard all about it. Gossip travels as fast as lightning in this town." She looked right at Faith as if warning her of what kind of thing could happen even to a man. "The poor laddie almost got shanghaied."

"Shanghaied?" Faith had never heard the word.

"Kidnapped. Men who are drugged, set upon, tied up, sometimes beaten and forced to work as sailors on oceangoing ships are said to be shanghaied."

It sounded dreadful. Mary put her hand to her mouth, showing her distress at the idea.

"Peter, it seems, was one of the lucky ones. He and another man untied the ropes that kept them prisoner and escaped, along with several others. Now he is back." She scowled at her husband. "And I would be hoping that you would show your appreciation for all he has been through."

"Bah! He lost my money, or mayhap gambled it away. Shanghaied! A likely story." He went off on a tangent of mumbling.

"I for one believe him. Peter has always been an honest man."

Ian was likewise scowling, but quickly backed down in the face of Maggie's potential outrage. "Well, mayhap he is telling the truth. What does it matter anyhow? What's done is done." He took a bite of potato cake, then another and another, mumbling with his mouth full. "I'll give him something."

"That's my hinny!" Rising from her chair, she gave him a kiss on the forehead. Before she sat back down, she whispered, "Faith is thinking of leaving us."

Ian nodded. "To go back to St. Paul. I understand."

Margaret shook her head. "No, she intends stay, to live on that land of hers—in the barn of all things! She wants to hire a man to help her."

"What!" His face turned bright red as he sputtered, "No. No, indeed not. I will not have it!"

If it had taken determination to convince Maggie that she had made up her mind, it took even more to soften Ian's objections. He growled and he grumbled, only giving in when Faith promised to take one of the family's dogs with her—Rob Roy, a gray Scottish deerhound.

"And I or one of the boys will be out to see you every other day, just so if you need anything, we can be of help." Ian looked down at the floor. *"Anything.* Anything at all. And not to worry about the money." For someone who was always frugal this was quite a statement.

"Thank you, Ian."

"And I will personally take it upon myself to help you find a hired hand. Someone of good character who isn't afraid to put in a hard day's work. Someone trustworthy—"

"Someone handsome," Mary cut in. Her mother's chastising look silenced any other outburst. Indeed, a strange, awkward silence swept over those assembled at the breakfast table. Though Faith wouldn't be that far away, though it wouldn't be a permanent goodbye, there was still a sadness. The closeness they had shared for so many days was coming to an end.

Faith's emotions were conflicted as she packed the few belongings she had brought with her. Staring for a long time at the wedding dress that had been a symbol of her love for Henry, she made the decision to leave it behind. She would have no need of it now, but perhaps Mary would.

"Oh, Faith, do you have to go?" Caitlin was the first to agonize her feelings as she said goodbye. "It will be lonely here without you."

"Lonely?" Faith tried to make light of it. "Without three in the bed?"

"I didn't care if it was a bit crowded. I liked having you here."

"So did I." Mary hung her head. "I hate it that you are leaving. It was like having another sister."

"I'm not going far. You can come to visit and I'll come back here from time to time." Still, it wouldn't be the same. Perhaps nothing really would. Henry's death had changed so many things.

Borrowing one of the MacQuarries' wagons, saying her goodbyes, Faith flicked at the reins and tried not to look over her shoulder as she set out toward Milwaukie. Though she would not have said anything to the MacQuarries for fear of hurting their feelings, she really did need time alone. Time to grieve. Time to give vent to the full depth of her emotions. Time to sort things out without anyone there to try and change her mind.

"Just you and me, Rob Roy," she said to the dog, reaching over to pat his wiry head. If she felt some fear at the prospect of being alone, she would not admit it. Besides, from now on that was going to be the way of things. She would have to get used to it.

Faith was deep in thought as she rode along, so much so that she scarcely took note of the scenery. When she saw the roof of her barn loom into view, however, she felt a warm glow replace everything else. Home. Her home now. Could she do it? Could she do all that she had planned?

Clenching her jaw as she guided the wagon toward the barn, Faith was determined that she could. She was strong, intelligent, and, best of all, she was used to working hard. Hadn't her father made certain of that? It was his legacy to her.

Unhitching the horses, Faith took a look around her property, not to appreciate the beauty this time but to calculate all that needed to be done. There were several large rocks that had to be removed before she could even think of plowing. And she needed to get a cow and some chickens and one or two horses and—

Rob Roy's barking startled her. Something was bothering the hound. Something or someone inside the barn. He was making a fearful racket. Having been cautioned to be wary, Faith ran back to the wagon and picked up the rifle Ian had insisted she bring along with her.

Carefully, she walked forward, then, pushing the barn door open with her foot, looked inside, holding the rifle steady as she did.

"Don't shoot!" Putting up his hands, a tall man inside the barn was quick to surrender. "I didn't mean any harm. Just wanted a place to spend the night. I've been through a hell of a time."

There was something familiar about the voice. Faith drew back, then gasped as the man walked into the light. Though the face she saw was unshaven, the hair tousled, the clothing dirty and torn, she recognized him in that instant. Dear God, it was Jonas Winslow!

Thirteen

Jonas stood for a long moment, unsure of what he should do or say next. Always having prided himself on his debonair appearance, he loathed being caught looking like a dirty street beggar. Nevertheless he forced a grin, bowing slightly as he said, "It's a pleasure to meet up with you again, Faith, ma'am."

Faith's blue eyes shone with an undisguised happiness. "And to see *you*, Jonas." Subduing Rob Roy, then putting down the rifle, she smiled. "How are you?"

In agitation he ran his fingers over his chin, disgruntled at the stubble there, then brushed at the dirt on his pants. "Better than I look."

Even disheveled, he was a handsome man. She had nearly forgotten just how pleasing to the eye he was. "You look fine."

"You're looking well," he said at the same moment, eyeing her up and down appreciatively from the top of her head to the hem of her dress. She had an hourglass figure, slim in the waist with full breasts and gently curving hips. "Oregon agrees with you." He'd forgotten just how pretty she was. Her cheeks were flushed, emphasizing high cheekbones. Her skin was smooth, her eyes wide. Even in the old faded calico dress and with her hair up in a bun, she was eye-catching. And *taken*, he reminded himself. He couldn't forget good ole Henry.

She tried to keep her voice calm and even, yet she was overjoyed to see him again. "Oh, Jonas, I'm so glad you came." Though she had issued him an invitation to visit, she hadn't really thought that he would actually take her up on it, at least so soon.

He shifted uneasily, more upset over this unexpected meeting than he would admit. He'd hoped to get a good night's sleep, clean himself up, and then catch a ride with Peter Seton into Portland to seek her out. Instead, here he was standing before her covered with grime, smelling like fish and a veritable pauper. Hardly the way to make a good impression on Faith and her soon-to-be or already-was husband.

So many questions ran through her head. What was he doing here on her homestead? How had he found her? Why was he in her barn? All she said, however, was, "I thought you would be in San Francisco."

136

"Well, I'm not," he answered curtly, then amended, "You spoke so glowingly of Oregon that I decided to change my plans. I took a boat to Astoria." He didn't mention that it was a fishing boat.

"You sailed up the coast?" Compared to her stagecoach ride, the thought of standing at the railing of a boat while the sea breezes whipped one's hair sounded so tranquil. "To Astoria."

"Where I'm afraid I almost got shanghaied."

"What!" She was taken aback, then remembered the talk at breakfast about Peter Seton. "Tell me."

He drew her to sit beside him on an old log. A slightly roughened thumb rubbed over the back of her hand. "I was discussing business with some 'associates' in Astoria," he told her. "When the meeting was over and I was walking toward my hotel, I was suddenly set upon by two men wielding a net. I walked right into their trap."

"Thieves?"

His touch caused a strange quiver to dance up and down her spine. In sudden embarrassment, Faith pulled away. She'd thought about Jonas often, wanted to see him again one day. Now that he was here, however, she felt uncomfortable, ill at ease. Something had changed between them. Her feelings toward him were different, but she had to remember Henry. After all, she was a widow of sorts.

Jonas noticed her reserve and solicitously drew back. He was careful in his choice of words as he revealed what had happened. "And worse. They hit me over the head. I woke up in a warehouse along with several other poor souls." Jonas told about how he and Peter Seton had untied their bonds and set the other captives free, exaggerating his bravery in the telling.

"Oh, Jonas! You really were a hero." To think that he had been in such danger troubled her. "How fortunate that you escaped."

"Or I would be far out to sea by now . . ." Jonas turned on all his charm as he added, "Instead of having the satisfaction of sitting beside you."

Something in his intense gaze forced her to meet his eyes but she quickly looked away. What was it about Jonas Winslow that made her feel so flustered?

Quickly he remembered himself. She was somebody else's fiancé. Maybe even a wife by now. Which brought him to the point of his visit. "Unfortunately when I was set upon, I was robbed as well. I haven't a nickel to my name. I was hoping perhaps you and—and your husband-to-be might consider using my services." Hurriedly he added, "I am very proficient in business matters and could certainly be of help as far as investments and legal—"

"Henry is dead!" Faith just blurted it out, biting her lip so that she wouldn't cry. She didn't want to lose her self-control in front of Jonas.

"Dead?" Jonas was shocked. He had never imagined this. All the time he had been selfishly talking about his own troubles he'd never realized how much she might be hurting.

"Yes." She nodded slowly, yet deep inside she still didn't believe it. She hadn't full come to terms with Henry's death. Perhaps she never really would.

"How?" Her face was etched in pain, her eyes were closed, but all Jonas could think of was how pretty she was. Pretty and vulnerable.

"He was shot by whiskey peddlers and—and *gamblers.*" She spoke the last word as if it were a curse. "A—a m—m—man from the railroad came to give me the n—n—news." Her words stuck in her throat as she remembered that terrible moment when her bubble of happiness had burst. Trying not to give in to utter devastation, she told him how she had learned of Henry's death.

"Killed by ne'er-do-wells!" Though he hadn't even known Henry Wingham, the tragedy of it all deeply troubled him. He couldn't help thinking of how happy she had seemed, chattering away about Henry and her upcoming marriage on the train. "I'm so sorry. So very, very sorry." And he was. For himself as well as for her. He had traveled all this way so that he could use his friendship with this lovely woman to his own advantage. He'd counted on making business contacts through her husband. Maybe even staking out some land for himself here once he saved a little money. He'd even dared to dream of starting his own saloon. Now it was too late.

His sympathetic expression was more than Faith could bear. Though up to now she had somehow managed control of her emotions, the dam finally burst. All the agony of the last few days poured forth from her eyes in a storm. "Oh, Jonas!"

Achingly moved by the sight of her tears, he reached out and brushed them away. "There, there, there." Then, as if it were the most natural thing in the world, he comforted her in the encircling haven of his arms. "Go ahead and cry. It will be good for you."

For a moment she was incoherent as her words mingled with her sobs. "Why? Why did it happen? How could fate have been so unfair?"

His arms tightened protectively around her. "Death is always difficult to understand."

"Oh, it is," she agreed, but just having him near seemed to ease some of the pain. "It makes a person feel so helpless. Poor, poor Henry."

"I wish there was something, anything, I could do to soothe you," he whispered.

Usually Jonas was glib in what he said, using his way with words to his own advantage, but at this moment he realized that he spoke right from the heart. He *did* wish that there was something he could do. Though Jonas rarely if ever had deep affections for people, something about Faith Tomkins tugged at his heart.

"If I could make it easier for you to get through all of this, I would."

She pulled away and looked up at him, her eyes swimming with tears, and in that moment it came to her. Of course. It was the only answer. "Would you really?"

He nodded. "Yes, I would."

Straightening her shoulders, she came right to the point. "Then stay here, Jonas, and help me run this place."

"Stay?" *And do what?* he thought, looking around him at the acres and acres of land. It was out in the middle of nowhere for God's sake.

"Yes. Stay right here." Her crying subsided and suddenly she was filled with a burgeoning enthusiasm. "I was going to hire someone to help me get this place going. To help

141

me oversee the building of a house and clearing the land, the planting. All the things that need to be done."

"All those things." Jonas shuddered. It sounded like an ordeal to him.

"The only problem is that I just don't know who to trust." She reached out and squeezed his arm. "But I do trust you. Completely." It was the perfect solution to her problem.

He drew away from her. "Well now, I appreciate your faith in me, ma'am. Really I do but . . ." Her belief in him was gratifying and at the same time frightening. He was a gambler who had lived by the code of fooling people and always keeping the upper hand. He had never trusted anyone and he doubted anyone had ever really trusted him. Until now.

"Then it's all settled." Faith felt as if the weight of the world had been lifted from her shoulders. "You will stay."

"Well now, I didn't say that." Stay here and be a farmer? The very idea filled Jonas with horror. Blisters and calluses were all a man got for toiling. He had never done a lick of honest work in his life and he didn't want to start now. "I just don't think that I can."

"Oh, Jonas, you must. Can't you see—"

Oh, yes, he could see it. Bending over all day working out in the hot sun, digging in the dirt, wearing himself out until he turned into an old man. Oh, no. It just wasn't for him. "Faith . . . ma'am . . ."

"Jonas, please." She sat up straight and looked him right in the eye. "I won't take no for an answer. You need money and I need a strong man. More importantly, I need a friend." She said it again. "You must stay."

Jonas meant to say no, and as emphatically as he could, but somehow, totally against his will, he found himself nodding in the affirmative. The sadness in those blue eyes of hers, he supposed. Damned if she hadn't completely entranced him, she and her tears. And yet perhaps it wasn't as bad an idea as he had first imagined it to be.

Jonas's mind whirled as he weighed the advantages to the situation he had been thrust into. She was a woman alone who owned a great deal of property. A woman in need of a husband. A vulnerable woman on whom he could use his charm.

All his life Jonas had been a wanderer. A man without roots. Like a tumbleweed. Now maybe he had been given the chance of a lifetime. Faith Tomkins was drawn to him. He would have had to be blind not to have noticed. And she was, as he had noticed before, very pretty.

"All right, I'll stay," he said, making the decision. It was crazy to even contemplate and yet he found himself thinking that when all was said and done he just might find out that he had just been dealt a winning hand.

143

Fourteen

Leaning back in the hotel's bronze bathtub, Jonas thought that at the moment nothing in the world felt as good as the water engulfing him. Closing his eyes, he luxuriated in the steamy warmth, emitting a long, husky sigh as it spread over his body. He felt contented. At peace. And damned pleased with himself. His decision to come to Oregon looked as if it just might turn out to be the best thing he had ever done.

"Yep, Jonas, you ole devil, if you play your cards right, you'll be sitting pretty from here on it."

He envisioned it all now, saw himself as a wealthy landowner like those haughty, strutting gentlemen he so often had the pleasure of besting at cards. His would be the easy life with nothing to do all day but give orders, make investments, and do what pleased him. He'd have the best cigars, drink the best whiskey, and dress in nothing but artfully tailored suits with matching vests. Why, he'd—

"Whoa! Hold on there," he admonished himself. Cupping his hands, he splashed water over his face and hair, scolding himself for getting way ahead of the situation. His lofty dreams were out of proportion with reality. The land didn't belong to him, it belonged to the lady. The lady *and* her husband if and when she chose one.

First he'd have to marry Faith Tomkins, and to do that he had to win her heart, a pleasant endeavor seeing as how pretty she was. Pretty, unmarried, and, at the moment, all alone.

Alone and responsive to his charms, he thought with more than a bit of vanity. "Oh, Jonas, I'm so glad you came," she had said, making him feel as if he were special. And she *had* been glad. It had been reflected in her eyes when she looked at him. Jonas had seen that look before when a woman was attracted to him.

Lathering the washcloth, he scrubbed his body vigorously, humming a tune all the while. It was a song he had made up in his head. A melodic song that put him in the mood for romance. He had it all planned out, knew just what he was going to do. This morning when he rode the wagon out to Faith Tomkins's property he would be prepared. It wouldn't be like yesterday when he was caught unawares. Today he was going to be all spruced up, wearing the new suit that he had signed a promissory note to purchase.

Lingering over his bath, Jonas thought the matter out. "I'll take flowers to her," he said to himself, knowing how susceptible women always were to a bouquet. "And a bottle of wine." That would relax her and make her all the more agreeable to what he was going to suggest—that she turn over the management of her land to him. After all, a woman needed a man to take control of things. That man might just as well be him. He didn't have a thimble's worth of experience at farming, but maybe it didn't matter. After all the years he'd spent playing cards he was a master at bluffing.

"Yes, that's it," he said aloud. "I'll manage the place for her and get one or two big strapped men to do the physical work." Jonas planned to use his head not his hands. He'd have much better things to do than plowing— managing the finances, for example, and showering time and attention on the lady in question.

Jonas stepped from the tub, wrapped himself in a large towel, dried himself off, and stared into the small oval mirror on the dresser as he shaved. Somehow, however, he couldn't meet his reflection as he whisked the razor over his jaw and chin. Now why was that? Why did he feel uncomfortable

146

with himself all of a sudden? Because he remembered how her eyes had sparkled with tears when she had told him about the death of her fiancé, Henry, that was why.

Staring long and hard at his image in the mirror, Jonas felt a stab of guilt for even thinking of taking advantage of the situation. Faith Tomkins was a good woman, a woman bereaved. She needed a friend, someone who cared for her, not a man thinking only of himself. He allowed himself to feel a tender spot in his heart for Faith, a warmth that radiated all through him as he envisioned those big blue eyes.

With a sudden surge of resentment he forced such emotions away. No one had ever given a damn about *his* feelings. He'd been kicked from pillar to post all of his life and had only survived by being tough and resourceful. A chance like this only came once in a lifetime. Unless he wanted to spend his life drifting, playing cards until his luck finally ran out, he better put sentimentality aside.

"Besides, just what was ole Henry doing if not feathering his own nest?" he said aloud, trying to placate his conscience.

Jonas had done a bit of questioning about the matter of owning land in the state and had learned something very interesting on the subject. Something that made Henry look more schemer than knight in shining armor.

Because of the Donation Land Act, the permissible size of a land claim had diminished from six hundred and forty acres to three hundred and twenty—*unless* a man had a wife. The new law allowed a man to claim an additional three hundred and twenty acres for his wife.

"So much for Henry Wingham's impulsive wooing," he said, finishing his shaving. Faith Tomkins might think of her deceased fiancé as a saint, but Jonas was certain the man was an opportunist. That thought eased his mind and set him to humming once again as he put on his clothes. He evaluated his appearance in the mirror with a grin, the cocky smile staying on his face as he rode out to Faith Tomkins's property on a horse rented from the Portland stables.

"Jonas!" Coming out of the barn followed by Rob Roy, she ran to greet him as he got down from the old brown mare. Likewise the deerhound showed exuberance, jumping on Jonas, getting dirt on his clothes. "Down, Rob Roy."

"Nice dog!" Jonas pushed at the big beast, trying to maintain his smile. Once when he was at the orphanage he had longed for such a dog, but now he saw the animal merely as a nuisance.

"It's so late, Jonas. I thought perhaps you had changed your mind and weren't coming."

"And disappoint a lady?" Jonas reached into the saddlebag for the bouquet he had wrapped in a sheet of newspaper. Unwrapping it and holding it out to her he said, "For you."

"Flowers!" Faith stared at them for a long time, reminded of the last time Henry had gifted her with a bouquet. It had been the day he had gone off to work for the railroad. He had promised her that the flowers they grew on their land in Oregon would put those posies to shame. "Thank you, Jonas."

Flowers, she thought. Once they had been a symbol to her of gaiety, romance, and life. Now all she could think of was that she hadn't even been able to lay a wreath on Henry's grave or to bid him a final goodbye. Death was what this bouquet reminded her of now. Even so, she didn't want to hurt Jonas's feelings by rejecting his gift, so she filled an old tin can with water and used it as a vase which she carried up to the loft. When she came back, she held out something for Jonas to take.

"Overalls," she explained.

"Overalls?" Jonas unfolded the blue denim package and held them out for inspection. Faded and patched, the garment looked to be the most hideous thing that he had ever set eyes upon. Not the sort of clothing he would ever want to wear.

"They're Ian MacQuarrie's." Faith gave him an impatient nudge. "Go put them on."

"Put them on?"

Faith touched the sleeve of his brown tweed jacket and laughed softly. "Why, Jonas, you weren't planning on working in this suit, were you?"

I hadn't been planning on working at all, he thought but did not say. Instead he broached the subject of acting as foreman and manager and hiring a workman or two. "Two pair of hands would certainly be better than one," he said, cocking an eyebrow. "And I would be free to use my experience in finances to make certain this property of yours becomes a profitable venture, Faith. Yes, quite profitable."

Faith shook her head. She had been hoping to keep the matter of her financial desperation a secret from Jonas, at least for a while. Now, as she stood looking up at him, she knew she had to tell him the truth. He deserved her honesty. If that caused him to change his mind and leave, well, so be it. "There is no money to hire anyone, Jonas, at least for now."

"No money?" For a moment Jonas thought he had misunderstood.

"The stagecoach was robbed during my journey to Portland," she explained. "Nearly every penny I had was taken. While I was waiting for Henry to join me, I used up almost all of what money I did have." Her voice lowered to a whisper. "And as you know, he never did come." Raising her chin, she tried to hang on to at least a shred of her pride. "But that doesn't mean that I planned to cheat you. You would have been paid. Somehow. Some way. I had hoped that you and I could get the farm to prosper."

Jonas felt as if his queen of hearts had suddenly turned into the joker. He had just assumed that Henry, being a man of honor, would have taken good care of the little lady who was going to be his wife. Now he learned that Faith Tomkins was nearly as poor as he. He had been robbed at the docks and the same had happened to her while traveling on the stagecoach! The revelation shed a whole new light on the situation. A whole new light. But though he wanted to turn around and leave, wanted to back out of the whole situation, he found himself walking toward the barn with the overalls slung over his shoulder.

Fifteen

Work. The more he thought of it, the more Jonas realized why he'd always avoided it. His days at the orphanage when he had been forced to do hard chores for his room and board had caused him to have a less than easygoing nature on the subject. Living in that awful place had robbed him of his childhood forever. Instead of playing with toy trains, boats, and kites like other boys, he had spent his waking hours working at the orphanage stoking the furnaces, sweeping and scrubbing floors, chopping firewood, carrying bucketsful of water or cleaning up the grounds—raking, cutting and digging. Enough drudgery to last a lifetime.

When he had left the orphanage at fifteen, Jonas had made a vow. He had promised himself that from that time on he would live a life of ease. "And yet here I am hard at work again," he mumbled to himself.

For the life of him he didn't know why he hadn't just turned around and bid Miss Tomkins a hasty goodbye when she had revealed to him that she had no money, Jonas thought sourly as he wielded an axe. Instead, here he was dressed in these scratchy overalls, shirtless in the blazing afternoon sun, straining his muscles and getting blisters on his hands. Hardly the easy living he had been hoping for when he head traveled all the way from San Francisco to renew his acquaintance with Miss Tomkins.

"Why didn't I say goodbye when I had the chance?" he mumbled, taking his frustration out on the poor hapless stump that he was chopping into firewood. There were other places he could have chosen to hide out. Why had he chosen Oregon?

Why? As his eyes strayed toward the slim figure dressed in faded blue calico, he knew in an instant. He, Jonas Winslow, a man who attracted women like honey attracts bees, had fallen for a pretty face. Fallen hard. Had right from the first time he had laid eyes on her at the train station, if the truth was told. Damned if that wasn't irritating. Worst of all, each and every time he started to renege on his promise to stay or thought to make a complaint, just one word of praise from her turned his backbone to jelly.

"Oh, Jonas, you don't know what a relief it is to have you here," she was saying now, coming up beside him. "You've accomplished so much in such a short time."

"Oh, it's nothing," he found himself responding like some besotted fool. The truth was, he ached in every muscle. There had been trees to cut down and stumps to be removed. Tough roots which were impossible to burn had had to be pulled or dug out. It was arduous work, much more so than playing a hand of cards could ever be.

Jonas had been laboring for several hours, all the while trying not to exhibit his foul temper or to let it be known that he had had very little experience with farming. Using common sense, and remembering his days working on the orphanage grounds, he had reacquainted himself with the proper use of an axe and how it should be sunk into a soft log when the cutting was done. That kept the axe blade safe and in good chopping shape, he remembered. Through trial and error he had learned to cross-stake cordwood so it wouldn't tumble down, to split a log by placing it in the crotch of a fallen tree, to use a maul to split a stubborn log.

Again she heaped praise upon him. "Why, it's nothing short of incredible."

"It's really nothing at all," he repeated, gripping the axe handle and taking another swing. A gesture done to show off how masculine and muscular he was. With each swing he sent woodchips flying high into the air.

He was disappointed when she didn't even look his way. She was gazing out at the land. Admiring every acre of her future homesite.

"Oh, but it *is something,* Jonas." Faith made a wide sweep with her hand at the area he had cleared. "Just look!"

Taking time out to lean on the axe handle for a moment, he did look around and had to admit that it was unbelievable what he had done in such a short time. "All right, I agree. I am incredible," he said with a grin, wiping his damp forehead with his arm. Leaning on the axe once more, he paused for a minute to breathe in the fresh air and nearly became intoxicated on the invigorating scent of pine, birch, beech, elm, and poplar mingled with the mustiness of the earth and the fragrance of wildflowers.

"It is beautiful out here, Jonas. Makes a person see things in a whole new light," Faith said softly. "Living close to nature makes one appreciate the simple things."

Like a glass of whiskey and a good hot bath, Jonas thought but did not say. Oh, yes, he had worked hard, but he knew that to be just the beginning. There was still plowing to be done, seeds to be sown, a chicken coop to be built, fences constructed, firewood stacked, not to mention putting up a house. Yet somehow he didn't have the heart to complain, perhaps because Faith Tomkins was working every bit as hard as he, picking up rocks that looked to be much too heavy for her, tugging at roots, lugging heavy logs.

"She has grit, courage, and resolve," he said softly, looking at her again from the corner of his eye as she fiercely worked with a shovel at digging up a stump. He had to admire her. Despite her soft, feminine exterior and her impeccable manners, she was tough and brave. Far different from what he had imagined a lovely woman like her would be like.

Her dedication and determination were contagious. Jonas had the feeling that with or without him she was going to make a go of this farm of hers. Somehow he wanted it to be *with* him. What's more, although he at first had thought this work to be distasteful, he was beginning to find some pleasure in the tasks, a certain sense of accomplishment in working alongside Faith.

The day seemed especially sunny to Jonas as he put down the axe and stacked the cordwood. Even with his shirt off he was hot. He felt exhausted and thirsty. Very thirsty. Picking up a bucket, he went in search of water, finding the perfect place in an area where several large rocks purified the stream. Filling the bucket to the brim, he quickly retraced his steps, but before drinking, he reminded himself to act like a gentleman. He offered the first dipper to Faith.

"For you, sweet lady." Their hands touched

and their eyes met for just a moment. But it was long enough for Jonas to come to a disturbing conclusion. Whether he liked it or not, Faith Tomkins fascinated him. The attraction he felt when he was around her was downright potent.

"Thank you, Jonas." Taking the dipper, Faith stepped back, troubled by the strange shiver that rippled through her. A strange sense of excitement that had set her heart pounding. A giddy feeling. When they were on the train together she had felt the same way, but had hastily attributed it to nervousness concerning her journey. Now she suspected differently.

What kind of a woman am I? she reprimanded herself silently, sternly. Henry, poor dear Henry. He was not even cold in his grave and yet here she was tingling at another man's touch. A man she barely knew. What did she really know about Jonas, this man with whom she had exchanged pleasantries on the train? Only that being with him made her feel vibrantly alive. Alive while Henry was dead.

Faith's body tensed at the thought of what had happened to her fiancé. Death had struck him so swiftly, so unexpectedly, that she hadn't completely come to terms with the reality of it all. Now guilt was added to her emotions. Guilt that she had so readily welcomed Jonas to work upon this land. Henry's land.

"I thank you and Henry thanks you," she said softly. Turning her back quickly, Faith felt the compulsion to mention Henry's name out loud again. Not so much to remind Jonas as to remind herself. "Henry would be pleased if he could see what you have done today, Jonas."

"Oh, he would, would he?" Jonas couldn't help but take note of the sudden coolness in her tone.

"Oh, yes." Faith forced herself to envision Henry's smiling countenance. "No doubt Henry would have been just as grateful as I am that you have so quickly transformed his acreage into farmable land."

Jonas' face flushed with annoyance—yes and *jealousy*. Damn. It was as if an apparition had suddenly appeared upon the scene. A cloud, ruining an otherwise sunny day. Henry Wingham's unwanted ghost. "Well, I'm so glad *Henry* would approve."

That's it! he thought. That was the end of this foolishness. He wasn't a farmer, didn't even want to be. Ever! Let her get somebody else. Someone ole Henry would recommend. Some other fool to do this drudgery. Tensing his jaw, Jonas started to tell her just that, but as he looked up, a cloud of brown dirt caught his eyes. A buggy or a wagon was coming down the seldom used pathway, stirring up a lot of dust.

Whoever it was, they were riding at a life-threatening pace.

Faith squinted, recognizing the family form dressed in calico. "It's Margaret! Margaret MacQuarrie." As the buggy rumbled up the road, Faith ran to meet it.

Pulling at the reins to bring the wagon to a stop little more than a foot away from Faith, Margaret said cheerily, "I brought you some freshly baked bread, a dish of just-churned butter, a jar of cherry preserves, a small ham, and a few other things I decided you would need."

"You are so thoughtful." Faith appreciated the concern.

Jumping down from the buggy and handing Faith a huge basket, she asked, "So, how is this farm of yours coming, Faith lass?"

"See for yourself." With unsuppressed exuberance, Faith took Margaret by the hand, leading her to where Jonas leaned against a tree. "Margaret MacQuarrie, meet Jonas Winslow. He's the man I told you about, the one I met on the train. Jonas this is my dearest friend, Margaret, who very nearly saved my sanity, if not my very life."

"Ma'am!" Jonas nodded, frowning as something about this Margaret MacQuarrie reminded him of the woman who had super-vised the children at the orphanage. The eyes perhaps. Or the set of the mouth. Or maybe the salt-and-pepper hair. Whatever it was, he felt an instant dislike for the woman and had the impression from the way she looked at him that the feeling was mutual.

"Jonas." Standing with her hands on her hips, she looked him up and down, taking in the denim overalls, his bare chest, his face, his hair. "Despite those clothes, you don't look much like an experienced farmer to me."

"That's because I'm not," Jonas admitted truthfully, seeing his chance to back out of his former agreement. What was he doing here? He didn't belong. This woman sensed it and he knew it. He should make a quick end to the pretense and be on his way. Taking the basket from Faith, he set it inside the barn, then flicked his fingers through his dark hair, brushing it free of the wood dust his chopping had created.

Faith's eyes sparkled as she looked at him. "Jonas is an entrepreneur," she said, remembering from previous conversations. "As well as a saint! Just look what he has done, Margaret."

Jonas had been close to telling Faith Tomkins to get another man to do her work, but now the words died in his throat. She did appreciate him. It was obvious by the way she was acting and what she was saying. Besides, she really did need him. How then

160

could he desert her? Henry's ghost or not he wanted to stay.

"Hmm." The older woman wasn't as easily impressed. She appraised him again, this time with the piercing eyes of someone trying to see deep into a man's soul. "A saint? I doubt it."

"Margaret!" Faith was shocked by her attitude.

"No man is, Faith," Margaret amended.

Faith felt the fierce need to defend Jonas. "Perhaps. But Jonas is as close to it as a man can come. Why, you should have seen how hard he worked, even after I told him that I couldn't pay him right away."

"Oh, he did, did he?" Margaret's look clearly said that what had been done wasn't enough.

Faith was perplexed. She had just assumed that Margaret would like Jonas. "Yes, he did."

"I see." Looking at the barn, then at Jonas, then back at the barn again Margaret Mac-Quarrie asked bluntly, "And just where does this 'almost saint' stay, when he isn't working? Where does he sleep?"

This time it was Jonas who answered, feeling the fierce need to defend a lady's honor. "Last night I stayed at the Portland Hotel, the one across the street from St. John's Episcopal Church, but if you ask me, I should be staying here. It isn't right for a woman to

161

be alone. Seems to me Faith could use some protection."

"Protection?" Margaret clucked her tongue. "Protection from the likes of him, lassie," she said beneath her breath.

"Margaret!" Again Faith was stunned. "Jonas has been a perfect gentleman."

"Indeed." It was obvious by the way she stiffened that Margaret didn't expect him to continue to be. Ignoring Jonas's presence, she once again tried hard to persuade Faith to come back and live with the MacQuarrie clan, but just as before, Faith insisted that her place was right where she was. It was her land, her responsibility to oversee it.

"If I'm not capable of doing that, if I need to be mollycoddled, then I might as well go back to St. Paul right this minute." And she meant every word.

"All right. But be careful." Taking Faith by the arm, Margaret drew her aside, her voice lowering to a whisper as she put words to her real concern. "You listen to me and you listen well. I've lived enough years to be a good judge of people and there is something worldly about that man. I read it in his eyes. He's far from the angel you see him to be. Far from it."

Glancing over her shoulder, Faith looked toward Jonas more critically. "Worldly," she repeated. To her, however, he seemed more

162

troubled. Lonely. Perhaps he needed a friend as much as she.

"Yes, worldly." Margaret's eyebrows drew together in a frown. "The kind of man who can be dangerous for a woman. The kind who will set out to charm you and win your heart, only to break it once he's had his way." Something in her tone hinted that she had met such a man once and had her own heart broken.

"Oh, I don't think—"

Putting her fingers to Faith's lips to silence her, Margaret issued a warning. "Mister Jonas is not the white knight you suppose him to be. Oh, no. He is after something, if I don't miss my guess. Either your farm or your virtue. Watch him carefully, Faith and don't for a minute let your guard down."

Sixteen

Faith lay on the mattress in the loft, staring up at the moonlight that danced on the barn's wooden beams. She was trying hard to sort out her emotions and that made it difficult to relax. Margaret MacQuarrie's words of warning troubled her but not as much as her attraction to Jonas Winslow. It bothered her, confused her. Was it any wonder then that she couldn't get to sleep?

If *she* couldn't sleep, however, the same was not to be said for the two slumbering down below. The sound of their snoring was a loud rumble.

"Jonas and Lachlan," she whispered, embarrassed by the situation. Jonas had insisted on staying the night at the barn to watch over her. Lachlan was there to keep an eye on Jonas. Margaret's doing, though young Lachlan had tried to make her believe it had been his own. And yet Faith couldn't really be angry. The Scottish woman meant well and perhaps it was for the best, at least until things settled down. Somehow being alone with Jonas at night in the close confines of the barn was troubling. Not because she didn't trust him. Oh, no. Because she wasn't certain she trusted herself and her own feelings.

She had been in love with Henry, hadn't she? Of course. He had been everything a woman could have wanted in a man—polite, gentle, kind, generous, caring, a man with a promising future and so much to offer. If kissing him hadn't made her hear bells, well, theirs had been a love on a more practical level. They had both wanted to start a family and to find adventure in the West. It had promised to be a perfect pairing, tranquil, stable, and secure.

Now, before they had a chance to share happiness, Henry was dead and she was in mourning. And very vulnerable.

Was that it? Was that all it was? Was Jonas just an escape from loneliness?

Jonas. He was so handsome, so charming, so sure of himself. Hadn't she noticed that right from the start? Yes. But was he, as Margaret had said, *worldly* as well? And if he was, did that make him dangerous?

Faith called to mind Margaret's reaction to Jonas. Although she appreciated her concern, Faith was bothered since it was so unlike the woman to be rude and outspoken.

Had she seen something in him that had escaped Faith's notice? Was there a flaw in his character she had not perceived?

"Mister Jonas is not the white knight you suppose him to be," Margaret had said. "Oh, no. He is after something, if I don't miss my guess."

Was it true? Had Jonas taken up with her just to "feather his own nest," as Margaret might say?

Faith thought long and hard about it and in the end had to give Jonas the benefit of the doubt. He had been gentlemanly, that was all. He had helped her with her baggage, shared his food with her, and his behavior had been above reproach. *She* had been the one who had issued *him* the invitation, he hadn't invited himself. And if he had accepted and actually come to visit, it had been with the thought in mind of visiting both her *and* Henry. How then could he have been after any gratification for himself? Nor had he insisted on staying when he had found out Henry was dead. Again, she had asked him and he, without promise of a guaranteed salary, had agreed to help her out.

Jonas had proved himself to be a friend. Faith couldn't fault him in any way. But what about her own feelings? Margaret couldn't see into Faith's heart, couldn't tell what she was thinking. But Faith knew and was pricked by a feeling of guilt. She had been drawn to Jonas right from the very beginning.

But just as a friend, she determinedly told herself. He was someone who had been kind to her. Someone who had cared. Someone she could talk to, rely on. Nothing more. Why then had the mere touch of his hand stirred her so? Why had the focus of her gaze touched for so long on his mouth? Why had the curiosity of what it would be like to kissed by him run through her head?

Faith sat up in bed, forcing any such thoughts from her mind. How could she be so disloyal to Henry's memory! She had to give him the respect he was due. Had to remember. Had to mourn. That meant keeping away from Jonas and yet . . .

Faith closed her eyes, trying to bring Henry to mind. She wanted to remember the moments they had shared, the walks and talks and kisses, the smiles. But it wasn't her fiancé's face she saw, it was Jonas's, and that deeply troubled her. She had been lovingly but strictly brought up. She was a lady, just as her mother had meant her to be, from the top of her head down to her toes. Ladies always remembered themselves and acted perfectly proper in all situations, therefore she had to get hold of herself, had to keep such feelings at bay. Had to keep everything in perspective.

But Henry is dead and that changes so many things, a traitorous voice inside her head whispered. *When you met Jonas on the train, you were on your way to being married and starting a new life. All that is ended now. You want Jonas.*

"I don't know what I want," she concluded to herself. That was the frightening truth. She just didn't know anymore. So much had changed. Her carefully planned future had been handed a crucial blow when the man she had thought to share her life with had been killed. But did that mean she wanted to live the rest of her days alone?

Lying back down, pulling the covers up to her chin, Faith tried to push such questions away. She had to give her heart a chance to heal, had to live day by day from now on. Had to be careful. She had been impulsive with Henry. She had met him, liked him, and promised to marry him right away. She wasn't going to do that again. She was perfectly content being on her own, being alone.

Content? Why then did two dancing shadows remind her of a man and a woman embracing. Why then did she lie awake feeling such a fevered longing to be held, to be touched, to be loved?

Seventeen

Jonas awakened just before sunrise, strangely anxious to begin the day. Was it to finish a task he had left undone, or because with daylight came the chance to be with Faith? Whatever the reason, he didn't linger on his pallet of straw but forced himself to get to his feet, a task that was no easy matter considering how stiff and sore he was.

Shuffling as he walked, he felt like a man who had suddenly turned ninety and realized how hard he had pushed himself yesterday. Even so, he did not hurry back to bed. Instead, he filled a pan with water from a tin pitcher, splashed some on his face, and, spying a sack of apples, grabbed two for his breakfast.

Jonas picked up an axe in one hand and a shovel in the other. He had something to prove—to Faith, to himself, and to that friend

169

of Faith's who looked at him as if he were a devil of some sort.

Just like that Miss Hathaway, he thought remembering a time in his childhood that was better off forgotten. Stern and reproachful, the orphanage headmistress had seemed to get pleasure from criticizing him.

"Your handsome, boyish looks won't make it easy for you here any longer," she had cajoled. "You will work and work hard."

As if to punish him for some unknown mistake she had made sure that Jonas got the worst chores, things that were demeaning and tedious. Instead of breaking his spirit, however, Jonas had set out to show her his worth, working extra hard, just as he intended to do today.

Pushing open the barn door, Jonas walked outside and stood for a long moment viewing the pink-and-purple horizon. Strange how few times he had looked upon a sunrise lately. Like an owl he had become one of the night creatures, gambling way into the late hours. Now in just a few days his life had changed and all because of a chance meeting on a train and a pair of wide blue eyes. *And a false accusation of murder*, he thought, troubled as he wondered what Mrs. MacQuarrie would think of that. No doubt she would assume that he was guilty. And Faith?

"It doesn't matter because I'm never going to be found way up here," he assured himself. Breathing in the early-morning air, Jonas felt as if he were embarking on a whole new life, as if the old Jonas was gone and a new one had taken his place.

Jonas put up his hand to shield his eyes from the rising sun. As he looked out upon the land he groaned. Trees, as far as the eye could see. The ground couldn't be tilled until they were removed, and that looked to be an endless job. Worse yet, there wasn't even to be a profit from the lumber. As Faith had revealed, the trees belonged to Ian MacQuarrie, given to him to pay off her debt.

Though the MacQuarries were friends to Faith, Jonas didn't get along with them one damn bit. In fact, having met the husband last night, he thought him to be even more irritating than the wife, if that was possible. Ian MacQuarrie was grumpy, quick-tempered, and, worst of all, stingy. Jonas couldn't forget the chastisement he had suffered from the man over the matter of using the head of his axe as a hammer.

"Axes are too valuable to ever be used that way," he had been told.

As for the MacQuarrie lads, Lachlan and Cameron had eyed him as if he were some kind of ogre. Only the girls seemed to like him. Mary was always smiling and Caitlin followed him around, doting on his every word, gazing intently at his broad-shouldered frame. Sometimes even imitating his wide-legged stance.

Walking across the area he had cleared just the day before, Jonas put down his shovel, flipped the axe so that the smooth, curved handle slipped through his hand, and began to work. Disturbing the early-morning silence with the thump of his axe, he chopped at a tree that would be in the way of the plow. All the while he tried to think of a way he could help Faith build a house. Living in a barn was rustic at best, inconvenient and difficult. Simple household chores such as cooking, washing, and ironing were made twice as hard for her. He wanted to do what he could to help.

But what? The only money Jonas had ever made was by gambling and he didn't want to take a chance on doing that here. Didn't want Faith to learn he was a gambler.

"Mister Winslow! Mister Winslow!"

Stopping the axe in midswing, Jonas swore violently as Lachlan MacQuarrie ran up to him. The solitude of the morning was shattered by the boy's chattered desire to help, which Jonas agreed to. As Jones worked, he had a small shadow.

Meanwhile, Faith was awakening to a cheerful blending of early-morning bird songs, a chirping that was accompanied by the sound of metal striking wood—melody and syncopation that she enjoyed as she stretched. Suddenly she realized how later it was. It had taken her so long to get to sleep that she had done the unthinkable. She had overslept.

"Jonas?" Leaning over the loft, she affirmed that he was up. And Lachlan, too. Tugging at her quilt, she rose from the mattress and hurried to get dressed, then brushed her hair, fashioning it in a thick braid atop her head. She dangled her legs over the side of the loft, and lifted up the hem of her green calico dress before climbing down the split pole ladder.

Right outside the barn was a rock fireplace. Starting a fire, she filled the coffeepot with water from the stream and put it on the fire to boil. Though she had never drunk coffee before coming to Oregon, she did so now with gusto. With it she ate one of the biscuits Margaret had brought. Filling up two tin cups, putting several biscuits in the pockets of her apron, she went out to where Jonas and Lachlan were working.

"How is it going?"

Jonas's scowl seemed to say, not very well. He grumbled as he ate a biscuit, washing it down with hot coffee. "I could get a lot more done," he rasped, "if *he* was out of my way. I have to worry about a tree falling on him."

Young Lachlan was defiant, showing some of his mother's spunk. "You worry about me?

173

Why, I've been cutting trees since I was just a baby."

"So long ago," Jonas said behind his hand to Faith. "Why, he doesn't look to be more than eleven."

"Thirteen," Faith corrected.

"And I'll bet I could teach you a thing or two about trees. I work in my father's sawmill. I can cut a tree with my eyes closed." As if to prove it, he picked up Jonas's discarded axe and, shutting his eyes tightly, took a swing at a nearby tree. He missed it and fell in the process.

Jonas was uneasy around boys of this age. Perhaps because of all the rights he had gotten into at the orphanage. Twelve- and thirteen-year-old boys could be very cruel. "Send him home, Faith." Remembering his manners he said, "Please." He wanted to have Faith all to himself without worrying about spying eyes. He was pretty sure that was why the lad had come.

Faith could see the impossibility of a truce. Lachlan or Jonas, she had to choose. She chose Jonas. "Lachlan, Jonas has cut several trees that need to be transported to your father's sawmill," she said, trying to be diplomatic. "Would you please do it."

Though he looked rebellious, young Lachlan agreed, though he did stick out his tongue at Jonas as they loaded the lumber aboard. Then in a cloud of dust he was on his way.

"Good riddance!"

Faith came to Lachlan's defense. "He's a good boy, but he is at a difficult age."

Jonas shrugged, not wanting to talk about Lachlan anymore. "Did you sleep well?" *He* had. Working himself into exhaustion, he had dropped off to sleep the moment his head hit the clump of hay he had used as a pillow.

Not wanting to confess her disquiet last night, Faith merely said, "Like a log."

"Good." Usually glib when it came to words, Jonas suddenly found himself tongue-tied. He had wanted the boy to leave so he could be alone with her. Now that he was, he couldn't think of a thing to say. Moreover, he was strangely aroused as he looked down at the ground and noticed her bare feet peeking from beneath her skirt.

"I felt like going without my shoes, just like I did when I was a child."

Ankles and feet had always acted upon him as an aphrodisiac. Turning away, picking up his axe, he resumed his task.

Faith threw herself into work also, with a twofold purpose—to fulfill her dream of making her land suitable for farming and to forget. Forget Henry's death, her financial woes, and, most of all, the way she felt about Jonas. Every once in awhile, however, when they literally "bumped into each other," it all came flooding back.

Now, as they worked side by side removing branches, he with an axe and she with a hatchet, their eyes met and Faith's heart started pounding so loudly she was certain he could hear.

"You are working much too hard, Faith. Are you tired?" he asked.

"Not at all."

"Are you hot?"

"No, but I *am* thirsty. Aren't you?" When he nodded, Faith moved toward the bucket before he had the chance. "I'll bring you water this time," she said, heading for the spring. It was a reminder to Jonas that it was time to dig a well so she wouldn't have to walk so far. In fact, he found himself wanting to do many things for her. He who had always thought first and foremost about himself was surprised at the warm glow that formed around his heart at her thankful smile.

Returning, she held the dipper out to him, letting him drink first.

"Delicious!" Jonas winked, wondering what she would think if she knew that until now, whiskey was the drink he preferred to share with a woman. But then, since he'd met her, his life certainly wasn't at all like his usual routine.

The pause was brief. Both Faith and Jonas

returned to their separate tasks taking pride in the fact that things were beginning to shape up. For the first few hours they seldom saw each other because both of them were busy, hard at work on their own chores. Taking a break for lunch, however, Faith caught him up with reports on the progress she had made.

"Tomorrow we must soot the fruit trees to get rid of the insects." She explained that they would take two shovelsful of soot, one of lime, mix them, and place them beneath the tree. Once they put some water on it, the gas from the mixture would kill the small, ugly creatures without harming the trees.

Faith kept track of the number of hours Jonas worked in a small notebook. She wrote in his time with brown ink that was homemade from mashed, boiled walnut hulls to which salt and vinegar had been added. It was amazing, Jonas thought, how inventive this young woman was. She seemed to find a way to improvise on so many unavailable items. For example, after writing, she sprinkled the page with sand to quickly dry the ink.

Strange, Jonas thought, how quickly time went by when you were with someone whose company you enjoyed. He and Faith talked as they worked.

"Have you heard from your family?" Jonas asked, curious to know.

"Several letters."

He wondered what it would be like to receive letters from home. In all his life Jonas had neither sent nor received one.

"There are times when I get homesick for St. Paul and my family," she confided. "Or at least for my mother."

"Not your father?"

"No. Not him." She explained how he had always wanted sons and had been disappointed by daughters. Furthermore she told him that they had quarreled over her decision to come West. "Sometimes I think that he was right, but then I take a look at what you have done and I know I could never go back."

"Never?" A breeze had come up, loosening her braid and whipping strands about her face. Jonas so wanted to brush them out of her eyes but he held back.

"Never."

"I'm glad." His voice was low and husky. "I like being with you, Faith. So very much."

Something in his voice touched every nerve in her body, make her feel dizzy. "Jonas . . . I . . ." With an inner groan she jerked her thoughts away from him and turned her concentration upon a small branch in her hand. If in that moment she could have brought Lachlan MacQuarrie back she would have.

As it was, a flash of lightning and a roar of thunder interrupted what might have been a revealing moment. Looking up at the sky, Jonas watched the gathering clouds and warned Faith of the impending storm. "Better run for the barn."

Within seconds the clouds burst, rain pelting them as they made a dash for it. They weren't quite fast enough. Within minutes they were both soaking wet.

Jonas closed the barn door behind them, then turned around, struck by how very lovely Faith looked with her auburn hair in wild disarray. Her damp bodice tightened across her firm breasts as she raised a hand to push back a stray wave, revealing the peaks beneath the wet material. A tantalizing sight. Could he be blamed if he didn't look away?

Faith felt Jonas's eyes upon her and something warm and shivery fluttered through her limbs. "Jonas . . ."

It was difficult for him to draw his gaze away from her beauty. God help him if she decided to wrap him right around her little finger. Searching for a blanket, he wrapped it across her shoulders. "You're shivering. I wish I could start a fire." But of course he couldn't. With all the hay, it would have taken just one spark from an inside fire to burn down the barn.

"We'll just have to dry off without one." Faith hugged her arms around her body, wishing for just a moment that they were *his* arms. It was a soulful yearning. A traitorous thought. Traitorous to Henry.

"Yes. Dry yourself off." He had her alone, Jonas thought, in a situation just perfect for seduction. Why then did he go to such great lengths to avoid touching her? Because he felt responsible for her. She imagined him to be her protector. How then could he act like a heel? Accordingly he heard his voice saying, "You had best go on up to your loft so you can change." To the loft so that she wouldn't be so tempting, he thought, watching as she climbed up the ladder.

Jonas knew now what torture was. It was being alone with a beautiful woman, a woman who was undressing just a few yards away, and not being able to touch her. It was a thought that plagued him as he stripped off his sodden clothing. He tried to keep from thinking of Faith unbuttoning each one of her little pearl buttons but it was nearly impossible. He wondered if the skin on her shoulders was as flawless as he imagined. Would her breasts be as soft to his stroking fingers as he supposed? The sensation of her nearness taunted him, teased him.

"Damn!" Realizing his train of thought, he knew he had to get out of there, and quickly. Gentleman though he thought himself to be, he was also a man.

As hurriedly as he tugged and pulled off his garments, now Jonas worked feverishly to put his wet clothes back on. A walk in the rain would cool him down. With long, purposeful strides he moved toward the barn door, opening it wide.

"Jonas, where are you going?" Draping a blanket around her nearly naked body, leaning over the loft, Faith was taken aback to see that he was preparing to leave.

"Out."

"Out? In the rain?" It seemed to be a ridiculous thing to do. "Why, it might be raining for hours."

"The ground will be soft. It will be a perfect time to dig a well," Jonas shot back.

"Dig a well? Are you crazy?" Certainly the agonized expression he wore on his face seemed to hint at that fact. "You'll catch your death of cold, Jonas. Jonas!" The sound of the barn door slamming was her only answer. All Faith could do was stare in disbelief, wondering why he had gone.

Eighteen

It was dark in the barn, and quiet. Only the drip, drip, drip of rain stirred the silence, beating against the roof and splattering on the ground. Dampness seeped through the walls. Though Jonas wrapped a blanket tightly around himself, he couldn't seem to fight the chill that spread through him, prickling his skin, going all the way down to his bones. It was a gloomy kind of night, the kind that did little for a man's mood.

"Damnable rain!" Jonas punctuated his expletive with a sneeze. He had come back to the barn, tired and wet after a long walk. Stripping off his wet clothes, he had put on a pair of Ian MacQuarrie's borrowed red long johns and settled down for the night. Sleep, however, seemed an impossibility, especially considering that he could not help thinking of the soft, forbidden body just overhead.

Jonas had felt frustration many times in his life. As a boy in the orphanage he had known that feeling when he was still hungry but only allowed one portion of food, or when he needed new shoes but had to make do with ones that pinched his feet. Once he had found a large red-and-white kite and had hidden it for himself only to be made to share it with boys who had mischievously let it drift over the orphanage wall and off into the clouds.

"Just out of my reach," he whispered to himself, looking up toward the loft. During his boyhood there had been many times that something he wanted had been denied him. Never before, however, had it bothered him like this.

Putting his hands beneath his head, Jonas closed his eyes. He wanted Faith Tomkins. Wanted her so badly that it was nearly an obsession. Wanted her with a passionate hunger that not even a long walk in the rain could cool. Wanted her and needed her with a different kind of longing than he'd ever felt for a woman before.

"A woman grieving over another man. A woman I haven't even known for very long."

A decent woman. A woman of good character. A woman not at all like the kind of easy-loving females Jonas was used to. That kind he could have at the wink of an eye, a dimpled smile, and the snap of his fingers.

He couldn't get Faith that way. Perhaps he couldn't get her at all. Maybe all he'd get for all his hard work and drudgery was aching muscles and a good case of pneumonia, Jonas thought, sneezing again.

"And it would serve me right," he grumbled.

Rolling over on his side, Jonas vowed that he would be gone first thing in the morning. He was out of place here, just as Margaret MacQuarrie had known the moment she saw him. As out of place as a leaf in a deck of cards. Faith Tomkins needed a different kind of man, a steady, reliable sort from a good family like dear old Henry or some strong bloke who liked the feel of farm tools in his hand. Someone to share her life and her dreams, a man who loved the land.

Jonas's eyelids flickered as he thought long and hard about his past. First there were his unfortunate years at the orphanage, then his rebellious adolescence, a time when he had taken up with bad company, and that had been followed by his gambling days accompanied by whiskey and women. Hardly recommendable qualifications for a high-class woman such as Faith. And what of his future? What could he really offer her? What did he have to give? Love? Never having experienced it in any form, Jonas wasn't really certain even what it was. Even if he did, would it be enough?

"Jonas?"

At the sound of her voice he sat up, wondering why he hadn't heard her climb down the ladder. "I'm here."

"I'm—I'm glad you came back. I was worried." It was so dark that he didn't realize she held a lamp until she lit the wick with a match. The glow illuminated her face, her auburn hair, and her slim figure, clad now in a white nightgown. He thought in that moment how she looked just like an angel.

"I had to come back. It was raining so hard that if I hadn't, I might have drowned." In spite of himself, he smiled.

There was a long moment of silence before she spoke again. "I brought you another blanket." She was puzzled by the way he had acted, rushing out into the rain like that.

Jonas realized he was staring at her and looked away. "Thank you, but I'll only take it if you don't need it."

"I don't. Margaret gave me a heavy quilt that keeps me warm enough." She stepped closer and, bending down, covered him with the quilt.

She was mothering him, that's all it was, yet just this simple gesture stirred him. He was a gone goose all right. "I think it's time for me to leave, Faith." There, he had told her.

"Leave? You mean leave here?" She was totally unprepared for this.

"Yes. It's just not working out very well."

To the contrary, she thought it was working splendidly. So much had been accomplished in such a short time. "Why?"

Jonas knew he could have made up a reason, could have been glib, but decided to tell her the truth. "Because I think I'm falling in love with you, that's why."

"Falling in love with me?" Her voice was a mere whisper.

"Oh, I know we haven't known each other very long, but I guess it just happens that way sometimes." He hesitated, then said gruffly, "Anyway, I'm not the type of man who likes to be a loser. That's why I want to go."

She reached out and took his hand, clasping it tightly as their fingers entwined. "Don't go. Please." Her touch was a shock.

"You don't understand, Faith." Or perhaps it was he who didn't understand. How could a grown man, one experienced with women, suddenly feel so much the fool? "A man—I—I have certain feelings."

Her confession touched her heart, causing her to make a confession herself. "I have feelings for you, too, Jonas."

But not like his. Oh, sure, she liked him, thought him to be an attractive man, that he could tell, but Faith Tomkins wanted a relationship where he kept his distance. A friendship. That just wasn't what Jonas had in mind. "I have needs, Faith." He came right to the point. "Whenever we're together, I find myself wanting to make love to you."

Just as he did now. He was mesmerized by her gentle voice, charmed by the vision she made in her white flannel nightgown. Her long auburn hair was hanging loose, framing a face that with its large eyes, high cheekbones, and well-shaped nose was nearly perfection. She was so utterly lovely.

She blushed at his boldness. "Jonas . . ."

"I've embarrassed you." But he didn't regret saying the words. It felt good to get it all off his chest.

They looked at each other steadily for a long time. His eyes caressed her, embraced her as firmly as if he touched her with his hands. He imagined what it would be like to slowly slip the nightgown from her body, to bring her down to lie beside him, to touch her breasts, her stomach, her thighs.

"I care for you. Very much, Jonas." If *he* was making confessions, then how could *she* hold back? But oh, how confusing it all was. She wasn't really certain just how she felt.

Jonas felt his heart jump out of rhythm, felt his blood pound through his veins. "Well, I'll be damned. Then wishes really do come true."

"But it's too soon." She couldn't let him get the wrong impression. Faith didn't want to lose Jonas, but she did want to be cautious and take it slowly. She was still coming to terms with Henry's death.

He could see the sadness in her eyes and felt like a heel. Just what had he expected? Had he wanted her to be so callous as to just kick her feelings for Henry Wingham aside?

"I'm just not ready for what you want, Jonas. Not yet." But her eyes seemed to offer him a promise.

"Then I guess I'll just have to learn to be patient." Even if patience wasn't one of his virtues.

Nineteen

Never in all her life had Faith been in such need of someone to talk to. The necessity of discussing Jonas's declaration of affection coiled within her, winding itself so tightly she was certain she was going to burst. She just *had* to tell someone. He was falling in love with her, he had said in a tone of voice that oozed with sincerity. Dare she believe him? Maggie had warned her that Jonas was dangerous, that he was a worldly kind of man. Did that nullify what he had said? Was his vow of love only meaningless words that he had spoken many times before, or had he meant it? And if he had, did she really want him to?

"I do declare, lassie, if you don't stop peeling that same potato you will have it whittled down to the size of a pea." There was a hint of laughter in Margaret MacQuarrie's reproach.

"What?" Faith flushed as she looked down at the unfortunate tuber. "Oh!"

"Something's on your mind." The Scottish woman paused. "Is it Henry or something else that's troubling you?" Her eyes were all-knowing. "Your handsome hireling, for example."

"It's—it's nothing!" Faith picked up another potato. She wanted to tell Maggie, needed her advice, but Maggie's prejudiced feelings toward Jonas meant that she would not give Faith an objective answer.

"Nothing?" The graying eyebrows shot up in disbelief.

Faith was quick to respond. "I was just worrying about finances, that's all. It's going to be a while before Jonas and I can even think of planting seeds, much less harvesting. In the meantime, there is very little money."

" 'Jonas and I,' " Margaret mimicked, frowning all the while. "Just listen to you. I'd have to be a fool not to know that he has already gotten to you. Just as I'm sure he had planned." Picking up a long wooden spoon, she stirred the bubbling iron pot of stew.

Faith immediately went to his defense. "Jonas has been very good to me, Maggie. He's been working for two solid weeks without even a hope of repayment and he hasn't complained once."

Putting an onion down on the chopping

190

block, Margaret gave vent to her hostility, slicing it into several tiny pieces. "Perhaps because he has something other than money in mind, hinny."

"Jonas is always a gentlemen." After his confession on that dark, rainy night a few days ago, he had fashioned a crude lean-to across the stream several yards away from the barn. It was there that he slept. Close enough to guard her, yet far enough not to put himself in the path of temptation. Hardly the actions of a philanderer.

"Jonas. Are you talking about Jonas?" A basket of laundry bounced in her arms as Mary pushed through the kitchen door with her younger sister following two steps behind.

"Jonas? Oooooooh," Caitlin echoed, closing her eyes dreamily.

Margaret shrugged her shoulders as if realizing she wouldn't get any help from her daughters on the matter. "Well, bonny is as bonny does, my grandfather always used to say. Besides, he isn't the only fish in the ocean."

Faith was annoyed, but tried to keep it out of her voice as she asked, "Is that why you invited Peter Seton here for dinner?"

Margaret's face flushed. "I'm a hopeless matchmaker."

"And you're wasting your time." Putting the knife and peeled potato down, Faith wiped her hands. "It's too soon for me to consider anybody. *Anybody*, Maggie!" It seemed to be an affront to Jonas that he was not also invited, but then Margaret Mac-Quarrie had her reasons.

"A woman needs a man. A good man," Margaret emphasized, nodding her head toward the doorway where the redheaded Peter Seton was standing, involved in a conversation with Ian. "Peter Seton is truthful, hardworking, generous, kind, and—"

"Probably just as embarrassed as I am to realize what you are up to." Reaching up, Faith took a stack of plates from the kitchen cupboard.

"I'll take him, if he wants to wait for me to grow up." Caitlin's green eyes sparkled. "I like big, muscled men."

"Hush!" Margaret silenced her daughter by gently swatting her on the hand with the spoon, then turned to Faith. "To the contrary, he's not embarrassed at all, he's looking for a wife."

"Oh, is he? Well, I wish him luck but do declare it won't be me." Faith was emphatic on the subject. "I will not marry just to find a man to take care of me. I can take care of myself." She felt pride in what she had accomplished. She had worked every bit as hard as Jonas every day.

Margaret blocked Faith's way as she started to leave the kitchen. "It is good to be independent, strong, and self-sufficient, I'm all of those things, but Faith, a woman needs much more than that. A woman needs companionship. A partner. Someone to share her life with."

Faith's voice was soft as she answered. "I know. And I do want that." Her eyes moved to where Peter Seton was standing. He was a pleasant enough looking fellow but something about him left her cold. "But not without love."

Hurrying from the kitchen, Faith busied herself setting the table. Peter hovered at her elbow, all smiles as he tried to instigate a conversation.

"So, you're from Minnesota, Miss Tomkins. I've never been there, but I've heard it's mighty green. And that there are lots and lots of cows. Did you have many?"

"Oh, no. I come from St. Paul. My family and I were city folks." Putting the plates down, she looked up into his kind brown eyes, deciding he was an amiable young man. "And you?"

"I'm a southern boy. One of those who came west to make my way after the war." A sudden cloud passed over his face. "But then let's not talk about that. What's over is over."

The subject seemed to be taboo so Faith asked, "How long have you lived in Portland?"

"Three years. I met Ian MacQuarrie my

first day here and he hired me on the spot to work for him. I'm hoping to open up my own lumber mill soon, though." He nudged her in the ribs and winked. "I think he needs some friendly competition."

Faith was diplomatic. "Well, from what I've seen, the town could profit from another mill. I've never seen so many trees. Henry always says . . ." She stopped herself, remembering.

"Oh, yes, your fiancé." Peter Seton hung his head. "I'm sorry to hear about your loss, miss. I know firsthand just what a tragedy it can be to lose someone you love."

"You lost someone, too?" She was instantly sympathetic.

"My wife. When the Yankees swept through . . ." He stopped himself. "Maggie tells me your fiancé worked for the railroad." As she moved toward the settee, so did he, taking a seat beside her.

"He did. As a surveyor." Somehow it seemed another lifetime ago, and yet only a month had passed since she'd seen him last.

"Well then, no wonder he picked such a choice spot of land." Reaching in his pocket, Peter Seton pulled forth a wrinkled piece of paper which proved to be a map. "Seems he was privy to the railroad's plans." He traced a line on the map with his finger.

Faith moved closer, trying to see. Female

intuition told her this wasn't just chitchat. "What do you mean?"

Flicking at the map with his finger, Peter's voice lowered to a whisper, as if he were revealing some deep dark secret. "Why, only that you are either sitting on a gold mine or a powder keg, miss." Again he traced the penciled line. "The railroad is going to run right through the corner of your property."

Jonas threw himself into work with a fury, doing the chores of two men. Rising before dawn every morning, he purposefully forced himself to keep on going until it was much too dark to do anything but sleep. When he closed his eyes he only hoped that he was too tired to dream, for when he did, the dreams were always of her.

"Lovely, lovely Faith," he whispered, bending down to pick up a shovel. Things were beginning to shape up, thanks to his determination to keep an arm's length away. A well had been dug near the place where Faith had decided to build the house and Jonas had built a makeshift bridge across the stream for hauling materials across.

He was quickly acquiring a collection of tools, including axes of every size, hatchets and hammers, a chisel, shovel, and hoe. Borrowed tools all, much to his chagrin. He hated being indebted to the MacQuarries. Faith's friends, but no friends to him.

Whenever they had the chance they always snubbed him, just as they had this afternoon when they had come riding out to the farm in the buggy to issue Faith an invitation to dinner. It didn't take much for Jonas to realize they hadn't wanted to include him. "As if I care," he mumbled, even though he did.

All his life Jonas had been ostracized by folks just like that hoity-toity Scottish clan. People whose newfound prosperity made them think they were better than anybody else. He had made up his mind to show them. He'd prove himself. Before he was through, he'd make Margaret MacQuarrie change her opinion of him.

Anger surged through him as he thought about that first encounter, but just as quickly it subsided. Hell, the fool woman had done him a favor. She'd goaded him into staying, and for that he was grateful.

Jonas was secretly pleased with the effect this work was having on his body. His muscles were becoming powerful, his skin bronzed and his waist leaner. What's more, he was becoming more skilled in his every move. Now when he wielded the axe he did it with a grace born of practice, making the tool whistle as it cut through the air.

More importantly, Faith believed in him. Strange how that had changed so many things in his eyes. She believed in him, so strongly that he had even heard her arguing with the MacQuarries in his behalf just this very afternoon.

"Faith . . ."

Even the very mention of her name stirred him. Though she had been gone only for a few hours, it seemed like a lifetime. Perhaps that was why he so eagerly craned his neck when he heard the sound of hoofbeats. It was not the MacQuarrie buggy, however, that thundered down the road. It was two of the scraggliest-looking men he had ever seen. Dusty and unshaven, they reminded Jonas of the kind of men who had played poker with him at the White Whale in Astoria.

"Evenin'," one of them greeted as he rode up to where Jonas was standing. Beady-eyed, pockmarked, and mustached, he seemed the very epitome of danger, or so Jonas thought.

"Evenin'." Jonas eyed him warily, as well as the man who rode up alongside him. These were just the kind of men he was here to protect Faith from. Now he was glad she wasn't here.

"You the owner of this land?" The shorter of the two seemed to be even more brazen than his companion.

"No. The owner is away. I'm the foreman," Jonas answered.

"The foreman." With a grunt the man turned his back, then, deciding he wanted to leave a message, he whirled around. "Well, Mister Foreman, I'd like to leave a message for he who does own this piece of land. The message is that Doyle Cox would like to take this property off his hands."

"Sell it!" Jonas tensed every muscle in his body.

The small man was belligerent. "Yeah, sell it."

"No!" Jonas was surprised at his emphatic answer, but then he realized that working this land, even for a few days, had changed his way of thinking. He realized now that money just wasn't everything. "This land is not for sale, to you, Mister Cox—or anybody."

That should have been the end of the matter but it wasn't. Before Jonas even had time to blink, the short man's companion slid down from his horse and lunged at Jonas. The man who had ridden with him joined forces, making it a fist-flaying free-for-all. Jonas winced as he felt the full force of a blow cut his lip, then another hit him in the eye. Then he was down.

"Just a little something to help you change your mind," the short man chided. "Mister Cox always gets what he wants. You'd be wise to remember."

Jonas ignored his injuries, and though he was down, he came back up swinging. "And you'd be wise to remember that no means no." With a one-two-punch he sent the short man flying, to land in a heap near the newly dug well. "Now, both of you get off of this land before I count to three," he threatened. "One . . ."

With a snort of outrage, both men remounted.

Watching the cloud of dust they stirred up, Jonas felt triumphant. Even so, he knew he had made some enemies today. He also knew something else: that this wasn't the end of it.

Twenty

It was late when Faith returned from dinner at the MacQuarries' home. As usual, she was escorted by one of their sons, Cameron this time, though if Maggie had had her way, it would have been Peter Seton driving the buggy.

Faith didn't know whether to be amused or angry at the way her Scottish friend had so obviously thrown the two of them together all during the evening. She had placed Peter Seton in the chair next to Faith's at the table, had always centered the conversation around Faith and how difficult it was to run a homestead all by herself, shooed everyone in the family out into the kitchen after dinner so as to leave Peter and Faith all alone, then had unabashedly asked him to drive Faith home. Faith had staunchly refused. Not that she didn't like the amiable young man. She did.

"Maggie means well," she had confided to Peter. "It's just that I need some time to sort out my feelings before I go 'husband hunting.' "

"I understand," he had said, taking her hand in a firm grasp that didn't stir her emotions in the least. "It took a long time for me to heal, but . . ." He got right to the point. "Do I dare allow myself to hope that perhaps once you have had some time I might begin to call on you? You are, in case you don't know, a very pretty woman."

"Peter . . ." Strange, but in that moment she knew. It wasn't because of Henry that she didn't want to be courted by Peter Seton—or any other man for that matter. It was because of Jonas.

"I see." Peter's expression couldn't mask his disappointment.

Faith wanted to soothe his manly ego. "I enjoyed meeting you tonight, Peter. You are attractive, charming, and fun but—"

"But there is something missing. No magic. No fireworks when you look in to my eyes." His grin was lopsided. "I guess I'm just not the Prince Charming kind of guy."

Gently, she had touched his arm. "You will be for the right Cinderella." Standing up on tiptoes, she kissed him on the cheek. "And I would be honored if I could call you a friend." Faith smiled as she remembered how quickly he had agreed to that.

The buggy hit a bump, jostling her thoughts back to the present. "Sorry, Faith. I didn't see that hole." With a flick of his wrist, Cameron got the horses back under control, swerving to miss another uneven part of the dirt road.

"It's all right, Cameron. You're certainly doing much better than I ever could. I hate driving at night, even when there is sufficient moonlight." A full moon, she thought, looking up at the sky. A lover's moon. The sight of it made her feel very soulful.

"You should have spent the night at the house. Cait and Mary would have liked to have you there." Cameron's expression seemed to say that he would have liked to have her there, too. Perhaps because then he wouldn't have to make this late-night ride.

"I like living in my barn. It's warm and cozy." And Jonas was nearby.

"Maybe. But I agree with Ma. You need a house." He thought for a moment. "I think Pa would give you more credit."

Faith shook her head. She was already in debt to Ian for what he had done. "I'll live just the way I am living until I can afford to put up a house." Trying to soothe his worried look, she patted his hand. "I'm happy, Cameron. Really I am." And she was.

"You deserve better." He said the words with the fierceness of a protective bear cub.

"It isn't fair that you have to work so hard with so little to show for it."

"No one ever promised that life would be fair, Cameron." Nor that it would turn out as one had planned. Certainly when she had told Henry that she would marry him and go all the way to Oregon, she had never expected to end up alone. Alone? She wasn't alone. The image of Jonas's smiling face came quickly to mind.

As the buggy pulled up to the barn, Cameron started to get down, but Faith had had enough of the MacQuarrie dogs acting like guard dogs. It was insulting to Jonas and humiliating to her. Maggie meant well, but it was time for Faith to seize control of her own life, she thought.

"Go home, Cam. Sleep in your own bed. You don't need to stay with me." He was more an intruder than a protector. "I'll be all right."

"But . . . !"

"Jonas is here to watch over me."

"Jonas." He spoke the name like a curse.

"Yes, Jonas." Faith didn't know what came over her, but suddenly she felt rebellious. All her life she had been so prim and proper, doing exactly what the rules of society dictated. Now she had the urge to thumb her nose at propriety. "Go home," she repeated.

"But Ma—"

"—has more need of you than I do." When

he hesitated she repeated, "Go home, Cameron." If it caused a scandal when it was found out that there was an unmarried woman living in such close proximity to an unmarried man, so be it.

Cameron MacQuarrie sat there a long time, but when he realized that she meant exactly what she said, he wasted no more time. With a flick of the reins and a nod of his head, he was gone, rumbling down the road. Faith watched him go, then smiled as the went in search of Jonas. She had brought him a large slice of chocolate cake and was anxious to give it to him as well as to talk with him about what Peter Seton had said concerning the railroad.

Faith found Jonas by the well, sitting on a tree stump all hunched over. "Jonas?" He turned around at the sound of her voice and she gasped as she saw his face. His eyes was swollen and black and blue. His mouth, which usually was turned up in a smile that emphasized his dimples, was twisted at an odd angle. "What happened?"

"Nothing." Jonas turned his head, feeling ill at ease to have her see him this way. His pride stung at the thought of having been injured. It had been a long time since he'd been marked in a fight. Not since the days at the orphanage had he sported a black eye.

"Nothing?" She moved closer and gasped as she saw his face clearly in the moonlight.

"Who did this to you?" The sight of him brought out all her protective feelings.

"I don't know for sure," he mumbled

She sat down beside him. "You don't *know*?" She couldn't prevent herself from touching him. Before she realized it, she was sliding her fingers over his chin and up to his lips, wiping away a trickle of blood.

"Something about buying your land. That's what started it." The nearness of her, the slight scent of lilac soap that emanated from her, the touch of her skin, made him forget his pain. The hunger to be near her, to touch her, had been with him for a long time.

"Buying my land?" Faith took a linen-and-lace handkerchief from her pocket and moistened it with well water. Gently, she washed the blood from the gash on his lip, careful not to hurt him.

"The railroad's coming through." He winced as she touched the cut on his mouth. "Someone named Cox wants to buy your property so he can sell it and make himself a fortune." He looked her straight in the eye. "But you don't want to sell it." Jonas was beginning to have strong ties to this place even if it didn't belong to him. He was beginning to think of it as home.

"No, I don't want to sell it." Despite everything, she wouldn't have parted with the land for all the world.

That's what I told them, and in return I got this." He pointed to his shiner. "But I'd suffer even worse than that for you. I promised to protect you and I will."

"Oh, Jonas . . ."

Before she had time to think, he had gathered her in his arms, his mouth only inches from her own. Her heart hammered in her breast, beating in rhythm with his. She was conscious of the warmth emanating from his body, aware of a bewildering, intense tingle in the pit of her stomach.

Jonas closed his eyes tightly and clenched his fists, taking a deep breath as he fought for control. He started to pull away and was surprised when she slipped her arms around his neck. Then her arms tightened. "I missed you tonight," she said. And wished with all her heart that she had insisted on his accompanying her to the MacQuarries. If she had and he had gone, he wouldn't be hurting now.

"Missed me?" Something in her voice took him by surprise. He touched her, moving his hand slowly up her arm from elbow to shoulder as he explored, caressed. It was Faith who initiated a kiss, as she slowly raised her chin.

Jonas groaned, closing his arms about her as he pulled her into the curve of his hard body. Her hands reached out to touch him and the feel of those hands was his undoing. They swept all reason and caution from his mind. Jonas captured her shoulders and bent his face to meet her, ignoring the cut on his mouth as he kissed her. The pleasure he felt in the intimacy of their embrace far outweighed any discomfort.

The tip of his tongue stroked her lips as deftly as his hands caressed her body. She moaned, turning her head so that his mouth slanted over hers and his tongue sought to part her lips. She mimicked the movement of his mouth, reveling in the sensations that flooded through her. Faith couldn't help thinking that it had never been like this with Henry. His had been sweet kisses, yes, but they hadn't left her breathless. Hadn't made her feel as if the entire world shuddered and shook.

Jonas's desire was not any less fierce than hers. He had known desire before, but never like this. His reaction to Faith's nearness, to the soft mouth opening to him, trembling beneath the heated encroachment of his lips, was explosive. He shook, giving in to a shiver that was nearly as violent as Faith's. For one moment he nearly lost his head completely. His hands pushed her back slightly as his fingers fumbled at her bodice, searching for her soft flesh. Then just as suddenly he stopped. Pulling away from her, he held her at arm's length.

"Go up to bed, Faith." His tone was stern.

"Jonas . . ." She was trembling. Never in all her wildest dreams had she realized how powerful desire could be. Nor how fiercely and how quickly her emotions could get out of control.

He looked down at her for a long, aching moment, thinking how sweet and untouched she appeared. "I apologize for what just happened."

"Apologize?" She didn't want him to. "Why should you when it was really I who kissed you."

He stood up. "Because I'm the one who knows only too well where a kiss can lead."

"Oh!" She blushed.

It was time again for confessions. "You don't know how it is with a man. I can't be satisfied with just kissing. I want you, Faith. In the full sense of the word."

"Jonas, just now I wanted you, too." She was relieved she had spoken what was in her heart. "I care for you, Jonas. Very much. I realized that tonight."

"And what about Henry?" His eyes searched her face.

She was silent for a long time. "A part of me will always care for him, but, Jonas, I don't want to grieve forever. I want to feel loved again and I think I can feel that way with you."

Slowly Jonas reached out to take her hand and in that moment he knew his life had changed forever.

Twenty-one

One kiss. Just one kiss had completely changed everything for Faith, too. For the first time since Henry Wingham had died, Faith felt as if happiness was within her grasp, as if she could reach out and touch it. Her sadness was gone and in its place was a reawakening of what it was like to hope and to dream.

A pink glow was on the horizon, touching the trees, making them shimmer with rays of light. A glorious sunrise greeted Faith as she opened the barn door and looked out. Breathing in the fresh early-morning air, she thought about last night and couldn't help but smile. She had someone who would stand beside her, protect her. Someone who cared about her. Somehow that made her feel more alive and heightened her senses to the world around her. The song of the birds seemed more vibrant, the colors of the wildflowers looked more vivid, their heady perfume smelled much sweeter. Her every instinct had been abruptly awakened.

He kissed me, she thought, touching her lips. His warm lips on hers had awakened a host of sensations that she hadn't even known existed within her. Now she knew she could never forget. That one kiss had somehow changed her, made her realize that she didn't want to be alone. She wanted companionship and, most importantly, love.

Faith hummed a tune as she gathered wood for the small stone outdoor fireplace. Lighting a fire, she put a pot of coffee on to brew, then looked out toward the land he was clearing. He had been a great help. Despite what the MacQuarries said, Jonas did seem suitable for a life of farming.

"Good morning!"

She whirled around at the sound of his voice and found him staring at her with a look that rekindled what she had felt last night. "Good morning."

It was obvious that he had been busy working. He clutched an axe in one hand and held an armload of wood against his chest. "More firewood if you need it."

Faith reached out to take a few small logs, but she missed and the firewood fell clattering to the ground.

Both knelt to pick it up at the same time. Fingers groping to retrieve the fallen wood brushed the other's hand, unleashing a maelstrom of sensations. A quiver danced down Faith's spine as all her senses came alive. Jonas was looking at her in a way she had only seen him do once before, a look that made his eyes flicker as if with sparks.

"Here, let me." Quickly, he gathered up the wood.

His mouth drew her eye, that perfectly chiseled mouth. She found herself wishing he would kiss her again. Slowly she stood up, looking at him as she rose to her feet. He was such an attractive man. She couldn't even think of one thing she would change about him. He was handsome, honest, patient, kind and caring. And most of all brave. Hadn't he fought those men when they had tried to intimidate him about selling her land.

"Is something wrong?" He tensed.

Faith realized that she was staring at him. "To the contrary, everything is right again, Jonas."

He sighed with relief. "Then you are just as happy this morning as I am."

"Definitely so." Faith felt her heart skip a beat as Jonas reached out and touched a strand of her unbound hair.

"Good."

They moved silently about their morning routine, drinking coffee and eating breakfast, but the looks that passed between them said far more than words ever could. If it was true

211

that they were headed toward love, then it was obvious that they were going there together.

As always when the sun was shining, Jonas stripped off his shirt and worked bare to the waist, tying the straps of the overalls around his waist. Though she knew it to be unfair she compared him to Henry. Jonas was muscular, Henry had been lithe and tall. Jonas dark, Henry fair. Jonas was strong, and although Henry was not weak, she doubted he could wield an axe the way Jonas did. Henry had been more the bookish type.

Faith had difficulty keeping her eyes from traveling over his dark haired head, his tanned torso, his lean hips, muscled arms, and his chest which was covered with just the right amount of hair—hair that tapered into a thin line and disappeared into the waistline of his overalls. With each stroke of the axe blade his arms bunched and hardened, the cords of his neck stood out, his buttocks tightened then relaxed. He looked comfortable as he chopped down that tree, even happy.

"You do belong here, Jonas," she breathed, quickly lowering her gaze when he turned without warning to find her watching him.

As Faith worked beside Jonas, heated glances were exchanged, wider smiles, more brushing against each other. Jonas made her feel all warm and tingly inside. Made her feel as if she were wrapped in a shimmering enchantment. If Peter Seton had told her he was not the prince she was looking for, well, she knew now that Jonas was. He was everything she had always wanted in a man. When she was with him she felt alive. Even working out in the hot sun was tolerable when she was with him. Today somehow it didn't seem like work.

"You are beginning to love this land nearly as much as I do, aren't you?" she said, putting down her shovel.

"The land and you," he answered, pausing in his task of digging up tree stumps.

It was Jonas who had suggested using the upturned stumps as a makeshift root fence around the barn until one of a more solid nature could be built. There was always something that needed to be done. Even when it was raining there was plenty indoor work, such as repairing equipment, cleaning tools, stacking firewood, or putting it out to dry. Pine and cedar had to dry for a year.

"I enjoy being here, working here, helping you."

"And I like having you here, Jonas." Reaching out, she let her touch speak for her when she found herself suddenly tongue-tied. What she wanted to say was how much she liked his smile, his teasing, his honesty, his love of the land, his sense of humor.

213

Jonas often made her laugh as he told her amusing tales about his journeys and the different kinds of people he had met. The longer they spent together the more she appreciated his keen sense of humor. Somehow he always managed to laugh at things that might have made other people angry. He even made light of his black eye and swollen lip, giving her a rousing account of how he had gotten his "badges of valor," as he called them.

"I gave as good as I got, Faith," he said, putting down his shovel and mimicking a boxing match. "You should have seen it. They went away limping and howling." Suddenly he grew serious. "And that had better be the end of it, if they know what is good for them. I don't want men like that setting foot on this land again." He draped his arm across her shoulder possessively. Jonas felt as if the years had been swept away and he was a boy again. She was his and he wouldn't let anyone or anything take her away.

"Even if they do, with you I feel safe," she whispered.

Jonas gazed intently at her, wanting to engrave every detail of her beauty upon his memory—the arch of her brows, the upward tilt of her mouth, the way the sunlight danced upon her auburn hair. He wanted to remember, just in case something happened and he lost her. Just as he had lost everything that he had ever really treasured.

So this is love, he thought, realizing that nothing could have prepared him for what he was feeling now. He had never realized how incomplete he had been until now, and the very thought of being without Faith was frightening. And yet there was every possibility that one day she would be gone. Nothing was forever. Hadn't he learned that by now? And yet looking at her, that was what he wanted. Forever. And all that went with it.

How do I make her love me? he wondered. What should he do to cause her to feel about him just as he did about her? Despite the fact that he had always been known as a ladies' man, Jonas now felt like an innocent when it came to this matter of love. Added to his predicament was the fact that he felt honorbound to protect her—even if it was from himself!

Jonas had never had a woman before who had not known a man's lovemaking. Despite her having been engaged, he was certain no man had ever possessed Faith Tomkins. That thought was both exciting, yet troubling as well. Above all else, he didn't want to hurt her. The newfound feelings between them were fragile and he didn't want to take the chance of spoiling anything. Even so, he hungered for her. What he wouldn't have given at that very moment to pick her up in his arms, carry her inside, and make love to her. It was a fantasy he carried with him as they worked beside each other all through the day.

The fantasy turned into a nightmare at night as he slept alone in his lean-to. Even though he was weary and his muscles ached all the way down to the bone, he couldn't stop thinking about her. Faith Tomkins was unlike anyone he had ever known. She was soft and feminine, yet at the same time strong and determined. She was generous, giving, beautiful, and virtuous, but until last night he hadn't realized the passion she possessed.

"Sweet, sweet Faith." He imagined her lying naked in his arms. It was a vision that haunted him as the night dragged on.

Jonas could never have known it but as she lay on the mattress up in the loft, Faith was thinking about such things and feeling wicked for her musings. What would it be like to make love with Jonas? To have him touch her, stroke her, to lie with her head against his chest?

"You belong here, Jonas," she had told him. He belonged with her. The thought moved through her mind like a melody, over and over again, so strongly that she didn't hear the sound of horses' hooves at first. Not until they were right outside. "Who?" Cameron? Lachlan? Ian?

Voices. None that she had ever heard before. Hostile. Shouting. Faith leaned over the loft and saw Jonas struggling to his feet. There was a crackling sound. A flash of sparks.

"Jonas!"

He looked up at her and then they both smelled it. Smoke! The barn was burning. Someone had set it on fire!

Twenty-two

Flames leaped in all directions, licking hungrily at the dry hay and straw scattered on the ground. Faith watched, transfixed in horror, as the fire spread rapidly throughout the barn, devouring everything in its path. All that she owned.

"No! No, no, oh please no." Like someone possessed she began reaching and groping, bundling her possessions together, holding them against her chest. "My pictures!"

She started toward the wooden box containing her treasures, watching in dismay as a blazing wooden beam fell near it. With a strangled cry she continued to move in that direction, disregarding the danger. The fire would ravage the entire structure in no time. She had to salvage what she could. She had to move now, and quickly, or she would lose everything.

"Faith!" To his alarm, Jonas could see

what she was doing. "Faith, leave it. Climb down. Now!" It would only be a few minutes before the flames completely destroyed the loft. She had to get away before she was trapped.

"I have to get the box!" The contents could never be replaced. Tangible reminders of so many memories.

"Let it burn." Flames leapt upward, threatening to demolish everything in their way. Even the roof was on fire. Timbers were crashing down as flames ate away at the foundation. They had to get out before the roof collapsed. "Faith!"

She faltered for just a moment, then realizing the hopelessness of saving her valuables, she dropped the bundle in her arms and turned toward Jonas. And all the while the flames from the burning barn danced higher and brighter. "I'm coming." Her hands trembled as she started her descent down the loft's ladder.

"Faith, be careful. The ladder has caught fire." The smell of smoke permeated the air, burning Jonas's eyes and obscuring his vision. He closed his eyes for just a moment. When he opened them, he gasped. Wisps of flame had caught hold of Faith's nightgown.

With a shout, Jonas lunged forward. Reaching up, he caught Faith in his arms and, falling to the ground, rolled over and over until the fire was out. Then instantly he was up again, pulling her with him. He cradled her close against him, realizing how very precious she was to him.

Thick smoke billowed through the air stealing their breaths away. The brightness of the fire nearly blinded them. All around them the fire raged out of control, licking at them with scorching heat. Stumbling over fallen beams and other debris, they slowly advanced toward the barn opening.

"The whole front of the barn is on fire!" Jonas gasped, choking violently as he tried to take a breath.

Greedy yellow-and-orange flames were attacking the door. A wall of heat blasted them as they pushed by. Dodging the falling, burning rafters, Jonas and Faith bolted to and fro, seeking a way out. Escape seemed hopeless, but their instinct for survival and love for each other were the driving forces that led them on. Somehow they would make it.

"Lean against me!" Making his body a shield, Jonas plunged through the door and into the night.

Cool air rushed to meet them. It was a balm to their lungs and their souls.

He cherished her with his eyes. "Are you all right?" With gentle hands he examined her and was relieved that despite her singed nightgown, there were no burns.

"I'm fine. A little shaken but fine. Are you okay?" she asked. They had survived.

Dark gray smoke swirled in the air like an ominous thundercloud. Pulling her against him, they watched from a safe distance as the flames consumed the barn. "Damn them!"

Faith leaned her head against Jonas's chest and tried hard not to cry as the charred logs and burning walls tumbled to the ground. Embers glowed orange where the fire had blazed itself out. Soon the barn looked like the ruins of a gigantic campfire.

Her breath escaped in a long, shuddering sigh. "I remember when it was put up. It took all day and the strength of several men. Now in just a few minutes, it's no more." And gone with it was the box that had held all her memories.

"I'm sorry, my sweet." It seemed natural to call her by that term of endearment. Turning his head, he nuzzled her hair.

The endearment was comforting to Faith, the only thing that could make her smile. "They want me to give up. To give them this land."

"And will you?"

She shook her head. "No. I'm even more determined than ever now, Jonas." She entwined her arms in his, snuggling against him. "If there is anything good that can come of this, it's that I realize that I am really strong. Strong and stubborn. I'm going to rebuild, the barn and the house. Somehow. Some way."

Jonas felt a twinge of fear for her. "They'll only burn them down and in the process put your life in danger. You might not escape next time."

"I'm prepared to take my chances." She looked over at him, saying softly, "But I'll understand if you decide to go."

"Leave?" He hugged her. "Not on your life. If you are going to stand up against them, then deal me in." It was a slip of the tongue, a reference to his gambling that he regretted. Still, as he thought about it, Jonas knew there was only one way to get the money to help Faith. Do what he did best. But he would think of that tomorrow. "Come, we'd best see if we can find my horse so that I can get you into town."

It was not to be. Either the horse had bolted and run away because of the fire or the culprits who had set the barn ablaze had stolen it. To his annoyance, Jonas realized that they were stranded, at least for the night.

"We'll have to stay here until morning."

Jonas remembered to be a gentleman. "You can sleep in my lean-to. It's warm and fairly comfortable."

Faith looked down at the ground, wondering how she found the courage to say, "I want you to sleep there, too." She wanted him to touch her hair, to let it slide slowly through his fingers. She wanted to lie beside him, to feel the comfort of his body pressing against hers.

"Faith, I'm only human." Slowly, his hands closed around her shoulders, pulling her to him. His heart pounded violently as he stood stonestill, looking at her.

Perhaps there were times when a woman had to make the first move, she thought. Lifting her arms, Faith encircled his neck as she rose on tiptoe. She melted against him, burying her face in the strong warmth of his shoulder.

He brushed the hair back from her face with an aching tenderness, then lifted a strand of her hair that had tumbled over her breasts. His touch was healing, his fingers strokes of velvet as he caressed her. "I love you, Faith." He had said the words to other women but he had never meant them before.

She felt his breath ruffle her hair and experienced the sensation down the whole length of her spine. "I love you, too."

Slowly his mouth came down on hers, the burning possession of his lips starting a fire of a different kind. Time was suspended as they explored each other's lips. Pressing her body closer to his, she sought the passion of his embrace and gave herself up to the fierce sweetness. The world seemed to be only the touch of his lips, the haven of his arms. She couldn't think, couldn't breathe. It was as if she were poised on the edge of a precipice, in peril of plummeting endlessly.

Jonas lifted his mouth from hers and held her close for just a moment. Dear God, what she did to him! Slowly, languorously, his hand traced the curve of Faith's cheek, buried itself in the thick red-brown glory of her hair. She was playing havoc with his senses. He wanted to make love to her, so much so that it hurt, yet with a fire that was tempered with gentleness. He felt a warmth in his heart as well as his loins.

"I don't want to hurt you. Never that."

"I know you don't and I know you won't." Her hand touched his, squeezing it tightly. "Come." Walking hand in hand, she led him to the tiny shelter he had created, tugging him down beside her. The soft, rounded curves of her breasts and stomach pressed against him as they lay down together. Once more her head rested against his chest.

The night was warm with just a hint of a breeze. Night birds serenaded the lovers. A perfect night for love.

"Faith, I wish . . . ." So many things. That he wasn't what he was. A gambler, a wanderer. A man on the run. He started to pull away, but her arms tightened around him, drawing him back down to her once again. "Faith, do you really know what you are doing?" Was she really over Henry? If not, then he would end this before it began.

Something warm and deep flowered instinctively at the sound of his voice. "Yes." Tomorrow she would return to reality.

He was relieved. Perhaps a ghost had at last been set aside. "I have never wanted anything as much as I want you now, Faith. Never!" There on a soft bed of blankets he held her cradled in his arms, sheltered beneath the outflung branches of two entwining trees.

She could feel the heat and strength and growing desire in him, giving proof to his words. "Then make love to me, Jonas."

How could he refuse when it was what he wanted, too?

Jonas held her chin in his hand, kissing her eyelids, the curve of her cheek. He kissed her mouth with all the pent-up hunger he had tried to suppress for so long. His tongue gently traced the outline of her lips and slipped in between to stroke the edge of her teeth. "Your mouth tastes so sweet," he whispered against her mouth, "and you are so soft."

His hands explored her innocent beauty. He felt her tremble beneath him and opened his eyes, mesmerized by the potency of her gaze. He found himself trembling, too, with a nervousness that was unusual for him. Anticipation, he supposed. Eagerness. Desire. The thought that this woman had never had another man filled him with a wrenching tenderness. He would make it beautiful for her, he vowed.

Slowly, leisurely, Jonas stripped Faith's nightgown away. His fingers lingered as they wandered down her stomach to explore the texture of her skin. Like velvet, he thought. "You are so beautiful."

She glowed under the praise of his deep, throaty whisper. "Am I?" The compliment pleased her, made her more sure of herself in this quest to experience the unknown.

"Very." He sought the indentation of her navel, then moved lower to tangle his fingers in the soft wisps of hair that joined at her legs. Moving back, he let his eyes enjoy what his hands had set free. "Do you have any idea how beautiful?"

"No. Tell me."

He told her with his touch, making her feel cherished. Precious. Faith tingled with an arousing awareness of her body, as if she was discovering herself through Jonas. The lightest touch of his hands sent a shudder of pure sensation rippling deep inside her.

Their lips touched and clung again, enjoying the sweetness of newly discovered love. As if it were the most natural thing in the world, Faith moved her hands over him, too, caressing him. Exploring. He took her hand and pressed it to his arousal. She felt the throbbing strength of him as her eyes gazed into his. Then he bent to kiss her again, his mouth keeping hers a willing captive for a long time.

Twining her hands around his neck, she clutched him to her, pressing her body eagerly against his chest. She could feel the heat and strength and growing desire of him with every breath. "Jonas . . ." Faith tried to speak, to tell him all that was in her heart, but all she could say was his name again and again, a groan deep in her throat as his mouth and hands worked unspeakable magic.

Jonas breathed deeply and though her hair smelled like smoke it merged delicately with the spicy scent of her. The enticing fragrance invaded his flaring nostrils, engulfing him. "Perhaps it was fated that we meet on the train," he murmured. "Do you suppose so?" His head was bent low, his tongue curling around the tips of her breast, sucking gently.

"I don't know." It was something she just didn't want to think about, at least not now.

Raising himself up on his elbow, he looked down at her, and at that moment he knew he'd put his heart and soul in pawn. Removing his shirt and trousers, he pressed their naked bodies together, shivering at the vibrantly arousing sensation. "Faith." Her name was like a prayer on his lips.

The warmth and heat of his mouth and the memory of her fingers touching his manhood sent a sweet ache flaring through Faith's whole body. Growing bold, she allowed

227

her hands to explore, delighting at the touch of the firm flesh that covered his ribs, the broad shoulders, the muscles of his arms, the lean length of his back. He was so perfectly formed. His masculine beauty hypnotized her, and for just a moment she was content to stare, then with a soft sigh her fingers curled in the thick springy hair that furred his chest. Her fingers lightly circled in imitation of what he was doing to her.

His lips nuzzled against the side of her throat. He uttered a moan as her hands moved over the smoothly corded muscles of his shoulders. "I like you touching me . . ." It seemed as if his breath was trapped somewhere between his throat and stomach. He couldn't say any more. The realization that she was finally to be his made him dizzy as he brought his lips to hers. Such a potent kiss. As if he had never kissed her before.

In fact, Jonas had the feeling that he was doing everything for the very first time as he made love to her. She was the only woman he would ever love. Burying his face in the silky strands of her hair, he breathed in the fragrant scent of her hair once more and was lost to any other thought.

"Jonas." Closing her eyes, Faith awaited another kiss, her mouth opening to him as he caressed her lips with passionate hunger. Faith loved the taste of him, the tender urgency of his mouth. Her lips opened to him for a seemingly endless passionate onslaught of kisses. It was as if they were breathing one breath, living at that moment just for each other.

Desire that had been coiling within Faith for so long only to be unfulfilled sparked to renewed fire and she could feel his passion likewise building, searing her with its heat. They shared a joy of touching and caressing, arms against arms, legs touching legs, fingers entwining and wandering to explore. Mutual hunger brought their lips back together time after time. She craved his kisses and returned them with trembling pleasure, exploring the inner softness of his mouth.

Desire writhed almost painfully within his loins. He had never wanted anything or anyone as much as he did Faith at this moment. It was like a dream waiting to come true.

Jonas cupped the full curve of her breast. He stroked lightly until the peaks sprang to life under his touch, the once-soft flesh now taut and aching. His breath caught in his throat as his hazel eyes savored her. "Lovely!" And now she was his. Bending down, he worshipped her with his mouth, his lips traveling from one breast to the other in tender fascination. His tongue curled around the taut peaks, his teeth lightly grazing until she writhed beneath him. He savored the expressions that chased across her face, the wanting and the passion for him that were so clearly revealed.

The night air caressed Faith's skin. Stars hovered about the sky like candles. *My bridal bed,* Faith thought, moving in sensuous fascination against him. Her hands crept around Jonas's neck, her fingers tangling and tousling the thick waves of his black hair as she breathed a husky sigh. How wonderful it was to be loved! She caught fire wherever he touched her, burning with an all-consuming need.

She shivered in his arms and, fearing it was from the night air, he gathered her closer, covering her body even more tightly with his to keep out the chill. With tender concern he tugged at a blanket, giving her the largest portion, tucking it beneath her.

"I'm not cold!" she whispered. It was something else that made her shiver.

Even so, he held her close, kissing, touching, rolling over and over on the ground. His hands were doing wondrous things to her, making her writhe and groan. Every inch of her body caught fire as passion exploded between them with a wild oblivion. He moved against her, sending waves of pleasure exploding along every nerve in her body.

"Jonas . . . love me," she moaned.

"Soon." His hands caressed her, warming her with their heat. They took sheer delight in the texture and pressure of each other's body. He undulated his hips between her legs and every time their bodies caressed, each experienced a shock of raw desire that encompassed them in fiery, pulsating sensations. Then his hands were between their bodies, sliding down the velvety flesh of her belly, moving to that place between her thighs that ached for his entry.

The swollen length of him brushed across her thighs. Then he was covering her, his manhood at the entrance of her secret core. With as much care as was humanly possible, he slowly entered her. His gentle probing brought sweet fire curling deep inside her with spirals of pulsating sensations. Then his hands left her, to be replaced by the hardness she had glimpsed before, entering, then pausing.

She felt his maleness at the fragile entryway to her womanhood as he pierced that delicate membrane. Every inch of her tingled with an intense, arousing awareness of his body. There was only a brief moment of pain, but the other sensations pushed it away. Faith was conscious only of the hard length of him creating unbearable sensations all over her as he began to move within her.

Jonas groaned softly, the blood pounding thickly in his head. His hold on her hips tightened as his throbbing maleness possessed her again and again. She was so warm, so tight around him, that he closed his eyes with agonized pleasure as he moved back and forth, initiating her fully into the depths of passion.

Instinctively, Faith tightened her legs around him, certain she could never withstand the ecstasy that was engulfing her body. It was as if the night shattered into a thousand stars, bursting within her. She was melting inside, merging with him into one being. As spasms overtook her, she dug her nails into the skin of his back, whispering his name.

A sweet shaft of ecstasy shot through Jonas and he closed his eyes. Even when the intensity of their passion was spent, they still clung to each other, unable to let this magical moment end. They touched each other gently, wonderingly.

"I knew that I loved you," he whispered, "but I didn't know how much." Far from quenching his desire, what passed between them had made him all the more aware of how much he cared for her.

Cradling her against his chest, he lay silent for a long time as he savored her presence beside him. His hands fondled her gently as she molded her body so trustingly to his. Jonas realized that for the first time in his life he was truly content. Money and power were said to be the most important things on earth but he knew differently now. Without someone who really cared, life was hollow and made of man a shallow creature. Faith made him feel alive!

But could he just forget his past? Or would it come back to haunt him? As he leaned his chin against Faith's soft, fragrant hair, he knew a moment of fear.

Twenty-three

Golden sunlight flickered on Faith's eyelids, awakening her. Yawning and stretching, she thought for just a moment that she was up in the loft but the sound of breathing reminded her of what had happened. "The barn!"

It was a remembrance that brought forth anger and joy simultaneously as the terror, the flames, the smoke, all came back so vividly. And something more came to mind. She and Jonas had made love with an exhilarating passion that made her heart race wildly just remembering.

A flush of color stained her cheeks as she recalled the words he had said, the things he had done, and how she had responded so eagerly. Beneath his hands and mouth, her body had come alive and she had been lost in a heat of desire. His hands against her breasts had not only warmed her but also comforted her, making her forget all about the fire—except for the one raging inside her.

"So much for being a lady," she whispered. She had responded without shame to Jonas, just like the wantons she had heard gossiped about. And what now? How would they both feel in the light of day? More importantly, what would she and Jonas be to each other now?

Lovers. Once Faith might have thought the word to have a tawdry ring to it, but feeling as she did about Jonas, she couldn't believe that the passion and joy they had found together last night was wrong. The world could be a much happier place when two people were in love.

Friends. She definitely wanted that. Despite the fact that their relationship had taken on a new dimension, Faith didn't want to lose the camaraderie they had shared. There were other things besides passion that drew her to him. Jonas was someone she could talk to, depend on, someone who could make her smile.

Turning over on her side, she stared into Jonas's sleeping face. His features were in repose, yet she could nearly imagine the dimples that accompanied his laughter, could almost feel again the softness of his lips as they brushed against hers.

Worldly. The word that Margaret MacQuarrie had used to describe Jonas flitted through her mind. Was he? His lovemaking seemed to prove that he was an experienced lover, that there must have been others before her. Did it matter?

A stray dark curl had fallen across his wide brow and she brushed it back out of his eyes with tender concern. Certainly he was handsome. Could she really expect that he hadn't attracted women? No. Nor did she want a monk. Worldly. If he had been, if he was, she didn't care. It was by the way he treated her that she would judge him—by his honesty, his strength, his gentlemanly manners, his kindness to her. Somehow, though she knew the coming days would be difficult, she felt hopeful because she knew that Jonas would be there, just as he was this morning.

Leaning forward, she touched his mouth lightly in a kiss. Her impulsive act awakened him. His eyes snapped open, then he smiled as he saw her bending over him. "If I'm dreaming I don't want to wake up."

"You're not dreaming, Jonas."

"Mmm." Finding Faith beside him, her auburn hair tumbling in wild disarray around her face and over her shoulders, made it the very best morning of his life. "What a welcome surprise." He drew her close against him.

"For me, too." She snuggled into his arms, laying her head on his shoulder, curling into his hard, strong body.

"Is it?" He wanted to believe that it was. Didn't want to think that he had taken advantage of the moment. Didn't want her to have any regrets.

"I wouldn't mind waking up every morning to find you next to me," she confided. She felt warm, content, and most importantly—loved. She belonged with Jonas.

"Perhaps we can do something about that." His hand moved lightly over her hip and down her leg. She was his! By her own admission. At last he had come to know the glorious sweetness of her body. And her heart? Had she given him that as well? Looking into her eyes, he knew that she had, and while that made him happy, it also gave him cause for concern. He didn't want her to ever regret caring for him, didn't want his past to trouble her in any way. Above all, Jonas never wanted to hurt her.

Unaware of his concerns, Faith closed her eyes. "Maybe we can stay right here like this forever." She didn't want to spoil the morning by letting reality intrude.

For just a moment Jonas allowed himself to hope for a happy forever. All his life he had wanted someone to care about him. Though his had been a wanderer's life, he had really wanted the same things as any other man—a home, a family, a woman to share his life. Until now it had seemed just a hopeless dream. Until he had met *her.*

"But we can't stay like this, can we, Jonas?" Though she had wanted to push all thoughts of the fire from her mind, Faith knew that she couldn't.

"No, we can't." He clenched his fist, determined to protect her. "We have to find the bastards who set the fire." From where they lay they could see the rubble. "And when I do—"

"And what if you don't?" In the quiet moments of early morning, Faith reflected on her life, realizing just how sheltered she had really been. Though her father had been a strict disciplinarian and had expected all his daughters to work hard, still he had protected them from the dark side of people's natures. Now, however, she was beginning to realize there wasn't always justice.

He touched his sore eye. "We will!"

She pressed her nose against his cheek, whispering, "Be careful," then wrapped her arms around him. For a long time she was silent, reluctant to move. It seemed important to keep the world at bay at least a little while longer. Her fingers threaded through his tousled dark hair, stroking gently to calm him. Instead, it had another effect as a rush of blood spread arousal through Jonas's body, replacing his anger. Capturing her face with his hands, he kissed her long and hard. When she didn't draw away, he moved his hands over her body, stroking lightly. With reverence, he moved them over her breasts, gently and slowly, until they swelled beneath his fingers.

"I wish . . ." he said against her mouth. That he had the world to give her. Instead, he had only himself. He wasn't a rich man. If he were, he would pay to have the barn rebuilt and, beside it, a house—the fanciest, grandest home she had ever set eyes on.

Faith closed her eyes to the sensations his touch created. Wanting to bring him the same pleasure, she touched him, one hand sliding down over the muscles of his chest, sensuously stroking him.

The feel of her hands swept everything from Jonas's mind. Their eyes met and held as an unspoken communication passed between them. He was ready for lovemaking and so was she. In a surge of passion, he rolled her under him. As a gentle breeze stirred the trees around them, they made love again, unaware of the eyes that watched them or of the trouble that fate had in store for them.

Part Two:

A Confrontation with
the Past
Portland, 1869

"Nor deem the irrevocable Past
As wholly wasted, wholly vain,
If, rising on its wrecks at last
To something nobler we attain."
LONGFELLOW—
The Ladder of St. Augustine

Twenty-four

The blare of the sawmill's noon whistle pierced the air, shattering Faith's reverie as she stood gazing out at the wagons, horses, and people that crowded the wide dirt street. There were people of every kind, of every shape and size. Gamblers, lawmen, lumberjacks, townsmen and women, miners, salesmen, bankers, and the newly arrived railroad workers. Were the men who had burned down her barn somewhere in the crowd? She could only wonder.

Whoever they were, they were responsible for the changes in her life. Changes both for the bad and the good—the good being that Jonas and she had found love, the bad that she had lost everything. Only the land itself belonged to her, acreage that was going to waste because she and Jonas just didn't have time to plant. Since the fire, they had both moved into Portland, she to live with the

243

MacQuarries temporarily and he to take a room at one of the hotels.

"Just until I get myself back on my feet," Jonas had promised, relating to her that he had several business deals pending. "Then we'll be together forever." His profession as entrepreneur had its "ups and downs," he said, and he was waiting for a time when it would turn lucrative again. "I'm going to get the money to help you build your house, Faith, and when I do, then and only then will I ask you to marry me."

That declaration was the only thing that kept her going day after day as she stood over the washtub cleaning the boarding-house's dirty linen. It was a job she had hoped never to have to do again when she had left St. Paul and her parents' own boardinghouse. But she had been determined to make her own way and not depend on Margaret MacQuarrie's generosity. If the job she had gotten at the nearby boardinghouse, with her odd jobs at the sawmill, didn't promise to make her wealthy, at least they gave her a sense of earning her own way. And freedom from Margaret's hovering. Faith had clearly told her Scottish friend that she loved Jonas.

"You're making a mistake," Margaret told her over and over.

"Jonas is the right man for me. I know what I'm doing," she had replied. And she did. Even with the hardship, the blisters, and her aching back, she was happy. More so than she had ever been in her life. Like a child waiting for Christmas, she looked forward to being with him, to having him touch her, kiss her, love her.

Turning from the window, Faith returned to the washtub, rubbing the sheets, table-cloths, and pillowcases on the washboard. Doing the laundry was an endless job, for when the linen was finished, there were the boarders' shirts to be done. She wondered how it was possible that she had any skin left on her knuckles. And when the laundry was done, there was always the cooking. Still, when she heard the jingle of her hard-earned coins hit the bottom of her piggy bank, she knew it was all worth it. Soon she would have Ian McQuarrie paid in full and, after that, every nickel would go toward rebuilding her barn. And woe be to anyone who thought to get anywhere near it with a match! To help defend her land, Faith was taking shooting lessons from Cameron. Next time any would-be arsonists came on her property, they would end up with holes in their bodies. That much she vowed.

"Ah, there you are, lass." Margaret Mac-Quarrie came sweeping through the door bearing a gift of cookies. "Oatmeal. The kind you said you liked." She held out the plate.

Faith wiped her hands on her apron and succumbed to the temptation, eating three. "Delicious. Thank you." Picking up a flat-iron, she put it on the wood stove, heating it in preparation for the stack of wrinkled garments.

"Oh, Faith." Margaret clucked her tongue, exhibiting her concern. "How I hate to see you work so hard. A young woman as pretty as you should be having a rollicking good time, at least once in a while."

"I do. Jonas is taking me to the theater tomorrow night to see Jack Langrishe's troupe perform *Alice, or the Mysteries.*" It was a polished professional group from Denver.

Margaret frowned her disapproval. "Jonas. The theater. A place for ruffians. Certainly not the place for a lady like you."

"Maggie." Faith didn't want to be drawn into another argument, but neither could she just keep silent. "Going to the theater is considered respectable, even by the most strait-laced matrons. Why, my mother always delighted in such entertainment."

Margaret seemed dubious.

"Besides, when I'm with Jonas, I'm happy, no matter what we do." She couldn't hide the sparkle in her eyes whenever she said his name. "I love him, Maggie."

"I know you do." She looked horrified at the thought.

"And he loves me, too." Faith smiled as

she remembered how just last night he had repeated the words again and again.

"He said so." Her tone seemed to say that he lied.

"He did. Many times." Taking the flatiron from the stove, she moved it over a white cotton shirt on the ironing board.

"Words, lass. To some men they come easily." She took a step forward, reaching out imploringly. "Faith, lass—"

"Jonas has proven it." She smiled mischievously, rebelliously, as she wondered what Maggie would think of the passionate nights she had spent in his arms, but all she said was, "He is working just as hard as I am so that we can get money to rebuild the barn."

"Working?" Margaret's cheeks flushed as she lost her temper. "If that's what you want to call fleecing the town's unfortunates."

"Fleecing?"

"Another word for cheating them." Seeing that her accusation had caught hold, Margaret kept up her tirade. "He's been gambling in the saloons in Oregon City. Gambling, lass!"

"I don't believe you." Faith knew that Margaret disliked Jonas, but she hadn't thought she would stoop to telling outright lies.

"Ian saw him when he was there to deliver a large load of timber." Margaret grabbed her arm. "We're only trying to protect you. You deserve better than such a man."

Faith's voice was cold. "Ian must have made a mistake. He saw someone else. Jonas isn't a gambler. He wouldn't know one card from another. He's an entrepreneur working on a business dealing." She wouldn't even tell such a story to Jonas for fear of insulting him.

"Oh, Faith, please listen."

"No." Turning her back, Faith stubbornly waited for Margaret to leave, but the smell of scorched cloth caused her to retrace her steps. The shirt was burnt, the dark-brown imprint of the iron emblazoned in the middle of the back. With a gasp, she grabbed the iron by the handle, then set it back on the stove.

"Och, 'tis a pity." The Scottish woman rushed forward to help. As she did, a square piece of paper fell from her pocket. Faith stooped to pick it up, staring as she saw Jonas's name written in black ink.

"Maggie, what's this?"

Snatching it out of her hand, Margaret Mac-Quarrie had a guilty look on her face. Like someone caught snooping, which was exactly what she had been doing, Faith was to learn. " 'Tis a copy of a letter I sent to the Pinkerton Agency concerning your friend Jonas."

"The Pinkerton Agency." Faith had heard of it before. It was an agency that served during the War between the States as a U.S. government secret service. General McClellan had used the agency to spy on southern troops. It was used in the West to catch mur-

248

derers, train robbers, outlaw bands, and counterfeiters. "And just what has Jonas to do with this?"

"Ian and I are hiring the agency to check on Jonas's background."

"Spying on him, prying into his personal life, you mean?" Faith was incensed.

"Whatever you want to call it!" Margaret put her hand on Faith's arm only to have it shrugged away. "It can never do any harm to be careful. Ian uses the agency all the time to check on his employees. It's really not as terrible as it sounds."

"Terrible?" It was worse. "It's an intrusion, a betrayal of Jonas, and of me."

"Of *you?* Oh, no. I want to protect you, Faith. Somehow Jonas Winslow has hypnotized you. I'm only trying to make you see the truth before you get hurt."

Crumpling the letter in her hand, Faith threw it on the floor. "It's not from Jonas that I need protection, it seems, but from you and your meddling." The MacQuarries had been good to her, it was true, but that didn't give them the right to interfere in her life. "If you want to use the Pinkerton Agency, Maggie, why not hire them to find out who set fire to my barn or who robbed the stagecoach. Leave Jonas alone." It was a plea and a command.

Twenty-five

People were pushing and shoving as the doors to the New Market Theater opened. The new building was filled to capacity and barely had room enough for all those who wanted to see the night's performance. Faith and Jonas had to push their way to their seats.

"This better be worth all the bruises," Jonas whispered in her ear as he shielded her from a wayward elbow. As they made their way through the excited crowd, Jonas held Faith against him, imprisoning her in his strong arms.

"I'm sure it will be," Faith responded optimistically, thinking to herself that it was as unruly a mob as she had ever seen. Certainly far different from the audiences in St. Paul, despite the fact they all seemed dressed in their Sunday best. She knew that thieves often roamed about an audience, waiting to find the right prey. She clutched her reticule tightly just in case. Certainly these days she held every penny dear.

Jonas was fashionably dressed in a black coat and buff-colored breeches, she in a dress of royal-blue velvet, a present from him. Faith's mother had said emphatically that a well-dressed woman or man never went out without gloves. Faith wore a matching pair. They hid her blisters and calluses, but she plucked them off now as she tried to make herself comfortable on the hard wooden seat.

The theater smelled of tallow and glue. The stage was lit by gas lights positioned behind the proscenium arch. The soft flames gave off a golden glow. "What do you think?" he asked.

Faith looked around her. The building was plain of architecture, built to be practical. There were few scrolls or luxuries, but she liked it nonetheless. "It's not as big as the one in St. Paul, though it has a certain charm. But what I'm more interested in is the play."

"Unfortunately, most of the people gathered here do not share your enthusiasm. If this is anything like some of the theaters I've been in, the onlookers will get fairly rowdy before the night is through." Already there were shouts for the play to begin.

The curtain, sporting a variety of advertisements from drugstores to jewelers, was still drawn, but the shuffling sound behind it hinted that the show was soon to begin.

"Look there. In the middle." Jonas pointed. "The curtain has a square announcing your friend Ian MacQuarrie's saw mill."

Faith turned to see the Scotsman's name in bold black letters, accompanied by the drawing of a large, round, sharp-toothed saw. Still bothered by Margaret MacQuarrie's prying, Faith kept strangely quiet.

"Faith, what's wrong?" Jonas knew her well enough to sense that she was troubled.

She started to tell him, then thought better of it. What was the use of stirring up ill will? "Nothing. I'm just a bit tired, that's all." She looked at Jonas out of the corner of her eye, noting his strong profile, the firm jut of his chin, the thickness of his hair. She tried to imagine him holding a deck of cards, but the image just didn't go with Jonas. The MacQuarries had to be wrong.

"Not too tired to see what's happening up on stage, I hope." Jonas knew that *he* was. Last night he had stayed up until the wee hours of the morning at a saloon in Oregon City, playing several games of poker. His efforts had paid off. In just two weeks of gambling he had won enough for the lumber and manpower to build Faith another barn. Now he was working on winning sufficient money for a house.

Faith took hold of his hand and gave it a

gentle squeeze. "No, not too tired to watch the play," her voice lowered to a hush, "nor to make love to you when it is over."

"Good." Leaning over, he nuzzled her ear.

Faith felt the familiar warmth flow over her body at the touch of his lips. Excitement swept over her, radiating to her very core. "If I can wait that long," she added, seductively teasing.

The murmur of their conversation died away as the houselights were snuffed slowly. Stillness settled over the large brown-and-tan room. A piano player struck up the first faint strains of a song. All eyes were focused on the stage, but Jonas's gaze was elsewhere. He was caught up in a web of enchantment, watching Faith and the hungry intentness in the smile that lit her face. It spoke of her passionate nature. He was consumed by a desire to kiss her but held himself under control. Later, he would have her all to himself without staring eyes.

"I would give you the world if I could," he whispered beneath his breath. He had a secret. Unbeknownst to Faith, he had been working on the farm nearly every day so the land wouldn't go to waste and he could surprise her.

Jonas had it all figured out. Although he knew very little about farming, he had kept his eyes and ears open to anything he heard at the general store, the barbershop, at the saloons, or even on the street. It had become a challenge to him to learn something new. Something he was bound and determined to master.

Faith had been very fair and good to him. He knew now that she was the woman he had been looking for all his life. He wanted to be with her until the day he died. But what could they do to make some swift money on her land? The least he could do was to help her with the money to build a new barn and a house. If he could earn enough money, they could hire the work done and get a return on the land even quicker. He had decided to win the money rather than work for it. Gambling money would come easy.

If they would plant a wheat crop now that the land had been cleared, by the time the wheat was full grown the house and barn would have been constructed and the wheat ready for market, killing two birds with one stone. Right now there was a great demand for wheat.

It would be a hot, tiring, dirty job, but he could rent four horses and do the work himself, saving more money. He was learning to be thrifty. He had heard that the Australian wheat called "blue stem" was the best, the most disease resistant. Her land was reasonably flat with good, rich soil. They could buy a plow and wheat seed and rent the horses until the barn was up, then they could buy their own horses. The first year they could plant forty or fifty acres and then increase as the demand increased.

He envisioned it in his mind. Holding the plow with both hands, reins thrown over his shoulder, he could walk and walk, then sow the seeds, cover, and wait for the crop to spring forth.

The curtain was slowly drawn up. Faith focused her gaze on the stage. The actors' voices weren't always clear, so she couldn't always understand exactly what was going on and the plot wove a tangled web, she was nonetheless enjoying herself, though it was a tearful drama.

"It was written by an Englishman, so I was afraid it might be stuffy," Jonas whispered.

"Well, it's not, which proves you can't judge a play by its author."

There was a growing sense of intimacy sitting beside Jonas. She sensed his presence with every fiber of her being. It was dark, only the gaslight casting a soft, golden glow over them. Jonas's knee was touching hers as they sat side by side and she was very much aware of him.

"Did you know your hair shines with magenta fire in the candlelight? Such lovely tresses. The darkest shade of auburn I've ever seen. In the shadows it's nearly as dark as a raven's wing." Even his voice drew her, rumbling with its low-pitched masculinity each time he spoke.

She was aware that his attention was being focused on her just as avidly as she had studied him, but she didn't answer. His eyes were caressing, moving from her head to her neck and lower, lingering on the rise and fall of her bosom. Though she tried to put the thought out of her mind, she couldn't help but wonder if there had been other women he had looked at in such a way. But that was silly. It was just the way of the world that women were expected to be virtuous and men allowed to "sow their wild oats," as her father always said.

"Something *is* troubling you. What?" he asked, seeing her sudden frown.

She reacted quickly. "Nothing." Nothing except the seed of suspicion Maggie had planted was beginning to grow, just as she had known it would, Faith thought sourly. "Or rather I was wondering if you have ever been to Oregon City."

"Oregon City!" He tensed, preparing to defend himself and his actions. Had someone seen him? If so, had they gone running to her to tattle on him? "Not lately," he said warily. "Why?"

Faith shrugged. "The theater company is scheduled to take their play there after they are through here. I was just curious to know how it compared to Portland."

"With all my traveling I've found that most towns are all the same," he answered quickly. Suddenly the evening was ruined for him, moving much too slowly for his liking. Guilt nagged at him. Why had he lied to her? Why couldn't he just tell the truth? That he was a gambler, a wanderer. That he had been to Oregon City only last night. Would she love him any the less? "Faith . . ."

His eyes moved tenderly over her thick lashes, her wide eyes. She was so different from the type of women he had met all his life in brothels and saloons. Refreshing and lovely. Just the kind of woman he had been searching for. How then could he take the chance of losing her? Besides, once he'd won enough money for her house, he vowed to give up gambling. He'd settle down, ·marry Faith, have a slew of children. And be respectable, he thought as he watched a stageman touch a foot-long match to the gaslights. The action signified intermission.

Faith's head darted this way and that as she watched the progression of theater patrons who moved about as they stretched their legs. She saw a pretty blonde on the arm of Peter Seton and recognized a few of Ian MacQuarrie's customers, but there wasn't anyone else who looked familiar. But a man moving about in the crowd suddenly caught her eye because of his height and mannerisms. She took a closer look, tugging at Jonas's sleeve. It was him!

"Jonas!"

He turned his head. "Faith, you're as pale as a ghost."

"As well I should be when setting eyes on the very devil." She pointed. "That's the man who robbed the stagecoach. I *know* it is." She stood up, determined that there should be a confrontation, but Jonas was quicker. Jumping over people and benches, he went in pursuit. Keeping his quarry in sight, he pushed and shoved through the crowd.

"Let me pass. Get out of my way." The hope that he would end up a hero in Faith's eyes goaded him into daring. Willing his legs to take long, swift strides, he pushed past a hooting, hollering human wall that stood between him and the man Faith had accused.

"Who's he after? What's going on?" Wondering if it was part of the drama, several people looked on.

Using physical force, Jonas was able to push his way through the onlookers. He moved stealthfully until he was just ten feet away from the man he was pursuing. So close. So very close that he was able to clearly see him.

"Well, I'll be damned." It was a man he had gambled with at the White Whale in Astoria. A shifty-eyed bastard to be sure. One who had given him an uneasy feeling.

As if sensing the scrutiny focused on him, the man's eyes met Jonas's, and in that instant, the truth was told. Jonas's intention of cornering him was all too evident. Scowling, the man hurried on through the crowd again. He was agile and cunning. In a pattern of pushing and ducking he quickly put Jonas at a distance as he fought desperately to escape from the theater.

He can't get away! Jonas thought desperately. If he did, it might be too late to ever find him again. Jonas hurled himself forward. "Catch him. He's a thief!" he shouted out. As the crowd gasped in surprise and fascination, Jonas gave chase.

Twenty-six

Jonas had never moved so fast in his life! Willing his legs to take long, swift strides he followed closely on his quarry's heels as the man dodged and darted through the crowd and away from the theater. Pushing over rain barrels, vaulting over anything in his way, Jonas ran until his lungs threatened to burst. Even so, the rogue managed to stay just out of his reach.

"Damn, he's a speedy weasel!" Jonas gasped. Changing his tactics, he took a short-cut and cut across the man's path as he headed across the dirt road. Jonas almost caught up with him but for a rickety hay wagon that rumbled out from an alleyway and came between. Just long enough for the man to get a head start again.

Jonas was exasperated as he watched the man disappear from sight. "Where in hell did the bastard go?" Two darkened streets led out of the square, like a Y, both slanting to his right. Jonas chose the path to the left.

Once away from the theater and the crowd, the streets grew silent. Most of the residents of Portland were already in for the night. Shops had been locked behind their heavy shutters, the street had only a few passersby. Glancing warily from side to side, he pushed onward, careful lest he be taken unawares. Something about the area raised the hackles on his neck. Just the sort of place where a snake could hide. It was undoubtedly here that the man had gone.

Jonas was on guard as he walked about. He was rewarded for his tenacity as he at last spied the rogue among a group of men who were lounging near a water trough. Now that he was among his companions, the man made no attempt at running. Instead, he grinned as if welcoming a confrontation.

Jonas realized at once that he had walked into a wolves' lair. These were rough and rugged men with the look of cruelty in their eyes. Gunmen. One of them, a sandy-haired man whose tousled hair hung to his shoulders, laughed softly.

"You seem to be in a mighty big hurry. Care to tell us why?"

Jonas had no quarrel with these men, nor was he in the mood for a fight when he was so obviously outnumbered. "Just out for a

261

stroll," he said sarcastically. "Anyone for a game of cards?"

A man who had until now been lounging in the shadows stepped forward, boldly pushing the others back, and it was then that Jonas knew he was in trouble. He recognized the man as one of those who had given him his black eye and who had undoubtedly set Faith's barn afire.

"Well, if it isn't the hired hand. Have you come back for another fight?"

Jonas shook his head, trying to act as if nothing was wrong. He was outnumbered ten to one. Though he was one to stand his ground, he thrust his hands into his pockets, turned around, and leisurely walked back in the direction he had come. Only a fool would take a chance on being maimed or, worse yet, killed. He wanted to catch the man who had robbed Faith's stagecoach, it was true, but not at the expense of his life. Then his name would never be cleared.

The sound of boot soles clicking on gravel sounded close behind him.

"Go after him!"

Jonas broke into a run. Weaving in and out, making use of his strength and agility, Jonas easily outdistanced the men chasing him, but his escape was cut short. Several two-storied buildings loomed in his path, forming a wall at the end of the dark alley. Now he would be forced to fight.

"Aha! We have you. Shall we teach him a little lesson, boys?"

Jonas was certain it was all over for him, but when he whirled around, he saw that only four of the men had bothered to follow after him. Far better odds than fighting the whole gang. "Oh, there will be a lesson taught, but not to me," he growled. His eyes blazed as in one agile movement, he sprang forward, his fists poised and ready for combat. He swung at his nearest attacker and had the satisfaction of seeing the man stagger and fall. "Next!"

The sandy-haired man rushed at Jonas's back with a knife, trying for a quick, crippling blow to Jonas's right side, but Jonas whirled and knocked it from his hand just in time.

"I'll take him off yer hands, Jamie, if you can't handle him alone." The third man rushed forward but Jonas thought fast, spinning to smash his fist into that man's face before he could draw his gun. The man staggered back, lifting his hand to his bloodied mouth.

Everything seemed to happen simultaneously, registering quickly in his mind. He no sooner felled one man than the second rose to take his place. But though the men were aggressive and brutal, they were no match for Jonas's experiences in the orphanage and his stubborn will to leave this match unscathed.

Scrambling wildly to retrieve his gun, one man muttered a violent string of swearwords. Gone, however, was the ruffian's fierce bravado. He slunk away like a wounded beast, making his escape around the corner of a saloon. Jonas started to pursue him, but just as he moved, he was tripped by one of the other rogues lying on the ground. Together they rolled over and over as they grappled. Jonas had his hands full, battling with first that man and then another. In the end he was victorious, watching as the men turned coward and fled.

Jonas had no time to congratulate himself. Hastily brushing himself off, wiping the blood from his hands, he hurried off in the direction the stagecoach robber had taken. This time, however, the man had truly vanished. The gathering darkness acted like a cloak to hide him.

Jonas searched and searched, but in the end had to admit defeat. He was gone. He might just as well try to find a needle in a haystack. But he vowed he'd find him. Some way! He had to. He would get Faith's possessions and money back for her and make certain the man and his fellow snakes were put in jail where they belonged. This time he knew just what they looked like so that it would be easier to catch them. If it was the last thing he ever did, he'd make certain they would never bother Faith again.

Twenty-seven

Moonlight streamed through the open curtains of the hotel room as the two lovers lay entwined. Faith lay perfectly still, savoring the utter contentment of her heart and body. Jonas's arms were around her, his head resting upon the softness of her breasts, his eyes closed. Faith felt a wave of love for him sweep over her, a longing to stay wrapped in his arms forever.

A tender smile lit her eyes as she looked at him, so strong and brave, yet such a remarkably gentle man. Tonight he had fought for her with a valor that could only be called heroic, yet he was also, honest, tender, and kind, always putting her well-being above his own. When they made love he knew just how to touch her, how to make her body sing a glorious melody to their passion, how to bring her to the very peak of pleasure.

Lowering her head, she kissed him. "I love you." Love. Such a glorious word.

"Mmm. What a pleasant reward. Makes me wish I had caught up with your scoundrel. What would you give me then."

"You already have my heart and my soul."

She heard the soft rhythm of his breath as he spread her hair in a dark cloak about her shoulders. "Beautiful. So very lovely."

His mouth was hungry as it took hers, plundering, moving urgently as he explored her mouth's sweetness. The pressure of the kiss drained her very soul, pouring it back again, filling her to overflowing. There was nothing in the world for her but his mouth. She surrendered to him completely, wishing the kiss could go on forever. Twining her hands around his neck, she clutched him to her, pressing her body eagerly against his chest. She could feel the heat and strength and growing desire of him with every breath.

As his hands outlined the swell of her breasts, she sank into the softness of the feather mattress. The coverlet beneath her was warm and soft, but she put it out of her mind as she became aware only of Jonas. His head was bent low, his tongue curling around the tips of her breast, suckling gently. She gave a breathless murmur and her body flamed with desire.

Jonas breathed deeply, savoring the rose scent of her perfume. The enticing fragrance invaded his flaring nostrils, engulfing him. His flesh felt as though it were on fire whenever it pressed against her yielding softness. Just touching her made him forget that he was ever lonely.

They lay together kissing, touching, rolling over and over on the soft bed. His hands were doing wondrous things to her, making her writhe and groan. Every inch of her body caught fire as passion exploded between them with a wild oblivion. He moved against her, sending waves of pleasure exploding along every nerve in her body. The swollen length of him brushed across her thighs.

She gave herself up to the fierce emotions that raced through her, answering his touch with searching hands, returning his caresses. Closing her arms around his neck, she offered herself to him, writhing against him in a slow, delicate dance.

Sweet, hot desire fused their bodies together as he leaned against her. His strength mingled with her softness, his hands moving up her sides, warming her with his heat. His lips burned a path from one breast to the other, bringing forth spirals of pulsating sensations that swept over her like a storm.

Jonas's mouth fused with hers, his kiss deepening as his touch grew bolder. Faith luxuriated in the pleasure of his lovemaking, stroking and kissing him back. Poised above her, he slid his hands between their bodies.

The tip of his maleness pressed against her, entered her softness in a slow but strong thrust, joining her in that most intimate of embraces. He kissed her as he fused their two naked bodies together, and from the depths of her soul, her heart cried out. Tightening her thighs around his waist, she wanted him to move within her. He did, slowly at first, then with a sensual urgency.

Jonas filled her with his love, leaving her breathless. Her arms locked around him as she arched to meet his body, forgetting all her inhibitions as she expressed her love. A sensation burst through her, a warm explosion.

Even when the sensual magic was over, they clung to each other, unwilling to have the moment end. Faith felt that surely the fire they had ignited tonight would meld them together for eternity. Smiling, she lay curled in the crook of Jonas's arm, and he, his passion spent, lay close against her, his body pressing against her.

"If finding you is a dream, I hope I never wake up." Jonas's voice was low and husky. He regarded her with his hazel eyes, his heart flooding with a fierce surge of love.

They talked about their dreams, their visions of the future. Jonas wished that somehow he could hold back the hours, keep them from speeding by.

"Why can't you stay all night with me?"

He wanted that more than anything in the world, to wake up with her beside him.

"I can't. Maggie would be scandalized. Besides, I don't want any gossip."

"Then I guess we'll just have to hurry and get married so that Maggie won't have any say in the matter." He traced her profile with his finger.

"Are you asking me?"

He crushed her to him, holding her to his chest for a long moment. At last he drew away, looking deep into her eyes. "Will you?"

She felt in a teasing mood. "I'll think about it."

"You are cruel," he countered, but he knew her answer to be yes. And then what? He wanted to be the answer to her dreams. Would he be? The thought worried him. He had a past. It was bound to catch up to him sooner or later. Would she understand?

"Then I'll answer quickly. Yes." Faith wondered what her parents would think of Jonas. Would they like him? Or would her father be as disapproving as he had been of Henry? And her sisters? No doubt they would be green with envy. But he was *hers.*

He cupped her chin in his hand. "Missus Jonas Winslow. Faith Winslow. I like the sound of it."

She sighed. "Me, too." Suddenly it came to her that though she had talked to him about her family, Jonas had been strangely secretive about his own. "Jonas?"

"Yes, my love." He took a handful of her glorious hair and caressed it with his mouth.

"You never mention your family. Where they are." She saw a shadow pass across his expression but kept right on. "Do you have any brothers and sisters?"

He knew the time for lying was over. "I don't know."

"What?" She hadn't been expecting this.

"I don't know who my parents are. I was left at an orphanage and spent my early years growing up there." Even now it was a subject that evoked unhappiness.

"Oh, Jonas. I'm sorry." Reaching out, she touched his cheek. "Was it really so terrible. Growing up in the orphanage?"

Usually when asked such a question he lied. This time he told the truth. "Yes, it was. I had no one. No one cared."

His thoughts tumbled back to those days before Faith had appeared in his life, empty days. How could he ever have imagined the pleasure he would enjoy in her arms that first day they met, or realize how very much he would grow to love her.

"But now *I* care." And she did. Very much. "We have our whole lives ahead of us, a lifetime of being together. I'll try to make up for your loneliness. I want to make you happy."

"You already have."

They shared a long and gentle kiss, a kiss that spoke of their love for each other, then reluctantly she rose from the bed. Her hands trembled as she got dressed and somehow she didn't know what words to say. Jonas, too, was silent as he slipped on his clothes. They walked to the door as slowly as they could. Before it was open, Jonas gathered her hungrily into his arms, his mouth sweetly, savagely, plundering hers.

"When can I see you again?" Jonas asked.

"Day after tomorrow. I'll be busy working until then."

"Two days!" It seemed like an eternity.

Gathering up her skirt, she walked out the door and down the stairs with Jonas right beside her. Hand in hand they walked down the boardwalk. When they were in front of the MacQuarries' house, he gave her one last kiss. "In two days," he reminded.

Opening the front door, Faith intended to sneak up the stairs, but Maggie's voice called her name. "Was the play a good one, lass?" Her smile was meant to be friendly.

"Oh, yes!" She related Jonas's pursuit of the man who had robbed the stagecoach. "You should have seen him go after him, Maggie. And he nearly caught him."

"Is that so?" Maggie bit her lip as if to keep from saying something snide. "Well, I

271

wish he was the knight in shining armor you think him to be, Faith."

"He is!"

Maggie issued a challenge. "If you think so, if you truly believe why not put him to the test. Come with us tomorrow night to Oregon City."

"I can't! I have too much to do at the sawmill."

"Ian will let you have the night off." Maggie repeated, "Come with us."

Faith thought long and hard. She didn't want to go. It was as if she didn't trust Jonas. She did. And yet if she did go and she could prove Maggie to be wrong, perhaps she could silence her tirades once and for all. Jonas wasn't a gambler. He was much too honest for such a profession. Even so, she found herself saying at last, "All right."

Twenty-eight

Jonas Winslow had been a gambler nearly a third of his twenty-nine years, but never in his life had he had a winning streak like the one he was on at the moment. Lady Luck was certainly smiling at him tonight. Though he had wagered only ten dollars so far, he had won nearly two hundred in just a few hours. What's more, he had done it honestly, without the help of marked cards. Such chicanery was a thing of the past since he had met Faith. Gambling itself would be, too, just as soon as he had enough money.

"Just a few more hands and then I'll quit." He'd help ensure his future and Faith's happiness, then lay down his cards for good.

That was a promise he had made to himself several times in the past month. He'd meant well. It was just that temptation had beckoned to him with all the allure of a beautiful woman. "One more time," she seemed to say. Thankfully he had obeyed.

Leaning back in his chair, Jonas tried hard not to smile as he looked down at the four bearded men who looked back at him, all wearing crowns. He had four kings and an ace. A hand just couldn't get any better than that. Was it any wonder then that he imagined he saw one of the kings wink at him? And to think he would not have come to Oregon City to gamble tonight if Faith hadn't had to work. Well, from now on she wouldn't have to get calluses on those pretty hands of hers.

"You can't keep on winning," the bespectacled man across from him grumbled. "You're bound to draw a poor hand eventually."

Yeah, that's the way with luck," Jonas retorted, deciding that he liked the Silver Shamrock Saloon. It had a better clientele than some of the others he'd been in.

Tonight Jonas was sitting at an oval table with a clergyman, a judge, a physician, two shopkeepers, and a mining engineer. An odd assortment of men with character traits from timid to bold, pious to ornery, generous to cheap. Men who would never have kept company with each other under ordinary circumstances. The itch for cards and the quick money that could be made had drawn them together for the evening. Eagerly, each one of them had elbowed his way to the gaming table, only to whine now that their expectations of quick riches had gone unfulfilled. Well, that was the way of things.

"Draw?" The physician, a gray-haired, paunchy man who considered himself an expert on poker, had taken the lead during the game. Now he looked at Jonas with a scowl.

"I'll stay," Jonas answered. He could nearly imagine Faith's new house in his mind's eye. They'd have it built in wood with stone trim so it would last throughout all the generations of Winslows to come.

"Do you want another card?" The same question was asked to all the players in turn.

"When my wife finds out I've lost a hundred dollars I'll be hogtied," the skinny shopkeeper was lamenting. "I can't lose any more. I'll fold."

"I'll take another card." Looking up at the ceiling as if saying a silent prayer, the preacher reached for his card. Whatever he had drawn, he looked cheerful. Too bad, Jonas thought, that he was going to have to ruin the young man's good mood.

"I'll fold." With a grunt, the black-bearded judge threw down his cards.

The mining engineer and the other shopkeeper each seemed to think they stood a chance at winning. They stayed and even raised the stakes. Jonas couldn't help thinking that it was like taking candy from two babies. Well, if they held the cards that he did, they wouldn't have a qualm of fleecing him, he thought, putting his conscience to rest. Besides, he wasn't doing this for himself, he was doing it for the woman he loved.

That very woman was at the moment pushing her way through the saloon, regretting having come to such a foul place. "Maggie, can't we turn back?" Faith coughed as she fought her way through the cigarette- and cigar-induced haze. "This is so foolish."

The fact that the bartender and several patrons gawked at Ian and the two women as if they were oddities made it even worse. Barked comments that ladies weren't allowed in saloons made Faith wish she could just disappear.

"Turn back? After we came all this way? Fie!" Margaret MacQuarrie was defiant. She took Faith's arm with a firmness that offered little chance for a last-minute escape.

"I have a trillion of things to do." Mentally Faith ticked them off in her mind—until something caught her attention in the corner of the large smoke-filled room. Not believing her eyes, she took a step or two closer.

"There. Didn't I tell you so." Margaret was triumphant. "A philanderer if ever I saw one."

According to Maggie, many an innocent, hard-working man had been ruined because of a professional gambler. They were evil. Dishonest. Greedy. Lazy. Her aversion was particularly fierce because she insisted that most won their games by cheating honest men. Lying in wait like spiders.

"It can't be." Jonas didn't even look like a gambler. His shirt wasn't ruffled. He didn't wear an embroidered vest. He didn't adorn himself with gold or diamond rings or stickpins. Nor did he carry a massive gold watch hanging from a gold chain. Even so, there he was. "It's some kind of a mistake."

"Oh, it's a mistake, lass. A mistake not to believe your own eyes. He's been caught."

"No." Faith hung back. She didn't want to cause a scene, nor to embarrass him. "All kinds of men gamble, Maggie. George Washington himself often gambled at cards, or so they say. It isn't a crime." She wanted to give Jonas time to explain before she judged him guilty.

"It is when it ruins a man's life," Ian MacQuarrie cut in. Then he confided just why they were both so bitter toward card players. "My brother, God rest his soul, poor Johnnie, lost every penny he had to a gambler. Shot himself, he did."

"Oh, Ian, I'm so sorry." But it wasn't Jonas's fault, which is exactly what she said.

"Perhaps not, but he and his kind have caused the ruination of many just like my brother." The look Ian cast in Jonas's direction was explosive.

"His kind!" Faith liked the MacQuarrie

family, but she wouldn't let them hurl accusations. One game of cards didn't make a man a gambler. She took several steps closer to where Jonas sat, anxious to come to his defense, but the scene she saw before her eyes stunned her. Jonas was raking in a stack of coins in a manner that made him look different to her eyes. As she watched him, she didn't recognize him at all. He seemed slick. Fast-talking. Not like the Jonas she knew.

"Now, now, now. Don't let a little bad luck stop you, boys. As you said, my good luck can't last forever. How about another game?" he was saying.

"Another game. And let you fleece us like sheep?" A thin young man with curly dark hair stood up.

"Gentlemen. Gentlemen." Putting his hand up in the air, Jonas was trying his best to placate them.

"You're a cardsharp. The best. Admit it," another man was saying.

"Well, I must admit to having played more than a few hands of cards." Jonas's smile was smug. "But, come on. Don't be spoil sports. I'll teach you all I know."

All he knew? Faith was stunned. So, he wasn't just out for a little game of cards. She had heard enough. With a swish of her skirts, she swept past Maggie and Ian and headed for the swinging doors.

"Faith. Dearie." Margaret was close behind. "Don't be angry."

Not until she was outside did Faith turn around. When she did, her expression was murderous. "Well, Maggie, are you happy?"

Margaret MacQuarrie shook her head. "No. But I couldn't let you hang on to a dream that never would come true. You had to know Jonas Winslow for what he is."

"A man who plays cards for money?" Oh, why hadn't he told her? It wasn't his gambling that was so disillusioning but his secrecy.

"A man who cheats others, Faith."

"Not Jonas." Despite what she had seen, Faith defended him. "There is no proof that Jonas was dishonest tonight or that he did anything wrong." He had worked hard for her. He had proven himself to be a friend as well as a lover. She wouldn't turn against him yet. In her heart she held the hope that he would confide in her.

Jonas didn't. Paying a friendly call early the next morning, he plopped the leather sack full of money right down in front of her, saying happily that at last his business venture had turned lucrative.

"Business venture." Wiping her soapy hands on her apron, Faith looked him squarely in the eye. "Is that what you call it."

He kissed her lightly on the lips. "Indeed it is. A venture that has made it possible for

279

me to help you not only build a barn but get a good start on a house."

"I don't want it, Jonas." As he held the sack out to her, she pushed his hand away.

"Don't want it." He was stunned.

Her tone was stern. Controlled. Scornful. "I know that it came from the Silver Shamrock in Oregon City."

His mouth fell open as he paled slightly. He didn't try to talk his way out of it but merely said, "You know—how?"

"I saw you last night." She was more disappointed in him than angry. "Oh, Jonas. Is that what you meant by being an entrepreneur. Is that just another word for gambler?"

"Faith!" He felt sick at heart.

"Oh, Jonas." Her voice was choked. "Why didn't you tell me?" Putting her hands over her face, she turned her back on him.

"Because." He hadn't wanted her to find out. His voice was soft. "Because I feared you would react just as you are doing now."

What was the use? he thought. What could he possibly say that would make her understand? *I've lost her,* he thought, feeling a great sense of sorrow. Still, his pride dictated that he would not beg. Turning around, he put the leather bag of money on the table, straightened his shoulders, and walked away.

Jonas left so quietly that Faith didn't know he had gone until she turned around. "Jonas?" For just a moment she thought of going after him but stubbornly held back. "Let him go," she whispered. Jonas was wrong for having kept silent on such an important matter. It was a betrayal of her trust. Was it any wonder she had begun to wonder if there were any more surprises in his past? Maggie's evaluation of him as "worldly" came quickly to mind.

"Faith?" Timidly, Mary peeked around the door. "May I come in?"

"Of course. It's your bedroom." Faith hadn't meant to sound so harsh so she amended, "And I always enjoy your company."

Mary plopped down on the bed. "I passed Jonas on the stairs. He looked upset. Did you two quarrel?"

Faith saw no reason to deny it. Certainly Maggie wouldn't keep the episode at the Silver Shamrock a secret. "I found out something about him and we . . . we talked about it, that's all."

"You found out that he's a gambler. I know. I heard." Mary laughed softly. "So?"

"He should have told me."

"Told you? Oh, pooh!" It was obvious Mary didn't share her mother's opinion on card playing. "He loves you. Does his gambling really matter?"

"Yes, it does." Could she forget that a gambler was said to have caused Henry's death?

"Well, then, I think you're silly." As if she were telling some kind of secret, Mary whispered behind her hand, "Nearly all the men in Portland gamble. It's the least of their faults if you ask me." She hurried to defend Jonas Winslow. "At least he doesn't swear, or get drunk and shoot up the town, or frequent the bawdy houses every chance he gets."

"No, at least he doesn't do that." Faith had to admit that Jonas had always acted like a gentleman when he was with her.

"But more importantly, he must love you to distraction to do what he has done. Working all by himself on your land, I mean."

"What?" Faith thought surely he must have misunderstood. Neither she or Jonas had been out to her homestead since the barn had burned down.

"He must be keeping it a surprise." Mary clapped her hands in delight, realizing she knew a secret.

"A surprise?" When Mary didn't answer right away, Faith tugged on her sleeve. "Tell me."

"Cameron and Lachlan have been going out to your land to see if those scoundrels who set the fire would have the nerve to come back. That's how they discovered what Jonas has been doing." Mary enjoyed making the story suspenseful, knowing she had Faith's undivided attention. "Jonas has cleared a large piece of acreage and planted

282

it with wheat, and he's been talking with Peter Seton about putting up another barn."

"He's done *what*?" Faith listened as Mary repeated herself, feeling now like the betrayer and not the betrayed. Last night she had been angry to think that all the while she had been working so hard Jonas had been gambling. Now she knew differently.

Picking up a brush from the nightstand, Faith hurriedly ran it through her hair, then without another thought she headed for the stairs.

"Where are you going?" she heard Mary say. She didn't take the time to answer. All she knew was that she had to go after Jonas, had to let him know that she loved him.

Twenty-nine

Jonas folded his belongings and put them inside the old brown suitcase that lay open on the hotel bed. He was leaving. There just wasn't any reason to stay. As some of his gambling cronies might say, "The game was over." Faith knew what he was and, worst of all, what he wasn't. How could he face her again now?

"Damn!" Retrieving a boot from under the bed, he stood for a long while just staring at it. Faith had bought him the boots after the fire, despite the fact that she had even less money than he. It was a sad reminder of the caring there had been between them and what might have been.

"But you can't make a rooster into a swan," he whispered.

It was something the headmistress at the orphanage used to say to him. Over and over again she had told him that he would never amount to anything. Anything at all. Oh, but how he had wanted to. For Faith.

Overcome by a sense of loss, Jonas dropped the boot and put his hand to his face. He had never really loved a woman before Faith. Now he had lost her. The crushing thought goaded him to anger at himself and gambling in general.

"And to think that last night I considered myself *lucky*," he thought in wry despair. Jonas tightened up inside at the thought.

For a moment he yearned to go in search of her, to try to make her understand that he had done it for her. But then he remembered the smug look on Missus MacQuarrie's face as he had left her house and he knew that such an attempt would be useless. Undoubtedly that Scotswoman was already poisoning Faith's mind against him, making him seem like the worst kind of rogue. Well, maybe he was. Maybe Faith was better off without him anyway. He was a man with a past. A man on the run.

A man wanted for murder. That fact came back to haunt him, putting an end to any fantasy he might have had for a happy ending to his dream. "Jonas Winslow, you are a fool," he admonished himself.

Suddenly he wanted to be away from this room. Away from the hotel. Away from Portland and any reminders of what a fool he had been to think he could belong to anyone, that anyone would care for him, that a woman like Faith Tomkins would love the *real* Jonas Winslow, gambler extraordinaire.

With frantic haste he stuffed his shirts, pants, and even the boots into the suitcase, closed it and latched it, trying not to feel any pain. It was just never meant to be. A wanderer was what he was and what he'd probably always be. It was a fact of life.

"Jonas . . ."

He stiffened at the sound of his name.

"Jonas, where are you going?" Faith panicked at the idea of never seeing him again.

"Away." Could he go? Could he really leave her?

"Oh, Jonas, no!" Her voice was choked. "Please don't leave." In a burst of emotion, she flung her arms around his neck. Jonas's arms went around her and he pulled her to him.

"Faith, I never intended to hurt you," he whispered against her hair.

She hushed him with a kiss, just content in being with him. In her heart she had already absolved him of any wrongdoing. He had already told her about the insecurity of his childhood. How could she, who had been raised in an atmosphere of affection, pass judgment on a man who had not had parents to guide him? Even if his way of getting the money hadn't been prudent, at least his intention had been to help her. That thought made her tighten her embrace.

"Will you let me help you unpack?" she asked at last, slowly sliding her arms down his chest and resting them around his waist.

He knew fate had given him another chance. This time he wouldn't spoil it. "I'm not going anywhere." He looked steadily at her than smiled. "Not now."

Hand in hand they walked back toward the bed, both of them trying to keep their thoughts on the suitcase and not on the pounding of their hearts. As Jonas opened the suitcase's latch, Faith propped open the lid, brushing her hand with his. It was all Jonas could do not to lose his head. Lord, what was it about the woman that always stirred him so?

"Your shirts are wrinkled." Faith held them up with a look of dismay. Had he really been in that much of a hurry to leave? "I'll take them back to the boardinghouse and iron them for you."

"Oh, no you won't." Jonas grabbed them and threw them on the bed. "You do too much of that kind of work already. I want to take you away from all that." He circled his arms around her waist and lifted her up to stand on a wooden chair. "You deserve to be on a pedestal."

"Like a statue?" Stretching her arms out, she struck a pose.

"Like a queen." He looked at her long and lovingly.

Faith jumped down. "Queens get lonely. I'd rather be one of the common lot." She busied herself unfolding his garments and putting them in bureau drawers and hanging them in the closet, taking note of the black embroidered vest and ruffled shirt she had never seen before. A gambler's apparel. A reminder of the Jonas she didn't really know.

"Jonas, what led you to gambling?" It had to be a touchy subject with him but she really had to know.

"Desperation." The moment came back quickly to him. "I'd reached the age when I had to leave the orphanage. I didn't know what kind of work I could do or have much of an education, so I just wandered around for a while. Then I met 'Royal Flush' Willie."

" 'Royal Flush' Willie!" It was a name that sounded, as Margaret might say, "worldly."

Jonas laughed as the balding, gray-haired rotund man came to mind. "Don't get the wrong idea. He was really a kindly old gentleman."

"Who trained you to be skilled at cards." She couldn't hide her disapproval as she imagined the scoundrel who would lead a young man down such a path. He must have been an old rogue.

Jonas shook his head. "Only after I badgered him and tagged along at his heels."

Jonas wasn't going to excuse himself at the expense of someone else, even though it might have been easier. A man had to own up to his mistakes. "Actually he warned me against the evils of gambling. Said he didn't want me to end up like him. But I was young and foolish. I didn't take his advice."

Faith couldn't help notice the pained expression on Jonas's face. "So he taught you all he knew. Then what happened to him?"

"He was shot by a man who accused him of cheating."

"And did he?"

"I don't know. Ole Willie always talked against using marked cards but maybe *he* did." Jonas scowled. "All I know is that the decent citizens of Ridger County wouldn't allow him to be buried in their cemetery, so he was cremated. I scattered his ashes in the Mississippi."

"How terrible." Now she was doubly glad that she had stopped Jonas before he had left town. What if such a fate were to befall him?

"It was. I really loved that old man," Jonas said beneath his breath. Wanting to put Willie out of his mind, Jonas reached for Faith's hand, but the reminder of the old man's fate troubled him. Was Willie the reason that he interfered in that argument in San Francisco? The one that had nearly caused his death.

Suddenly he wanted to tell her about that incident.

"If you are going to say anything more about what happened at the Silver Shamrock, don't." She wanted it to be forgotten. "Everyone has *some* secret."

He studied her carefully. He wondered what hers was and doubted that it could be anything much worse than drinking too much elderberry wine at the fair.

Again his conscience prodded him into making a confession. Shouldn't he tell her that he was a wanted man? Faith loved him. She would stand behind him. "Faith . . ."

Faith didn't want to talk. They were alone and the moment was right and she wanted Jonas to make love to her. Moving to his side, touching his face with her hands, she stood up on tiptoes and kissed him. A potent kiss that stopped the world from turning, at least for a moment. She was so much in love.

Time froze as they explored each other's lips with infinite appreciation. Faith locked her arms around his neck, her hands kneading the muscles of his back as if committing them to memory. She couldn't help thinking how right it felt to be in his arms.

"Mmmm." A moan slid from his throat as he picked her up in his arms and gently laid her on the bed. Silently he worshipped her body as his hands explored. He stroked her breasts, kissing each in turn as he bared them to his view. His tongue tasted the sweet honey of her flesh. All thoughts of San Francisco, of anything else but her, faded into obscurity.

They undressed each other with sensual pleasure and finally they were lying naked together, caressing each other's bare flesh as they moved. Then he was above her, his gentle hand making her moist, warm flesh ready. He entered her slowly, pressing deeper and deeper. She was warm and pulsing and beautiful.

Feeling him inside her, joining with him in love, Faith felt her heart move. As always, she felt first astonishment, then delight, in the joy of being together. The whole world seemed to whirl and spin around her as she moved in rhythm with him. Bringing her hips up to meet his, her body quickened its movements. Her body was aflame, then it burst into a hundred tiny flames.

As Faith lay naked beside Jonas in the aftermath of their loving, she knew how very lucky she was. They might not be rich in money, but being loved by Jonas made her the wealthiest woman in the world.

Thirty

The noise of pounding hammers, the scraping of shovels, and the low hum of men's voices floated on the breeze to Faith's ears as she stood at the well. She had made the decision to use Jonas's winnings to rebuild the barn and construct a small house on her property. It seemed the right time, considering that Jonas had proposed and she had accepted. Just as soon as the house was finished, she would be married.

"I'm going to be Jonas's wife," she whispered, wiping her wet hands on the white apron that covered her dandelion-colored poplin dress.

It was strange what changes a few months could bring. She had set out from St. Paul intending to marry one man, and yet in a few weeks she would be wife of another. A man who made her feel loved, contented and happy. A man whose lovemaking took her to the stars and back again. What more could she ask for?

Jonas had proposed in quite a romantic fashion. He had told her that he knew beyond a doubt that he loved her, that he wanted to wake up each morning and find her beside him, wanted to see her swell with his child, wanted to grow old with her. He had even bent down on one knee while taking her hand. He had said that there was no other woman who could ever make such a thorough claim on his heart. Then he had asked her if she would marry him. And of course she had said yes.

"You didn't. You wouldn't," Maggie had said. "Even after you found out?" When Faith had steadfastly stuck to her decision, Margaret MacQuarrie had vowed to put an end to her scolding, but she had insisted that one day Faith would regret it.

Never. As she watched Jonas hard at work with the others, his muscles bulging, his skin gleaming from the sweat of being out in the hot summer sun, she felt herself to be the luckiest of women. Jonas had never had a family or anyone who cared for him. Now he did. That thought made her smile.

"I heard the news, Faith. Congratulations." Coming up beside her, Peter Seton pulled on the rope that brought the bucket up to the top. "I wish you every happiness."

For just a moment Faith waited warily for

him to issue a warning against Jonas. But he didn't. "Thank you," she said sweetly. "And from what I hear, I may be offering the same to you very soon. Just how is the Widow Jamison?" It had been gossiped that he was wooing the lovely blond woman.

He blushed. "Congratulations may be in store. If she'll have me, that is." Putting his hands in the bucket, he splashed water on his face.

"She will." Faith wanted everyone in the world to be just as contented as she. "I've seen the way she looks at you. The same way I look at Jonas. I love him, Peter." Faith squared her shoulders as if settling in for a verbal fight. "That's really all that counts."

Peter took her hand. "I've been watching Jonas the last several days. He hasn't even looked at a deck of cards, hasn't done anything but come out here to work. And not just for show, as Maggie says."

Faith drew her lips together tightly at the thought. Maggie was her friend and they agreed on every other thing except Jonas. "Ah, yes. Maggie."

"I think Jonas has found a purpose in his life. He seems a changed man. One who loves you." Picking up his hammer from the ground, he started back toward the barn. "Don't be too angry with Margaret. She is only thinking of you."

"I know." If she didn't realize that, Faith

would have moved out of the MacQuarrie house long ago.

"Jonas will win her over. Give him time."

Faith could only hope so. She wished for the day the MacQuarries would welcome Jonas into their home and give to him the friendship that they had given her.

Filling a large bucket with water for the workers, she waved to Jonas as she came toward the barn. He looked happier than she had ever seen him. Gesturing with his arms, he engaged in a lively conversation with the man who had laid out the plans for the barn. She wondered if they were discussing new plans for the house. Both men were pointing that way. Her eyes were drawn to that area, too, a plot near the barn which was shaded by trees.

Jonas motioned for her to join him. "George agrees with me that if we build the house of stone as well as wood we'll thwart anybody who tires to set fires."

"And we can use stones from the pile we made while clearing the land." Faith thought it to be a very good idea. Though Jonas had searched, hoping to catch sight of those men again, he had come up empty-handed. They had to plan accordingly.

"Precisely!" Jonas took her hand, positioning it in the crook of his arm. "Come, let's pretend."

"Pretend?"

He whispered in her ear. "That the house is already built." They walked together around their imaginary home. "This is the smoke room. Right next to the cellar."

Faith picked up on the game, opening a make-believe door. She could almost hear the hinges creak. "And here is the kitchen."

"No!" Jonas picked her up in his arms, stepping over an imaginary threshold. "The parlor."

"Of course." She wrapped her arms around his neck. "I should have known. I can see the green velvet settee. Shall we sit down?" Though it was in actuality just an old pine log, pretending made it seem almost real. "Would you like a cup of tea?"

"Coffee. With a little shot of rum."

She laughed, miming the act of pouring coffee into a cup. Then, pretending to uncork a bottle, she "poured" in the rum. "Just a little." Then she poured some for herself.

"To us!" Jonas lifted up his invisible cup. "Your agreeing to marry me has made me the luckiest man alive!"

"It has made me the happiest woman," she countered.

Jonas suddenly swore violently as he looked up and saw the churning dust from Margaret MacQuarrie's buggy. His good mood was shattered. "What does *she* want!" He doubted that Margaret was coming to offer her best wishes for their marriage.

Faith put her hand on Jonas's arm. "Whatever Maggie has done, she thinks she's protecting me. I've become like one of her daughters. Eventually, she'll come to love you, too."

"Yeah, I'm sure that she will," he grumbled sarcastically. Still, for Faith's sake, he was prepared to let bygones be bygones. He was not prepared, however, to suffer the woman's company. Watching warily as the Scottish woman got out of her buggy, he kissed Faith on the cheek and hurried back to the barn.

Faith braced herself for a confrontation. Maggie's bold stride as she came her way seemed to clearly state that something was wrong. "Good morning, Maggie. Beautiful day, isn't it?"

"Too hot!" Taking off her bonnet, Margaret MacQuarrie fanned herself, then looked toward the barn. "I can see that you're making good progress."

Faith's smile was forced. "Oh, yes, we are." It was a source of contention between Maggie and her that Jonas had refused to use wood from Ian MacQuarrie's sawmill, insisting on using timber from a rival mill instead. Faith had tried to explain that it was because he didn't want to become indebted to them again.

"It's going to be big, lass." She sniffed her disapproval. "Sure and I hope it doesn't end up as firewood, like the other one did."

"It won't. Jonas is going to hire a man to act as lookout."

Margaret MacQuarrie shook her head. "Oh, Faith." Suddenly her surly mood changed to one of sadness. "Poor, poor child."

"Not poor at all. Not now!" Knowing that gave her a feeling of pride. Together she and Jonas could make this homestead work. She knew it.

"Faith. You must listen. I—we . . ." Though she had seemed determined to tell her something at first, Margaret was suddenly hesitant.

"What is it, Maggie? And if you are going to tell me I shouldn't marry Jonas, you can save your breath. I love him."

"I know." Maggie drew in a long, shuddering breath. "That's what makes this so hard for me." Nevertheless, she took a folded piece of paper out of her reticule. "I'm afraid your Jonas can hardly be called an upright citizen."

Faith was immediately suspicious. "Jonas hasn't been gambling lately. That is a thing of the past. Every man deserves a second chance."

"For some things." Slowly she unfolded the sheet. "Then there are things that can't be forgiven."

Faith forced herself to remain calm outwardly, but inwardly her emotions were in a turmoil. "Such as?"

"I'll begin at the beginning of this Pinkerton report." In a singsong tone Margaret MacQuarrie made a verbal list of Jonas Winslow's past sins. "He's been working riverboats, trains, and saloons for several years, has been accused of cheating more than a dozen times, has been in brawls on both sides of the Mississippi. He's an opportunist, taking advantage of rich plantation owners during the war," her voice grew louder, *"and* their daughters. The list of women in his life is much too long for one sheet of paper, including saloon girls, actresses, singers, and other women of ill repute, if you know what I mean." She coughed.

"Maggie—!"

The Scotswoman wouldn't let Faith interrupt. She plowed on, detailing romantic liaisons that Faith would rather not have heard about. "And he's been with other men's wives and has had mistresses, too!"

"I don't care. That was all in the past. I've forgiven Jonas, Maggie." Faith turned and would have walked away, but Maggie stepped in her path to block the way.

"Some things cannot be forgiven. *Murder,* for instance."

"Murder?"

Margaret lowered her voice, not wanting anyone else to hear. "He's wanted in San

299

Francisco for killing a man during a card game." She thrust the Pinkerton Agency report into Faith's hand. "Read it for yourself."

Faith did read it. "No!" It was as if a trapdoor had opened, hurling her downward. She stood there, staring. She was too stunned to say anything for a long, long time.

Thirty-one

Jonas watched from high atop the barn as Margaret MacQuarrie's buggy vanished down the road. He breathed a sigh of relief. Whatever the reason for her visit it had been a short one. Had she come to talk Faith out of marrying him? That seemed likely. Didn't the woman ever give up? Let her say what she might, he thought, confidently lifting up his hammer, love was a bond that words could not shatter.

Jonas melded into a routine as he wielded the hammer, helping the others put on the roof of the barn. It was hot and growing hotter. Stripping off his shirt, he worked bare to the waist, flexing his muscles from time to time. He knew Faith couldn't keep from looking at him, and that pleased him. Out of the corner of his eye, he could see her staring at him now, as a matter of fact—a stare that went on and on and on. Then she was running, as if a nipping dog was at her heels. Without even saddling one of the nearby horses, she pulled herself onto its back and galloped away.

"What in hell?" Jonas watched as she rode off, puzzled by her haste. For a moment he was tempted to go after her, but she disappeared so quickly he didn't have a chance. Still, he didn't like it. He didn't like it at all.

"Just where did the little lady go in such a hurry?" Peter Seton asked the question that Jonas had just asked himself.

"Knowing women I'd say she probably had a dress fitting," Jonas replied, not wanting the red-haired man to pry. "Wedding dress, that is."

"Or maybe a fitting for something lacy for the wedding night," Bart, a short little man, countered, winking slyly.

"Oooooh eeeeee," chortled another, a man who had recently been married himself. "Something red."

"Or black!"

"Lucky Jonas." Peter pounded him on the back. "I gave Faith my congratulations and I'll say the same to you. I've never been a poor loser, though I would have liked to have had her for myself."

"Thanks, Peter." Jonas felt just a twinge of jealousy. Had it been up to Margaret Mac-Quarrie, it would be Peter and not him preparing to share Faith's life. Still, he held out his hand. "I don't know very many men around here. Don't suppose you'd consider being my best man."

"I'd be honored."

They settled back down to working on the barn, heavy hammers called "commanders," pounding in the wooden nails.

"If I don't miss my guess, this one will stand." Peter could tell a lot about wood by merely knocking his knuckles upon it and listening to the sound. "This barn won't go up in tinder like the other one did."

"You're right it won't." It was a touchy subject with Jonas. "That's because I intend to find those men who set the fire and see that they're put in a place where they won't even be allowed matches!"

There was another reason why he had wanted a large barn. He'd learned that the size and condition of a man's land and barns influenced his standing in the community. He wanted Faith to be accepted in Milwaukie society.

The house was going to be a simple square structure built upon a stone foundation, in harmony with the design of the barn. There would be three bedrooms, a parlor, a kitchen, a washroom for laundry, and a sitting room. Knowing how often it rained, Jonas envisioned three fireplaces for warmth and a back porch with a roof.

"And to think we might both have been

on a boat far out to sea by now," Peter Seton reminded him as they carefully balanced themselves on their ladders. "I don't know about you, but I'd make a lousy sailor."

Remembering the *Al Di La*, Jonas grimaced. "I don't even want to think about it. Besides, I'm perfectly content to be a farmer." Marrying Faith, living here on this land, was more than he had ever dreamed of. Remembering "Royal Flush" Willie he knew the old man would call him very lucky.

"Must have been a speedy dress fitting," one of the men exclaimed, breaking in to the conversation. "She's coming back."

Jonas looked at the speck of dust coming closer and closer. But it wasn't Faith. As the figure on horseback came closer and closer, he could see that it was a tall man astride a bay horse. Across the saddle was a Winchester.

"Pooh, ain't her," said the short man. "If it is, she's suddenly gotten mighty ugly."

"And grown a mustache," said a man named Cooper.

All five men watched as the horseman approached, stopping in front of the barn. Dismounting, he took his rifle from the saddle and walked in long strides toward where the men were working.

"Who is he? Never seen him before." Bart was curious.

"Trouble, no doubt." Peter Seton was on his guard.

"Can we help you?" Jonas looked at the newcomer long and carefully, trying to see if it might be one of the men who had burned down the barn or threatened him.

"I'm looking for Jonas Winslow," the man said as he ambled over in his direction. Shading his eyes from the sun, he looked up.

"You mean the bridegroom?" Bart asked, leaning over the roof, giving Jonas a nudge that made his ladder sway.

Carefully maintaining his balance, Jonas climbed down. He thought to himself that if this was another attempt to get Faith to sell, this man was wasting his time. "*I'm* Jonas Winslow."

Taking a large piece of paper from his pocket, the tall man looked at it, then at Jonas, then back at the paper again. "Yep, you're him all right." He raised his Winchester. "You're under arrest."

"Under arrest?" Peter Seton was incredulous. "For what?"

Jonas knew. A sixth sense told him that somehow his past had caught up with him. "San Francisco," he said under his breath.

Faith sat in front of the living-room fire, staring hard at the flames. Wanted for murder! Jonas Winslow. *Her* Jonas. Nothing could soften the tight knot in her stomach at the

305

thought. Gambling was one thing, murder quite another.

"No! I don't believe it." And yet it had been down in black and white. A detailed account of the shooting Jonas was accused of. A cold-blooded killing, it had said. And all over a game of cards. Jonas was a wanted man!

"I'm sorry, Faith. You must believe me." Keeping a cautious distance, Margaret Mac-Quarrie stood in the doorway. "I never knew the Pinkerton agent would turn up something so . . . so serious."

"But they did. And now—and now . . . ." Faith couldn't control her tears. This was nearly as tragic as Henry's death. Perhaps even worse in some ways.

"Oh Faith, lass . . ." Twisting the hem of her apron, Margaret MacQuarrie was obviously distraught. "I only wanted to make certain that you weren't taken unaware by some unscrupulous rogue. I—"

"And what now, Maggie?" Suddenly everything was very clear to Faith. Jonas had come to Milwaukie after the shooting, remembering her from the train. He had been hoping to find a place to hide. But what were his real feelings for her?

"I don't know, lass."

Faith did. "The Pinkerton agent will know, Maggie. He'll come and take Jonas back to San Francisco." Jonas in prison was a terrible thought.

"Aye, I suppose he will." Maggie's voice was soft. "But Faith, lass, if Jonas killed a man that's the price he'll have to pay."

Faith blinked away her tears. "No!" No matter what he had done or why, she couldn't stand by and let him be taken away to some jail. Or worse yet, hanged! "I don't care what he has done!"

"Faith!"

She bounded to her feet. "I'll stand behind Jonas no matter what, Maggie!"

"You can't mean that."

"I do." She felt frightened for Jonas. Panicky. How much time was there before he was apprehended? "I know him. He would never kill anyone over a card game." Hadn't he decried his friend Willie's death? "If Jonas killed a man in San Francisco there had to be a good reason."

"Defending himself perhaps?" Maggie toyed with the corner of her apron as she thought this over.

"Or something else." Faith said again, "Jonas is not a killer."

Suddenly Faith knew what she had to do. Pushing through the living-room door, she took the stairs two at a time. She had what was left of her money hidden in a music box in the bedroom. She'd gather it up, ride back to the farm, and give it to Jonas. Together they'd flee Portland, go anywhere that Jonas would be safe.

Thirty-two

Faith urged Maggie's buggy horses up a hill. The sun hovered low on the horizon casting a soft glow on the countryside. Usually she would have stopped to enjoy the view, but today she didn't have even a moment to spare. She had to get out to the homestead and find Jonas before someone else did, that someone being a Pinkerton agent.

Faith had Jonas's escape all mapped out in her mind. They'd take the buggy to Astoria and there board a ship bound for anywhere but San Francisco. She'd planned it quickly with the help of Margaret MacQuarrie who had agreed to be her co-conspirator.

"It's not that I agree with you about running from the law now, lass. It's just that since your mind is made up about doing this fool thing, I want to make certain all goes well. I don't want you to get hurt. I'm not doing this for Jonas Winslow but for you," she had emphasized. "Sure and may I not live to regret it."

"You won't regret it, you won't," Faith whispered now, breathing a sigh of relief as she saw all the familiar landmarks come into view. Jonas had to be there. He just had to be.

Oh why had she just ridden off? It had been such a foolish thing to do. She should have talked with Jonas about what the Pinkerton agent had revealed. She should have told him she'd stand by him, should have spirited him off without another word. But all she could do now was cross her fingers that all would work out as she planned.

It didn't.

Faith knew the moment she rounded the bend and heard the silence that something was wrong. It was verified the moment she located Peter Seton. Unlike the others, he hadn't deserted the homestead but had waited around, hoping she would come back so that he could tell her gently, before she heard it in town.

"Where's Jonas?"

"A man with a gun took him away. Faith . . ." He reached for her hand.

She was too late! The realization was like a deep ache in her soul. She had let Jonas down when he needed her. He had been caught! She put her hand to her mouth muffling her cry of despair.

"Jonas was wanted—"

"I know about that," she said, pulling away.

"That it was a Pinkerton man who came after him. That Jonas is wanted in San Francisco. You know?" He tensed his jaw. "I never would have thought—"

"Don't believe any of it." Picking up a hammer from the ground, she clutched it with the fervor of her convictions. "Jonas doesn't have it in him to be cruel or spiteful. He wouldn't shoot a man down because he thought he cheated in a card game." Seeing that Peter still was doubtful she repeated, "He wouldn't!"

"I want to believe that, Faith, for your sake." Folding his arms across his chest, Peter hung his head.

Faith likewise hung hers. What could she do now? A jailbreak? Hardly. It would be dangerous and might jeopardize the outcome of Jonas's trial. But oh how she wished she were daring and resourceful enough to try it.

Going to the well, Peter dipped his handkerchief in the waterbucket and, bringing it over to Faith, wiped her forehead. "If there is anything I can do, Faith."

"There is!" She took him by the arm. "You can ride into Portland with me. Jonas is going to need a lawyer! While I'm at the jail you can help me by finding him the best possible one." As they made their way to the buggy, her mind was already formulating another plan. They'd get a smooth-talking attorney who would be able to talk Jonas right out of his cell. That was the only thing that gave her even a semblance of calm during the frantic journey back to town and down the bumpy dirt roads. The wood-and-stone buildings seemed to fly by in a blur as Faith sought out the jail. She hardly even remembered stopping the horses, but there she was suddenly standing before the door.

"Can I help you?" A dark-haired man with a drooping mustache and a badge as big as his fist stood in her way.

"I want to see Jonas Winslow."

There was a pause, and for a moment she feared that the man would deny her request, but then he stepped aside. "Come with me."

Faith called on every ounce of inner strength as she followed the lawman through the open doorway that led to the jail cells. Taking a deep breath, she forced herself to remain calm. Somehow she'd manage to get Jonas out. She didn't know how, but if she kept her wits about her, she knew she would think of something.

"Faith!" Though Faith couldn't see him yet, Jonas saw her. The moment was gut wrenching. What could he say to her to make her believe him?

Jonas was in the cell farthest from the door, separated by a wall from the one inhabited by an outlaw named Frank Irwin. Chilling laughter echoed from beyond the bars as Faith passed by. "Well, hello, hello, little lady," a raspy voice taunted. "Come to see me?"

It took all of Faith's control to ignore him. She sighed in relief as she heard the key's jangle. The thick iron door creaked open and Jonas feasted his eyes on the woman he so loved. Sunlight streamed in through the high, barred window to illuminate the highlights in her auburn hair. Dressed in a bright-yellow dress, her hair flying every which way, she was beautiful.

"Faith?"

The sound of his voice brought forth a sob. "Oh, Jonas!" She ran to his side throwing herself into his arms.

He moved her hand around to his lips and gently kissed the palm. He stared down at her face somberly. "Oh, sweet Faith, you give me hope." Just looking at her and touching her deeply affected him.

Her eyes seemed to burn his with blue light as they misted with tears. She was very dear to him. He would have never wanted to cause her pain and yet somehow it seemed the deck would always be stacked against him.

"You're crying. Don't cry, Faith." He

groaned and caught hold of her, tangling his fingers in her hair, his mouth hovering just inches from her own.

She raised her head, trying valiantly to smile. "If you have picked this place to spend our honeymoon I'll do it, but couldn't we go someplace with a big wide bed."

Jonas couldn't even pretend to smile. "I didn't kill that man in San Francisco. You've got to believe me."

"I do!" She kissed him on the lips. "It's all some terrible mistake. I'll stick by you."

He had expected anger. Hurt. Recriminations. Never in his wildest dreams had he expected her to be so understanding. He loved her all the more for it.

She looked scathingly at the man with the mustache. "I'll prove just how foolish this story about your shooting anyone really is."

"Foolish," he repeated. He wanted to believe it would be that simple, yet all his years at the orphanage when he had so often been blamed for something he hadn't done, soured him on justice.

"I love you, Jonas. Together we'll get through this."

"Together." It was a word that touched his heart. His fingers traced the soft curve of her cheek and tangled in her hair.

She clung to him, trying desperately not to cry. He was the one in need of comfort.

"Everything is going to be all right," she insisted.

"One minute more. That's all." The mustached man's voice was as booming as thunder. "Just one minute and then you've got to leave."

"Oh, Faith! Faith." Whispering her name, Jonas gathered her to him, his voice breaking as he asked why this had to happen. "We had our whole world before us!" He buried his face against her neck.

Faith didn't want to tell him, didn't want him to hate Maggie. "I don't know," she whispered instead, clinging to Jonas as if she would never let him go.

"Time's up!" came a harsh reminder.

Jonas squared his shoulders and said an emotional goodbye.

"I'll be back, Jonas. Sooner than you can imagine. And with a lawyer," she threw over her shoulder as she was pushed from the cell. "I promise."

Faith paced in front of the sheriff's office for a long time, then, hoping to find Peter, she walked briskly up the street. Though she wouldn't admit it, she was more than a bit apprehensive about what was going to happen now.

"Excuse me," said a hoarse voice.

A shadow crossed her path and Faith looked up, only to gasp at the irony of it all. As if there wasn't enough on her mind, there, walking down the boardwalk as if he owned the town, was the dark-haired, mustached man from the stagecoach.

"You!"

For just a moment the gray eyes stared at her, then recognition sparked within the cold depths. "Well, well, the little missy from—"

"St. Paul. We were on the stagecoach together. The one that you and your friends saw fit to rob." The moment the words were out, the man stepped directly in her path. Faith knew she had made a mistake and cursed herself for it.

"That is a careless accusation, one that should not be bandied around, sweet thing." If she didn't keep quiet he intended to silence her his expression seemed to say. "Surely you have made a mistake."

Faith's bravado faded as she looked around and realized the street was deserted. Though it galled her to back down she said, "Perhaps."

Minutes passed slowly as he froze her with his penetrating eyes. Then he smiled. "So good to see you again." He took off his hat, bowing in mock politeness.

As she stood there, Faith took in every detail of the tall, thin man's appearance so she could describe him to the proper authorities. He had a small mole under his nose on the left side, there was a tiny scar that crisscrossed his right eyebrow, his nose had a small bump on the bridge. Otherwise he was really quite ordinary looking.

"I wish I could say the same." She took a step forward. "Now, please excuse me."

He reacted quickly, standing in her way. "Don't be in a hurry. We're just getting a chance to become reacquainted."

"Reacquainted, indeed!" She seethed with indignation. This man should be where Jonas was, not walking the streets to intimidate decent citizens. "Suffering your company once was quite enough." Lifting her chin, she whispered, "You nearly ruined me, sir, but with perseverance I survived."

He laughed, and the sound was menacing. "So I saw. Which brings me to a very important subject: your little homestead." There was a pause. "I want to buy it."

Faith responded instantly. "Never!"

"Never? Something tells me you just might change your mind." He threw back his head and laughed, a sound that raised goosebumps on her flesh. In that moment she knew he had been responsible for burning down her barn. How she hated him!

"I will never change my mind. The land is not for sale!"

When he spoke, his voice was barely audible, yet the tone was frightening. "Then, so be it." It was a threat and a challenge.

Thirty-three

RAWLINS AND OLIVER the sign read, the last name appearing in the tiniest of letters. Faith crossed her fingers as she walked through the doorway, following after Peter. Jonas needed a lawyer immediately, but so far every lawyer they had approached had turned the case down. She didn't know why. Had it become know that Jonas was a gambler? Or was there another reason? She could only speculate.

"Let's give it another try."

Peter's soulful tone did little to put Faith at ease as she entered the small office. Nor did the appearance of her surroundings. This drab, plainly furnished room did not give a very good recommendation of its occupants.

There were no rugs on the wooden floor, no large leather chairs, no chandeliers, no paintings or wall hangings. The only furniture was a large mahogany table with two straight-back wooden chairs and a bookshelf loaded to the ceiling with books. Only one lone oil lamp gave the room any light. Its flickering flames illuminated a hunched-over figure scribbling on a small piece of paper.

"I don't know, Peter . . ." Had the situation not been so desperate, Faith would have turned right around and headed back toward the door.

"We have to give it a try." His expression seemed to say that they had no choice. Besides, as the seated figure turned around, it was too late to flee.

"May I help you?" A petite tawny-haired woman wearing a suitcoat, tie, and spectacles addressed them politely.

Faith was anxious to get this matter over and done with. "We're looking for either Rawlins or Oliver," she stated, looking around for either one of those attorneys.

"I'm Oliver," the woman said.

"You?" Peter voiced his surprise, not ever having seen a woman lawyer before.

"Yes, me." The woman laughed good-naturedly. "I'm Clara Oliver, a bonafide lawyer, I assure you." Putting her small hand to her temple, she smoothed the tendrils that had escaped from her chignon.

"But you are much too pretty!"

Again she laughed, taking his astonishment as a compliment. "But not so much so that I didn't have to work, and work long and hard to become a part of a field traditionally barred to my sex, sir."

She had studied at Hastings College of Law in San Francisco, she told them. More importantly, since few lawyers ever graduated from a law school, she had apprenticed herself to Chester Sawtelle, a noted attorney. Absorbing all the knowledge that she could from that association, she had passed the California bar examination.

"Alas, despite my accomplishment, California law restricts the legal profession to 'any white male citizen' who can satisfy the requirements of age, moral character and legal knowledge. I came here to Oregon to establish my new career. I want to be more than a glorified legal clerk. I want to be a lawyer in every meaning of the word." She pointed toward the sign. "Edward Rawlins has given me that chance."

Faith felt an instant kinship with this woman. She quickly revealed the reason for their visit. "Jonas Winslow, my husband-to-be, has been put in the Portland jail, but I know in my heart that he is innocent. Please, can you help us?"

Clara responded without hesitation. "I can and I will! It will give me a chance to make a name for myself." Enthusiastically, she reached for a piece of paper and a pencil.

"Faith, don't you think . . ." Peter Seton pulled Faith aside, whispering in her ear, "I don't like this. I don't like this at all. It's obvious that she is desperate for clients. That's why she is taking Jonas's case. She freely admits it's to earn a reputation."

"I don't care what the reason is, Peter. My intuition tells me to give her a chance."

"Intuition." He scoffed at her reasoning.

There was no use discussing it. Faith had made up her mind. Still she said, "It's true Clara Oliver wants to make a reputation for herself. As someone who wins her cases. She must for Jonas if she takes him on, Peter. Can't you see?"

He was gruff. "I suppose so."

Faith turned toward Clara Oliver. "What do you intend to do?"

"If I can keep the San Francisco authorities from getting their hands on my client I think we have a chance. I'll fight the extradition."

"You mean you're going to try and keep Jonas here?" That idea was appealing to Faith.

"That's what I mean. It can be done if I can establish either that his identity was mistaken or that there was a lack of evidence."

"But there *is* evidence." Faith remembered. "Jonas told me that his pearl-handled revolver hadn't even been fired, but they are using it to prove he shot the man."

"It's clear he's being set up. I'll stall for a while. I need more time to work on his defense." Clara Oliver scowled. "How many witnesses were there?"

"I'm not really certain, except for the men involved in the poker game." Jonas had only vaguely talked about that night. Now she wished she had pressed him to tell her everything.

"Then I need to talk directly to Mister Winslow." She looked troubled.

"Is there a chance?" Faith had a moment of doubt.

Clara Oliver was so sure of herself that it was contagious. "If I have to go all the way to San Francisco I'll see that Jonas Winslow is set free." Her eyes gleamed. "On that you have my promise."

The jail cell was so small that Jonas felt boxed in. He had hated closed-in places since his days at the orphanage when he had been punished by being locked in a linen closet. Then he had known he would eventually get out. Now he was not so certain.

"Murder." It was something they stretched a man's neck for. "Or worse."

The very thought was frightening. How was he ever going to clear himself? He had played cards enough to know that the deck was stacked against him. He felt helpless. Frustrated. Just when he had found everything he had ever wanted, when life looked as though it was going to come up with a winning hand, he had been cornered.

How had that damned Pinkerton agent found him? The answer was suddenly as plain as the nose on his face. Margaret Mac-Quarrie. It had to be. She had come out to the farm in her buggy and a little while later the Pinkerton agent had appeared. He doubted it was a coincidence. Jonas felt betrayed. Suspicion hardened his heart and the bitterness showed plainly upon his face.

"Damn her!"

Her prying had ruined him. In just two days time Jonas was being transferred to the jail in San Francisco. He might never see Faith again. That more than anything else troubled him.

Through the tiny window in the jail cell Jonas could hear the night sounds of Portland: clattering wagon wheels, tinkling piano music and drunken laughter from the saloons, and barking dogs. Lethargically he just lay on his cot not even bothering to get up until one sound pierced through the ruckus.

"Psst. Jonas!" It was Faith's voice, coming from outside.

Jonas bolted to his feet and ran to the small barred opening. Clinging to the bars, he looked out at her, laughing softly when he saw that she was standing on a box so that she could reach the window.

"I hope you brought a saw from your friend Ian MacQuarrie's sawmill."

"A saw?" She saw his smile and knew he was kidding her. "Not a saw but something much better." Reaching up, she touched his hand, holding it for a long poignant moment. He looked so tired. There were deep circles under his hazel eyes and a stubble of beard on his chin. "We're going to get you out of here, dear heart."

"Out?" Jonas was afraid to hope. Still he asked, "How?"

"The other day I hired a lawyer who is going to try to keep the authorities in San Francisco from—" Faith tried to remember the term, "from . . . extraditing you."

"Extrawhating?"

"Extraditing." She quoted Clara Oliver. "That means surrendering an alleged criminal to the authority of another having jurisdiction—in this case the state of California."

"Keeping me here, you mean." It seemed too good to be true.

"By having the case thrown out for lack of evidence."

Jonas was thoughtful. "I hope this lawyer of yours knows his law."

"*Her* law," Faith corrected. "And she does."

Jonas was taken aback.

"Your lawyer is a woman, Jonas. Clara Oliver by name." Motioning to the attorney to come forward, she introduced her to the incredulous Jonas.

"Faith . . ." His whisper seemed to ask her if she had suddenly lost her mind. "I've never been one to have the opinion that a woman's place was nowhere but the confines of her husband's house but—"

"But you have your reservations about my qualifications," Clara Oliver said softly. "Don't. I've had to be twice as good as any man in my profession to even be able to hang out my shingle. To put it bluntly, I'm the best."

Jonas started to protest, then thought better of it. He remembered playing cards once with a woman named Poker Katy in Kansas City. He had been certain he could best her, but she had won every hand. Twice as good as any man, she had taken everything of value that Jonas owned.

"I don't have any reservations." To the contrary he could only hope that the attractive woman could outwit Sam Cummings, the guard who held all the keys, into letting him go.

"Good." Clara Oliver readied herself for taking notes. "Now, tell me exactly what happened that night in San Francisco."

Jonas quickly called the events to mind. "I was in a fancy-pants hotel, smoking a cigar as I played cards. I remember thinking that a man could get used to the luxury of the surroundings."

"What game were you playing?"

"Poker as usual." He sensed her question before it was asked. "I was playing with three other men. Ordinary-looking men."

"Was there anyone else present? Anyone at all who could be an impartial witness?"

Jonas shook his head, then he remembered someone. "Yes. A slim red-haired woman dressed in a black satin gown. Her name was Red."

"Red who?"

"I don't know, but I do recall she was a singer and that she dealt the cards. And that she had a man friend. A rich man by the looks of him. He didn't like the attention I paid to Red. He didn't like it at all." He'd never forget. "He was the one who insisted I was the killer."

"So you might have been set up because of jealousy?" Clara Oliver hastily scrawled down Jonas's affirmative answer.

Jonas detailed the events of that tragic evening as quickly as he could. "The winning hand was three aces and two jacks. The man to my left threw down two aces, saying that there weren't five aces in any deck of cards."

"And then?"

Jonas ran his hand over the stubble of his chin. "The man across from me reached for his gun, but he wasn't fast enough. The man to my right pulled out his revolver and fired." He still remembered his confusion. "I pulled out my pearl-handled gun, but I didn't cock the trigger. Yet suddenly I was being named as the murderer."

"Of Randolph Vanduvall."

"Yeah. Yeah. Come to think of it, that was the name." He was impressed that she had found out his name. He himself had forgotten it until he had been reminded.

"You see, Jonas, she really is very knowledgeable," Faith felt convinced that Clara Oliver was the person to settle the matter of Jonas's innocence once and for all.

"I peeked in the Pinkerton agent's file," Clara answered. "But do go on."

"I was surrounded by policemen, all of them pointing pistols at me. They didn't even give me a chance to explain. They just took my revolver and began hurling accusations. Damn fools! If they had only done some investigating they would have seen that my gun hadn't even been fired."

"Maybe they didn't want to know that."

"They didn't." Jonas told of how he had heard his gun fired. "I was confronted with the smoking pistol, then pushed into a police wagon."

"But you escaped."

"Precisely."

"And you came here."

Jonas's eyes touched on Faith, who stood

just a few inches from the lady lawyer. "To see Miss Tomkins. And to fall in love." His voice lowered to a pitch that was barely audible. "And no matter was happens, I will never be sorry that I did. I want you to know that, Faith. You are the greatest joy of my life."

"And you of mine." She wasn't able to get close enough to Jonas to kiss him through the bars, so she did the next best thing and touched her fingers to her lips, then touched his mouth. "I'll do anything necessary to see that you are set free, Jonas. We will be together again. Please believe that."

At that moment, seeing the love clearly written in her eyes, he felt hope.

Thirty-four

Waiting. That was the difficult part. Faith had marked the days off the calendar with big, bold red Xs as they passed by. One day. Two days. Three days. A week. Still, a decision had not yet been made on Jonas's fate. Would he be forced to go to San Francisco? Or could Clara Oliver work a miracle?

Faith had never been particularly interested in legal proceedings before, but now, in the hope she might in some way aid Jonas, she assimilated as much as she could. A sworn statement had been presented to a magistrate giving the facts of Jonas's alleged crime and identifying him as the person accused of committing it. Now it was up to the magistrate to hear the proofs offered for and against Jonas and then decide if he should be released or if there should be a trial.

"Any news yet?" Maggie looked up from

her cross-stitching, watching as Faith dipped the pen in red ink.

"No." Faith crossed another day off the calendar. "Clara is meeting with the magistrate this afternoon."

"Oh." Maggie returned to her needlework. Since Jonas had been taken to jail, Faith had noticed a change in her friend. She was quiet, subdued. A woman of few words. Faith missed the spunky Maggie.

"It's not your fault!" Faith stood up and walked over to where the Scottish woman sat. A pitcher of lemonade rested on the table beside her. Pouring a glass, she held it out.

Margaret MacQuarrie declined the lemonade. "Och, but it is."

"You couldn't have possibly guessed what was going to happen because you employed the Pinkerton agent, Maggie." She took a sip of the lemonade and decided it needed more sugar.

"I've never been a busybody." Sticking her finger with the needle, Margaret MacQuarrie swore softly. "I've always minded my own business and let others do the same. Except this time. And just see where my prying got me." She sucked at her finger to stop the blood. "Or rather where it got your Jonas."

"You didn't purposefully try to cause Jonas harm. I know that, and for all his blustering Jonas does, too." At first Faith had held Margaret MacQuarrie accountable for Jonas's fate, but she had since forgiven her. Whatever had occurred, Margaret hadn't done anything maliciously.

"I love you as if you were my own daughter," Margaret proclaimed as she took one stitch, then another.

"I know." Faith called to mind that night she had first arrived. She had been nearly penniless, had been wet from head to toe and so frightened. "Right from the very first you were kind to me."

Plunging the needle in and out of her cross-stitching in agitation, she confided, "I only wanted to make certain you knew all there was to know about Jonas Winslow so there would be no surprises. How was I to know . . ." That he was accused of murder, she was obviously thinking but didn't say.

"Jonas was set up. That's the truth, Maggie." It was important to Faith that Margaret MacQuarrie believe in Jonas's innocence. "I think so and Clara Oliver thinks so, too."

Maggie was hesitant, as if she really didn't know what to think. "I suppose it wouldn't be the first time something like that happened. Nor the last." Cutting the green thread, she picked up a spool of brown, her fingers shaking as she threaded the needle. "All I hope is that whatever happens now, you will not be made to suffer."

"I'll always stand behind him, Maggie." Faith looked to see what Maggie was working

330

on and smiled to see the replica in colorful threads of her new barn and the surrounding shrubbery. Two figures stood nearby—a woman with auburn hair and a man who was obviously meant to be Jonas. "It looks lovely."

"We Scottish are a superstitious lot at times. In medieval times it was considered good luck to create a tapestry of a home or a castle." Holding it up, she exhibited her handiwork. "This is just my way of saying that I hope all will go well and that you will be happy, hinny!"

Faith was deeply touched. If she hadn't completely forgiven the Scottish woman before, she truly did now. "Thank you from the bottom of my heart, Maggie."

Faith stood for a long time watching as Margaret worked on her cross-stitch. "Oh, Maggie, I'm on pins and needles wondering what is happening at the hearing. Hoping. The magistrate could decide to release Jonas if he considers the evidence insufficient or false." But would he.

"Then let us hope."

"And think good thoughts. He will free Jonas. He *will!*" Faith spoke with more bravado than she felt. Later in the day as she and Clara Oliver sat together in the magistrate's chamber, her hands were trembling as she waited for the decision.

"He looks to be a stern man," Faith whispered in Clara's ear as she appraised the man with his tightly curled dark-blond hair and shrewd, piercing blue eyes. Samuel Thompson seemed to be an unsympathetic sort of man, one who seldom smiled.

"Let us hope he is a just one," Clara responded.

It was a tense moment. The room was dimly lit. Dark and gloomy. As Faith and Clara sat across the table from Samuel Thompson and the prosecution attorney, Gerard Bradford, they were besieged with hostile glances. If the magistrate seemed grim, the prosecution's lawyer, a short, thick-browed man with a sarcastic leer, was even more so. Clara had assessed him as a "nasty little man," which seemed an accurate description as he rose to speak before the magistrate.

"I scoff at my . . . uh—" his look in Clara's direction was condescending "—my *opponent's* contention that there is no evidence against the defendant, Mr. Jonas Winslow. No evidence? A murder weapon and a room full of witnesses." He laughed scathingly. "Now *really*, Miss Oliver. This is no dime novel but reality we are dealing with here. Jonas Winslow is nothing but a cold-blooded murderer as I shall prove."

Clara stood up exhibiting determination and poise as she answered him. "A murder weapon, you say? No murder weapon at all but a revolver drawn to stop a murder, not commit one." She turned toward the magistrate. "I have learned that the victim, Randolph Vanduvall, was shot twice—once in the chest and once in the shoulder. Jonas Winslow's revolver was a single-shot model which I contend was not missing a bullet until long after the shooting."

"What are you saying?" Bradford was furious.

"That someone else fired his gun, to make it appear that he was the culprit."

"There were witnesses!" he sputtered.

"Ah, yes. The witnesses. As to them there are, in fact, only four who can be accounted for, two of whom will be suspects to the shooting themselves if Jonas Winslow is found innocent. What better motive is there than that to lie. I repeat, Jonas Winslow is innocent—"

"Innocent, you say!" Gerard Bradford interrupted. "He is as guilty as Adam was of taking the first bite of the apple." He eyed her up and down. "And as guilty as Eve was of tempting him."

Clara Oliver's voice was calm. "In case you have forgotten, Mister Bradford, in these United States of America a man is presumed to be innocent until proven guilty. It is one of the oldest principles of our common law and one of the most substantial protections against improper verdicts. This presumption exists until a verdict is found against the defendant. If there is a reasonable doubt, which I declare that there is, he is entitled to an acquittal."

Faith appreciated Clara Oliver's skill with words. Gerard Bradford had started out on the attack, but as both attorneys argued before the magistrate, it was soon the prosecution who was on the defensive as it was pointed out that he was prejudiced against a man still assumed to be innocent. The burden was upon him to prove the guilt of the accused.

"Beyond a reasonable doubt." Clara Oliver then quickly sought not only to rebut the evidence offered by the prosecution and to attack its veracity, but to show that reasonable doubt *did* exist. "Suspicious circumstances, surmise, and speculation are not sufficient to convict. I therefore am requesting that Jonas Winslow be released until such time as there is sufficient evidence or proven motive for his accusation."

"Sufficient evidence, is it? Motive?" The grin on Bradford's face was devilish as he reached into his pocket. "I submit a motive in the form of an IOU signed by Jonas Winslow which shows him not only to be in Randolph Vanduvall's debt but to be an old acquaintance of the victim. His loss of the game that night would have ruined him."

"An IOU?" Clara was taken aback. She

looked at Faith, whispering, "I was told nothing about this."

"Nor was I. I think he's lying. Jonas told me the game took place the first and only night he was in San Francisco. He said he didn't know anyone there."

"Let's hope so." Trying to maintain her poise, she said softly, "Or if it exists, let us hope it can be proven to be a forgery." Squaring her shoulders, she continued the battle to get Jonas free, but it was obvious to see by the magistrate's change of expression, from grim to grimmer, that Bradford's accusation had made an impression. Worse yet was his assertion that there was indeed an impartial witness.

"I have in my possession another document which I will present now: the statement of Miss Red Danberry, who makes clear that she saw Jonas Winslow pull out his revolver and fire at Randolph Vanduvall. She further states that Mister Vanduvall was not carrying a gun." His tone was sarcastic. "Shooting at an unarmed man in any state or territory is considered murder, Miss Oliver, just in case you didn't know."

Quickly Clara consulted her notes but Faith knew she had been taken unawares. The lawyer pleaded for time to reconsider the evidence that had been presented by Gerard Bradford, but her request was denied. As Faith sat there listening, her hopes were dashed as the magistrate declared that he had found probable cause to believe a crime had been committed and that the defendant Jonas Winslow had committed it. He ordered the prisoner held in custody without chance of release until such time as there could be a trial.

The cot was uncomfortable. Jonas tossed and turned on the rock-hard mattress, not tired enough to sleep yet too bored with his surroundings to want to stay awake. Damn. He wasn't going to be out of this place soon enough.

He had never really appreciated his freedom before now. Just the ability to come and go as one pleased seemed the greatest luxury. When he was released he would never complain about foolish and trivial things again. *If* he was released. The possibility that he might be kept here was a harrowing thought that played on his mind—until he heard a door shut.

"Jonas . . ."

Relief and happiness washed over him as he saw Faith standing right outside the bars. He sensed, however, the moment he looked into her eyes that something was wrong. Her walk, her downcast eyes, the set of her shoulders, reinforced that impression. Instantly he rolled from his cot and, standing, crossed the small distance that separated them. "What is it?"

"May I speak with Mister Winslow alone," she asked the jailer.

"I suppose so." The jailer who was little more than a boy stood there trying to decide, then compromised. "But you can't go in."

"All right." Faith wasn't in a mood to argue.

"And you better not cause any trouble." He was hesitant.

She affected her most ladylike demeanor. "I promise I won't."

He stood watching her for a long time, then shrugged. "OK, then." He left with an awkward gait, though he did turn around several times before pushing through the outer door.

"He acts as if he thinks you are dangerous. Do you suppose he fears you are going to help me make a jailbreak?" Jonas sounded far more jovial than he felt.

"I wish I could." Faith clung to the bars, longing for his arms around her. "Oh, Jonas . . ."

He thrust his hands into his pants pockets. "The magistrate didn't accept Clara Oliver's plea that there isn't enough evidence against me, did he?"

"No." A stricken silence followed as their eyes locked in sadness. At last Faith found her voice. "The lawyer for the prosecution handed over two things Clara wasn't counting on: an IOU from you to the man who was killed and a signed statement from a woman named Red Danberry saying that she saw you pull the trigger."

"It's a lie!" Jonas was incensed. "I've never signed an IOU in my life. Not to anyone. Never needed to. Somehow my luck always changed for the better before I had to. And as to that woman saying I fired the shot, she must be blind."

"That's what I thought, but unfortunately the magistrate believed the evidence." Oh, how she hated to have to tell him. "He's . . . he's going to hold you for murder."

Their eyes locked and held again as Jonas reached out to touch her face with gentle, probing fingers. "So, the thing I feared the very most has happened. I'll be imprisoned for life—or worse."

"Oh, no. Clara says—" She tried to be optimistic, but in truth she was frightened. What if they took him away and she never saw him again?

"Clara tried her best, for that I am appreciative. But she just doesn't understand a lot of things. Neither did I. Until now."

"The truth was that the moment Red Danberry had set eyes on Jonas Winslow, he had been a marked man. A murder had already been planned and he, a man strange to the town, had been picked as the one to blame it on. He hadn't stood a chance. He knew that now. He knew something else as well. Whoever had set him up would make certain he never got the chance to be exonerated. His life wasn't worth a nickel now that his whereabouts had been found out. And those around him were likewise in danger.

"You've got to forget me." If he was going to make certain Faith didn't come to any harm, physically or emotionally, that was the brutal reality.

"Forget you?" His voice sounded so cold.

"You have to."

She clutched frantically at the bars. "Jonas, don't even say that. I couldn't. Not ever."

Her unhappiness touched him, and he reached out to stroke her hair. "You are a beautiful woman. You have your entire life before you. A life that needs a husband and children." The very thought of her with another man tore at his soul, yet he knew he had to make such a sacrifice. He couldn't let her suffer because of his bad luck. "I want you to forget what happened between us. I want you to find someone else to love."

Faith felt tears sting her eyes. "I don't want anyone else. I want only you. Only *you*, Jonas."

"Me? A man in a cage?" And if the worst happened and he was executed, what then?

She felt rebellious. "It's not for you to tell me who to love, or what to do, for that matter. I'm stronger than you realize, so if you're trying to be noble, you can just forget it."

Turning his back, he walked to the far side of the cell. "You can do much better for yourself."

" 'Do much better for myself?' " The words were like a physical blow. A betrayal. Faith's face flushed with sudden anger at him. "Perhaps you're right." Her voice was choked with misery. "Perhaps I could do better than to love a man who has already given up on himself."

He turned around to look at her, sadness in his eyes. "I haven't." Ah, but he had.

She heard the hopelessness in his voice. "Listen to me, Jonas Winslow. I love you. I trust you. I believe in you."

"It seems that you do." And for that he adored her. "But there are times when love just isn't enough."

"It has to be!" The moisture of her tears sparkled like diamonds. Reaching up, she brushed them away.

She looked so unhappy, so miserable, that he couldn't keep himself from moving toward her. "Don't cry, Faith."

"Oh, Jonas!" She didn't want to fight, didn't want any hostile words between them. Pushing her arms through the bars, she circled his neck.

Somehow, despite the metal gate between

them, they managed to kiss, a fierce probing of mouth and tongue that was very arousing.

"Damn these bars!" he whispered against her lips. Oh, what he wouldn't have given to spend just one more night with her. "If only the jailer could be bribed—"

"Bribed!" Faith pulled away knowing in that moment exactly what she was going to do. "Undoubtedly the witnesses against you have all been bribed. But people who can be bought are sometimes available to a higher bidder."

Jonas knew by the gleam in her eyes that she was planning something. "Faith, tell me . . ."

Faith heard the footsteps of the guard, so she had to speak quickly. "I'm going to San Francisco to talk to the witnesses myself and to do a little detective work."

"San Francisco? You're not!"

"Oh, yes I am." She was determined. It was the only way.

"The men who framed me are dangerous. You'll get yourself killed."

She blew him a kiss. "I'm not afraid! If I have to go to the ends of the earth to prove that you are innocent, I will." Picking up her skirt, she pushed through the door.

"Faith! Faith!" He called her name again and again but she didn't come back and Jonas knew there was no way he could stop her.

Part Three:
To See Justice Done
San Francisco

"Justice is a machine that, when someone has given it a starting push, rolls on of itself."
—GALSWORTHY, *Justice, II*

Thirty-five

The shadowy outline of San Francisco's many hills looked ghostly viewed through the fog. Leaning over the rail, Faith squinted, trying hard to see through the haze, but it enveloped the harbor making it difficult to assess her surroundings. That, added to the eerie two-note song of the fog horn, caused a shiver to run up her spine as the small ship pulled into the harbor.

"Are you sorry we came?" Clara Oliver pulled her shawl tightly around her shoulders to combat the cool, moist early-morning air.

The salt spray of a wave splashed her face as she gazed toward their destination. "Not at all."

Faith knew she had to come to San Francisco for Jonas and for their future. It was her hope that somehow she and Clara Oliver could find a way to prove that he was being

345

framed. For that purpose they had both braved the dusty stagecoach ride to Oregon's coast where they had boarded a passenger ship en route to San Francisco. Now, after an exhausting and turbulent journey, they were finally here.

"I just wish that the fog would lift so I could see where we are going." Instead, the fog was like something greedy, gobbling up all the trees and buildings so that only the brightly colored rooftops were visible.

"Maybe it's better that you don't see," Clara said softly. "If you did, you might turn around and hurry back to Portland. There, it is safe. Here, anything can happen."

"I'll just have to take that chance."

She knew what Clara was saying and didn't have to be told again that San Francisco was dangerous, rife with gambling, murder, robbery, drunkenness, and prostitution. She would have to be very careful lest she find herself in as dire a predicament as Jonas. Faith was nevertheless impatient to arrive.

Faith was dressed sensibly for the journey in a full-skirted gray wool traveling suit with fitted jacket. Beneath it was a high, lacy-collared white blouse, chemise, corset and two petticoats. She did not wear the restrictive corsets that were a woman's woe. A woman ahead of her day, Clara had lectured her on the evils of corsets and advocated that women should exercise frequently to keep themselves trim so they would not need such artifacts.

Clara likewise was dressed in a traveling suit, hers of brown tweed. At the neck she wore a tie that was a replica of the kind many businessmen and male lawyers wore. Her hat was similar to Faith's but had a wider brim. She gripped firmly the satchel containing documents and notes she had brought along to aid her on Jonas's case.

Despite the fog, the barrel and bale-strewn docks were bustling with activity as the ship pulled in. Robust sailors dressed in canvas pants, striped shirts of various colors, and jaunty caps could be seen. They were busily unloading their ships but not too busy to wave cheerily at Faith and Clara. Without thinking, Faith lifted her arm.

"Ignore them!" Clara's voice was stern, but it softened as she explained. "Showing even a bit of attention to those poor woman-hungry souls can bring on trouble. It might even target them for being shanghied were they to follow us into town."

Faith remembered the close call Jonas had told her about in Astoria and nodded.

"Poor devils. If they only knew what was good for them they'd stay away from the saloons, gambling halls, and brothels. But some of them won't and they'll suffer for it. Just as Stephen did."

"Stephen?"

"Oh, just someone I once knew . . ." The faraway look in her eyes seemed to say that once he had been someone special.

Having lived in San Francisco, Clara had been a knowledgeable source of information about the city during the journey. She was the daughter of a doctor and a pretty blackjack dealer he had married. Clara was well versed on both kinds of people who made up the city's citizens—the law-abiding and those who lived outside the law. She had always been interested in helping those who were victims of the criminal element of the population. Now as they waited for the ship to unload their belongings, Clara seemed to be reflecting on days gone by.

"Did you love him?" Faith didn't mean to pry, yet she was curious.

"Stephen. Yes. Very much." So much so that it seemed to be a part of her life Clara couldn't bring herself to talk about. Tensing, she changed the subject, reminding Faith once again to be very careful now that they had arrived in the "city of sin," as she called it.

Sodom and Gomorrah did come to Faith's mind the moment she and Clara Oliver arrived in the gambling area of San Francisco. It was a bawdy, bustling, turbulent bedlam of thieves, shady ladies, gamblers, and other parasites who clamored together to reap a profit off other people's weaknesses. It seemed that vice and greed were the heart and soul of this part of the city.

"It's hard to believe this den of debauchery was actually named for a saint," Faith declared, as she quickly stepped out of the path of a painted lady.

"The Alcalde's doing twenty-two years ago. Actually it was called Yerba Buena when it was first founded as a settlement. That means 'good herb.'" Clara paused and put down her leather suitcase for a moment to adjust her hat, though she did not let go of her satchel even for a moment. "Once this was a peaceful hamlet but the gold rush brought gold-hungry men who transformed it into this."

As the two women roamed the streets looking for a decent hotel, they noticed that the billiard rooms and gambling saloons were all filled to capacity with men driven to cards and dice. They were not the kind of places that proper ladies were found. Faith and Clara had decided to disguise themselves as dance-hall girls when it was time for investigating. They could only hope that they would not be propositioned too forcefully.

"Where are we going to find a hotel?" Faith asked, anxious to sit down and rest her aching feet. "One that is at least marginally acceptable."

"Let's stay near the hotel where Jonas played that card game," Clara decided.

"Someplace where we might be able to garner some information." Clara had in mind discovering the true identity of the mystery woman "Red" Jonas had mentioned and all the pertinent facts concerning the late Mister Vanduvall.

Clara insisted that they avoid Morton Street, however, where the most notorious district of prostitution was located. "From dusk to dawn the women lean from their windows, naked to the waist, soliciting passersby with explicit and provocative promises."

"Hardly the place for a lady, I dare say," Faith exclaimed, hurrying to stay in step with Clara.

"Hardly."

Even though they avoided the worst areas, however, it was impossible to completely avoid the reality of the city. They passed garishly lettered signs that beckoned passersby into brothels, saloons, and opium dens. Music and bawdy laughter filled the air, as well as the visual reminders of men wallowing drunk in the streets, and women with painted faces and brassy hair openly selling their favors. Faith felt totally out of place. Coming face-to-face with the evil that existed in the world was unsettling.

"This one looks as if it might do," Clara said, heading in that direction of a sign that read THE GAMBLER'S PARADISE.

350

"Here?" Faith didn't like the looks of the hotel.

"It's right next door to the Golden Palace, the place Jonas talked about."

That made a difference. Dragging her single, heavy leather suitcase behind her, Faith made her way up the steps looking nervously around her as they stepped inside.

At first it was difficult to see. Smoke from cigars and cigarettes was as thick as the fog shrouding the city had been. As her watering eyes grew accustomed to the haze, however, Faith could see the tall bar that was well stocked with bottle after bottle of liquor. Behind the bottles was a huge mirror that reflected all the men drinking, gambling, or both.

"Take a look around, Faith. It's up to you to decide if we stay or go."

Slowly Faith walked around. All the tables seemed to be crowded. The players stood around them in lines three or four deep, elbowing their way to the gaming table to throw down their coins.

"There was a law passed against gambling fifteen years ago, but its only effect was to close a few of the smaller establishments. Ten years ago it was repealed."

Clara told her that the most popular games were monte, faro, rondo, and roulette. There were many who thought poker was too slow a game. Some wanted the immediate action

351

and insisted upon staking everything upon the spin of the wheel or the turn of the card.

"The stakes range from fifty cents to ten dollars. Sometimes considerable sums are wagered on a single play. Fortunes are won and lost in the course of a single evening."

Faith jerked away from a sudden hard poke in the ribs. Turning, she found herself face-to-face with a frowning blonde, her face thick with makeup.

"What's a matter. Slumming, dear?" the woman hissed. She reeked of cheap perfume and whiskey. Wavering on her feet, she was obviously inebriated.

"No . . . I— I . . ." Faith stammered. "I'm . . ."

The woman's dark-rimmed eyes raked Faith head to foot. "Your kind ain't needed here. Do-gooding troublemakers every one of you." She gave Faith a shove that nearly knocked her down. "Get out of here."

Faith held her ground. "I will not." Bracing herself, she put down her suitcase. If she was going to do Jonas any good she had to be strong. Any kind of weakness would be, as Clara had said, lethal.

Putting her hands on her hips, the blowsy woman stared her down. "You must not have heard what I said. Do I have to speak some other language? Leave!"

Trying to hold her temper, Faith shook her head. "No!" She had faced stagecoach robbers and a life-threatening fire. She wasn't afraid of this woman.

"Faith, be careful. She's trying to start a fight." Hurrying forward, Clara came to her aid but it wasn't needed. As the blonde lunged, Faith remembered all the scuffles she'd had with her sisters in childhood and put up her fists. She was just in time to block what would have been a punishing blow. Reacting quickly, she parried another.

"Why, you . . . !" With a screech of anger, the woman launched herself at Faith, lashing out with her hands, kicking with her feet. What followed was a jabbing, slapping, hair-pulling, pinching bout, a fight that appeared to have no rules.

Men stopped their gambling and formed a ring around the battling pair. As Faith rolled over and over on the wooden floor, she heard men making wagers.

"A dollar on the newcomer."

"Two dollars on Queenie!"

"They'll last two minutes."

"Four dollars says they'll last five."

The fight lasted *six* minutes, and during that time Faith was more than able to hold her own. Unimpaired by liquor, younger and more agile than her opponent, she was better able to react to the other woman's blows. That, added to her anger at having been set upon without a reason, gave her the strength and determination to at last pin her adversary to the floor.

"The winner." With a laugh, one of the onlookers, a balding man with large black handlebar mustache, pulled them apart. It was only then that Faith felt the sting of humiliation. What had she done? Fighting like some drunken lumberjack or sailor. Her cheeks flushed bright red as she stood up, shakily straightening her hair and small feathered gray hat.

"Oh, dear!" The last time she had fought like that she had been eleven years old. It had been a fight with Prudence, she recalled, over some foolish thing.

"And I worried that you couldn't take care of yourself," Clara whispered in her ear.

Faith started to make apologies for acting like anything but a lady, but she wasn't able to get a word in among all the chattered congratulations. She was being hailed as a celebrated person. Then before she knew what was happening she was being pushed and pulled toward a thick oak door.

Thirty-six

The room on the other side of the oak door was what Faith would have described as opulent. The walls were paneled with wood, the floor was covered with thick decorative rugs that looked as if they came all the way from Persia, from the ceiling hung a large crystal chandelier. Paintings of women in various stages of undress hung along one wall. In the marble fireplace a fire crackled, giving warmth to the otherwise chilly room. It was, however, the strikingly attractive gray-haired man seated in a large overstuffed Victorian chair who drew her eyes. Imposing was the word that came to her mind.

"What is it, Jamison?" His voice was authoritative.

"Excuse me, Mister Aubry, Sir," she heard the mustached man say. "I thought you might be interested in this little lady."

The pale-blue eyes that stared at Faith were

cold and unnerving. A tight ball lodged in her stomach. "Oh, indeed," she heard him say. "And why is that?"

"She took on Queenie just now and gave her a good licking. I thought maybe she could take her place." With familiarity the man slapped Faith on her behind. "She sure as hell is better looking. And younger. And sober."

"Bring her closer." It was not a request but a command. In answer the man shoved Faith forward.

"Now see here!" Indignantly she slapped his hands away.

"And spunky," the man said with a laugh that made the ends of his mustache dance.

The man named Aubry raised his brows. "So I see." He toyed with his gold cuff links. "What's her name?"

Perturbed at being spoken of and not to, she answered quickly, "My name is Faith."

"Faith?" The name seemed to amuse him.

Thrusting back her shoulders she returned his icy look with confidence. "Yes. Faith."

"Faith, who?" Picking up a cigar he ran it under his nose to judge its aroma and freshness, then using a gold cigarette lighter he lit it. "Do you deal?"

"Do I what?" Faith was taken unaware by the question but Clara, who had been hiding in the shadows unnoticed, hurriedly stepped forward.

"Yes. She does and I do. We're the best."

Puffing slowly on his cigar, Aubry let out the smoke in big smoke rings as he asked, "And just who are you?"

Clara boldly put her hands on her hips. "Claretta, and I'm the best damn blackjack dealer you'll ever find." She winked at Faith. "Next to *her,* that is."

"Well, well, well." The man named Aubry was obviously interested. "And just what, may I ask, is your price?"

Getting in to the mood of the lie Faith blurted out, "Twice what Queenie made."

"For each of us," Clara added.

Leaning back in his chair, Aubry took another puff on his cigar, then his lips curled in a smile that was more of a sneer. "All right. But you better be worth it." Snapping his fingers, he dismissed them. "See to it, Jamison. They start this evening."

"This evening." Faith was aghast. She'd never even held a card, much less dealt one. Her bravado was shattered and she wondered if Clara Oliver had lost her mind. That was the question she put into words when at last she and Clara were alone in their room.

"No, my sanity is quite intact." Carefully unpacking her suitcase, Clara held each article of clothing up for inspection before she put it in the closet. "I saw just the chance we needed and I jumped on it. With both feet."

"But I don't know how to deal cards." Faith

loosened the buckle on her suitcase. "They'll realize in an instant that we are both frauds."

"No, they won't." Clara took a deck of cards from the bottom of the suitcase. "Because I'm going to teach you. We have all morning and all afternoon."

"You mean that you know how?" But of course she would, Faith thought, remembering her mother had dealt cards in that very game. The story of her parents' meeting must have been quite a romantic one. She would have to ask Clara to tell her some time.

Without bothering to answer in the affirmative, Clara shuffled the cards and gave a very impressive demonstration. She almost made the cards dance. Her nimble fingers kept them intertwining with each other, first one way and then a reverse to the other.

"Except for making a show when you shuffle, blackjack is easy. You only need to deal one card at a time." She demonstrated the shuffle again, then dealt out the cards in a make-believe game. "Being dealers will give us the perfect chance to gather information. What better way than being out among those who are actually playing cards?" Shuffling the cards one more time, Clara then formed them into a tightly packed deck again and handed them to Faith. "Now, you try."

Faith was all thumbs. Her fingers trembled as she handed back the cards. "I can't. I just don't have your skill."

"And so you'll give up just like that?" Clara snapped her fingers. "Poor Jonas. And to think that I believed you when you told me how much you love him."

"I do love him."

Clara threw the cards down on a table near the bed. "Then you had better at least try."

"All right." Taking off her hat, shoes, and jacket, Faith sat down on the bed, picked up the cards, and looked at them for a long time. "Show me again," she finally said with determination.

Clara exhibited her dexterity, explaining to Faith the rules of the game. "The object for the gambler is to be dealt cards having a higher count than those of you, the dealer, up to but not exceeding twenty-one." She explained that jacks, queens, and kings were worth ten points each. The aces were worth either one or eleven.

With only a pause for something to eat and drink, Faith mimicked Clara's actions over and over, making mistakes again and again. It was difficult at first to make the cards do what she wanted them to. Certain that she was going to fail miserably and ruin their whole scheme, she wanted to cry. As the hours progressed and she relaxed, however, she slowly developed skill that earned her Clara's praise. But was she good enough to fool men who made their livings playing cards? she wondered.

The chance to find out arrived much sooner than Faith would have liked. Faith looked dubiously at the sapphire-blue dress slung over her arm, the dress Jamison, the bartender, had given her. Now that the time had actually come, she felt queasy and just plain scared. Even reminding herself that she was doing this for Jonas didn't calm her uneasiness.

"Blue. And feathers. You're going to look like a bluebird." Clara slipped her red satin confection trimmed with black lace over her head. "Aren't we going to be quite the pair. I wonder what they would think of us in Portland."

"I can just imagine," Faith answered, trying to lace up the back of her dress herself. "Certainly Margaret MacQuarrie would be scandalized . . . but oh, goodness gracious!" She was having no luck at all with her fastenings. Giving up, she turned her back to Clara. "Not too tight. I wouldn't want to faint."

"Or look so alluring that you get yourself in trouble," Clara teased, trying to make light of the situation. "Though seeing the way you wrestled with Queenie I have no doubt but that you could hold your own."

Faith laughed despite her nervousness. "I guess I can fight quite well when I'm provoked. But hopefully I won't have to do it again." Fixing her hair atop her head, she appraised herself in the small mirror on the dresser, cringing as she saw how low cut her dress was and how short. It was so low that it showed a great deal of flesh. The bodice was tight, pushing her breasts together in an ample display of cleavage. "I do look like a bluebird, Clara. An indecent one."

Clara's dress was just as revealing, though it showed less bosom and more leg. "Just the kind of outfit to wear at Jonas's trial, don't you think," she said, turning round and round to model it. "And I must insist that the other lawyer wear the same style. Perhaps in green."

Faith laughed at the image of a man wearing such attire, complete with garter. The levity of the moment took her mind off her jangled nerves, soothing her like a calming potion. By the time they descended the stairs, she was surprised to find she wasn't scared anymore.

"Just remember to act confident even if you make a mistake and no one will guess that you haven't done this a hundred times or more," Clara instructed, throwing her feather boa over her shoulder.

Faith did the same, pausing to look around her at the opulence she hadn't really noticed before. *Grandeur* was the word that came to mind but tinged with a garishness that looked as if someone had gotten a bit carried away. Couches, divans, and settees were scattered along the sides of the room, heaped with cushions of green, gold, purple, crimson, and blue. Marble tables were topped with oil lamps of porcelain and glass of every hue, veiled so that their light floated in the air giving an aura of mystery to the room. Just as in Aubry's office, paintings were hung on the walls of women and of pastoral scenes but there was no carpeting, only a plain plank floor. Chandeliers hung from the ceiling. What surprised her most of all, however, was the tiny orchestra of nine men who were playing operatic music.

"It seems our Mister Aubry does at least have a touch of good taste," Clara said softly. "And undoubtedly he is very rich."

"Rich enough to have a man murdered and blame it on any one he chooses," Faith whispered, her eyes riveted on the dozen or more tables in the room. Again each table had a compact crowd of eager bettors around it. The patrons were men of every class, exhibited by their manner of dress. There were top hats, slouch hats, cowboy hats, and no hats at all.

Standing and sitting around the tables were well-dressed, respectable-looking men in frock coats rubbing elbows with flannel-shirted miners fresh from their diggings. Sailors sported their striped shirts, canvas pants, and tams. There were Chinese men with long pigtails and Mexican men with sombreros.

Food lay on the long bars, free for the taking—apples, boiled eggs. And of course there was plenty of whiskey, rum, and beer. The clatter of the bottles, clinking of money, and the low hum of men's voices blended with the music as Faith and Clara entered the gaming area.

"Oh, there you are." The mustached bartender took each woman by the arm. "You in the blue take that table. Blondie, take the one over there."

Faith moved to an empty table on the right, located right under a huge crystal chandelier. "Anyone for blackjack, gentlemen?" she asked, feeling strangely calm considering the situation. Instantly, the table was crowded, coins jingling as the gamblers made ready to place their bets. Remembering all she had been taught by Clara, Faith began the game.

Suddenly all eyes turned toward the door as a woman dressed totally in black entered the room. Faith stared at the woman's bright red hair. "Who is that?" she asked a bearded miner who had just received one of her cards.

"Her? Why, that's Red. Red Danberry. Barbary Coast's nightingale and Wyatt Aubry's mistress."

Red. That name sounded over and over again in Faith's mind. It couldn't be a coincidence. It had to be the woman who had sworn on oath that Jonas was a murderer!

Thirty-seven

Jonas winced at the stale odor of rotting food as he watched two rats fighting over the leftovers of his uneaten dinner. "You're welcome to it, boys," he muttered. "I certainly found it inedible."

Jonas was in a less than pleasant mood. The food was terrible, his bedding was dirty, the mattress was lumpy, and the little toad of a jailer taunted him night and day. Most troubling of all, however, was time. It moved so slowly as he languished in his damnable cell that he could never be certain what hour it was. There was nothing to do but think and reflect as one day blended into the next. Boredom, he thought, was perhaps the greatest plague of all. How long had Faith been gone? Two days? Three days? Four?

Not a man who could be idle for long, Jonas got up from the small wooden stool. There was barely enough room to pace his cell, yet he walked back and forth. What if everything went wrong in San Francisco? What if there wasn't any evidence to clear him? What if Faith got herself in trouble?

"What if the sky falls down?"

Tapping his foot in agitation, he plotted his escape. He'd wait until the jailer brought his dinner, then he'd pounce. Oh, how he'd like to get his fingers around that skinny little neck and squeeze! He'd take the keys and . . .

Despite his frustration he knew that would be the worst thing he could possibly do. It would be a confession of his guilt just when Faith had risked her safety to try to find a way to get him free. No, he had to keep a cool head no matter what the provocation and stay right where he was. But how he wanted to smell the fresh air, look at the blue sky, feel the wind on his face.

Trying to occupy his mind, Jonas went to the windowsill and wrote down a list in the dust—things that needed to be done once he was set free: a new fence, a bridge over the stream, a cellar dug. And, of course, he needed to tend to their crops. He also listed items needed on the farm: a maple-sap bucket, a hay fork, a scythe, a reaping hook, a buck saw.

A rattle of keys jarred him from his thoughts. Turning around, he saw the jailer peering at him through the bars. "I have a visitor for you."

"A visitor!" He thought immediately of Faith. She was back. Why so quick? Was that bad news or good? But it was not Faith. Margaret MacQuarrie stepped from behind the jailer. "You!"

"Mister Winslow, please. I'd like to talk with you a moment," she said politely.

"Well, I don't want to talk with you!" The nerve of the woman. "Haven't you done enough?" He turned his back.

"Go ahead and get your anger out, but I will not be going anywhere. Not until you listen to me." Folding her arms across her chest, Margaret didn't budge.

Nor was *he* going anywhere for that matter. He was locked up like some damned parrot. "Well, then, spit it out." Undoubtedly she had come to say that she was sorry, that what she had done had been for Faith's own good. Hell, he'd heard all that before.

Margaret took a step forward. "I've found out some information, Mister Winslow. Information that once this . . . this unfortunate matter is cleared just might help us to make amends. I believe it will make you happy."

"Information?" He couldn't imagine what she was talking about. How could he possibly be happy, even for a minute, being cooped up in jail.

"About your heritage." Reaching in the

366

pocket of her apron, she pulled out a folded piece of paper.

"If that's the Pinkerton report, you can—" He had to clench his teeth to keep from being boorish.

"It is. A new report that came in just today." Clearing her throat, she started to read it aloud.

He swore under his breath. "Save it, lady. If it says that I'm Jesse James, they're lying." But even though he pretended he wasn't interested, in truth he was very curious about what was written down on that piece of paper she now folded into four perfect squares.

"So that's the way you're going to be. What a shame." Without so much as a blink, she put it back in her pocket.

The two of them faced each other silently. And all the while the clock just outside the tapping of Jonas's foot ticked the time away. Tap, tap, tap . . . In the end it was Jonas who weakened.

"OK, so I suppose I do want to know what it says." Still the silence. "Please . . ." It irked him that he was the one to back down.

Margaret MacQuarrie took out the piece of paper once more. " 'James T. Wakefield Senior died May 30th of this year of our Lord nineteen hundred and sixty-nine after suffering apoplexy. Mister Wakefield was a prominent New England investor who made millions of dollars investing in the Erie railroads during the War Between the States. Later he invested in the Northwestern Railroad, which is slated to run through Milwaukie, Oregon, once it is completed within the next year," she read. "It had been a bold maneuver in order to gain and secure the business the immense quantities from the West to New York."

"Very interesting, but what has this got to do with me?" Jonas asked suspiciously. James T. Wakefield. The name didn't sound familiar. Jonas couldn't remember his name among those men he had played cards with, nor did he remember any Mrs. Wakefield that he might have seduced at some time during his youth.

"What has this got to do with you?" Margaret MacQuarrie smiled. "James T. Wakefield was your father."

"What?" Jonas reached out and clung to one of the bars to steady himself. "What are you saying?"

"It seems that your mother, Anne Collins, a New York debutante, and your father eloped. They got married in Cornwall, Connecticut and later returned to New York society, or so it says here." She tapped at the paper with her forefinger.

"You don't say." All the years of loneliness and bitterness welled up again inside Jonas. How could he ever forget that he had been unwanted. Dumped on the orphanage's doorstep. "Well, it's too bad that I'm a little late in offering congratulations to the happy couple," he said snidely.

Margaret ignored his barbed sarcasm and continued the story. She told him that his mother had wanted children desperately. After several miscarriages she had conceived a child, a son whom they had named James T. Wakefield, Jr. Anne, who had always been frail, suffered greatly from the birth of her son.

"She died when you were little more than a tot, Jonas." Being a mother herself, Maggie's voice quivered with emotion.

"Died?" Jonas thought to himself that he should feel some sorrow, but it was difficult to mourn someone he couldn't even remember. It had been so long ago. So many heartbreaking years ago for him. "But my father was alive. Why was I given up?"

"Your father never remarried." She looked up and her eyes were filled with tears. "It—it seems that he blamed you for your mother's death and, not wanting to be burdened with childrearing, placed you in an orphanage."

"The son of a bitch!" Anger welled up so tightly in Jonas's chest that he was certain he would explode. "I'll never forgive him for that. Never!" He had spent years feeling unwanted, suffering under the strict discipline of people who didn't care about him. And

369

all because a man was so selfish that he just didn't want to be burdened.

"Perhaps he was. It's not for me to judge, but you are his only living heir, according to the papers that were found in his safe." Her voice got louder. "All the money and the land he owned now belongs to you."

"I don't want it!" On that Jonas was firm. Money couldn't bring him restitution for what he had lost. All the riches in the world couldn't bring back his youth or grant him a happy childhood. "At no time did my father even try to contact me. Not even one letter." He felt cheated. "I don't want anything that belonged to him!"

"Don't want it?" Maggie nodded. Her eyes were sympathetic. "I can understand."

"No, you can't." Jonas's eyes were cold. "You have a family. You have always belonged to someone. I didn't." How could he ever forget all the Christmases he had spent alone, all the birthdays without presents—the unhappiness he had felt, his sense of isolation. That was something that couldn't just be swept away because of an inheritance.

"You're right. I can't fully understand. No man can walk in someone else's boots, my father used to say. But Jonas, I do sympathize with you and I *am* sorry!"

Jonas met Margaret MacQuarrie's eyes and in that moment he realized that the time for hard feelings was over. What was done was done and could never be undone. The future, however, was another story.

"You're angry at me and at your father for giving up his tiny laddie, but think, Jonas. Think! What about Faith?"

If he accepted the money it would make her life so much easier. Even if he had to stay in prison for the rest of his life, he could see that her future was secure.

Margaret went on to tell him that the railroad, which he, James Wakefield, Jr., now owned, was the very same one that had been trying to buy up Faith's land. "Ah hah! I can see that you know what I mean."

"I'll be damned."

Never had so many feelings gripped Jonas at one time. Even after Margaret MacQuarrie had left, he felt the potency of his emotions. Anger for the misery he had suffered, for the lonely years he had spent. Remorse at never having known his mother. Relief at finally finding out who he was. Happiness knowing that he could at last give Faith the kind of life that she deserved. Confusion, wondering how he really felt about it all.

"James T. Wakefield. Railroad tycoon," he whispered. For a long time he stared out the window, laughing at the irony of it all.

Thirty-eight

The room had quieted to a hush as Red Danberry flounced into the gambler's den. Immediately she became the center of masculine interest.

"Give us a song, Red!" someone in the back called out.

"Show us some leg," another man requested. In a gesture meant to convince her, he threw a handful of gold coins at the stage. His act of generosity was mimicked and soon there was a shower of coins, a golden rainfall.

Faith's fingers froze in the process of turning over a card. She was distracted as the red-haired "Barbary Coast nightingale" moved through the room, her hips swaying provocatively as she walked.

Throwing back her head so that her hair cascaded wildly around her shoulders, Red Danberry appeased her worshippers by sauntering up to the stage. " 'Barbary Nights,' " she requested huskily to the piano player, who ran his fingers up and down the keyboard in an arpeggio pattern of chords. He began the song, slowly at first, then with a bouncing rhythm.

It was a seductive song, meant to get the attention of any audience. And it did. The men were spellbound. Hypnotized. For just a moment all movement within the room froze. All eyes watched the woman in black as she swayed from side to side, her long hair swirling about her shoulders as she sang. Raising her arms toward the ceiling, she became a part of the music, moving with a liquid heat that set every man's heart aflame.

"Ain't she somethin'!" The man across from Faith nearly swooned.

"I'd do anything to have a night with her," breathed another man.

"Why, she's nigh on to perfect."

"She sings like an angel."

But Faith wasn't as impressed with the redhead's talent. Having attended operas, concerts, and ballets in St. Paul, she observed that Red Danberry was a mediocre singer and dancer. But she had to admit that the woman was pretty and moved her body in a way that was sensual yet in the same time graceful.

"Look at her dance!" The man beside

Faith clutched his cards, distracted for a moment. "She's plumb wonderful!"

It seemed that all of the men at her table had something to say about Red. Hoping to learn all about her, Faith asked some questions. She was careful not to look as if she was just being nosy. "I think I may have seen Miss Danberry on stage in New York. Has she ever been there?"

"New York? Naw. She comes from Colorado Territory. Denver, to be exact."

"Denver."

"She's a widow. Came out to California a few years ago hoping to better her life."

"Shh!" Putting their fingers to their lips, several of the men around the table hushed any more talk but not before Faith learned of the woman's scandalous reputation. Her past lovers were said to be the King of Bavaria and one of the princes of England, not to mention several renowned generals who had made their reputations during the War Between the States. Some said she had even been a spy for the North. Now she was the paramour of Wyatt Aubry, owner of both the Gambler's Paradise and the Golden Palace, the man who, for the moment, was Faith's boss.

Aubry suddenly seemed to materialize out of thin air, whispering in her ear, "You, whatever your name is. Stop gawking and deal. That's what I pay you for." There was the hint of a threat in his voice.

"Of course, Mister Aubry." Hurriedly, Faith turned a card up for the man standing to her left. It was an ace, which, added to his ten, came up twenty-one to the dealer's eighteen.

"I won!" The man excitedly collected his coins.

Though at first Faith had been sure of herself, Wyatt Aubry's presence right at her elbow made her nervous. Her fingers trembled as she dealt out one card to each man in turn. Unfortunately, two other gamblers also scored a win.

Wyatt Aubry hissed in Faith's ear, "In case you don't already know, the dealer is supposed to win. The dealer. *You.*"

"I know who I am," Faith retorted, hotly, wishing Wyatt Aubry would just disappear. "And I know what I'm doing." Or at least she wished that she did. She hated having him so close, watching her every move. He was going to see through her facade. He was going to know that she was a fake and would throw her out before she even got a chance to find out anything.

It was as if Wyatt Aubry's eyes were burning coals, scorching her as he stared. Faith's muscles tensed and her back stiffened as she dealt out the cards for the next game.

"If there is one thing I hate, it's to lose

money." He grabbed her by the arm. "Understand?"

Faith shrugged his hand away. "I understand." She wondered what the punishment would be if she were to cross him and decided that Wyatt Aubry would be the kind of man who would play rough. But how rough? Would he stoop to murder? That question troubled her as she began the game. Looking at her own cards, she saw that they added up to twenty-one.

"Hit me!" The miner was smug as he asked for another card, but his smile faltered as he saw that his cards added up to twenty-two. "Damn!"

"Sorry. You broke," Faith informed him, snapping another card down on the table for the man standing next to the miner. Seeing his cards, she asked him, "Double down?" He nodded, but luckily for Faith he lost, too. She had heard Jonas talk of Lady Luck and knew as each man around the table broke, that she was in her favor.

Thank God, she thought, starting another game. Once again she as dealer was the winner, raking in the money of all these unfortunates who had hoped for blackjack.

Turning to Aubry, she asked sweetly, "Satisfied?"

"Not yet." For just a moment his eyes left her slim form as he glanced toward his paramour.

"Red . . . Red . . . Red," The men were chanting as Aubry's red-haired songbird took her bow. "Encore. Encore." She charmed them all by throwing them a kiss, then starting another song.

Faith tried to ignore everything but the game, but this time a tall, bespectacled man in top hat took the pot. "Five cards without breaking wins," Faith said regretfully, but it was the men at Faith's table who were the losers during the next round. She redeemed herself during the next game and the next as the music came to an end.

Red Danberry's finale was greeted with a burst of applause before the last note ended. The men shouted and stamped their feet, then those who were sitting stood up. Some even threw their hats in the air. Red Danberry was the sweetheart of every man there. But when her performance was over, she left on the arm of only one man: Wyatt Aubry.

"I thought he would never leave!" Faith said under her breath, thankful to be out from under his piercing eyes. She settled in for a long but hopefully more relaxed evening.

It turned out to be one which soon took a toll on her physical being, however. Her back hurt, her feet ached, her eyes watered from all the smoke in the room. It seemed that the night would never end. From the pained look on her face, it seemed as if Clara was just as miserable.

The evening still proved successful. When at last the night had blended into the wee hours of the morning and they were safely sequestered in their hotel room, the two women revealed their information.

"Red Danberry has quite an interesting past that includes being Wyatt Aubry's mistress. I'm certain that's why she lied about Jonas. The question is, why was Aubry after Jonas?"

"Jealousy," Clara answered. "From what I've learned, he resents any man better-looking than himself, particularly if Red has been caught flirting with him."

"Red Danberry and Jonas." The idea of their being together even for a moment was strangely disturbing, though she knew that to be silly. Faith quickly pushed away her twinge of jealousy. "But would he resent someone enough to set him up for murder?"

"If the timing was right," Clara suggested. In talking with some of the gaming room's patrons, she had found that Jonas had arrived in San Francisco at a dangerous time. There was competition in the gaming industry. A struggle for money and political control. "Vanduvall was not just a man gambling the night away. He intended to challenge Aubry's monopoly. His death was very convenient."

"Aubry had Randolph Vanduvall killed. And needed a scapegoat," Faith whispered.

"Exactly!" Now it was up to both of them to prove it.

Thirty-nine

It was foggy, but not so hazy that Faith and Clara couldn't see the Stars and Stripes as it fluttered in the breeze from high atop the wooden flagpole. It was the Fourth of July, a time of commemoration, yet they weren't in the mood for celebration.

"You know Wyatt Aubry is behind Vanduvall's murder and I know it, but how are we going to get others to believe it?" Picking up a brush, Faith agitatedly stroked her hair.

"Or if they do believe it, how do we convince them to go up against their fears of the man and help us put him behind bars." Clara couldn't keep from pacing up and down in front of the window. "From what I hear he has the whole city in his pocket. Why, even the fireworks for tonight's show were a gift from him. A patriotic gesture, of course."

"Of course!" Oh, it was so frustrating. At

times it seemed as if there was little hope. When she and Clara had boldly decided to come to San Francisco, they had never suspected that Jonas's adversary would have quite so much power.

"He's like some gigantic spider," Clara exclaimed, seeming to read Faith's thoughts.

"And we are like gnats who have to be careful not to get too close to his web." It was a worrisome thought. Not only did they have to worry about Aubry but all those under his influence as well.

During the last two days she and Clara had been doing a lot of detective work and what they had found out about Wyatt Aubry made it very clear that the corrupt former banker was involved in many shady deals. That his gambling establishments often used marked cards was only one of them. Faith had heard whisperings that he held a large share in most of the whorehouses and cribs, that he had dealings with many of the criminal bosses, and that he even got a profit from the opium dens. Hardly an upstanding citizen. Worse yet, he had used bribery to ingratiate himself with the law officials, the city government, and even the lieutenant governor of the state.

"If you make Wyatt angry, you might as well write your obituary," one old gambler had confided. And so it seemed. Last night a drunken gambler had openly quarreled with Aubry, condemning his gambling house as being a den of cheater and thieves. This morning he had been found floating in the bay. The morning papers said he had taken his own life, though Clara and Faith suspected otherwise.

"Do you think he suspects us?" There were times when Faith was certain that he did. Or at least her. "He's always looking at me."

"Maybe that's because he thinks you're pretty." Clara stopped pacing for just a moment. "Maybe that's the key. If he's attracted to you, perhaps you could use that to . . ." She shook her head. "No. Too dangerous."

Faith set down her brush. "Nothing is too dangerous, Clara. I'll do anything." She shuddered as she thought of Wyatt Aubry touching her even for a minute. "Well, practically."

"There has to be another way." Clara began her pacing again.

"If we could only find out who really shot Randolph Vanduvall." The sudden boom of fireworks sounded like exploding shells, shattering the silence of the night and making conversation difficult. Faith had to raise her voice to be heard. "But how?"

"That redhead knows."

"Red Danberry!" Faith nearly shouted it.

Clara shushed her, fearful she might be overheard. Still she nodded. Coming closer, she whispered in Faith's ear, "If we could only get her to rescind her testimony, Jonas would be cleared."

"But of course she won't." Poor Jonas, Faith thought. It was looking worse and worse for him unless she and Clara quickly found a way to get what they had come for.

"She would never go against Aubry, even if her conscience bothered her. She must be afraid of him."

"Or maybe she loves him."

"Heaven forbid!"

Faith and Clara were in a somber mood as they went to the window to watch the fireworks. Though neither wanted to admit it, saving Jonas seemed a hopeless cause. Even so, Faith knew in her heart she would never give up. Somehow, some way there had to be a way.

It was hot in the cell. Uncomfortable. Jonas was thirsty, but though he had rattled his tin cup on the bars, no one had come to give him water. Nor had he had anything to eat since breakfast. The leftover cornmeal mush in the wooden bowl was already crusty, though not too unappetizing for a small brown mouse who eagerly feasted.

"No water. No food. A fine way to treat a railroad tycoon," he said to himself sarcastically. He could only hope that his incarceration would not be for much longer.

Something had to happen or he was going to go stark raving mad cooped up in jail.

He plopped down on the cot, gathering up the deck of cards he had bribed the guard into giving him. Dealing them out, he began his hundredth game of solitaire.

"Red queen on the black king, jack of hearts on the queen of spades, four of diamonds on the five of clubs . . ."

The pop of firecrackers outside his window startled him. It was unnerving and did little to calm the turmoil of his emotions. For just a moment he had thought it to be gunfire until he remembered it was July Fourth.

"Black ten on the jack of hearts and so on and so on and so on," he mumbled, getting back into his game.

Three games later he threw down his cards, bored with the game. He wondered if once he got out he'd ever want to play again and scoffed at the thought. Of course he would. Once a card player, always a card player. Going to the tiny window, he looked out as fireworks shattered the sky.

Oh, Faith. Where are you now? he wondered wistfully. Closing his eyes, he envisioned her beside him, remembering what they had shared. He wanted to touch her velvety skin inch by inch, explore her loveliness. At that moment he would have given every penny of his newfound inheritance just to have her there.

The cell door behind Jonas creaked as it opened. Thinking it to be the young jailer, he didn't even bother to turn around but just said sternly, "Leave the supper tray by the door. I hope it's something edible this time." Only when he didn't get an answer did Jonas turn around. To his surprise it wasn't the jailer at all but a tall, thin tawny-haired man he'd never set eyes on before.

"Good evening." The voice was hushed.

"Good evening yourself." Jonas wasn't in a friendly mood. "Whoever you are." From the looks of him, bookish and reflective, Jonas concluded that he must be a judge or a lawyer. The huge briefcase the man held in his hand seemed to confirm it.

"Who I am isn't important." The man's eyes behind his spectacles moved over Jonas appraisingly. "It's what I'm going to do for you, that is."

"And just what is that?" Jonas asked coldly. Though he didn't really have a reason, he felt an instant distrust of the man.

That man's tone was conspiratorial. "I'm going to let you out of here."

"Let me out!" Jonas snapped his finger. "Just like that?"

"Yes, just like that." He held out the briefcase. Opening it, he proved that it wasn't a briefcase at all but a suitcase stuffed with men's clothes. He set it down on the cot. "Here are your clothes and as many of your

385

possessions as could be retrieved without arousing suspicion."

"My clothes." Jonas smelled a trap. "And just why are you doing this for me?" As if he had to ask. Undoubtedly Faith had stumbled on something down in San Francisco. Whoever had really killed Randolph Vanduvall was scared. This man was obviously his crony.

The man's eyes narrowed. "It doesn't matter why." He took a ring of keys from his pocket that Jonas knew to be to the outer door.

"Oh yes it does!" Jonas wasn't going anywhere. He could smell a setup. Undoubtedly the moment he walked through that door he'd be shot and it would be shouted all over town that he had been trying to escape. He looked around for the jailer, but he was nowhere in sight. "Where's that kid who was guarding me?"

The man's smile was cold. "Let's just say that he is . . . occupied elsewhere."

"Occupied." Jonas's body tensed. "Alive, I hope."

The visitor was quick to assure him. "Oh, yes. He's tied up somewhere, but don't worry, he won't be any trouble. I've made certain of that." He dangled the keys enticingly before Jonas's eyes.

The more time that passed, the more Jonas disliked this man. "Of course."

"I see you understand." He swung the cell door open. "Now, let's get down to business. There's a horse right outside with a gun in the saddle holster."

"No!" Jonas shook his head as he sat down on the cot. "I'm not going anywhere. When I get out of here it will be all legal. You can tell that to whoever sent you." That should be the end of it, he thought.

But it wasn't. Jonas's ears perceived the distinctive click of guns being cocked and knew he was in trouble. Two other men had entered the cell and both seemed ready to pull the triggers of their guns. Most troubling of all Jonas recognized the two men as those villains who had set fire to Faith's barn.

"Can I shoot him, Henry?"

"No. Not now," the man named Henry answered. "We don't want any trouble. Besides, there are a few things I want to talk with him about first. Man to man you might say." His smile was chilling.

"I can't imagine that I would have anything to say to you." Jonas wanted to wipe the other man's grin away, but he didn't get the chance. As the barrel of a gun was pressed into the small of his back, he was forced to his feet and marched out the door.

Forty

Clara and Faith decided upon a plan. Clara was to concentrate her efforts on Red Danberry and Faith would cautiously keep an eye on Wyatt Aubry.

"We'll make a notation of everywhere they go, everyone they see. Hopefully we'll find out something. We have to, Faith." Jonas's case was scheduled to go before the judge in six days.

"Less than a week." Time was running out. That thought gave Faith a feeling of desperation. She feared for Jonas, enough to throw caution to the wind. Clara said that Wyatt Aubry had been giving her the eye. If that was true, then she intended to use any attraction he might have for her to get what information she could. If that meant openly flirting with a man she detested, so be it.

"Good evening, Mister Aubry," she said, smiling as seductively as she could as she passed by him at the door.

"Good evening." He followed her as she made her way to the gaming area. "I see that you took my advice and wore black. It becomes you."

Wyatt Aubry had insisted that she wear dresses with a low neckline to, as he put it, "show off her assets." Tonight Faith wore a dress of black silk that was low-cut and clung to her slim curves. Around her neck she wore a white cameo, tied with a thin black velvet ribbon.

"My aim is to please. And to bring in as many customers as I can." Again she smiled. Faith had already charmed the clientele and her table had begun to draw an impressive patronage.

In just the short time that Faith had worked as a dealer she had learned a great deal about the rules of San Francisco gambling. The first female dealer had been hired nearly nineteen years ago and since then the other saloons felt obliged to hire women to meet the competition. Faith was surprised to learn that most of the major gambling houses in town had at least one lady dealer.

"If women dealers are caught making a few mistakes in favor of the house or even caught cheating, the customers laugh it off and go ahead with their game." No so with Faith's male counterparts who might very well lose their lives for such a sin.

There were many gambling houses clustered in and around Portsmouth Square, once the central plaza of the town in Mexican days. Because of Wyatt Aubry's competition from the El Dorado, Bella Union, Mazourka, Fontine House and La Souciedad, he had found it necessary to offer enticements to lure customers away from the other establishments. That's why Red Danberry was so valuable to him and also why he had hired Faith and Clara. Attractive women were a sure draw, she heard him say. Having women deal blackjack, or "vingt-et-un" as it had first been called, pulled in customers, some of whom were happy just to admire the fairer sex from afar.

"Shake these gamblers loose of as much gold as you can." Aubry winked, knowing full well that she understood his meaning.

"Oh, I will." He wanted her to cheat if it was necessary. Though that was completely against Faith's principles Wyatt Aubry insisted upon it. "You know what to do. All professionals know tricks in order to protect themselves and their houses. I'm asking you to use your knowledge to protect my little place here," he had said just yesterday.

"A card up my sleeve, is that what you are saying?" Faith had only narrowly held her temper in check. Using a sewing needle to raise bumps on the cards that she could feel while passing them through her fingers, she increased the house's winnings. If only Jonas could see her now!

Faith was quickly learning the gambling trade. Her dexterity with cards amazed her. There were even times when she actually *liked* playing. It was a challenge. Now she could understand Jonas's fascination with gambling.

"All right, gentlemen. Gather around."

Bets were made in gold or silver coin rather than the paper money issued by banks. San Franciscans distrusted paper money, so there was always the clinking and clunking sound of coins when the playing began. Faith was becoming used to the sound.

"Sorry." The pinholes on her cards helped Faith deal an ace and a jack to herself and losing card to the others. "I'm the only one who has twenty-one."

She dealt again, but this time her attention was diverted by Wyatt Aubry. He was angrily engaged in conversation with a short, squat, bespectacled little man who reminded Faith of a gnome. It was obvious that they were quarreling and that made her hope that perhaps this man might be of use to her.

"Who is that man?" she asked one of the players.

"Adolph Schwartzman. He runs the Fontine House."

She made a mental note of the name. "Ready for the next hand, gentlemen?"

It was a long and tedious night, one Faith was only too glad to see end. Her legs ached, her eyes watered from all the smoke, and she was exhausted. Even so, during the course of the game she had kept track of the name of everyone Wyatt Aubry had talked with that night. Clara had watched Red Danberry and had done the same.

"Tomorrow we pay each and every one of them a call." It was at least something to make them feel that the time they had spent in the gaming hall hadn't been wasted.

"Now we can hurry up to our rooms and relax on our beds." Anxious to do just that, Faith had taken off her shoes.

"Not just yet." Cautiously, Clara looked over her shoulder, then lowered her voice to a whisper. "I have a friend named Ed who works at the telegraph office. He came in to-night to tell me I received a telegram earlier today."

"A telegram!" Faith put on her shoes, her fatigue suddenly vanishing.

"He said he would leave it under the tele-graph office's doormat in a brown envelope."

"Under the doormat?" Faith was dubious.

"Don't worry. It will be safe there. Ed and I have always used that place for secret mes-sages." Arriving at the telegraph office, Clara found the envelope just where she said it would be. She tore it open. Her confident mood all too soon soured as she read it under the streetlight.

Clara's raised eyebrows, her look of surprise, her frown told Faith that something was wrong.

"Clara, what is it?"

Clara held the telegram out to her.

Faith's fingers trembled as she took it. Somehow even before she read the telegram, she knew that it was bad news. Still, as she read the words she wasn't prepared for what it said, that Jonas Winslow had escaped from jail.

Forty-one

"Jonas would never run away!" Faith was adamant.

"No, I don't think so, either." Clara tore the telegram into pieces and placed the shreds into her reticule. "But I wish that he had."

Faith's heart was racing. Something terrible had happened to Jonas. "We have to go back right away!"

Clara shook her head. "No. We have to finish what we came for. If Wyatt Aubry is behind Jonas's disappearance, we have to find it out and have him confronted with the evidence." Impatiently, she tugged at Faith's sleeve.

"Where are we going?"

"I think it's time we did some late-night spying." She pointed toward the Golden Palace. "Come on." Hurriedly, they retraced their steps but didn't go in the front door.

Ducking into the shadows, they moved through the alleyway. "According to one of the gamblers at my table, Aubry has a secret gaming room. We have to find it."

Coming to the back of Aubry's establishment, Faith located an unlocked door. "Let's go through the kitchen entrance."

"No." Clara kept looking for another entrance. "Let's use this one. It looks like a forbidden portal."

Faith reached for the knob. "Of course, it's locked."

Clara took a hairpin from her bun, exhibiting great patience as she worked it back and forth for what seemed to be a long time. "Ah ha." Triumphantly, she opened the door just a crack.

Suddenly Faith was hesitant. "If we're discovered we could be in a lot of trouble." The thought of Jonas, however, goaded her into daring action. She peeked inside to see a dark and empty space. "I don't see anyone lurking about. It looks safe to me." They entered the room, which upon exploration seemed to be just another gaming area.

"Look, there's another door."

"One with a tiny peephole." This time it was Faith who moved boldly forward. Carefully she positioned herself so that she could look within.

Inside the inner room smoke was thick, curling up in spirals toward the ceiling like rising clouds. There was only one table. Around it were six men. Faith tensed as she saw Wyatt Aubry. He was sitting in such a way that she could see his profile. Taking a puff on his cigar, he narrowed his eyes as he surveyed the others.

"Yes, sir, this little place is thriving," he was saying, reaching up to run his fingers through his thick silver-threaded dark hair. "Despite the competition. Even those damned Chinese and their fan-tan haven't hurt me as much as I feared."

"It's those two new dealers of yours," a man Faith recognized as one named Baker said. "Pretty. But then if they weren't, they wouldn't be here."

"If there's one thing Wyatt knows it's how to pick good-looking women," a man named Brown answered.

Aubry leaned back in his chair and put his feet up on the table. "Yeah, good-looking. And maybe dangerous."

"What do you mean?" Baker was instantly wary.

"There's something funny about both of them." Nervously, Aubry drummed his fingers on the arms of his chair. "If this was Richmond, Virginia, and if we were still at war, I'd say they were spies."

"Spies?" One of the men laughed.

Another didn't think it was so funny. "Maybe they are—for La Souciedad or the El Dorado."

Aubry shrugged. "I don't know. What I do know is that I have a nose for trouble, always have. The prim and proper one bothers me, that's why I've been watching every move she makes."

Faith determined than he meant her and felt a bit queasy in the stomach. How she wanted to get this all over with and go back to Portland.

Baker relaxed. "And here I thought you were staring because you intended for her to take Red's place."

Aubry grinned. "Who said a man can't have two women at the same time?"

Faith covered her gasp with her hand. Never! She was relieved when the conversation turned toward business matters. As she listened, she learned a great deal about the man who owned the gambling house. Aubry had profited by his quick wit, deviousness, and business sense, but he was especially proud of his latest venture. He was going to take a small, run-down waterfront eatery and with a little imagination and money turn it into one of the city's poshest night spots, a place where men could live out their fantasies.

"Nearly all men at one time or other dream of a life in the West. I intend to capitalize on that, in creating the Frisco Corral—

an establishment with a western setting, down to a scaled-down replica of a gold mine. Leaving their coats, hats, gloves, and ties at the front door, donning boots, gun-belts, and ten-gallon hats, the customers of the Corral will enter a western world, a place of pretense and fun where they can get away from their stuffy lifestyles, at least for a while and pretend they are gunslingers, sheriffs, goldminers, or cowboys."

There was a guffaw from Adams. "As they mingle with those who are!"

Aubry sternly silenced him. "This establishment will cater to the elite, wealthy upper-class patrons with money to spare. Men with power who have a need to be lavishly and creatively entertained."

"Oh, I get it. And that's why you asked us here. To invest in it."

Aubry flicked the ashes from his cigar on the floor. "Exactly."

"What about Schwartzman? Are you going to let him in?" Rodgate smirked.

Aubry glowered. "What do you think?"

Rodgate's voice was high-pitched and irritating as he answered. "I think the same thing is going to happen to him that happened to Vanduvall." Raising his hand, he pointed his index finger, pulled in his thumb, and pretended he was shooting a gun. "Bang."

Faith squeezed Clara's arm as they exchanged "I told you so" looks.

"Hey, Aubry. You want us to invest. Why don't we play on it. A little bit of poker. What do you say?" Strange that even though he owned several gambling dens he had to be goaded into gambling himself.

"Lost your touch, Wyatt? You becoming an old man? Or have you just turned coward?" Obviously knowing Aubry's attraction for gold, the bald-headed man across from him hefted a large bag of coins. "Now, how about it? Just one hand."

"Which will lead to two, then three, then four. Isn't that so?" Clenching the cigar between his teeth, Aubry squared his shoulders, gave his perfectly tailored coat an impatient tug, and picked up a deck of cards on the table in front of him. "Well, don't complain to me when you lose your new silk shirt, Trumbell."

" I feel lucky tonight," Brown was saying as he shuffled the cards. Like Aubry, he was smoking a cigar. The others smoked cigarettes. "Real lucky." He grinned as he dealt out the cards.

"Well, you won't be as lucky as me. I've been wanting to beat old Wyatt here for as long as I can remember. Tonight I will." Adams was cocksure.

"Oh, is that so?" Aubry's left eyebrow shot up.

"And then again maybe I'll win," Rodgate spoke up. Peering through the smoke, he said, "Let's get started."

What followed was the usual bluffing and bidding. "Five dollars!"

"Hit me."

"I fold."

"Draw?"

"I'll raise you four!"

They bickered back and forth, each man taking his turn. It seemed to be a cordial game, but suddenly it turned ugly when Brown won the hand.

"I beat you, Wyatt. Care to try another game? Or are you afraid I'm on a winning streak and that you'll lose again?"

Aubry bristled at the challenge. "Let's play again."

The cards were gathered up, shuffled, and dealt. This time, however, it was Adams who won, followed by Rodgate. Brown won the fourth time. Thoroughly disgruntled, Baker rose from the table without even trying to win back his money.

"You cheated!" His accusation was directed at Brown.

"Cheated?"

"Yes, cheated. And I say it before every man in this establishment. George Brown had an extra ace up his sleeve. The oldest trick in the world."

"Take that back!" Grabbing Baker by his

shirtfront, Brown looked determined to throttle him, but the other men intervened, pulling him off.

"Stop it!" Aubry was adamant. "I don't want anyone hurt tonight."

Baker's eyes sparked fire. "Unless you order it, right? Like you ordered me to kill Randolph Vanduvall." In the face of Aubry's fury he regretted his words the moment he said them. He would have regretted them even more had he know his confession had been overheard.

"So. Now we know." Faith felt relieved. The mystery of who had pulled the trigger had been solved in a timely manner. Now it was up to Clara to make use of what they had heard. If it wasn't too late. "Oh, Jonas, wherever you are, please be safe and know that I love you," she murmured plaintively.

Jonas was struggling like an angry bear against the ropes that held him tied securely to a chair. "I'll get loose, you bastards, and when I do . . ." The direction of his gaze targeted the man named Henry as the victim.

The way he had been marched out of jail with the barrel of a gun poking into his ribs made him furious. His very life had been threatened and he had been certain he would be shot. Instead he had been taken to Faith's new barn, of all places. Now he was being taunted with the threat that the men who held him would set it afire. With him in it, of course.

Jonas tensed his shoulders and clenched his teeth. "Just what are you after?" he asked his captors. Although he recognized three of the men he could swear he had never met this Henry before. What vendetta did he have against him? "Is this about San Francisco?" When none of the men answered, he yelled, "Damn it! What do you want with me?" If they were going to kill him, why hadn't they just shot him and been done with it?

"I'll tell you what we want." Henry stepped forward. "We have a little deal going, you see. A chance for all of us," he gestured toward his cohorts, "to profit significantly."

"Yeah, yeah, yeah, you want to buy Faith's land!" Jonas was more perturbed than anything else. He was tired of it all. "But that doesn't really have much to do with me. It belongs to her."

"No, it doesn't." Henry's face looked like a thundercloud. "Not entirely."

"What do you mean?" Jonas was puzzled.

"Quiet!" The command was shouted.

One of the men wasn't quite as secretive, however. "Seems ole Henry here had it all planned out, but he miscalculated a bit," he said, stepping forward. "He thought he could get his hands on the deed, but when Dickie here," he pointed toward one of his companions, "robbed the stage, he couldn't find it."

"I mean it. Quiet!" Henry's warning sounded serious enough for the other man to do just that. Taking a step backward, he quieted. He had, however, given out at least a little information.

"So," Jonas said, looking Henry right in the eye, "you're the one who set it up for Faith to be robbed. It wasn't just a matter of fate." Something niggled at the back of his mind, something about this Henry, but he couldn't figure what it was. "You took a gamble and lost. It wouldn't be the first time. Why take it out on me?"

Henry's expression was chilling even though he smiled. "It's not a personal matter. Let's just say that you are being held in hopes of being our trump card. A gambler like you should understand."

"A trump card. An ace up your sleeve. How so?" Jonas was trying to second guess Henry and having a hard time of it. Just what was his plan?

All of a sudden he understood. He was being held as a hostage to blackmail Faith. They were going to use him so that they could force her into selling out. Then these double-dealing ruffians could buy the property and turn around and make a profit from the railroad when they delivered it into their hands. For a lot of money, of course.

"My life in exchange for the deed." He spoke it aloud. As Jonas looked slowly around at his captors he felt far from secure with such a bargain.

Forty-two

Clara and Faith waited until there was quiet all around them before attempting to leave Wyatt Aubry's establishment. They moved like lightning when all they heard was silence.

"Quick, go to the door and see if anyone is lurking around," Faith whispered to Clara as she struggled with the latch on her suitcase, the same one Jonas had helped her with the day they had met.

Clara opened the door just a crack but enough to be satisfied that no one was about. Gathering up her bag, she opened the door wider and crept out, motioning for Faith to follow.

Faith at last got her suitcase fastened and slowly slipped through the doorway. She paused a moment in the corridor to listen. Hearing muffled voices, she felt a moment of panic. It turned out, however, to be just a couple of men in their cups, discussing winnings and losings. As noiselessly as she could, she moved past their door.

It was strange how much heavier her suitcase seemed to be, Faith thought as she and Clara started down the hotel's stairs. Nervously, she descended the stairs, which seemed to squeak with every step, her chest tight with apprehension and anticipation.

They had it all planned out. They would cheerfully "borrow" one of the carriages housed in the hotel's coach house and two horses, of course. Would borrow them just long enough to get to the docks where Clara had already booked passage on a homebound ship.

Faith knew that she would never really feel safe until they were on their way to Portland but tried to put that out of her head.

"Going somewhere, ladies?"

Wyatt Aubry's voice thundered from the darkened area behind the bar, startling Faith so much that she nearly dropped her bag.

"Isn't my hospitality up to snuff?" It was too dark to see his face, but she knew his eyes were on Clara and her.

"No." Faith retorted, realizing that she had to say something. "No. In fact we were miserable here."

"Too smoky, too boisterous, too loud," Clara exclaimed.

He shook his head as he moved toward

them. "What a shame." Meeting them at the bottom of the stairs, he took each woman roughly by the arm. Though he wasn't a big man, Faith sensed a restrained power and violence in Wyatt Aubry. Enough to know that they were in danger.

"Please . . ." A surge of panic swept through her. They were trapped, and all the glib words in the world weren't going to do them any good.

Aubry ignored Faith's plea. "Just who are you and why were you here?" His face was taut with the determination to find out. "I want to know why you told me you were dealers."

Frantically, she searched for an explanation. For the love of God she couldn't tell him the truth, but what *was* she going to say? "We . . . we're both widows. We needed employment."

The sound that came from his throat was almost a growl. "Don't tell me you were just two poor unfortunates in need of a job. I don't believe you." He moved his hand up to grasp at Faith's throat with a strength that caused her to choke as he pressed hard.

Faith could hardly breathe. Unsuccessfully, she tried to pry his fingers away, locking her nails in his flesh as she did. It only made him increase the pressure.

There was tension in Aubry's hands, his words, his posture. "I'm not going to ask you again. Just who are you?" It was obvious he wasn't going to believe anything they might say. They had condemned themselves in his eyes by their attempted flight. "Trouble to be sure. But just how much of a threat I don't know. Yet!" He turned his attention to Clara. "Just how much do you know?"

Faith took advantage of his distraction. Violently, she pulled out of his grasp and, remembering her fight with Queenie, lunged at him. They had to get out of the hotel before he called out to his hired hands.

"Uuuuuuuh!" Aubry's breath came out in a grunt as Faith's shoulder pressed into his stomach.

"Get him, Clara." Not waiting for reinforcement, Faith brought up her cupped right hand and smashed the heel into the underside of his chin. Reaching for a bottle of whiskey behind the bar, Clara brought it down forcefully on his head. This time his breath came out in a groan as he slumped to the ground.

"Run!" It was a command Faith didn't even have to give. Leaving their suitcases behind, snatching up only Clara's business satchel, they made for the front door.

"It's locked!" Faith shuddered. They had to get out before Wyatt Aubry regained consciousness. Her fingers were all thumbs as she fumbled at the latch. In what seemed like hours she had it unhooked. Then they were out and running as fast as their legs would carry them. Avoiding the flickering gas lamps guarding the streets, they darted from shadow to shadow.

"God bless the fog!" They couldn't have planned it better if they had tried. Just as fog had greeted their arrival, it was now safely enshrouding them as they attempted to leave.

"Can we find our way?" For a moment Faith was concerned that the fog could easily be as much a curse as a blessing.

"Find my way?" Clara pretended that she was offended. "Why, my dear Miss Tomkins, how can you even ask?"

The fog was so thick it was nearly impossible to see one's hand before one's face, yet Clara proved that she spoke the truth. Taking Faith by the hand, she led her up and down the streets, pausing for only a second.

"We're being followed!" Clara alerted Faith to that troubling fact.

They fled down the wooden boardwalk, their soft footsteps echoed by booted feet that made a thudding sound. For what seemed like an eternity they ran, all the while glancing over their shoulders. At last the smell of the ocean told them that they were at the docks.

"Clara, they are still behind us." Thinking quickly, Faith pulled Clara down to hide with her behind a large barrel. The sound of running feet passed by them. Peering over the edge, they watched as the darkened figures sped by. As soon as they had passed they were up and running again.

"Hurry!"

Faith reacted quickly. Too quickly. Something in her path tripped her and she fell in a sprawl. The fall knocked the breath from her body and she lay motionless upon the damp ground for a moment. Pain shot through her ankle but somehow she managed to get back up. Limping, she sped down the docks.

"You're hurt!" Clara observed in concern.

"My ankle. I must have sprained it." Biting her lip to keep from crying out, Faith leaned on Clara. They made their way clumsily down the wooden sidewalk, breathing in the scent of triumph as they spied the shadowy silhouette of the ship and its sails.

Ignoring her discomfort, Faith followed Clara up the gangplank. Home. Never had the word sounded so good, more so now that she and Clara felt for the first time that Jonas really would be proved innocent. *If* he could be found.

Forty-three

Jonas had loathed being in jail, but being held captive by a band of cowardly land-grabbing thieves for the last two days was even worse. They were boorish, hateful men who undoubtedly liked to pull the wings off butterflies and hold cats up by their tails. How he hated to be within their power. Totally. As bad as these men were, however, their leader was even worse. Coldly devious, he was obviously skilled at manipulating their thoughts and actions.

"Sign your name to this!" Standing in front of Jonas like some medieval lord, he dangled a piece of paper in front of his face.

"In case you haven't noticed, I can't. My hands are tied," Jonas shot back sarcastically.

There was something more to all this than the desire for land. Each time the man named Henry came face-to-face with Jonas

411

there was hostility in his eyes, as if he had a personal vendetta against him.

"Tied. So they are." With mock politeness Henry took a pen out of his pocket and held it out to Jonas. "What a pity. Promise to be cooperative and we'll rectify that right away. Will you sign this?"

Jonas tried to read some of the words, but the paper was bobbing up and down. "What is it?"

Henry shrugged. "Oh, just a little letter from you to that pretty young woman of yours requesting that she sign a bill of sale to her land to make certain you remain healthy. I'm sure you know what I mean."

Jonas did. It was blackmail, pure and simple. So that was the game being played, he thought. In a show of disdain, he spit on the piece of paper. "Go to hell!"

His actions infuriated the usually controlled Henry. He bounded forward, raising his hand as if to stroke Jonas. Instead, however, he motioned to one of the other men. "Hit him, Willy," he ordered.

The command was obeyed and Jonas felt a punishing blow to his chin. Despite his pain, however, he refused to cower.

"Now will you sign?" Henry loomed over Jonas in a threatening manner.

"No."

Again Willy was ordered to give punishment.

So, that was who he was dealing with, Jonas thought. A man who let others do his dirty little deeds. The kind of man who was only brave when he had others to back him up. Alone he was undoubtedly a gutless weasel.

"He can hit me again and again, but it won't do a damn bit of good!" Jonas was cocky. "But I might agree to pay a little game of poker. If I win, you set me free, if you win . . ."

"You'll sign."

Jonas shook his head. "No." He gritted his teeth. "If you win, I just might consider not pushing your face in the moment my hands are free." How he wanted to do that right now.

"You'll never touch me." There was such finality in his voice that Jonas wondered about it. Would Henry resort to ordering his murder?

"Don't be so sure," Jonas responded. "Anything can happen."

"Yes, anything." In an obvious attempt at intimidation he took a match from a gold cigarette case. Deliberately, he lit it on the arm of Jonas's chair and held it right in front of his nose. "For example, there could be another fire with an unfortunate casualty."

It was a threat that had been used many times during the last two days. At first it had frightened Jonas, but it had begun to lose its effect. "I really don't think that there will be. You see, you look like an intelligent man," he gestured toward the others, "not like this group of jokers. I'm betting that when all is said and done, you won't even singe the hair on my head."

"Oh, no?" Henry held the lighted match so close that Jonas winced as he felt the heat, but in the end he snuffed it out and threw it to the floor. Keeping his eyes riveted on Jonas, he paced back and forth.

"What are you going to do now?" Willy questioned as he followed after his leader, keeping one step behind. "Maybe you should just return from the dead and tell everybody this land is yours."

Return from the dead. Just what was Willy saying? A suspicion nagged at the back of Jonas's mind. Henry. It couldn't be! Or could it? Faith's Henry?

"Henry. Henry Wingham," he exclaimed, watching for a reaction. As Henry turned his head at the mention of the name, Jonas knew for sure. "Well, I'll be damned. I'm being held prisoner by a ghost. Amazing."

It was difficult to tell just who Henry Wingham was angrier at, Willy or Jonas, but surely the expression across his face was murderous. "Yes, a ghost," he snarled, losing all semblance of composure. "Which is

414

what you will end up being now that you know more than you should."

Remembering the heartache Faith had suffered because of this man's supposed death, Jonas was likewise furious. "Why? Why would you pretend that you were dead?" It just didn't make sense. Faith had loved this man. She had been planning a future with him. Why then this macabre pretense? So many questions echoed through Jonas's head.

"Because it became clear that the little fool was actually serious about keeping this motheaten land." Henry's laugh was mocking. "Imagine *me* a farmer!"

"Yeah," Jonas scoffed. "Imagine." This man had probably never done a lick of honest work in all his life. He tried to imagine what had happened. "So, in order to get twice the land, you took advantage of the Donation Land Act and proposed to Faith, knowing that having a wife would be to your advantage. You planned to turn around and sell the land to the railroad. You had learned it was going right through the land. Faith, however, was so eager to make a home here that you knew you had misjudged everything. So you sent her on ahead, having already set it up for one of your little friends to steal the deed from her during a stagecoach robbery. But she outfoxed you. She had it safely hidden." Jonas grinned.

"In the hem of her wedding dress, as a matter of fact."

"In her wedding dress." The dark-haired man standing behind Willy was agitated at that news. "Damn. In that satchel."

"You fool!" The man responsible for the error in judgment was skewered with Henry Wingham's eyes.

Jonas continued. "What I can't understand is why you made Faith think you were dead?"

He answered the question in his own mind even as Henry Wingham answered it verbally. Henry had taken it for granted that the poor bereaved young woman would flee with her tear-stained handkerchief, leaving the precious land far behind. But she hadn't. She had stubbornly and bravely held on to it and in so doing had innocently thwarted the vilest of plans. The fear that Henry Wingham might have another sinister plan up his sleeve coiled in Jonas's stomach.

"What now?" He was nearly afraid to ask the question. Certainly by figuring it all out he had put himself in danger. Had he put Faith in danger as well? He still had one ace up his sleeve! He now owned the railroad. Little did these men realize that no matter what kind of deal his father had made with them, they were bargaining with someone else now. Him.

* * *

Portland was a seething mass of noise and motion as the stagecoach groaned down Second Street, but to Faith the hodgepodge of buildings was a welcoming sight. "At last," she said.

"Amen," Clara responded.

It had been an exhausting journey from San Francisco. Hunger tugged at their stomachs, they were tired, dirty, with hair and clothing that was messed and rumpled, but foremost in their minds was getting to Clara's office where they could begin to put all the bits and pieces of information they had gathered into perspective. Especially the most important one: that Nicholas Baker was the man who had killed Vanduvall.

"Just wait until I tell Maggie!" Faith had quite a story. She had seen a side to the world that she hadn't really known existed before. The sordid side.

"Are you going to tell her about being a dealer?" Clara teased.

"That and a few other things." Suddenly feeling the need to freshen up, she took her leave of Clara, promising to meet her at the office as soon as she had changed her clothes and eaten breakfast.

Opening the stagecoach door, Faith merged with all the people treading the boardwalk. Walking past the depot tearoom, she remembered the first time she had come here and her meeting with Maggie. That had been a fateful day that had influenced the days to come. Days that had changed her from a naive girl to a woman.

It was a short jaunt to the MacQuarrie house. Faith arrived just as breakfast was being served and was given a warm welcome. Maggie made her usual motherly fuss, Ian was stern and fatherly, Lachlan was eager to hear all about San Francisco, and Mary and Caitlin fought over who was going to sit next to Faith.

"Tell us everything that happened," they both exclaimed, seeming to echo each other.

Between mouthfuls of pancake Faith related the story, beginning with her not-so-cordial introduction to Queenie. "Though my experience as a fighter is certainly limited, I held my own," she was quick to say. "My tussle with that woman made it possible for Clara and me to get a job right at the hotel."

"A job?" Maggie's look was decidedly disapproving. "Doing what?"

Faith smiled as she wiped her mouth with a napkin. "Dealing blackjack."

"You didn't!" Maggie was aghast.

"I did." Faith proudly held up her chin.

"How exciting," Caitlin and Mary agreed.

"And as a matter of fact I became rather good at it." Hurrying to finish the food on her plate, Faith then helped clear the table, continuing to talk all the while. "But to tell

418

the most important part of the story, Jonas didn't kill Randolph Vanduvall and we can prove it."

"I'm so glad." Margaret answered, looking around for Faith's baggage and realizing that she had none.

Faith answered the woman's unasked question. "We had to leave in quite a hurry. I left my suitcase behind."

Raising just one brow the Scotswoman answered, "Did you now?"

Even now the memory was upsetting. "We did, and it was terrible." Faith intended to tell the whole story of their hasty escape but first she had to ask, "Where is Jonas, Maggie? Does anybody know?"

"No one. But I can tell you this. He didn't run away, Faith. He wouldn't. Not after what I told him." Maggie gently touched Faith's shoulder. "The Pinkerton Agency located Jonas's parents. He's—"

Maggie didn't have time to finish. Cameron came banging into the room, his face flushed with excitement.

"Something strange is . . . is happening out by the barn." He was out of breath, panting. "Intruders of some kind."

Faith's heart lurched. "Intruders? Who?" Was it the men who burned the barn?

Pausing to catch his breath, Cameron was flustered. "I crept closer and peeked through a crack in the door. They're holding Jonas."

Forty-four

It was going to be a murderously hot day. Already that was evident. Inside the barn it was stuffy and uncomfortable, a situation made worse because Jonas was famished. He hadn't been given any food since yesterday. His nerves were taut, yet for the first time in his life he gave thanks for his years at the orphanage. He had been taught patience there. Though it was quickly running out now. He was damned tired of being trussed up like a turkey waiting for Thanksgiving.

Last night instead of trying to sleep, Jonas had given a great deal of thought to his situation. He had debated revealing his new-found identity as James T. Wakefield. On one hand he knew it was risky letting these gun-happy men know who he was. Contrarily, he might also be able to convince them that he would strike a deal with them, blackmail as it were. An unsettling thought.

"Hey, Willy!" Jonas sniffed the air. "That coffee smells good. Mind if I have some?"

"Naw." Pouring some coffee into a tin cup, Willy stepped forward, then took two steps back. "Henry says we're supposed to keep you tied."

Henry Wingham was always in command. What he said was law. That rankled Jonas. Unlike the others, he had no respect for the man. It wasn't just Henry's behavior toward him as a captive but how he had treated Faith. She was a good woman who deserved far better.

Willy shrugged. "Too bad."

"Yeah, too bad." Jonas looked around for Henry and caught sight of him climbing down from the loft, which he had requisitioned as his "office." Jonas thought it was time to play a different kind of game. It was time to play his ace if he wanted to be set free. "All right, you win, Henry. It's time to negotiate.

"You'll sign the note to Faith." Snapping his fingers, Henry motioned to Willy to bring it forward.

"Oh, no." Jonas shook his head. "I'm not talking about that. I'm talking about a real deal."

"What kind of deal?" From his tone of voice, Henry was at least curious.

Jonas's voice lowered to a whisper. "Come closer and I'll tell you."

Pulling up a stool, Henry waited. "Well?"

Jonas purposefully let the anticipation build, then he said, "I'm talking about a business negotiation with the new owner of the R and R."

"New owner." Henry Wingham's usual poise cracked a little. "What new owner? What are you talking about?"

"You mean you don't know?" Jonas clucked his tongue. "Shame, shame, shame. And you call yourself a businessman." His voice got a little louder. "James Wakefield is dead. Or didn't you know?"

"Dead" Henry Wingham was stunned. "No."

"Oh, yes." Jonas was enjoying his captor's unease. "But not your kind of dead. He won't be coming back to haunt the living."

For a long time Henry Wingham just sat there thinking, looking angrily at Jonas from time to time. Finally, he barked out an order. "Ride into town, Tom, and find out if what he says is true."

Like a puppet, Tom moved toward the barn door.

"And Tom," Jonas added, "while you're there, ask them about the new owner, James T. Wakefield. Ask them." The slam of the door punctuated his request.

Turning over the stool as he bolted to his feet, Henry Wingham was livid. "What is this all this nonsense?"

For the first time since he had been taken from the jail, Jonas felt confident. Ready to take a chance. As a gambler he had certain intuitions of when he was on a lucky streak. He felt that way now. What a good feeling it was.

"Boss! I'll be damned," Tom reported when he returned, "he's telling the truth. The old bastard did die. Probably of apoplexy the way he was always carrying on."

"Wakefield is dead?" Again Wingham's bravado was shaken.

Glancing over his shoulder at Jonas, Tom went on. "His son is the new owner."

"His son!" It was obvious that the wheels had begun turning in Henry Wingham's head as he frantically tried to salvage all his plans. "We'll have to find out who he is. Gussy up to him. Get in his good graces. Maybe we can still come away with something."

"I doubt it," Jonas said wryly.

"Boss!" Tom's grin was sheepish as he pointed toward Jonas. "It's him. I swear to God it is. Jonas Winslow is James T. Wakefield, Junior. The gossip must have started up while we were holed up here."

Henry Wingham looked like a boy who had suddenly found out there was no Santa

Claus. "Why didn't you tell me?" he asked Jonas.

"Because you didn't ask" was Jonas's reply. He had gambled and won. But what now?

What a difference his new fortune made. Though he was still held prisoner, but it was now under entirely different circumstances. Suddenly his hands had been untied, he had been given a cup of coffee, and damned if he hadn't even been given a cigar which he was avidly puffing on now.

"I hope that there are no hard feelings. I'm certain that we can come to some kind of agreement, Mister Wakefield." Henry Wingham could be obsequious when it was required. Even so, he drove a hard bargain. "But of course you realize I can't just let you go. You have learned things I'd rather . . ."

Jonas clenched the cigar with his teeth. "Believe me, I'll be quiet if you promise me you'll leave here without looking back." Jonas wanted to protect Faith more than he wanted to see Henry Wingham punished. It would break her heart if she found out about her Henry's scheme. Better for her to think him dead. "Agreed?"

Henry refused. "I've invested a lot of time and money in this scheme of mine. I have to profit somehow."

Yep, blackmail, Jonas thought. He'd pegged this SOB right away. "How much?" At the moment he was willing to agree to just about anything to get out of there.

"Five thousand dollars."

The cigar fell from Jonas's teeth. "Five thousand dollars?" Certainly Henry Wingham was no petty thief.

"Five grand. That's what . . ." He paused for just a moment, listening to a sound that no one else perceived. "What was that?"

"I didn't hear anything," Willy answered.

"Well, I did." Henry Wingham was insistent. "Up in the loft. Check it, moron." Instantly all of the men reached for their guns.

Jonas shrugged. "Squirrels."

"Or something bigger," Tom growled. Cocking his gun, he looked as if he welcomed trouble. "Whoever it might be would have had to ride out here from town, following me maybe." Cautiously, he went in search of the noise, slowly climbing up the loft's ladder.

Forty-five

"Stay close together," Ian MacQuarrie breathed as he motioned toward his wife, Faith, and his children. Fearing to call upon the sheriff for fear it might in some way endanger Jonas, it had been his decision for all of them to ride out to investigate this matter themselves. The women were armed with pitchforks, axes, and shovels, the men were brandishing guns. Cameron had gone on ahead to enter by way of the tiny window up in the loft.

"You're a foolish man, Ian MacQuarrie. You're going to get all of us killed," his wife breathed. "We should have let someone who knows what he's doing take charge of this."

"Pooh!" Ian MacQuarrie seemed to be stimulated by the danger. "Maybe we can make it up to poor Jonas for being so steadfastly against him by saving his hide." Stealthfully, he moved from a small grove of trees to an old tipped-over wagon, the others following in his footsteps.

"How many are there, do you suppose?" Mary whispered.

"And if there are men inside how do we know somebody else isn't prowling around out here? If there was one roaming about there could be other lookouts." Caitlin wasn't was brave as her father.

"We'll just have to take that chance." Not agreeing with Ian who was leading the group, Faith slowly inched herself away from the others. Moving hurriedly she had soon reached the front corner of the barn before she realized that Mary was behind her.

"I wish I had a gun," Mary mourned.

"You won't need one if we can take them by surprise," Faith decided. Rounding the corner, she inched toward the door, putting her ear to the thick wood. She could hear voices. One she recognized as Jonas's husky tone. But how many others were there? It didn't matter. She had to do something.

Her journey to San Francisco had changed her to a bolder, braver person. Still, she didn't want to be foolhardy. Men, like rats, could be vicious when cornered.

"Careful . . ." She stepped soundlessly toward the barn door as she came to just inches from the opening. Before she even had a chance to open it, however, it was opened for her with a yank that caught her off balance. Breathlessly, she looked up at the culprit.

"Hello, my dear."

For a long disbelieving moment Faith stared at Henry Wingham, her eyes widening as a frown tugged at the corners of her mouth.

"No!" It couldn't be. Oh, but it was. "I thought . . ." Faith stood deathly still as realization dawned over her. Henry was alive. She didn't know how or why there had been such a dreadful mistake, but she was happy that there had been. "Henry . . ." She moved toward him, her eyes sparkling with tears. "I was told that you . . . that you . . ."

He didn't even touch her, just stood there looking at her coldly. "That I had been killed by desperadoes. Yes, I know."

So many questions tumbled past her lips as she sought to learn everything she could about what had happened. First and foremost, "Why didn't you get in touch with me, Henry?"

His smile was cynical. "Why? Because it didn't look to me as if you were lonely, my dear." His eyes moved toward Jonas.

Guilt washed over her, threatening to drown the happiness she felt. "Let me explain." Somehow she wanted to make Henry understand that although she had great affection for him she truly loved Jonas. But how?

"Explain?" For just a moment there was a flicker of emotion in his eyes, but then, once more, he regained his icy control. "There is no need."

"Oh, but there is." Faith closed her eyes. When she opened them she was shocked to see Cameron struggling with two brutal-looking men.

"I'm sorry, Faith. Guess I wasn't quick enough," Cameron apologized. He cowered as one of the men put a gun to his shoulder.

"Henry, don't! What are you . . . Cameron."

Suddenly noticing that the other men in the room were armed, Faith looked helplessly around her. She had been so stunned at seeing Henry again that her thoughts had been all jumbled. Now she realized that something was terribly wrong.

"Jonas . . ."

Fearing for Faith's safety, Jonas merely said, "Get out of here, Faith. Don't ask any questions. Just leave."

"No!" She wouldn't. Not without Jonas and Cameron. Not until she found out what was going on. Why was Jonas here in the barn with Henry of all people? Why were the men brandishing guns? Was Jonas being held captive or was he here of his own free will? She had to know.

"Let her stay. We'll have a little party."

Henry took her by the arm, drawing her farther inside.

"No!" Jonas was prepared to fight for Faith if need be. Or negotiate. "If you want me to make good on paying you the money you want, let Faith go."

Henry was just about to agree when one of the men stepped out of the shadows. Faith gasped as she recognized the man who had robbed the stagecoach. "You. You're the one who stole my money." In confusion, she looked at Henry, then at Jonas, then at Henry again.

"Henry isn't the man you thought, Faith." Jonas looked at her helplessly. "It's a long, complicated story."

Not so complicated that Faith couldn't guess. "You put that man up to robbing me," she said in a cold, controlled voice, accusing Henry Wingham. "But why, Henry. Why?" Because of the land, she thought, her face flushed with anger. It was all some kind of hideous scheme. Henry Wingham wasn't a hero at all but a man not much different from Wyatt Aubry. The question was, how dangerous was he?

Henry Wingham's voice was as hard as his eyes. "You are a dreamer, my dear. You just wouldn't understand. Perhaps things might have worked out differently if . . ." For a moment he seemed regretful, then all traces of remorse vanished as he motioned Willy

430

and Tom forward. "They know too much. We can't let them go now."

Can't let them go. The meaning was all too clear. Jonas realized he had to act quickly. With a snarl he lunged savagely for Willy, knocking his gun to the floor. He picked it up, turned and grabbed Henry Wingham around the throat. Now he had a hostage.

"Tell them to drop their guns or by God you will be a dead man." At that moment he was deadly serious.

"You heard him." Now that he was cornered there was a quiver to Wingham's voice. "Drop them."

Crazy, chaotic moments followed in which Faith hardly knew what was happening. Everything happened at once with dizzying rapidity. She was aware of the sound of splintering wood, knew that Ian and Lachlan Mac-Quarrie had pushed through the door. She found herself reaching out to grab one of the gunman's wrists as they tried to get their guns. She heard the gun fire, but the bullet hit the ground.

There were curses, a scuffle, the sound of flesh against flesh as the combatants came to blows. Then thankfully it was over. "Caitlin rode to get help. We'll turn these brutes over to the law," Ian was saying. "Faith, are you all right?"

"Yes." At least she would be now, she

thought, entwining her arms with Jonas's. For what seemed like forever they stood there, wanting to be alone but surrounded by others. At last when the sheriff's men rushed in to take their prisoners away, their wish was granted.

"Jonas, my boy . . ." Ian came forward, reaching out a tentative hand. The gesture of truce was acted upon by Jonas.

"Ian." Maggie tugged at her husband's sleeve. "That's all well and good, but—"

"But what?" Ian was grumpy until he understood. "Oh . . ." He followed his wife out the door leaving the two lovers behind.

Faith reached up and brushed her fingers across Jonas's face, tracing the lines and hollows. "I felt so proud of you today." Faith leaned back against him with a contented sigh.

"I love you, Faith. Never doubt it."

"You have proved it tonight, my love." Taking hold of his hands, she gave them an affectionate squeeze.

"Faith . . ." He was troubled about the situation with Henry, but when he tried to talk about it she wouldn't listen.

"It's over and done with." Gently, she kissed him on the mouth. "Henry Wingham ceased to be important to me a long time ago."

There was so much they had to tell each other, but somehow the moment didn't seem right for talking. Jonas's hands lingered on the soft curves of her body. They had waited so long. Too long.

"I'll have to give myself up."

"I know. But in the meantime . . ." For the moment they were together. It was a thought that was much too tempting. "Jonas, lock the door."

He didn't have to be told what she meant. Instantly he complied, then reached out to her. "Come here." He gathered her into his arms, kissing her with all the hunger of his soul.

Forty-six

The large room was a sea of faces. Some were sympathetic, some amused, and others just curious, wanting to see how a woman lawyer handled herself. Clara Oliver was viewed as an oddity, a woman trying to do a man's job. Some whispered that her poor client was doomed, that she would turn the courtroom into a circus. Clara, however, ignored any criticism, handling herself with poise and decorum. Dressed in a fashionable jacket and matching skirt, she looked slim and almost fragile, but her expression showed that she definitely intended to win.

Faith sat between Maggie and her daughter, Mary, choosing an inconspicuous place, hoping to see without being seen. Dressed somberly in a suit of dark brown, she hoped to blend in with the crowd. Jonas sat at the defense table. He looked tough, lean, and sure of himself. Looking back over his shoulder at Faith, he boldly winked as if to say that everything was going to be just fine.

Maggie gave Faith's hand a gentle squeeze. "God in his wisdom and mercy will reach out and touch the hearts of those who sit in judgment, lass," she said. "Besides, Jonas isn't just a gambler now. He's James T. Wakefield, Junior, a man of influence and power. That makes a difference."

"I hope so." Faith was still overwhelmed by what Margaret had revealed. Jonas, her Jonas, wasn't really who she thought he was at all. Not an impoverished gambler with unknown parents but the son of a wealthy railroad tycoon. She was having trouble getting used to that fact, though she was happy that Jonas had finally found out his identity.

"Oh, Faith, everything has to turn out right . . ." Mary suddenly hushed as the large double doors at the far end of the room opened. There was a stir in the courtroom, and people stood up as the judge entered. Faith assessed him. Dressed all in black, he looked awesome and unforgiving.

"You may all be seated," he ordered sternly.

Faith barely heard the opening words of the officials of the court, her heart was beating so loud. To her consternation she saw Wyatt Aubry passing by her as he walked down the aisle. Sweeping into the room like a king, he arrogantly ignored the disturbance

435

he was making as he trod over the feet of those in the crowd. How was it, she wondered, that she so easily saw the evil in him while missing it in Henry?

"Let him feel confident," Maggie said, pointing Wyatt Aubry's way. He was obviously amused by the turn of events, certain that no one would take a woman lawyer seriously. "Little does he know what our Clara has in store for him."

Indeed, when Clara had insisted that Aubry be called upon as a witness she had given little away. Neither he nor his lawyer knew that she had likewise called upon a mystery witness, none other than Red Danberry. As for the murderer, Mister George Baker, a warrant for his arrest had been issued making certain that he, too, would be at the trial today. If nothing else, today's proceedings would be interesting.

The prosecution went first, offering up evidence against Jonas. He called Wyatt Aubry to the stand. His voice was loud and clear, carrying throughout the hushed courtroom. Faith leaned forward with a curiosity that soon turned to anger at the blatant lies he told. Lies that were quickly made evident when Clara took her turn.

"Look at his face," Mary hissed. "He recognizes Clara now. It can't help but make him nervous."

"If he is wise, he will be shaking in his

shoes," Faith answered, smiling as she saw his calm serenity was fading. Before he was excused from the witness chair, Clara had managed to make Wyatt Aubry sweat.

Jonas focused his attention on the remarks of the woman who held his life in her hands and the men who would decide his fate. For the first time since this had all happened he actually felt that he would be freed. Clara's sharp mind had been trained to notice everything at once, a gift she exercised now in the crowded courtroom.

The trial was short and sweet. What touched Jonas's heart most of all was that Faith stepped forward as a witness in his defense, revealing his honesty, his kindness. When the prosecution revealed his past as a gambler, she was his fiercest advocate, clearly showing her love for him with every word.

"There is a little bit of the gambler in each of us," he heard her say. "Most of us hide it, Jonas openly enjoyed it. There is no ill in that." She revealed her journey to San Francisco, her job as a dealer to glean information. Then in a trembling voice she told of overhearing the real murderer of Randolph Vanduvall made his confession.

Maggie, Ian, Mary, Caitlin, Lachlan, and Cameron were called upon next. They all spoke highly of Jonas, told of how hard he had worked and of his integrity.

It was then that Clara pounced. All eyes

swept toward the back of the room as the mystery woman appeared. Dressed all in black, her bright red hair hidden under a hat, Red Danberry was nonetheless breathtaking.

"Why, you doublecrossing little bitch!" Wyatt Aubry sputtered his outrage.

"Sorry, darling," she calmly replied, "but I'm not lying for you any longer. One thing I know for certain is that I wouldn't like to be in jail."

Pandemonium broke out in the court as Wyatt Aubry's misdeeds came to light. Despite the prosecution attorney's indignant statement that Wyatt Aubry was not on trial, it was apparent that he soon would be.

The excitement was only beginning, however. As she perceived that the time was right, Clara called George Baker to the stand. Over the pounding of the judge's gavel, she condemned him as the real culprit, a charge that was met with the buzzing of voices all around the courtroom.

The jury debated for less than ten minutes, and when they returned, a verdict of not guilty was read. *Not guilty.* The courtroom broke out into wild applause and hoots congratulations. Though the citizens of Portland had first doubted Clara, it was clear that now they loved her. She would never have any trouble getting clients.

With a smile that was rare for him, the

judge rapped his gavel. At last Jonas knew he was really free. What might have ended in a great sadness had ended in a triumph.

"And all because of Faith and Clara." His eyes were filled with love as he saw Faith coming toward him. Then she was in front of him, her face a mixture of worry and of love. Wordlessly, he gathered her into his arms. "I do love you so, Faith," he said at last. "More than anything in the world I want you to be my wife."

"Are you asking me to be Missus Jonas Winslow or Missus James Wakefield?" she asked, fearing for just a moment that his newfound status might change him.

"Both. No matter what my name is, I will always love you." In the expression in his eyes was reflected the truth of his words.

"Then, yes." She kissed him and caressed him and murmured over and over again how much she loved him, too. "Come . . ." she whispered, leading him through the crowd.

Borrowing Maggie's buggy, she and Jonas fled from the attention that was quickly brewing from the case. All the newspapers in town wanted an interview with Clara, and with Faith and Jonas, too, but they had to find the happy couple first.

"Where are we going?" Jonas grinned as he realized they were heading out toward the barn. "You're thinking the same thing I'm thinking."

"Uh huh." She leaned against him, urging the horses into a frantic pace. Then at last they were there, the site of so many memories.

It was quiet inside the barn except for the sound of their breathing. "So, you worked as a blackjack dealer," Jonas teased.

"And I was quite good at it, if I do say so myself." Slowly, she unbuttoned her bodice, striking her most provocative pose. "Care to play a hand, sir?"

"Oh, no, I have it in mind to do something else."

Standing before her, so close that there was barely an inch between them, he leisurely undressed her. Her bodice was the first to go, sliding to the hard earthen floor with a swish. Her skirt was next, slipping from her body to fall in a heap at her feet. He tugged at her chemise, watching as it slid down her body. His eyes touched lovingly on her full breasts, narrow waist, and slender hips.

"You are so beautiful," he whispered against her hair. "All the time I was in jail I imagined you beside me. It was the only thing that kept me sane."

"I thought of you, too. I couldn't believe that fate would be so cruel as to keep us apart forever." Naked and burning with passion, she flung her arms around him, holding him close as her mouth returned his kisses with a frantic urgency. All the days of

440

anguish, of searching, of wanting, all the questions in her mind drifted into oblivion.

Ruled by his desire, Jonas peeled away his own clothing, letting the garments fall where they might.

Faith moved her body against him, feeling the burning flesh touching hers. A shiver danced up and down her spine as he stroked her skin. She leaned against his hand, giving in to the stirring sensations. The hunger to be near him, to touch him, to make love to him, had been with her for so long that somehow this moment seemed more dream than reality.

"There is no bed, only a pile of hay." His voice was low and husky. It reminded him of another time and he smiled.

"It will seem as soft as a feather bed if we share it," she answered, burying her face against his chest as he swept her up in his arms. He carried her to their makeshift bed, gently lowering her to lie upon it.

Staring up into the mesmerizing depths of his eyes, Faith felt an aching tenderness for him. She clung to him, drawing in his strength and giving hers to him in return. She could feel his heart pounding and knew that hers beat in matching rhythm.

"You went all the way to San Francisco just for me."

"Because I believe in you, Jonas." She started to tell him about all her trials, but he silenced her with a kiss. She responded with a natural passion that was kindled by his love. Her entire body quivered with the intoxicating sensations he always aroused in her. After so much time apart, she wanted only one thing—to feel his hard warmth filling her, to join with him in that most tender of emotions.

When they had made love before, Faith had been just a bit shy, holding back a small part of herself. Now she held nothing back. She boldly explored Jonas's body as he had done to hers, his hard-muscled chest and arms, his stomach. His flesh was warm to her touch, pulsating with the strength of his maleness. As her fingers closed around him, Jonas groaned.

"Faith!" Desire raged like an inferno, pounding hotly in his veins. His whole body throbbed with the fierce compulsion to plunge himself into her sweet softness and yet he held himself back, caressing her once more, teasing the petals of her womanhood until he could tell that she was fully prepared for his entry. Her skin felt hot against his as he entwined his legs with hers.

"Love me. Love me now," she whispered. Her frantic desire for him was nearly unbearable. Parting her thighs, she guided him to her with a fierce ardor she had never shown before. Writhing in pleasure, she was silken fire beneath him, rising and falling with him as he moved with the relentless rhythm of their love. Hot desire fused their bodies together, yet there was an aching sweetness mingling with the fury and the fire. In the final outpouring of their love, they spoke words with their hearts and hands and bodies neither had ever uttered before.

In the aftermath of the storm, when all their passion had ebbed and they lay entwined, they sealed their vows of love with whispered words. Sighing with happiness, Faith snuggled within the cradle of Jonas's arms, happy and content knowing all the ghosts of the past were at last safely laid to rest.

EVERY DAY WILL FEEL LIKE FEBRUARY 14TH!

*Zebra Historical Romances
by Terri Valentine*

LOUISIANA CARESS   (4126-8, $4.50/$5.50)

MASTER OF HER HEART   (3056-8, $4.25/$5.50)

OUTLAW'S KISS   (3367-2, $4.50/$5.50)

SEA DREAMS   (2200-X, $3.75/$4.95)

SWEET PARADISE   (3659-0, $4.50/$5.50)

TRAITOR'S KISS   (2569-6, $3.75/$4.95)

Available wherever paperbacks are sold, or order direct from the Publisher. Send cover price plus 50¢ per copy for mailing and handling to Penguin USA, P.O. Box 999, c/o Dept. 17109, Bergenfield, NJ 07621.Residents of New York and Tennessee must include sales tax. DO NOT SEND CASH.

PASSIONATE NIGHTS FROM
PENELOPE NERI

DESERT CAPTIVE   (2447, $3.95/$4.95)
Kidnapped from her French Foreign Legion escort, indignant Alexandria had every reason to despise her nomad prince captor. But as they traveled to his isolated mountain kingdom, she found her hate melting into desire . . .

FOREVER AND BEYOND   (3115, $4.95/$5.95)
Haunted by dreams of an Indian warrior, Kelly found his touch more than intimate — it was oddly familiar. He seemed to be calling her back to another time, to a place where they would find love again . . .

FOREVER IN HIS ARMS   (3385, $4.95/$5.95)
Whispers of war between the North and South were riding the wind the summer Jenny Delaney fell in love with Tyler Mackenzie. Time was fast running out for secret trysts and lovers' dreams, and she would have to choose between the life she held so dear and the man whose passion made her burn as brightly as the evening star . . .

MIDNIGHT CAPTIVE   (2593, $3.95/$4.95)
After a poor, ragged girlhood with her gypsy kinfolk, Krissoula knew that all she wanted from life was her share of riches. There was only one way for the penniless temptress to earn a cent: fake interest in a man, drug him, and pocket everything he had! Then the seductress met dashing Esteban and unquenchable passion seared her soul . . .

SEA JEWEL   (3013, $4.50/$5.50)
Hot-tempered Alaric had long planned the humiliation of Freya, the daughter of the most hated foe. He'd make the wench from across the ocean his lowly bedchamber slave — but he never suspected she would become the mistress of his heart, his treasured sea jewel . . .